Ann Patricia Turner-Savage grew up in the West Country; however, her ancestry is North East European. Being denied an education after the age of fifteen, she rebelled strongly and set about obtaining one. Her first opportunity came when she travelled across Europe in 1976 and took the ferry out of The Pireus at Athens to the Port of Heraklion on Crete. She took a bus to Matala and lived in a mountain hut without electricity or running water. Laundry and honey cakes, etc., were delivered by donkey. Feral goats would wander into her bedroom and try to eat her washing from the line in the garden. Patricia learned to converse, read, and write Greek and loved every minute.

Later in Paris, she studied the *Impressionists* and worked hard to reach 'Fine Art' standard in painting oil on canvas. Patricia is also fairly confident painting using watercolors. These skills opened a whole new world to her. She still retains a few French phrases from her time in France. Gaining an Access Course Certificate, she attended Birkbeck and studied Ancient Lives Textual Evidence. This led her to Egypt, and her passion for this astounding country and its amazing history has totally fulfilled her life.

Arabic-speaking and diplomatic by inclination with a mischievous sense of fun, Patricia had no trouble fitting in with the Arabic-speaking communities along the Nile and flourished. *The Invention of Forever* found its way into print due to a very unusual experience in the tomb of the teenage Pharaoh of the 18th Dynasty Tut Ankh Amun. Patricia is still haunted by this amazing and insightful experience.

Patricia claims that true insight of the Sahara can be gained by constant study of *The Lost Oases* written by the intrepid explorer A. M. Hassanain Bey. Her love for the desert and the Bedouin people is well known. Patricia returned to Egypt last Autumn to 'fine-tune' her research for a sequel to *The Invention of Forever*. She has just celebrated her 80th birthday.

I would like to dedicate *The Invention of Forever* to all the kind, lovely, friendly people of Egypt.

A special thank you to the Egyptian Army Soldiers who were manning the tanks in the Sharas of Luxor and looked after us all in a terrible time.

Special dedications go to Ahmer, Salah Bogarde, Mona Bogarde, Hosna, Bassam and Mahmoud.

Also, my dear pal the Sufi dancer and Captain Ashraf Farag of 'Moon Valley'.

Ann Patricia Turner-Savage

THE INVENTION OF FOREVER

AUSTIN MACAULEY PUBLISHERS™

LONDON * CAMBRIDGE * NEW YORK * SHARJAH

A CIP catalogue record for this title is available from the British Library.

ISBN 9781398492110 (Paperback)
ISBN 9781398492127 (ePub e-book)

www.austinmacauley.com

First Published 2024
Austin Macauley Publishers Ltd®
1 Canada Square
Canary Wharf
London
E14 5AA

Acknowledgement and special thanks go to my dear friend and neighbour Clinton Peck.

For all the excellent help, patience, and fortitude.

The father of all the rivers is calling his children home.

Table of Contents

A Short Presentation

The wheeling constellations of 'The Milky Way' are a source of constant fascination. Long before anyone alive today, there were those who constantly watched the skies for the smallest change. The Ancient Egyptians were held in a kind of bewitched and passionate fascination of such depth and purpose that their whole lives became 'United' and intertwined every way possible with the great river of stars in the Galaxy. They observed all with an obsessive fervour.

So interconnected were they within their philosophy of mankind's true destiny within the Universe, they never ceased from this toil towards uniting themselves with their chosen deities.

Within sacred divinity is a kind of terror. Constant and sophisticated artistic interpretation with a godlike status…takes its toll. Unique in their reading of all symbols and signs towards the incredible inventing of a life beyond their Earthly life led them to create a life within the Circumpolar stars for their Pharaoh—and hence for themselves. To add to this, they named them The Indestructible Ones due to their fixed point.

Nothing was considered insignificant. Every manifestation of life was precious and held a sacred divinity within the elite of the Ancient Egyptians, who were held in thrall by the mystery of the sun, moon, stars and mankind's part in the enchantment of the universe.

This exotic civilisation continues to draw thousands of people from all corners of the world. Among those fascinated by the lives of the ancient Egyptians is Amira Kinov, an historian… who is slowly building her career and reputation within the Antiquarian Department of Cairo. Amira a lively divorcee lives with her daughter Sally in her grandfather's old house, and together they enjoy an incredibly close bond.

The story opens with Amira who, after completing a 'paper' to add to her talks on Egyptian History, is as always shocked by the way that time has completely run away with her and she must get to the local shopping mall in Toronto to choose a particular book for Sally, before meeting her from school.

While she is totally absorbed in this happy task, armed terrorists attack the mall and everyone begins screaming and running literally for their lives.

Amira is wounded during the shooting, but instead of turning right with the crowds that have caught her up and are dragging her along in their blind panic. She is almost fainting but is somehow held within their terrified stampede; Amira is somehow caught up in the bottleneck of the melee and as they all rush to the right, Amira turns left. This absolute split-second decision changes everything…

Amira is soon located in a skiff on the nearby river by the skilful lifesaving Agusta Westland Cormorant Helicopter rescue team led by Flight Commander Pierre Tremblay. There is also the absolute determination and humanitarian philosophy of Detective Alain, Nurse Vicky Mackellen and the hospital team all involved in the making of a story of defiance in the face of terrible loss.

We travel to Cairo, with its vibrant, exciting and intriguing people. To Yasmin Mubar a rebellious fellow historian from a strict Muslim family. Amira and Yasmin spent a good deal of time together as students, but now Yasmin is developing animosity towards her own stifling culture.

Yasmin is meant to help Amira look after a very wealthy and privileged Japanese group. However, on the first morning of this vital itinerary, Yasmin is a 'no show'. Amira has to cope alone with this very influential super rich group. Top of the schedule being a visit to the stunning Peng design of the Grand Egyptian Museum out on the Alexandria Desert Road which is an amazing futuristic architectural showpiece for treasures of the 18th dynasty. Tut Ankh Amun plays a powerful role within the unfolding of the strangest of tales…due to the most respected of the group…Riku Takeo…an aristocrat of the warrior class of Japan's very own ancient history. His very name translates to 'Wise Sky Warrior'.

The Invention of Forever is skilfully interwoven with myths, mysteries and the powers of the past that intertwine with ancient beliefs. A terrible snake goddess haunts Amira…revealing how past horrors can and do still manifest today…proving they can shake us out of our laughter even on an innocent sun-filled day.

However, it is a voyage on the fabulous sailing yacht—Pagan Arrow—with her unusual crew which includes Mattie, a wonderfully insightful First Nation man with a penchant for renaming things with puzzling labels. I call them The Mattie Labels!

I hope you enjoy reading this exciting adventure with its unusual outcome as much as I have had such pleasure creating the lives of those within the tale. Naturally, I have 'dusted off' some of my own true experiences from my life and adventures within my beloved Egypt.

Chapter One
A Runway to the Stars

Regarding our 'selves' is a one-off to us and a handful of other creatures. (Apparently, dolphins know who they are and can identify their individuality in a mirror!) Our place in the universe encapsulates us through our history of perceptions. We are manipulated by our own history and just reading about colonising other planets…evokes alien thoughts.

Catching up on line with the latest machinery that can dig the surface of Venus, the excitement of seeing our fabulous Earth star from thousands of space miles away through a camera lens whilst living in space ships gives a tremendous lift to our cosmic spirits. We are told constantly by song and verse of our being children of the universe. Watching the outcomes of worldwide recent space programmes assures us constantly of our 'home' in the stars of The Milky Way Galaxy.

There is a civilisation that took this extremely seriously.

The ancient Egyptians perceived life and their place within the universe as 'unique'. From the first time we pick up a book about them and the pyramid of Khufu, who actually sought a space travellers' path through time and space to the circumpolar stars, we hear ourselves say, "What were they thinking?"

The Foundation of Their Thinking

On trembling nights filled with stars, there were those who felt the cosmic flow like a great river of star clusters overhead. They fancied this energy could carry them out, out, out there to where great Gods ruled in an empire of brilliance.

From a time long before the pyramids there is a small amulet depicting a man with a star for a head. Within African stories surrounding the desert nomads are peculiar myths.

The tribal people of the Dogon claim categorically they have a metal ancestor who fell to earth. This figure is made of metals in their significance of his or her arrival. They are too sophisticated to explain all. This ancestor 'belongs' within their framework alone. He or she has iron shoes. They have a concomitant belief system which defies all explanation. Many anthropologists are mystified. David Attenborough has described their beliefs within his intriguing book, '*Behind the Mask*'. There never has been recorded a satisfactory explanation regarding this. It lies within a science not yet explored.

Let us return to Egypt…to Kemet and Deshret.

Sky watchers' horizon scanners and astrological priests appointed themselves a role which guided the King whether he be in the role of Pharaoh warrior, father, artist or engineer. They viewed life 'in the now' as precious perfection with exact moment to moment of vital experiences utterly valuable.

They sensed a wonder of their place within the stars. They knew something magical had happened all along. Today too many ignore our exquisite fortunate alignment within the solar system. Our fragment of beauty and life in the vastness.

The ancient Egyptians philosophised towards the formation of our being brought into existence…by sky reading, and discussions with astrological charts. Applied Mathematics and divinity of a most adventurous kind…within the early dynasties of those precious dwellers along the Nile and surrounding savannahs, for savannahs they were. They appointed essential sky watchers. All changes and phenomena were measured, calculated and took their place within a strict code of their unique physics and mathematical workings. Timely records were kept of any shifts in visible star formations also and uncannily they knew we were not flat. They knew there was a disappearing time and a calculation of hours that produced a new dawn and a new millennium. The planets drew their absolute attention.

Odd

They gave power to the dung beetle we refer to now as a scarab. He or she was named Khepri and treated as a godly divinity who they believed thrust the ball of the sun out of the earth every new dawn.

How was this strange thinking achieved? They 'invented' a long set of labours, monsters, obstacles and trials.

Some record (32) in all for the Pharaoh to solve and overcome from a solar boat which glided through the twelve hours of night and darkness. The weighing of the heart, quicksand and whirlpools, flesh eating monsters to name a few. All this belonged to an eerie underworld of...

'That which is in the Amduat'.

They believed in a life beyond the 'now'.

Within the life of life, the ka and the ba and a third 'essence' which is unwise to print the name of even here. Nothing was deemed too insignificant. Every creature had a role and a part to play under the great watchful eyes of Amun Ra...this stunningly beautiful phrase evokes our tenderness...

"Oh, thy tears shed mankind and they shed their own tears."

Interference

The true name of the great lion at Giza...Harmakhis Kephri Atum Ra...

Greeks renamed it Sphinx. Because they did not know what they were talking about. Tragically, the ignorance of their 'Interference' has stuck. What were they thinking?

Let us revise...

The simple dung beetle became the scarab and Khepri...a vital god...who rolled the sun out of the earth every dawn. A symbol of pure mystery to us here in this century.

However, we should not judge. For we grasp with a sort of vague inaccuracy at the world around us. Plundering and destructive. We could say. What are we thinking?

A unique and mysterious approach performed the wondrous foundation of a civilisation of great influence.

Today, our own sky watchers of the great horizon are valued in the deepest spiritual and scientific sense and we are in turn astonished by each 'discovery'.

For within those ancient lives came about the great (deep curiosity) whilst regarding questions and knowledge of the cosmic wonder. Nothing phased them...rather, this great mystery seemingly out of its time frame of knowledge from (our viewpoint) held an essential seed they needed to grow with. Since we in this century look up at the sky automatically many times a day...these ancient sky watchers did so with a fervour. They consistently cooperated within a field of visual and non-visual understanding of creator god spirits within their manifestations of expressive art, building the pyramids required mathematical genius. There was nothing too minute, nothing too grand but that they recorded it and treasured it with mindfulness and gave everything great significance.

The list of observatories, telescopes and space programmes today is vast.

The ancient Egyptians began a journey for all of mankind to seek another life in the stars. The most powerful of 'their life dynamic' became invested within a complete complex spiritual essence. Looking along the Nile while observing 'The Milky Way Constellation', there is such a mirror and to them an echo of the greatness.

The wonder of every visible fascinating star.

Their 'Art' incorporated all the influences…of the cosmos…take as example… Nut the goddess who holds up the starry night sky and is (composed) of stars. Fortunate rich Pharaohs gave artists great leeway in decoration of their tomb's ceilings and some survive today to show us the true wonder of their reverence towards a sky filled with uniform stars. Laid out for those who lay down and looked up.

A blue sourced from natural pigments and against this, gold stars. Not unlike the stars I received as a small child for handing in (very neat, careful work).

There is beauty in the Egyptian's story of how Nut slept with Jeb…a beautiful man…so handsome no woman could resist him and how together they made mankind. (We are stardust…we are golden) to quote a famous song by Joni Mitchell. We are creatures of air, water molecules and earth. We can still feel the reverberation within us from the big bang.

The stars gave mysterious magical yearnings to priests, whilst high in the night sky brightest of all of these shines the circumpolar stars. The guide stars.

The ancient Egyptians believed these to be vital to the afterlife and named them accordingly as 'The Indestructible Ones'…the very home of gods. They linked this belief to their Pharaoh for he was starlight and golden.

Part of the Pharaoh's work and its most essential was the 'INUNDATION' of the Nile…they called Eteru.

The river. Life or death came from its flood carrying silt to grow crops and provide life giving water.

Even today is coined the phrase…Egypt is the beautiful gift of the Nile she is every man's mother. In ancient Egypt if the Eteru did not flood correctly, the Pharaoh was blamed. Anarchy could follow.

However, the drama around the sky at night is only part of the drama.

The sun held all the aces.

19

Khonsu Moon God of time and fertility.

The moon god Khonsu often referred to as 'The Traveller'. Within the Papyrus of Ani also referred to as…Lah and is painted in a stunningly beautiful representation of rich colours. Green painted body and face, white mummy wrappings or windings. This figure holds a tall staff banded with colours. The staff has an unusual fixture for within the adze at the top is the ankh or vice versa. The crook and the flail held to the breast in the Pharaonic manner. The headdress or crown is a cradle curve holding a pure white sphere.

Khonsu has a wife called Mut.

Within the Papyrus of Ani.

Lies spine tingling lines…Chapter 2…A spell to come forth by day and live after dying—Words spoken by the Osiris Ani:

"Oh, one bright as the moon god Lah.

Oh one shining as Lah.

This Osiris Ani comes forth among these your multitudes outside.

Bringing himself back as a shining one He has opened the netherworld."

In my experiences, the Egyptians of today love to wander around and gather in the dark and cool under the watchful gaze of 'gummar'… The Arabic word for moon. During winter nights, they light fires in the sharas of Luxor and happily chatter through the dark sipping chai smoking shisha (water pipes). Their children play without fear in the dark streets lit by the moon stars and streetlamps.

Part of the answer to these mysteries. Everything about the life of Pharaoh within his 'earthly form' was one of service to his people conveyed through chant, music, incense, ritual, ceremonial clothing and specific crowns…which required much attention to detail.

The Magician's Cloak with stars, moon and magic wand…comes to mind. Add heat, dust, strange music from the most unusual handheld instrument called a sistrum…with incense burning to carry skyward a devotional message by chanted request and thanks for things granted by the gods… Add the moon gods' shining presence perhaps partially hidden behind mist.

All the ingredients for power and wonder.

And all this in the fourth dynasty…with Harmakhis Khepri Atum Ra and shining white pyramids.

They were surely touched by the divine. Priests and Priestess chanting raising the incense burners on high to aid the message and song of praise to the gods.

Add a huge pantheon of gods goddesses and self-suggested grandeur stirred with showmanship and combine the whole to create awesome splendour.

Priests were very powerful and none more than the Djedi.

Interestingly, it was Khufu (via his own son) who—according to the decipherment of the Westcar Papyrus was drawn to the Djedi…A combination of their sacred learning and wisdom transformed and manifested into a design that was directed into the very fabric and architecture of a great pyramid on the Giza plateau…this we refer constantly to as the Great Pyramid of Khufu. Which was absolutely engineered to take Pharaoh Khufu to join the other gods within 'The circumpolar star' via a fantastically devised resurrection machine.

When the final cap stone was ceremoniously laid and the great 'machine' with its immense size and pure white, sheer, smooth polished sides dazzled in the sunlight or glowed pearlescent by the moon's light for miles in every direction within its desert setting… astonishing spectacle as description does not come close. They surely invented 'Awesome'!

Believing this would indeed take their Pharaoh and eventually themselves to the final destination to live forever. The great pyramid shone out as beautifully as the stars against the cobalt blue of an Egyptian desert night sky. No contemporary words express its description. The sheer sides and pointed cap stone would have sparkled like a great star and it does not take a great leap of imagination to suppose at certain hours this 'star on earth' was enabled to join point to point with a cosmic star shining through eternity together.

Indeed, these particular pyramids were called Houses of Eternity!

They were creating as much as was within their power to build below to recreate and mirror all they saw in the constellations above.

Indeed, the river overhead in the cosmos had its twin on planet Earth the…Eteru—The River…we call The Nile.

Amira saved this introduction for her new lecture and closed the laptop. Glancing at her watch she gasped…then closed the blinds in the study. Running up to her bedroom she threw off one set of clothes and changed into another then rushed to the bathroom tucking a towel around her to protect her clothes and brushed her teeth. Glancing into a mirror, she pulled a face smoothed her wild tumble of blonde hair and ran downstairs. Finding her boots and jacket, she plucked a bunch of keys from their hook which said 'TAKE ME 'and jumping back to the stairs sat there and stuffed her feet into a pair of exquisite boots…which were in marked contrast to the jacket which let the look down by a long way. Starting up the old station wagon which her wonderfully comic daughter Sally had named Mumblechuckler…she drove carefully out…then swearing like a Yukon miner backed up and went back to close the front door.

She needed to get to the mall find the book for Sally and then whiz along to the school to meet her at the school entrance. At the mall, the park up was far too easy…where was everybody. Amira ignored all the tempting stores and saw few people…more of a scattering than a crowd. One woman was staring at her…Amira was used to this…probably a parent. Her students called her Amira sometimes…she never corrected them. This apparently was undermining authority at home. Amira was alone in the children's section of the beautiful bookstore. There was no time to dreamily browse. The Noel Streatfield book was there…excellent! As she leaned forward to select a copy of 'The Red Shoes', a strange metallic sound startled her…she felt as if a horse had kicked her and slumped clumsily into the shelving. There was of course no horse.

A screaming crowd of shoppers surged into the bookshop as they reached her aisle, they caught her up in their stampede of terror…carrying her in a relentless herd response. As they reached the sortie, there was a terrible scrabbling and the door eventually opened and they spilled out in a melee of shouts and screams. Amira found herself hanging onto the edge of the door in a daze desperately holding herself upright. A terrible throb in her side urged her to simply give in and fall in a crumpled heap, but yet another more powerful flight instinct surfaced and from a strange place in her mind screeched 'RUN!'

Careening away like a drunk, she stumbled into a clumsy run. In her mind her legs were running like an Olympian but in reality, she was barely moving. Then logic kicked in and she managed to hobble run.

It was ridiculous but worked. Screaming and machine gunfire…yes it was bloody machine gun fire assisted her hobbling also a primal fear. Noises were coming from the right, so she turned left. The beautiful river flowed majestically ahead and its diamonds in the sunlight sparkle invited…small crafts moored there were calling her and the nearest was a sound, spanking new skiff and even more unusual oars laid out neat and sweet.

Grabbing the painter, she gasped with pain and panting half fell half fainted into the shallow belly of the craft.

Blood oozed now forming into a beautiful sticky rose pattern through her clothes.

Slumped on the seating gasping and vomiting with a terrible agonising fire spreading in her side she grabbed at the icy river water throwing it in the general direction of her face. She simply must not give in to the agony she must find something deep within to row away…get away. She vomited again this time a burning acrid bile…another icy water splashing, she gritted her teeth. Another volley of terrifying gunfire and screaming from the car park told her what she must do.

"Get the fuck out of here!"

Thin eddies of the current caught and teased at her oars she adjusted to the pull and was violently sick over her clothes. Ignoring everything else, she plied the right oar and the main swift river current caught her craft sending it rapidly to the middle.

A fainting fit so strong pulled her down with its black central spiral yawning wider and wider until it all but engulfed her. "Kind river spirit aid me now," she whispered, then the black.

The river spirit must have heard her because the skiff swung erratically into the bend of the river and instead of flying on downstream it purposefully plummeted into the far riverbank with a thud.

Not moving more than an inch. Stuck fast in trailing tree branches which obligingly caught up in the craft and held it there.

This was how the Helicopter Medic spotted her as he delicately manoeuvred the bulky ass of the Cormorant with a clatter of whirring rotor arms overhead.

The radio contact babbled excitedly in triumph.

"Female with what I think is bullet wound in skiff…looks like a live one. Over."

There was a blur of pale rainbow colours…and a beaker…a nurse and a watch…Amira opened her eyes fully. She couldn't figure anything—so fell asleep again.

When she woke up the next time, there was darkness outside but a glow of light imposed itself lightly upon the room. Soft, pearly, comforting. A beautiful young face came into focus.

"I'm very thirsty."

"Gawd in heaven I bet you are…good sign though."

She was so lovely. Amira found herself gawping and was about to struggle up when the nurse…raised her hand.

"No, Mrs Kinov, you have had the bullet removed and the surgeon has left me strictest of instructions you must stay in this position…the sutures."

Amira's voice was a hoarse whisper…

"My little girl."

"Sally, she came but we thought it best you rest properly. Sleep after this is good. Keeps you in one position…literally. She left this."

A card with a little dog saying 'Get Well Soon Mummy' in a bubble above its nose.

"She's my darling just seven…a few days ago in actual fact."

"Seven, tut! Oh, those were the days."

"How long…I was in a river I think…thought I saw people running screaming so I ran to a river. The skiff oh my god oh no I stole someone's skiff!"

"The owners have already called and said they hope you're soon better. Amira they totally understand and are truly glad it saved you."

"Oh, what a relief…my daughter…who is…where is she staying."

"A fabulous mum Julia Gagnon who has a daughter called Sadie…Sally's age has very kindly taken her home. Because you see it all happened so fast. Detective Alain Veldour. I know great name…I'm thinking of changing mine from Vicky Mackellen to Alana Veldour. Sorry…well he was assigned to your case and naturally is taking it very seriously. He contacted the school and they thought it best Sally was not upset more than necessary."

"Oh poor love, oh tell me Vicky is she with good people…please I beg you."

"Absolutely, they are normal nice and cheery…no twits and no religious cranks."

"Thank goodness. When will I see her…?"

"Alain is coming in an hour he will need to see you Amira…it's the law I asked for another 24 hours but he's adamant. Fresh in your mind."

"Nurse Mackellen, the only thing on my mind is my daughter oh and my car my old Station Wagon Mumblechuckler she's our lifeline."

"Yes…Alain guessed at that…brilliant mind he has. He took the liberty of driving it to your home for safety. Your neighbours will keep an eye on things."

"He sounds like a man who might be worth being hitched up to."

"He has two poodles. Indie and Bindie."

"Ha ha ha ha…oh no don't make me laugh."

"No, you must not laugh."

"So, stop telling me funny things."

Vicky who was the best tonic on the ward ran a pretend zipper along her lips. Walked to the window and looked out on the Grey Dominion.

"Would you like some water."

Amira nodded and Vicky opened a new straw and helped Amira drink.

"Oh jeez that's better."

"Good, now how about a mouthful of breakfast."

Amira actually managed two but nausea prevented any more. Vicky cleared the tray and called a sullen-faced girl who could have come directly from the set of Zombie Nation. 'Zombie Girl' tidied the room and left.

"Yes, she's working up to… The Miserable Girl of The Year Award."

"Please Vicky no, my stitches…I think she might win."

Amira lay back and tried to focus sufficiently to read the report of the surgeon, he'd acted on her behalf to 'Administer…all medical needs deemed vital for life'.

"Thank goodness you did…what is your name my dear life saver…ah Mr D'Arcy. But of course."

She slept involuntarily until a light tap on the door alerted her to a visitor. A well-built man early fifties with strong features and dark green eyes…nodded and walked about two steps into the private room.

"Ah Nurse Mackellen told me I can only talk for five minutes…if you don't mind."

He handed her a neat white card. Amira read out.

"Detective Alain Veldour…plus two poodles named Indie and Bindie."

"Correct…I see Nurse Mackellen has enlightened you. How are you feeling?"

"Grateful. You not only arranged for my Sally to be cared for…but rescued old Mumblechuckler."

He was puzzled…then the penny dropped.

"The faithful family vehicle…yes guilty as charged. What a racket and yet so reliable…started first turn."

"Yes, and swearing in her general direction also aids the engine whenever real reluctance is displayed."

"Are you in pain?"

"No, I don't think Nurse Mackellen allows the 'p' word into her domain."

"I was told you were witty and sharp. I don't think you will get angry with me when I explain…Sally is safe at school sitting with Sadie Gagnon…same class apparently. Mrs Julia Gagnon is a very responsible and calm mum…Mr Gagnon an architect, a totally decent sort and both have sent best wishes and get well soon. They know you are naturally worried so."

"When can I meet Julia and her husband, I am so grateful so impressed how quickly they stepped up to help."

"Leave it with me. I will do what I can to arrange this."

"Thank you, such a relief… Everyone is so good. Oh yes did anyone mention my stealing a skiff."

"No charges…the owners are delighted to be of benefit. It comes roughly under 'Force Majeure' and the police think it the actual brilliant move that saved your life."

Amira began to cry.

"I think that's going to be enough for one day. Besides Nurse Mackellen already has my number…a veritable tiger when protecting patients."

"Mmm."

"If anything at all comes to you no matter how trivial it might seem… Write it down on this…please."

He handed her a neat black book…which had a pen attached by a chain.

For some reason, it amused Amira. She didn't see or hear him leave…sleep claimed her so many times and so she missed Sally's visit. Again.

Nurse Victoria Mackellen rang the school, and they allowed Sally to pop over as soon as Amira woke up from the drugged sleep…she was much more lucid now.

Sally was brought to the bedside and the staff left them to it.

Tearful gentle hugs of joy made them both smile. Sally had brought Binx. A much beloved toy of indeterminate age and unknown design. A description of grubby would definitely be a compliment.

Sally was bursting with joy and hiding her fear really well. Dear little soul.

Outside in the corridor…

Ward Sister was berating Nurse Victoria Mackellen…nothing new in this of course. The main gripe being Sally seeing her mum outside of visiting hours.

"The rules are in place for a reason. Nurse, you do not create them to suit yourself…you are forcing me to put you on report. I will let the Board of Governors deal with you."

Nurse Victoria Mackellen knew better than to say one word. Ward Sister had personal issues…she was childless, petty and outside of the hospital hours lived in the family home left to her. She had hobbies of grumpiness and cleaning.

She also felt permanently cross with sparkling-eyed, cheeky Nurse Mackellen, who was constantly ogled and admired. In other words, Sister was very disliked, plus no warm-blooded man or woman was ever interested in her. Outcome unchanging.

Nurse Victoria Mackellen saw herself as the buffer zone between her patients and any rules of stupid inflexibility and dragons…in general… Oh yes, and she did not give a fuck.

In fact, a large part of her argument was that if the old sour puss was shouting at her then Victoria must be doing something right.

Detective Alain Veldour had intellect, humour, sixth sense and a nose for the strange twists and turns of his cases. This one was a religious intolerance crime through terrorism. There was no sense looking for it to be changed that was a waste of manpower.

Tighten up security, educate and train more officers to defend the country. The enemy is enabled by weak people with evil motivations. He didn't go along with the theory of…oh he, she, used to be nice until they got their hooks into him or her. He was convinced this misanthropic psychological and illogical response was hidden. And waiting to be awakened. These killers hated beyond all reason. Literally.

A misread line in a book…someone looking at them the wrong way, just any reason to turn on mankind and destroy. Evil Imams were grooming the hatred and sealing the fate of so many without defence. Generating such cruelty. It had to stop.

He was, along with his team just picking up the pieces. Sometimes these pieces were human remains. Gruesome disorder. Critical, was becoming too often the norm.

He heard the demented Ward Sister with her one-sided shouting tirade.

How did Nurse Mackellen put up with such abuse at her place of work. Yet how to shut up such a miserable tyrant…without upsetting or affecting the innocent. This was the complexity of detection. Of reduction of harm done.

It was the constant pursuit of the ghost in the machine.

Unable to stand the shouting a minute longer…he strolled to the pair and looking directly at Ward Sister he said.

"Why don't YOU be quiet…just for a change. You might enjoy the peace."

Shut up one more bully…successfully applied.

Ward Sister's mouth made a perfect (oh) a silent one.

He walked towards room number 22—Amira's. Thinking as a heavy peace fell like a cosy warm curtain…mmm so that's how to deal with you!

The door was open, and Sally had taken off her sturdy boots and heavy school coat and was lying alongside her mum with the snuggling ability that only girls of seven can truly accomplish. They were whispering to each other it was so lovely to see. He looked at his watch thinking. Five more minutes won't hurt.

He found the hospital visitor chill zone and bought two latte's and some hot chocolate.

Threw a handful of cakes on a plate and a snow cake for Sally. Then paid up at the till. Returning to room 22. He knocked politely.

"Come in come in whoever you are…"

"I come in peace and have cakes and coffee."

"Oh my yes you do and most welcome."

"Sally darling go and find a chair for our chum."

They all settled down. Amira had her drink poured into the beaker…nibbled the snow cake.

"This is a surprise picnic thank you, detective."

"Can I eat two, Mummy?"

"Looks like you need a treat hon…so why not."

"May I look?"

The detective opened the little black notebook, but only a few lines met his eyes.

"Ah yes there is a reason…my eyes are not focusing…not an excuse, a reality."

"Oh of course the morphine. Do you recall anything."

"Yes, when I lay quietly thinking there was a 'flash of recall'… I think you call such moments; like when you wake from a dream…just for those few seconds, there is a picture…when I walked into the mall there was a woman staring at me, or at the very least in my direction. Then it's just the book…"

"The book."

"Sally had some money left over from her birthday, so I thought to pick up a book she wanted…I was in the shop looking through the titles when I thought a horse had kicked me…it was the bullet of course."

"Sorry, Amira, but I don't see the connection."

"I knew the woman, I think it was someone from Cairo."

"Oh, your work as a guide."

"Don't say that in front of Yasmin…we spend years researching as Historians. Tour guides often just pick up a quick degree…or just the patter by ear. We bring the unbiased research you see, the real stuff. Tourists rarely know Akhenaten from Seti the 1st. We are bound by the factual, as proven as deep as the textual evidence allows. Champollion, we bow to you stuff."

"Sorry, I am lost."

"You're meant to be."

"Ah the deeper knowledge."

"Yes, but we are flawed. These insights produce smug attitudes and secrets kept, especially from colleagues. Producing (THE WORK!)—Do you trust quickly in your profession?"

"Absolutely not…"

"There you see."

"I truly had no idea this study had such an adrenalin of mystery and secrecy."

"Read about the inter-departmental battles to locate the tomb of Tut Ankh Amun…the teenage Pharaoh of the 18th Dynasty…"

"Oh yes that was all over the news when he was found…Theban hills. Am I right?"

"Valley of the Kings November 22, 1922…by Howard Carter. A genius of understanding. He had this insight. Belzoni and Champollion also. My very own life was changed forever by I.E.S. Edwards, another Egyptologist with a genius for understanding ancient lives."

"Who is that? There are strange connotations surrounding that name."

"He wrote… 'The Pyramids of Egypt'."

"Ah you have alighted upon a subject that I find fascinating."

"So you should. So many go there for two-weeks holiday…what nonsense," They say to me.

"We want to see as much as possible. At home, they see one documentary, fly out to Cairo see a pyramid or two then talk rot. The problem starts for some as they get home A creepy feeling and a dissatisfaction, then the yearning to return. The spell has been cast. The magnet is pulling them like a tiny helpless pin. While others say they hate it…but what they hate is the way Egypt makes them feel."

"Oh, you are serious."

"More than you dear detective. When you retire, that's it. We historians do not. Egypt will not let go." Amira lay back and closing her eyes quietly and promptly fell asleep.

Sally was mystified and gathering up Binx, she held him tightly.

Chapter Two
Snake Woman

Detective Alain Veldour had a determined look as he left Room 22.

Sally tearful now in spite of a picnic of hot chocolate and cake was going back to school.

He drove her slowly, handing out tissues from a box in the car. Sally sniffled. This awful thing that had her mummy and kept changing her mummy was not letting go.

Sadie and Binx were her one consolation; Mr Gagnon of course was kind.

Her own father was calling every evening after his work was finished. Her meals were placed with Sadie's, all beautifully prepared. Mummy was not a good cook, but Sally wanted the slightly unusual flavours of her mistakes. Perfect isn't perfect…not really.

She struggled out of the big car and waited miserably while the detective answered his mobile. There were such a lot of lights along his dashboard. He took her hand and walked her to the Head's office where he filled in a form. Walking back to his car he waved to Sally who stared out of an upper floor window through a space between a badly drawn capital 'L' and a Llama. All in reverse of course.

Later that day, he drove home collected the excited poodles and shopped at the Auto Mart…let the dogs run in the local park…which they loved. He went on to Amira's house…he was known for his unusual approach during investigations. So why not live up to quirky behaviour. He spread out the tool kit of the year and started to repair, service and fine tune lovely old Mumblechuckler.

At nine in the evening he had her purring. So he locked up and took Indie and Bindi home…waved to neighbours who had curtain and blind twitched merrily, but to give them their due had brought him and the poodles snacks and hot drinks. Declaring him, in private of course, a possible candidate for the next husband. They had witnessed Sally's father being horribly aggressive towards her mother. Old gossip dies hard.

In the spotless private room Nurse Vicky Mackellen had helped Amira into the chair by her bedside. Therapy sessions were now on the schedule. Reluctance also on same schedule.

Across the corridor, a young man sat in her office. Liam Mackellen who… volunteered as a reader for some of the patients, writing and correspondence for others.

When Amira was as comfy as the sutures allowed, Vicky called him in "Amira this is my brother Liam he reads to people, if you prefer of course, he will sort correspondence…it's your choice." Amira had her mouth in the 'Oh bloody hell position'. Either that, or lock jaw.

Liam should carry high vis warning hazards…(totally overkill in the handsome male department.)

He drew up a seat and delved about in a rucksack. Held up—'History of Deep Angling'.

'The on Trend Greeny'…Shakespeare. Then as a grand finale…

'Memoirs of a Paris Madam'.

Amira chose 'Deep Angling'. Grinning madly, Liam opened at random and began:

"Yawn yawn splash yawn."

"Stop it you are not to make me laugh."

"Ah truly sorry about such an ill-judged beginning. Now, I have always found Martine the maid of Boulevard des Capucines a very rewarding second choice…"

"I was expecting a serious reader with a calming manner."

"Yes, well I was expecting a vision in lace…so looks like we are both set back on our heels."

"Oh well so sorry, Prince Liam…but I don't have my make-up case… There was also a bullet to deal with as a bloody priority but hey…"

Liam rummaged about in his copious rucksack produced a flask of hot chocolate, sarnies, a Tupperware case of cake and Amira's make-up case.

"Oh, how did you?"

"Burglary pure and simple, that and a desire for mascara in any form."

Amira took the case.

"You shame me into an apology."

"Apology accepted…hot chocolate?"

Vicky came in with some more books and a few letters.

"Ah I see you two are hitting it off."

"We didn't have the heart for Angling…but Martine is stripped and ready for action. Amira is keen to turn that page."

"Oh, were in first name city…so refreshing."

"Liam brought me my make-up."

"Ah well that is how to win over any woman. Sonia and Jack called by on their way to work and dropped off several things they thought you might need mail and stuff…you were in therapy."

"That was a shame did they say when they might come back."

"Tomorrow yes, Saturday. They can bring Sally and take her on to her father's place later."

"Oh him, he didn't visit I suppose."

"You supposed correctly."

"What is your job, Liam?"

"Oh, teaching the very resilient to learning and training cats to pee in window boxes."

"Amira take him off our hands please. He needs a wife and gawd in heaven with that face he's gonna find it impossible."

"Hey that's enough Vickamonstrousness I am here you know."

Vicky straightened up the bed and gently brushed Amira's hair, applied a little blusher.

"Right, I'm off duty now until Sunday."

"Have a lovely time Vicky thank you for making me feel better."

Nurse Mackellen left with a flourish and jazz hands. Amira smothered laughter settled back in the chair and pointed to her correspondence.

"Do you mind opening those please, Liam?"

The next hour was taken up with Amira being helped through the practicalities of being divorced and running a home…she was tired of it and had to admit that it was a tough call…when they had finished…Amira fell fast asleep.

She woke to the clatter of the evening meal being delivered by Misery Annie…

Who was now on track for two medals in grump and one in (Ignore All Patients.)

Amira didn't care she was hungry for the first time in a week. Sadly, the timing was seriously off. So often life lines up the goodies and we can't indulge.

After four mouthfuls she felt nauseated and shoved the plate away irritated.

Sonia and Jack arrived with Sally on Saturday and Jack was ecstatic holding Amira's hand very gently and looking totally pleased she was looking so much better.

Amira and Jack were both rescued from alcoholic parents. His father was vindictive and brutal at the drop of a hat. Sometimes, without the hat dropping.

Amira's grandfather had taken them both in. They owed him their excellent attitude to life.

Jack owned his own paint supplies warehouse and had proved himself business-like. A good husband very capable, good natured and homey. His wife Sonia in contrast was a flirtatious comic. They were oddly matched and yet it worked. Sonia had brought glamour nighties and hair products…she set Sally the task of laying out curling tongs and fetching drinks.

Jack told Sonia.

"Darling, this is not a beauty salon!"

"Oh but sweety it is."

A tonic. They closed the door to keep out Ward Sister. Luckily, the ticking off from Detective Alain Veldour hadn't worn off yet.

"We have seen 'The Liam'…Now listen to Mummy darling Amira. What does Mummy know?"

"Mummy knows best."

"That's right."

Sally was happy. She was flushed with excitement and lining up toys along the pillow. Sonia cleansed Amira's face and made her up…brushed her hair and applied the magic tongs to the music of an unseen and unheard orchestra of transformation adverts…for before and much later.

Jack entertained Sally and for his pains was given a facial of the worst kind "Sally you are very heavy handed with that cosmetic sponge…go easy, Jack is not a rubber toy."

"But he is, Mummy, he is."

"Jack, you are allowed to protest."

"Oh I think he's used to a bit of rough treatment Amira."

Amira blushed. Jack was like an older brother…Sally was very over the top with her administrations.

Sonia stood back and admired her work.

"Not bad considering you were half dead last week."

They all laughed and then stopped as the door opened.

"Liam!"

Amira was obliged to hold her side and grit her teeth. She was very much afraid she may well resemble Bride of Frankenstein.

Sonia forever impossibly wicked…stood in front of Amira and arranged her hair to perfection all the while pulling grotesque faces of…wowee and yes please. She leaned in and whispered in Amira's ear.

"We are going now…you have permission to roll him on the floor."

Then straightened up and taking all her bits and bobs went to the door and in a terribly good southern drawl announced…

"I have had just about all I can take of this dump."

Sally kissed her mother repeatedly and all toys in turn. Jack raised his brows, and the men did a hello and bye with nodding dog understanding of the all-male and back slaps club. Jack turned Sally around by her head and marched her out the door…which of course she liked. Liam approached the bed.

"Hey, you're looking good that is some wig you're nearly wearing."

"Thank you, a compliment coming from you."

"Now don't adjust your corsets…it's nice to see you wellish I hope they didn't go because of me."

"No, Sally is due at her father's house…access visit."

"Made you this."

"Oh, you are so kind."

They tucked into still very warm cheese melts and washed them down with illicit beer.

"My guess is Ward Sister is on break. Better crump those beer cans."

"Gimme yours, I'll take them home. No evidence is the best. Now where was I, did Martine have clothes on or off at the last session."

"Off!"

"Now, Amira, I can see trouble ahead with this Paris nonsense."

"It's your novel, Liam, may I remind you."

"There is far too much discussion about this very naughty girl from Montmartre."

"The Shakespeare then not much can go wrong there I should think."

"Tcccch how about the Taming of The Shrew. You can't say that can tease or corrupt."

"Well, this bit in French is a close shave with porno… She is up the duff. Do you read this to the single mothers in the maternity ward, Liam?"

"Well, there's a moral lesson."

"A little late in the day wouldn't you say."

"Not at all there is a great deal of eloquence in the line… He reached across to undo her lacy negligee and it slid to the floor with a silk rustle."

"No that is not to my taste; this is much more louche…"

"Louche belongs with wine and cognac…not cheese melts and cold beer."

"You read that somewhere?"

"Eloquence has nothing to do with pregnant maids."

"No but I think adding up might."

"And taking away."

Amira was stuffing a tissue in her mouth to prevent outright guffaws of laughter.

She felt like a schoolgirl.

"Liam…you're impossible."

"That's just what I told her."

Amira handed him her book…

'Hatshepsut… A Woman Who Would Be Pharaoh'.

"Oh my this is different."

"If you read this, I won't go to sleep."

"No, but do you know something, I just might."

"If you read this now…I promise to listen to… The life and loves of a Paris Femme Fatale."

"Deal."

Hatshepsut, a Woman Who Would Be Pharaoh (1473–1425)

The early part of the 18th Dynasty heralded a great change in the gender of rulership.

As Tuthmosis 1st held his first daughter Hatshepsut in his arms he had the most amazing thoughts that this child would, he was convinced, create a very different style of life for the people living along the banks of the great crop-giving wonderful Nile.

So…

He gave her a childhood of inclusion and all the discussion of the nomes and smaller groups of agricultural farms that spread through the two lands. Everything was open to her. Her tutor Senenemut was respected and beloved by Tuthmosis the 1st her father. When on her much beloved father's death Hatshepsut was crowned co-regent with the underage prince Tuthmosis III, there was resentment and the citizens of Thebes must have witnessed much anger displayed due to this co-regency.

In time, this female ruler would lay a new path for other women through boldness and statecraft. Being strong-minded would be insufficient. You must know the needs of your people and set about supplying them. Or rather, answering them. Adventures and great lives begin by astute planning and usually in youth. Hatshepsut learned much from her tutors…however, by royal custom at the time she was obliged to marry her half-brother Tuthmosis II …she soon found her abilities lay in statecraft. Also, through listening to the debates of men around her she was eventually able to give direct orders and they were carried out.

Her proud father placed a brilliant tutor to guide her through the labyrinth of Royal Court life, death and lies.

Young Hatshepsut soon became adept at seeing how the ambitious manoeuvred themselves into powerful key positions. How death constantly stalked the corridors of power. Senenemut her tutor and later her vizier was a very big influence—

Who cared for her and obviously nurtured her naturally imposing and commanding presence.

This, and having in her own right great wealth and lands…most certainly elevated this very progressive princess.

Also, the ancient Egyptians were masters in the art of grandeur, spectacle and panoramic settings.

They had such ability in how one creates 'Wonder'.

Egypt's vital advancement as a great civilisation was made by such as these.

All the known world around the Mediterranean ports traded to and fro with Egypt.

Hatshepsut knew her people and called them her rhekit (Lapwing) for they were as plentiful as the Lapwings that flirted and called through the verdant trees and flowers along the Nile the…'Father of all the rivers'.

All the pantheon of gods goddesses, some with the heads of animals some as small as the dung beetle…Khepri. Some with superpowers like the falcon Horus described in this quotation…

- 'My command stands firm like the mountains, and the sun's disk shines and spreads rays over the titulary of my august person, and my falcon rises high above the kingly banner unto all eternity'.

The falcon is the key to ancient Egypt. For this bird of prey is like no other as it gives the observer great pleasure during its magical flight in hunting. Much admired also for its beauty displayed whilst at rest.

The falcon and royalty have connections going back many thousands of years. Few lay claims to the falcon's power more deeply than Egypt…within the Egyptian pantheon, the falcon is famous as Horus who actually is several gods in one… A celestial god with close relationship to the Solar God reigning over the sky and the stars.

Horus takes on the personalities of so many gods…equally presented in the form of a falcon and Hurun, Harakhty, Haroeris, Harmahkis.

During the reign of the Tuthmoside Pharaohs, there was a period of peace, stability and harmony known as Ma-at. After the many battles the Egyptians had finally entered a period of feasting and happiness for they had finally driven the Hyksos out. Now the building of and the great unification of Egypt began.

When seeing so many deities carefully reinstated, there is a definite feeling that the rejoicing began as the last chariot of the Hyksos turned the corner amidst a flurry of desert dust. Subsequently, in this their introducing the chariot into Egyptian life…

they left an encouraging battle toy…for the chariots were drawn by magnificent highly skittish horses.

All the walls of tombs and temples began to express this new exciting mode of travelling.

Egyptians fell in love with this…clattering of hooves and wheels.

Well, the very wealthy such as the Pharaoh and his commanders did.

This love affair was on a par with a young rock star and his first Lamborghini.

A new age was dawning, this was fact. With this new phase of splendour for the land of Kemet and Deshret came a prophecy as unusual as it is unearthly.

Close and early investigation is required when understanding a little of the 18th Dynasty Queen/King Khenmet—Amun-Hatshepsut—(1473–1458 BC) had herself drawn, carved, painted in a most unusual way-wearing the entire regalia of a MALE Pharaoh. Building monuments, sending expeditions to foreign lands (the expedition to Punt sailed down the Red Sea to the East African coast). Perhaps it was situated at modern day Somalia. She took part in the athletic games, or jubilee festival just as other Kings had before. Taking the title 'son of Re'.

Going further than even this, she had her 'divine birth' recorded along the walls of her funerary temple at Dheir el Bahri. Depicted as a royal religious tradition her divine conception—as is expressed in this story. (The god Amun disguised himself as Tuthmosis I—c 1504–c1492 BC. He found the lovely Queen Ahmose sleeping…woken by the God's powerful perfume she saw only her husband Aakheperkare (Tuthmosis I) so, gave herself willingly, smiling upon his majestic presence, he went to her at once, his penis erect before her. He gave his heart to her, his love passed into her limbs. The palace was flooded with the God's fragrance and all his perfumers were from Punt. The god's pronouncement. Khenmet-Amun-Hatshepsut shall be the name of this daughter I have placed in your body. She shall exercise kingship over the whole land.

We must remember that the matriarchal bloodline relied upon the constant contact with conception of a child with the blood of Amun in their veins. Golden bodies and gold itself was the very 'soul tissue' of the gods and goddesses. We see this now as excellent (P.R.)…in addition, however, was a certain mysterious canon. A spiritual quality which cannot be explained. A divinity. Hatshepsut knew how to add dignity to her reign… Her father had much to do with giving her great confidence and tactics may have had a part to play in her donning the false beard and the full regalia of a king. These wily tactics could aid Egypt in her place upon the worlds stage. Alas, there is always some peculiar mischief on behalf of ambitious men 'hanging about' the crowned Pharaoh.

Life in a royal Theban household is full of 'Whispers around the pillars'. The Pharaoh certainly wielded great influence. We, in an age so far removed can still well imagine jealousy especially in Tuthmosis III. Who due to his age was obliged for many years to be in the shadow of her great power. Great building projects are attributed to her reign which stretched over some twenty-one years. If we still doubt her abilities. We have her stunning Mortuary temple at Deir el

Bahri and the beautiful relief depicted along the processional ramp area. This provides evidence of a highly regarded Pharaoh.

Such expeditions as the trading journey to Punt had also happened during the reign of 6th dynasty Pharaoh Pepy. There is proof that he wrote to members of his expeditions that of all the treasures...that they had found. The safe return of a tumbling dancing pygmy was of the greatest of his wishes. (He must be guarded at all hours of the day and especially as the pygmy sleeps.) In regard to Hatshepsut's reign. The expedition to Punt which is so beautifully depicted along the processional way.

The frieze shows men with massive baskets strong enough to hold whole trees and their native soil. The pots themselves designed specifically for the purpose...had special handles which enabled the very strong young men to pass poles through these handles and safely carry the trees on board the boats. The boats themselves are depicted beautifully along the frieze. The whole picture is one of great triumph...which tells us of a whole planned procedure to trade for specific trees. Myrrh and incense were, and still are, greatly prized. Hatshepsut dedicated much time to worship and ceremonial display within her temples to Amun Ra the goddess Hathor and her father Tuthmosis I...this required the burning of valuable incense. The gods and ancestors were believed to use the intermediary of the perfumed and exotic smoke to connect with the priests and Pharaoh with each plume of smoke, a spiritual conversation could take place...between the earth and the heavens the smoke rising perfumed, edifying, rich.

The shadowy temple's exotic interior lit by torchlight dancing over the figures of Hatshepsut her priest and her serving women in their gossamer fine clothes. The drama of the great dish of fire and stunning sistrum music drifting with the incense through the great pillared temple to Amun at Karnak. Hathor also appears to play a massive part in Hatshepsut's life. Hathor at Djeser-Djeseru played a vital role in the ritual spiritual life of the court at Thebes.

A ritual combined in 'The Feast of the Valley'. Which took place during summer under the new moon at Shemu the second month of summer. Amun, who usually dwelt alone in his very own sanctuary at Karnak. Anyone who has passed through this high energy temple can imagine its beauty captured by thousands of years of forceful ambience... Amun would spend his time attended only by his priests.

The perfuming washings and dressing…of the cult statue was their duty alone. No ordinary person ever entered the sanctified room where the god 'resided'… He was visited only by the priest with offerings of fine meat bread wine and beer. On the appointed day, he would be carried from his dark sanctuary where all would be torch lit and taken with his companion statues of Mut and Khonsu…across the river Nile to spend a night with beloved Hathor at Djeser—Djeseru. Hatshepsut adored this festival…escorted by priests in the fine Leopard skins of their station, with musicians dancers and sistrum shakers. Incense would be carried by the specially chosen. Acrobats gave thrilling performances and those around would gasp…all the excited Theban people would be delighted at this amazing procession.

Amun with his own special servants would be carried shoulder high in his very own golden barque.

When they reached the Nile, all would be assembled on the great barge. Crossing the water and guided with great care through the specially dug canal systems through to the mortuary temples of the West Bank.

Djeser-Djeseru was set out with lovely gardens…religious rites performed at points along the journey. Sadly, the small Valley Temple is no longer visible.

Theban families stayed at their own tomb chapels and feasting and drinking would be especially happy. Amun's servant bearers made a stop at a small shrine along the way if necessary and finally carry him along the processional way of beautifully painted sphinxes. As the night progressed he would be with Hathor and the people would feast by torch light…What an amazing sight and sound this must have been.

Sunrise brought a special climax ritual then Amen would be returned once more across the Nile with sunlight glinting on pools and the Nile River.

PUNT…Myrrh, Incense bark and perfumed oils.

The fabulous trees with their exquisite perfume brought all the way from Punt would have added greatly to the pleasures of the now exhausted people.

Those same trees may well have brought back wonderful memories of the news of the expedition returning from Punt. Perhaps, they returned at night and the great boats were sighted from a long way off and runners came with great haste to the Palace of Hatshepsut. She would have dressed carefully attended by her ladies in the costume room with its fabulous wigs, which did she choose? How her hands must have hovered over each wonderful Aegis necklace which did she select?

Each careful decision of the luxurious bangles and earrings hair adornments and crown. We can imagine the scurry the shouting of "They have returned…at last, they have come". Such excitement in the voices calling through the night from the great river. The sweating straining oarsmen…their heavy breathing and relief in this the coming by night by torch flair with tiny sparks flying into the celestial night filled with the all-encompassing stars.

The ultimate in homecomings after perhaps years of absence. The unloading of the strange animals their cries and calls. Fires lit to prepare food…bread made, meat roasted. Fruit laid out beer poured.

The myrrh trees precious as gold to every Pharaoh priest and noble…unloaded and Hatshepsut hastily gathering her gardeners to prepare the ground in the garden of the mortuary temple for the careful placement of each tree it's watering in, care and protection. Their careful removal from basket and pot. When all was completed…oh the joy…Hatshepsut would have walked with her serving women through the garden with its lushness all around.

A fragrant experience. Cooling shadows and the glow of the pomegranate. Grapes and as always, the pink flowered tamarisk, acacia, willow, cornflower, mandrake, poppies, daisies…and the lotus.

The cow and the lotus. The lotus is depicted time and time again. With incredible self-cleansing properties…representing all that is good and pure. Hundreds of scenes within all the Pharaoh's life show its beauty and importance…constantly represented in reliefs and within the designs of artistic furnishings used in their daily life. The richness a lotus holds within its bloom is still valued. Blue Nile lotus perfume is the most exotic alluring perfume one can ever experience. The sacred lotus Hathor.

Hathor also held a vital role in Hatshepsut's life… The goddess is described within a complex structure of roles… Daughter of Ra, considered as the eye of the sun…wife of Horus …also mother of Horus sometimes. Several functions are…linked to her…celestial deity, the lady of the far lands, Goddess of joy, Lady of the Sycamores…her principal place of worship today is at Dendara in Upper Egypt.

Hathor is a very artistic representation and there are echoes of the cow and lotus used in ritualistic house-warming parties today in India. In Egypt she is a woman with two horns surrounding a solar disc. Hathor's origins go so far back in the mists of time—she is synonymous with the oldest of history. A documentation known as the Narmer palette…which was carved from schist—a votive palette, recalls the unification of the two kingdoms by first dynasty ruler Narmer. Hathor the goddess is present in the form of cows...her absolute symbol. Also, as if to draw emphasis, is depicted at the top of the palette on both sides.

TODAY...

The Hathor column is beautifully visible to those visitors who have followed the processional ramp at Hatshepsut's Mortuary Temple at Dheir el Bahri on the West Bank of Luxor...turn left and you will find this column within the temple dedicated to Hathor. Exquisite in its formation with the capitol sculpted in the form of a sistrum.

Hatshepsut always referred to Hathor as 'my mother'. And incorporated worship of this goddess within her vision for Egypt.

We must also be inspired as her actions were mostly that of defiance towards the accepted views of a 'feminine station' and a turn in the road of destiny within the preparation for her role as a determined acceptance as a male Pharaoh...the first woman to be called Pharaoh.

She adored her father and the tutor he had chosen for her, one—Senenemut. Respect was obviously present on all sides.

We can imagine her walking with great deliberation about Thebes and her people prostrating before this truly enigmatic ruler.

Later in her reign the stepson Tuthmosis III...must have felt great frustration when she had the upper hand as an all-powerful co-regent. Especially when she planned the unique expedition to Punt.

For upon her death, he exacted a peculiar revenge by a desecration of nearly every statue or cartouche containing her name and likeness. Beware present day guards in the lovely Mortuary Temple built for her by architect Senenemut who, as a very old man had followed the 'blueprint' of Mentuhotep II's architect. These guards will point to Hathor and tell you Hatshepsut...with great and emphatic spit to accompany this untruth. The fact that they hold out hands to expect money for this misinformation, is 'rarely' seen as a wonderfully unique accessory to your visit.

The Mortuary Temple reflects a time of much grandeur. Thebes was a tremendously significant religious centre on the West Bank city of the dead.

The East Bank...

The city of the living, temples built in dedication to gods situated on the East Bank of the Nile.

The West Bank ceremonies displayed great devotion to the dead. Kings having been buried there since the 11th Dynasty. (c. 2055–c. 1985 BC) This meant that Western Thebes took a particularly important place in the New Kingdom (c1550–c1069). The Valley of the Kings stirs the imagination of thousands of people world-wide. In the much-documented Ramesside period (c. 1295–c. 1069 BC). The Kings ruled from their Northern Capital of Per-Ramesses…but were buried in Western Thebes. (Take note there is an exquisite mortuary temple at Medinet Habu.)

And the Ramesseum which served the Ka of Kings buried in the Valley and spread out along the desert fringes. Hatshepsut's is the best preserved and imitates the architectural lay-out of Mentuhotep's II—(c. 2055–c. 2004 BC)-very grand and especially intricate funerary complex…south of the deep Theban Hills recently, much more has been excavated and new writing offers fascinated insight into his reign.

Liam closed the fascinating book. Drank deeply of some water then as Amira also sipped water he stooped and scrabbled about in his rucksack…took out a stunningly lovely bookmark depicting a Pharaoh dressed in the grandest pleated kilt of white cotton…filmy, revealing, exotic, sensual.

"Oh! Liam how fabulous and what an excellent reader you are."

He blushed up faintly as he packed away his things.

"You are a little tired I think…I have to go now as well, a tricky tutorial on the schedule. Your subject is the biggest surprise."

"Thank you for making it a great time for me. When will you be coming again?"

"I have to wait for Vicky to sort of okay it all…but very soon."

Amira waved…she fell asleep in minutes after he had gently closed the door behind him. Therapy woke her again and persuaded her to go for a walk in her backslide to a wobbly Jemima Puddleduck impersonation a little way down the corridor. Therapy Nurses Gemma and Drew were full of pride.

"Very good Amira, this may not feel like it but you are healing nicely. We have to get the balance right for you as an individual. Those sutures are in a tricky area. We all have to work with what we have."

"I am so weak…it's all so new…my life was so lively before…you know running after a six-year-old. Correction, seven-year-old."

They helped her to sit in the chair and she actually ate her supper watching television. The news was still crammed with the terrorist attack at the popular shopping mall. She watched mouth open as her favourite anti-terrorist detective was interviewed on screen with dozens of reporters, and bustling film crews who pushed forward and gathered in front of him. His lovely voice calming and sensitive.

"We have a very big task ahead and are still collating evidence, information, and caring for the bereaved of those who tragically lost their lives…this is our paramount role…we are learning the modus operandi of these murderers."

"Detective…how many survived this atrocity."

"Two."

Amira gulped, there was another survivor. A hundred questions rattled through her mind. She knew forty people had been callously mown down in the carpark…they had run to the right. She was only alive now because she had turned left!

A nurse bustled in and cleared her tray.

"You have visitors Julia Gagnon and your little girl…and the handsome Helicopter Medic Pierre Tremblay hopes to see you…if that's okay. He's off duty later."

"Oh yes. My hero! I owe my life to his sharp eyes."

"Well ease up on the kisses; his wife is a bit of a jealous type. Actually, she is more than a bit."

"I will keep it to a handshake."

A little girl peeped around Amira's door.

"Hello, are you Sadie? Do come in."

She withdrew and grubby revolting Binx peeped around waving a paw.

Sally came in giggling and plonked herself on the bed. She was obviously in a 'this is my lovely mummy so I intend to show off mood'. In other words, normal stuff.

"Hello, this is a lovely surprise. Is Mrs Gagnon with you?"

A stocky, dark-haired very friendly woman came in carrying a bag of goodies.

"Yes, but please call me Julia. How are you…oh my god they've sat you out in a chair already. Now, I took the liberty of bringing you a little bit of normality and contraband at the same time."

Julia handed her a takeout of a juicy burger with delicious barbecue sauce and some incredibly expensive strawberries. A glossy magazine finished off the treasures.

"Wow thank you, Mrs…sorry Julia…I'm ultra spoilt. The food is so basic here…of course, but all of the staff…apart from…" Julia leaned closer.

"Ward Sister. But we knew her from when I had that bundle of mischief over there." Inclines her head towards Sadie.

"Oh, that must have been quite an experience…but excellent end result."

Julia swelled with pride. Sadie was a striking little girl with gentle wide set lovely eyes.

"Thank you, Julia, for all you're doing for us. We will need to talk about expenses…eventually…"

"Oh, good lord no, no, this is our opportunity to give back…we have loads of space…do you two girls mind buying us all cool drinks…which is your favourite, oh sorry would you like a hot one rather than a cold?"

"Cold please…and my purse is over there." Julia shook her head vigorously. She gave Sadie money and Sally wriggled off the bed kissed Amira and ran off giggling with Sadie.

"They are good at entertaining each other. Sally loves to cuddle up to Sadie they whisper about boyfriends and makeup. They think we don't hear."

"Oh, I'm sorry Julia my daughter is a bad influence…I bought her a lip salve and you know how precocious they become at seven."

"Mmmm they are lovely and keep us laughing."

"Well, a big thank you is in order. Detective Alain is behind all this and when he told me I felt so relieved."

"How is the therapy? Do you feel like you're making headway."

"Ah that…I'm walking very oddly, but at least it is a sort of walking."

She touched her side involuntarily.

"We can't help with that, but you might need to stay somewhere, when you're signed off out of here, do consider us please we would be easy going."

"You have done so much for us already…Jack and Sonia want to put us up…Sally must have mentioned them…and by the way where have those two got to."

Julia frowned and hurried off to find them…she passed through the door as a trim man in his early thirties was about to tap on the door. They both laughed and Julia said something Amira couldn't hear.

In came Pierre Tremblay. Amira knew instantly who he must be…he was in full medic helicopter pilot gear…festooned with badges and a trustworthy (I can do) air floated around him.

"My hero!"

"Oh, you've made my day…ooh you're looking very different today Amira this is surely not the little drowned pussycat we hauled out of that skiff—it can't be."

"Oh, let me give you a little hug…the stitches won't stand for a big one yet."

He squeezed her shoulders ever so slightly. He was very personable and warm.

"I just saw the Brittle Bluebottle—mon Dieu! She's a pill…"

Amira had to hold her side…

"No no this room has collected all the black marks for laughter and she cannot stand Vicky…I mean Nurse Mackellen…I must ask how did you ever find me on that riverbank."

"Oh, I have this piece of equipment that really does the sweep for me."

"Sweep…"

"Yep, the colour of your clothes stands out against all the greenery so unless you're in camouflage well…here you are alive and kicking."

"Thank you and thank all your crew."

"Hate to sound you know weird but you're looking so fit and so fit. Ha!"

"Oh, thanks yes, I'm feeling so much better. Everyone is marvellous here…I suppose even the Brittle Bluebottle may have her good points. Oh, and I'm sure I heard you fly over once or twice."

"Yep, we deliver pizza to the doctors when we've got nothing else to do!"

"They must be thrilled, but why don't I believe you. Tell me Pierre the news gave out there is another patient that you rescued from the mall…what happened to them."

"Ah that'll be young Tristan…he dived under a table or unit or some such. Badly damaged his ankle. He was hoping to join Cirque de Soleil as an acrobat. Well, he can say goodbye to that for six months, probably longer."

"You're kidding how awful for him…must be a bad break."

"Sadly yes. He used to be able to do tumbles, handsprings flying cartwheels. Now, he can barely walk on it even with it all strapped up and each day he is impatient to be in therapy…his impatience will be his undoing."

"Can't anyone…er calm him down make him listen."

"Therapy here are doing the best they can. I'll tell Vicky perhaps as you both survived something very terrible and unique…he might listen to you."

"Pierre you should know I can't often persuade my seven-year-old to listen." Pierre pulled up a chair and answered the lively trill on his mobile link.

He nodded and replied, "Got that, sweetheart. I'm visiting our patient Amira so speak later."

He closed the phone and looked at her with a 'yes' expression.

"What kind of helicopter do you fly?"

He pulled out a wallet and she saw a fabulous crew grinning broadly in front of an Agusta Westland Helicopter. Huge lettering declared…it to be a…CH 149 CORMORANT. Famous for her flying capacity in Air Sea Rescue conditions. Humanitarian missions. Medical evacuations. Impressive. Pierre Tremblay… Tactical Rescue Pilot grinned out as the top man.

"Wow how amazing did I really go in that?"

"Yes, you sure did. She saved your life."

Amira kissed the photo.

He removed the photo from the wallet.

"Oh no that's your special one."

"Nah we have some more…she's our baby she can really get down and get cracking in the worst of weather."

"Well, kiss her for me…thank you so much for saving my life."

He touched his forehead.

"Right, I'm away to my dinner and an impatient missus."

Then he was gone. Amira looked at the photo for a long time. Sally Julia and Sadie also looked carefully at the photo…they all became very sombre and sipped cool drinks, made small talk…Sally could not get close enough to her mother. Julia and Sadie whispered, "We'll be just outside, give you a few minutes."

Sally was tearful and Amira kissed her over and over then brushed her hair ever so carefully.

Trying not to wince. She wanted normal.

They both did.

That night for some unknown reason the staff forgot to close the blinds so Amira lay watching the dusk float through trees in the hospital grounds. Shadows were stealing along the interior branches of the oldest trees. A few birds were settling down and gradually dusky light no longer touched their delicate feathers…instead an eerie purple light fixed itself very gradually, delicately and artfully painted as if by an invisible hand. A feeling of calm had replaced the nausea. Amira felt that Pierre had somehow brought her old self in with him…perhaps on his clothes. A reassurance.

He had given her real comfort… When he had talked so frankly and openly. It was good to be able to thank the person who had seen her in that skiff all wet and bloody. His expertise had restored her. Humbling. She watched out of the window. The birds were oblivious of her and were gradually happily settling down for the night. The antics of their pushing and shuffling about along the tree bough was amusing.

They had bright little eyes and although thick glazing on the windows prevented any sound. Amira sensed their silence fall with the darkness. Their last tidying of stray feathers the move over nudges. Soon their eyes closed. No breeze stirred the leaves…just a gentle breathing came from the night. Amira also slept soundly and deep comforted by a poem…

Drifting.

Walls steal the shadows from unsuspecting trees.

And the Nagla palm caresses the sky

the longest river holds a conversation

with the drifting mist of dawn.

A heron rises,

wing beats disturb pollen into lazy swirls.

Egypt is stirring.

The ward was bustling about with morning staff. Nurse Vicky Mackellen is back on duty. Liam is also in the busy hospital helping a frail elderly man with some challenging correspondence. Government bureaucracy sucks at directing its missives at real people. They are seemingly incapable of detecting the possibility of a real person being behind a name.

This elderly patient is more forgiving of their stupidity and 'crap speak'…than Liam will ever be. He basically, sees too much of it. This will be over soon, and he will drive over to his college and give a lecture on literature at the turn of the millennium. What's not to love. Amira is in Therapy and stretches her legs slightly easier with each passing day. Eating better has given her energy. An attractive male is eyeing her constantly from the benches. She is convinced it is Tristan…he sports a support boot on his right leg. She however, dare not break concentration and manages with superhuman effort to stop walking like Jemima Puddleduck.

Her therapist notices at once.

"Amira well done this is a huge improvement…"

She left Therapy on a cloud of pride. Vicky had come for her and was pushing her back to Room 22 Amira managed to eat half her lunch. She felt the worst might be behind her. A corner was turned…and Liam was coming to see her tomorrow. He arrived and they watched the local television's coverage of the first of several memorials to those who had lost their lives at the mall. Vicky held Amira's hand…as she cried. The loss of life was so horrific from teenagers to mothers and fathers. The pictures of those responsible were the greatest shock… A young woman in a black head covering was amongst them.

Vicky was called away and Liam had no words. There were none.

The routine in the hospital became Amira's steady source of influence. Therapy over one day, she managed with the aid of a walker to return to her room. Tristan was waiting outside in the corridor. His athletic frame slouched a little. Even so the moment he stood up although rather awkwardly, there was an underlying lithe animalistic ease of movement.

He opened the door for her let it swing in slowly.

"I'm Tristan…we have more or less the same therapy timetable."

"Yes, where were you today?"

"Oh, a doctor wanted to check me out… Would you like a cold drink from the café…"

"Mmm that's a great idea, give me a minute and I'll get some money."

"I won't be long."

He was very different to what she had expected. His manner was easy and those eyes a dark lustrous brown almost black which charged his looks with a kind of sultry challenge. She felt heat rise to her face and stay there. For reasons unknown, she cleaned her teeth and tousled her hair. Scrabbling for make-up she managed to apply mascara…very lightly. The polite tap made her jump.

"Please come in…I'm making myself presentable."

He sat down and yanked open the cold cans handing her one. The effervescent rush was embarrassingly sexual. She knew what it was then, what it was about him…he was damned sexy he had an immediacy to him. She felt the air charge up between them. She was so glad the door was closed at this winding down part of the day. Before she sat down in the chair by the bed, she brushed past him…the zip of a thrill went right through her. He looked up at her and she eased herself into the higher chair. Their eyes were locked.

"Mmmm you are something else Amira."

He bent his head towards hers and she caught a little of his look it was not a difficult choice…her blood was pounding, and she felt his forehead on hers. This was it…the past receded and she touched the side of his mouth and kissed him, there was never any doubt in this part of the desire. She pressed herself to him and he caressed her neck and breasts. They had no choice. Life is like this…

"We seem to like each other."

She kissed him again.

"Yes."

A noise in the corridor made them sit back slowly. They sipped the coolness of the drinks and she had to straighten her clothes.

"Unexpected outcome to a stroll in the corridor."

"I want to undress you Tristan and…"

"Fuck me."

"I was going to gentle it down rather nicely to 'make love' to you."

"If you like."

He laughed out at her pretensions.

"I have a feeling Tristan you prefer crude realities to…"

"Anything else…yes. Why pretend, we want the same thing. Perhaps it's the survival thing celebrating what we survived. This even by itself is a kinda destiny."

"You are smouldering even as you sit there with that can in your hands."

"I am proud of my smoulder ability but I don't do it alone…"

She kissed him and fondled his torso fishing around inside the shirt finding him caressing him. He sat back slowly with a thoughtful look.

"Which side are your stitches where did the bullet."

"Here…"

"Must be gentle with you then, mustn't I?"

An erratic knock at the door silenced them. In walked The Brittle Bluebottle… with Misery Annie who carried a supper tray.

"Ah there you are. Mr Logan…would you mind returning to your own ward this instant. A supper tray is there…also your mother is waiting, this is a busy hospital not a meet and greet."

The sarcasm and venom was loaded so heavily in her voice…a look of dislike seemed to make her nose rise higher on her face, it was weird.

Amira lifted herself up slightly her voice was not strong, but she suddenly found a strange defiance mechanism from deep within…

"You rude, horrible woman who do you think you are we are survivors of an atrocity you bully you nasty, nasty piece of humanity…YOU return to YOUR office…this is MY VISITOR."

The silence that followed was larger than the room the ward the hospital. Larger even than Toronto.

The whisper, because that was all it was had changed everything. Horrified the Brittle Bluebottle began shaking from head to toe and scurried away. Misery Annie burst into the biggest smile… "Oh, you did it YOU YOU of everyone here it is astounding. Not one of them not one of us, we are so cowardly but not you…" She came to Amira and put her arm gently around her shoulders kissed her forehead. Squeezing her shoulders gently once more she hurried away. Tristan bent over Amira kissed her forehead.

"Absolutely right, well done. Better see what mum wants cannot wait to tell her…see you soon."

Amira nodded and for the rest of the evening was in a state of 'whatever will happen now. 'The next morning… Liam brought in Amira's Antiquities Newsletter easily spotted with its lovely Egyptian envelope, colourful stamps. Amira opened it excitedly, there was a letter and a neat post it note sticking out from the middle section declared…'

Egypt's Lost Golden City

"Oh, look, Liam, at last it's been found. Amazing, isn't it?"

He read the heading and sat down with the air of someone who has waited for this moment all his life.

"This is a serious bit of good news, Amira, do they want you to go over?"

"Not yet, but you're a good guesser they want me later. I told them what happened here but you can imagine it was all over the department they take terrorism very very seriously indeed."

"Do you miss it a great deal?"

"I have to keep a lot to myself because Sally can get distressed and god knows how she will react to my next mission." She sat quietly reading her letter.

Liam watched patiently he had mixed feelings when it came to Amira. He only slept with waitresses or college dropouts. He had a strangely reserved manner with those he dubbed 'thinking females'. Also, he saw there was a new and unmistakable confidence in her manner now.

Misery Annie whose real name 'Marti' was now finally displayed on an identity tab came in with two hot drinks. Also, on the neat tray lay a box of chocs with a note tied on.

"Oh, at last you are smiling…are things really that improved."

"Thanks to you we have had a much needed re-shuffle…I can at last wear this. She was keeping it telling me I hadn't done enough to earn it."

"Marti, that sounds ominously like she is mentally unhinged. Stressed… she's not here anymore surely."

Liam scrabbled about in the rucksack which Amira fully expected a three-piece suite of lounge furniture to come out of.

"She's not shown her face. As far as staff gossip goes…early retirement is bandied about."

"Oh, Marti, you are a very different person…I'm pleased things have improved so much."

"Thanks to your brilliant intervention do let me know what you need…the meal is a celebratory one today…fabulous, isn't it? All due to you standing up to her…nobody dared for fear of…well basically losing their position here…not having an income, plus the possible loss of a home. She was obviously well aware of her vile power. What a…" There was a silent agreement.

Marti winked and said with added new confidence…

"Oh, I am so happy here now. I couldn't do anything she had such control. By the way, you are looking much better and you have another good-looking man it's like a night club in here."

Laughter followed…just as it should…laughter after all is the best of medicines, isn't it. Another little knock and Tristan peered around the door.

"Marti this room has seen it all, come in Tristan…"

Marti stood aside for him…

"Oh, hi Tristan how's the walking today."

"Not too good. Therapy can't do much more. Amira here's my number and stuff. I'm spending a couple of weeks in this Aqua Clinic or something…mum and dad located it. They're brilliant as always. They'll be picking me up in a few minutes so thought I'd come over."

He approached the bed and plonked a bag of goodies and a few magazines on the locker. Bent over kissed Amira on her cheek. Marti had found her chirp and piped up…

"Tristan, I see there isn't much wrong with your other equipment."

Tristan totally un-phased gave out one of his smiles which had Marti fanning herself…saying… "Stop it sssssoooo sexy…"

Amira speechless gave a weak wave. It was all happening too fast.

Marti followed Tristan outside…of course.

Liam was looking very steadily in her direction as she tried to look normal, unflustered.

"Not quite able to carry the cool cats trick Amira are you."

"Oh, I dunno just a bit out of practice I suppose."

"He's a flirtatious chancer Amira…doesn't bother me but women are usually fluffed up by him."

"Perhaps I need a fluffing up right now…"

"Yes, but do you really think a man like that is a good bet."

"I'm a bit out of the scene I admit, Liam, but you know getting back on the horse is always…"

"It's your life, Amira."

"I have to start somewhere, sometime. Years since I yunno."

"Beautiful women can start again on quieter mounts. If they wish. Anyway, you have a brilliant bit of news from Egypt."

"Yes, I was hoping you might read it."

"I would love to."

Amira was so flustered, she was as Liam had very rightly pointed out probably out of her depth with the Tristan Logans of this world. Luckily, the article provided an immediate refuge. Liam dived right in.

'EGYPT'S LOST GOLDEN CITY…'

ATEN has at long last been successfully excavated by an Egyptian mission. ATEN named after an Egyptian Sun god lies in the desert at Luxor. ATEN has been dubbed already probably by journalistic enthusiasm as the Pompeii of Egypt due possibly to the way the sands had covered and preserved the remains. Archaeologists broke the news last September. The city built in the reign of Pharaoh Amenhotep III. Tut Ankh Amun's grandfather…who ruled for four decades until c. 1353 BC. A reign of great opulence and grandeur. This period in Egypt's history holds great fascination…the excavation originally was in search of a mortuary temple.

However, what has come to light is causing a stir. The complex contains several neighbourhoods, including a bakery with ovens. Several of the remains of dwellings measuring up to twelve feet high. Jewellery, colourful pottery, painted pottery animals, mud bricks with the seals of Amenhotep III. Scarab beetle, amulets…tools for spinning and weaving. A massive vessel for the storage or carrying of meat. Dr Zawi Hawass proudly announced the Egyptian mission's discovery…under the sands remarking, – "*Many foreign missions have searched over the years for this…but failed to locate the city. The city at present has been referenced as 3,000 years old…Tut Ankh Amun and Ay are said to have used it. Work continues to excavate the site further. There is naturally hope to uncover further vital archaeology to greatly enhance this dynasty. A further glimpse into the life of the ancient Egyptian's lives. Many have searched for this site in the past.*"

"You must be thrilled, Amira."

"Yes, there is always follow-on discoveries once anything like this happens. Look at this."

She handed him a letter. He scanned it quickly.

"Will you be well enough it's a long flight."

"An opportunity to take Japanese businessmen around the new Egyptian Museum out on the Alexandria Road…how many of those do you think a lowly researcher Egyptologist gets in one lifetime."

"Yes, but this is only some five weeks or so away."

"Quite."

Liam was called away to help another patient and Amira thanked him.

She pulled open the bag Tristan had left. There was a notebook, useful but puzzling as a present. A card with a bunch of bears rubbing their bottoms on trees—inside there were two contact numbers, email and web site. A new tee shirt pale blue in the softest cotton.

"Mmmm this is nice actually. Thanks, Tristan." A gold wrapper caught her eye…it was chocolate. She hid it quickly in the locker. She had a feeling the hospital shop was the only gift area open to him and it was very thoughtful. The card was fun and cleverly non-committal. She read the message:

Get better soon. As you guessed the hospital shop is a bit light on romantic gifts.

Love, T.

Even so, there was kindness behind the gifts. Sweet guy. Liam had been too quick to dismiss him. She had to work hard now on that release note from the consultant. She had plenty to work towards-. Back to Egypt. She mentally punched the air. YEH!

Chapter Three
An Astrological Country

All that followed Amira would recall with such surprise. She was so much better and tried her best to be calm but little bursts of merriment kept breaking out.

All the staff were in a great state of wondering what might or might not come out of 'The showdown in Room 22'. As it was now constantly referred to. Ward Sister was suspended. That was obvious. Later, retired or fired was talked about quite naturally.

Those tyrannical and over the top reactions she had so readily applied to every situation. A woman in her position was meant to exude calm and confidence so making those around her full of confidence. Fired was Amira's guess. Tension vanished out of the wards…Amira was waved at by everyone. Amira soon made brilliant progress and the wonderful day arrived when she finally got the word to go home…Sally, Sonia and Jack were thrilled, and slowly drove her to their ultra-modern home which was severely minimalist. This made life very easy for Amira her right leg was playing up and kept going into painful spasm…she was told it was a temporary thing. Sally was over the moons of Saturn and declared their temporary room in Sonia and Jack's fabulous home…The Biz…Amira wondered where such expressions came from. One of her first tasks after settling Sally in at Sonia and Jacks was to thank Vicky and Liam Julia and Edward for the great care and kindness. She sent special cards and chocs to the various hospital departments via reception. They responded quickly with phone calls. Amira wanted to give a party once she was back home but felt wary in case her finances were too screwed up. She had just waved off Sally in Julia's car, when an old Chevy rolled up. Liam jumped out and Amira put on some fresh coffee.

"What a great surprise, Liam, sit down and let me spoil you for a change."

"Jeeze what a place this is… Thought I had the wrong address then spotted you in your clothes."

"Rephrase please Liam, you make it sound like we met under sexually provocative circumstances."

"I thought we did. You were in bed in a sheer what not."

"Oh, that exciting number that opens up the back and is modesty incarnate at the front."

"Yes drives men wild that sort of thing."

"Yes Liam, I grant you that especially with the tears on my cheeks and the vomit bowl."

"Quite earthy and real I'd say."

"Now though you feel that my glam on trend surroundings are a turn off."

"Oh well with this kitchen worktop between us there is an overkill of domesticity."

"You are all talk Liam, words create false worlds so often. This is near to the real me…a mum and…"

"Yes, I have my refuge in words and jokes."

"Yet in the silence of meditation free from exterior torment and the temporary kaleidoscope of life all around us. Words cease to have meaning."

"They come and they go."

"Desire maintains its hold though."

"Liberation from Samsara is in resisting."

"Buddha found the middle way…not too much of extreme deprivation. No excess and a recognition of the changing world. All effort to find a permanent self-failed."

"Also, permanency is delusion. Our individual suffering. Self is to be extinguished. Free our self. Aged 35, the Buddha entered a deep meditative state and experienced many previous lives. One truth remained; all forms were subject to Samsara. Buddha went through a force of the liberation of his mind to find a solution. No need for gods or earthly status. Fundamental change was required. A new mission—He made his way to Varanasi which was to became a school for the clarification of the four noble truths. He found his old friends there. They were astonished at the change in him, he had indeed become the Enlightened One—One who recognises—Suffering. Craving. End of suffering, the eightfold path…wisdom leading to Nirvana the end of suffering, and end of Karma.

"Philosophical freedom is ridding yourself of samsara induced by greed driven concepts. Democratisation of Karma allows everyone the opportunity to reach Nirvana via a moral life. Be your own lamp. Master of your own fate."

"How does this work with your career within the history of the Ancient Egyptians."

"They were trying to develop Ma-at. Harmony and balance."

"They were so war-like."

"They had no thought process to bypass the self-invented gods."

"So, they failed."

"They wanted to live beyond."

"Beyond what."

"Death."

"Oh of course they went to extreme lengths to retain self."

"Yes, and so sought the cosmic energy of sending Pharaoh to the stars…to the circumpolar stars… They called them the Indestructible Ones."

"Got you…"

"People see the pyramid of Khufu as huge stone blocks or a destination for a holiday."

"They saw a forever."

"A resurrection machine and a journey through the cosmos to life hereafter."

"Wow."

"A lesson in the fragility and yet the power of the human mind."

"All over again."

"Proof of Samsara, proof that compassion and empathy can direct change…for the betterment of our brief experience in this our form in this life. Reincarnation is inevitable but it is how we conduct ourselves…in this life."

"Why did the Pharaoh have such a hold over the people."

"They saw him or indeed her as literally a god on earth…a golden divinity the one way they could go to the god in the stars."

"Not with you."

"If he got there, he would take them too."

"But he was a mummy!"

"You will need to read… 'That which is in the Amduat'."

"I'm bowing out sorry Amira."

"Most people do."

"I can't get my head around any of it."

59

"No…Egypt draws only those to her with a rich curiosity. A spirit of ecstasy that will follow with a great thirst to know for its own sake."

"I think too much you would say."

"Resist too much I would say."

"Vicky thinks highly of you."

"Which is another way of saying."

"You have me there."

"I will never have you. What happened to the trying a gentler horse after so long…out of circulation then?"

He went crimson to the roots of his beautiful hair.

"A lesson for me Amira…my Achilles Heel exposed."

"Well think lightly of yourself, dear Liam…but you should wear a badge saying. 'Look but don't touch'."

"Supernatural instincts such as yours, Amira… It's me that's out of my depth."

"I wanted to cuddle you the other day, but the frost was too much for me."

"I suppose Tristan has no frost…but he's also not here is he."

"He throws aside convention enough to get the girl."

"Crude."

"But effective."

"You just want a roll in the hay."

"Let's not fall out, Liam…intellectual arguments are peculiar forms of foreplay in my book."

"Why don't you just ring him up and…and and…"

"Good idea thanks for dropping by."

He did not close the door quietly…Amira ungratefully perhaps was glad to see the back of him…and was reminded of Goldilocks and the three bears. One was too hot, one was too cold, and one was just right. She looked forward immensely to the third.

Sonia came back early and Amira told her all that had happened.

"Oh what a plonker! Did he get all het up and then go on a sour note…just to prove what for fucks sake."

"Literally, precisely, stupidly."

"And there was me thinking he would be sweet and sweaty between the sheets. Oh well, let's have a wine before we make the supper… Where's Sally, upstairs…?"

"Music lesson with Sadie they both love the flute."

"Oh, do you remember when you and Jack used to play the recorders together, it was like old tom cats having kittens. Rose' wine do for you."

"Come here Sonia, you darling normal bundle of fun. Yes Rose' is fine thanks, but gentle hugs first."

The Sonia, Jack, Sally, and Amira with visits from Gypsy the cat…was a rich and happy household…Jack took Sally out to the local kids club one Saturday to give Amira chance to study and revise for the up and coming trip to Cairo. Her visa was sorted and the Antiquarian Department had arranged for her to stay with a fellow Egyptian historian in their visitor flat near the old Museum of Antiquities. Amira was obliged to call on Sally's father who luckily wanted a holiday and so it all fell into place. Which had to be a first.

Amira had worked like a Trojan and was winding down with a shower when on emerging and wrapping a towel around herself the front doorbell went into overdrive. Sonia was showing buyers with big bucks around a huge property over at a new development and so Amira went to the door expecting the mail man…she peered around a six-inch opening…and Tristan stood there friendly saucy smile and smoulder ability all turned up to full capacity.

"Right, I'm not wasting this golden opportunity on small talk."

He laughed out loud as she yanked him in. He followed her upstairs where she cleared her bed of books and he had already thrown off his clothes. He was fantastic and said zero.

Actions speak louder than words.

"Amira you."

"Tristan you."

"Best surprise ever."

"Can't bear waste Tristan and you were on top smoulder form."

"Your breasts fit exactly in my hands."

"And your stomach fits exactly on top of mine just wriggle a bit. Mmmmthaassit."

"I'm in the mood for more how about you."

"Smoulder city again."

"Perfect sex here we come again, you're hard to please Amira Kinov."

"Don't you just love it when that happens."

Hunger eventually drove them to hunt around like mice in the kitchen. They never recalled what they ate that day. Next morning, Jack was looking very puzzled.

"What's going on Amira, you look lit up and there is a snap to your step which was not there before."

"Oh, do I? Am I? Well, that's good."

Sonia sipped coffee and pulled faces.

"Mmmm this needs Sherlock Holmes investigations with a Nosy Rosy thrown in for good measure. Surely not The Liam." Sally piped up with grown up in two seconds thinking.

"All the nurses fancy 'The Liam'…don't they, Mummy?" Then proceeded to readjust Binx in his chair as he was on a downward slide again.

"Liam's just all looks surely Sonia, I can't see him…you know."

Sonia pulled a face.

"Jack why did Sonia pull a face. Mummy, what's that mean…you know."

"I am lost in a seven-year-old city, darling. And by the way, what happened to getting ready for school…we don't want a two-minute dash."

"Sorreeee."

Jack pulled on his heavy coat.

"Phew, close shave that one. Right, you two ladies of the nose in the air leisure classes, it's time for the blue-collar sex slave to check out."

Amira walked carefully upstairs to (One) give Sonia and Jack their bye see you later snog and (Two) make sure Sally had the correct books and clothes for school. Kids now had to drag trollies to school to accommodate mobiles, lessons with more than one book, changes for gym and tablets.

Fashion accessories of the devotion to materialism kind. Snacks, flask and mini first aid kit…oh and lots and lots of money. Swim day added even more. The days of a small school bag. Gone.

Amira waved a cheery Sally into school where a bunch of kids were dragging their trollies like weightlifters in miniature—into a circle of greetings with her little daughter centre stage. Glory through near to death association. Amira was spoken of in hushed tones of great admiration.

"You go girlie," whispered Amira and steered Mumblechuckler towards home to read post, pretend to dust which was in fact impossible. She also had to run the gauntlet of neighbours who said puzzling things like… 'He is such a great

mechanic. Older men are usually more stable. And the even more mysterious—
Poodles are great in the house'.

She so wanted to be 'home' home.

But also wanted to be with Sonia who was the best mate ever. Plus, their house was very good for Tristan trysts…she was seeing him again this morning…they wanted a long time together before reality took him for more treatment and 'Clown Tumbling School.' And Amira to Cairo. She simply had to marry him and have him with her every night. There really was no alternative. Clearing the high-tech kitchen took a while. Those polished counters need rubber gloves and expensive products…glossy high status good looks…no need for explanation. What happened to release from drudgery in kitchens.

When Tristan arrived…

He rang the bell with an adorable impatience. Amira opened the door carefully. She was wearing the palest pink lace teddy.

"Oh baby."

She sensed immediately that she had ordered it online that it was the kind you don't keep on for very long.

"Amira, I'm like a cannon about to go off."

"Easy does it my handsome."

How they made it to the bedroom and closed the door would remain a mystery all of their lives.

"This is amazing. I'm not sure even the Kama Sutra knows this one."

"Let's not mention it to them."

"You are."

"So are you."

At three in the afternoon, they had to pretend to be good as Amira and Sally were invited to Julia's birthday celebration and therefore a family get together. Amira wisely had made a cake the day before and Tristan cut veg for a casserole to pop on slow cook for Sonia and Jack…while she frosted a delicate sponge with a delicious icing recipe. Five candles complimented it while two white orchids gave it an air of the correct age being coyly withheld and yet still giving an accepted appropriate look.

Life is weird.

"I am taking you with me Tristan…"

"Is it time for a statement."

"Er yes…we are well acquainted…so yes, it's a good time for the reveal."

"I'm so lucky…come here."

"A few minutes upstairs?"

The drive over to the Gagnon house was like no other. The whole of town seemingly was steering to stare into the car, all wearing gold lame and tinsel tiaras, clown makeup and shameless hussy dresses. Then they recalled a fancy-dress gala was being held to raise money for the hospital's new wing to be furnished.

The Gagnon's drive was chock a block so they parked up on a neighbour's drive this kind woman was outside and beckoned Amira to drive in by smiling and nodding. Tristan waved his thanks. Old Mumblechuckler mysteriously silent now but scruffier than ever slid to a halt behind an expensive, shiny new S.U.V.

All the nubile girls gawped at Tristan. They spent the entire party flickering eyes at him. He was not handsome in any conventional sense…no, he was better looking than that. Julia joined Amira as she washed her hands in the bathroom.

"Thank you for the lovely cake Amira so sophisticated. Ed thought a pink elephant might do…I said—bloody hell no."

"Men sometimes get a bit like that from time to time."

"I don't think yours will ever get like that."

"I know Julia, and yes I earned him. After that first misery in jeans."

"Oh yes you're first, he's a pill."

"I wish he'd swallow himself, Julia…well at least he left early."

"Yes, I think when every female in the room lit up like a row of fairy lights and watched Tristan cross the room, – including his own wife…was his exact moment for retreat."

"Sorry, shock is a wonderful thing."

"Yes, what a party. Sadie has taken dozens of photos many blurred, too many too close. We will make a new album later and call it –The Nostril Collection." Amira laughed and Julia hugged her with great care and they rocked very gently literally with laughing. Ed eventually gave out the goody bags for the kids…called for silence and was booed out into the chill of the patio. Amira Tristan and Sally said their goodbyes and an entourage of teen girls followed Tristan longingly to the car. To add to the piquant moment he kissed Amira when he sat next to her in the car. A group whisper can be very encouraging.

Amira was never happier. Sally was cooing over the delightful contents of two goody bags. She was a little angel at bedtime and Amira read her a story, then waved Tristan off. Sonia was wiping down in the kitchen. She had watched him go. Amira looked across at her puzzled.

"Sonia you are never speechless."

"What a…I don't hear violins I hear jungle drums and feel the heat of…"

"A thousand suns."

"Adjust your Lycra ladies, it's all about to kick off in the old West."

"Well, that was the way it was won."

"No wonder 'The Liam' beat a hasty retreat."

"What do you think it is about Tristan that unnerves men and sends girls and women a little nutty?"

"Well, you know the answer to that; you're his love interest."

"True."

"And."

"He's totally irresistible."

Sonia opened the fridge and poured two chilled wines. They sat at the island in the kitchen and clicked glasses. "To family, love, sex and Dolce and Gabbana."

Moving back to grandfather's house was accomplished through the miracle of a most dreadful muddle brought about by careful planning. Amira recalled the morning of her packing off Sally to school and the courtesy of a clean-up…in the fashion magazine photograph called a kitchen…not her own of course. She carefully packed their accumulation of 'things' into Mumblechuckler but before the drive to the food market, Amira left a carefully worded and rather beautiful thanks for all the wonderful times. We truly appreciate all you do… Love forever message. Her concentration on the job to find supplies was intense. After all she had truly been off the scene.

All of the shoppers were in bash and grab mode. Amira realised that this had always been the case…but her recent sphere of experiences had shrunk. Lists are marvellous and she planned healthy meals. Of course she did, and then ruined the plan by trundling slowly to add forbidden foods and a good wine. Her Bank Manager wished to see her… Well, he would, wouldn't he? The muddle came when she arrived home and picked up her mail and saw how much time she didn't have left before Cairo. Tristan had gone to Clown Tumble School… (his description). A day of sorting two lives and waving to neighbours. All love comes at once and she ploughed gracefully dishevelled through chores and eventually flumped into the study with half opened and misunderstood correspondence. Her bullet wound throbbed horribly. She rested with a snoring accompaniment for friend in the study until a sort of violent hunger grabbed her. The larder invaded and the doorbell ringing in a Wagnerian manner. Surely Bank Managers do not make home visits.

Opening cautiously, she saw Indie and Bindie and her favourite Detective.

"Hello, dear detective, come in come in… You recall Sonia's fab home…well this place is shabbily chic…only the wrong end of it."

"Homely and comforting let me make you supper. Where is Sally?"

"Sadie always gets picked up directly from school today for flute lessons so my girl gets to enjoy the same."

"You're flushed and it's taken years off. Now where is the big pot."

Amira treated this as a compliment followed by a conditioning practicality. Also, she knew a genuine heart beat in this brilliant man's breast. He was very easy company. They soon had the soup bubbling gently and the dogs fed…content to throw off shoes and spread out with the far superior wine that Alain had brought with him. Indie had his head on his master's knee…adoration melting from every pore. Bindie was on 'security' watching birds out of the window.

"Better Amira?"

"Excellent wine prevents overwork that's my new mantra."

"Perfect conclusion… I meant to ask, are you and Tristan a sort of item…do tell me if my curiosity is inappropriate."

"How did you know this."

"Oh Marti told me about all the latest happenings in Room 22."

"Oh, Detective…"

He gestured open handed into the air.

"Live to love and love to live. He's just what you need right now."

"You are reflecting what most are hinting toward."

"We need people Amira and don't you fly out to Cairo soon."

"Mmmm there is a directive from the head of 'You will do this' He announced I am to have help from Yasmin my old Uni' chum and fellow historian to accompany and advise six Japanese businessmen on a tightly scheduled itinerary."

"Ah and this is exciting and exacting."

"Only you could say that."

"I will check on the supper. Do you mind if I nip to that new deli, my radar picked it up on the way here?"

He left quickly as the delicious supper was near to perfection. Indie whined softly and snuffled the air under the front door. Amira fondled the beautiful dogs' ears, but he was not to bought off his quest.

"Oh, it's all right darling...oh Bindie you like following. You shall get an honorary title. Sweet shadow!" She heard the slam of the Detective's door and he came bustling in with a pile of wonderful foods.

"Wow this is amazing...Indie took up door duty and cried for you."

"Oh, mon petite not to cry not to cry."

Indie did a tail waggle dance that would have shamed an exotic dancer.

"FOOD!"

When Sally was dropped off, she came home to a magnificent feast and ran upstairs to wash up and change...

Bindie galloped eagerly behind her...his expression said...

(At last! Someone nuts like me.)

"You are such a big hit with my daughter and I sense pleading for a puppy will be next." She listened for various sounds and when the right one for descending by stair began, Amira laid out Sally's delicious supper. Detective Alain Veldour left with a greater reluctance than he ever thought possible. Sally was fast asleep, and the dogs rushed out the front door and the cold air rushed in. Amira wondered whatever was going to happen next. She locked up and went to bed. She was reading the new email from Cairo regarding a request to know a little something about Belzoni and his wife. One of the Japanese men had a particular penchant for this unusual circus strong man.

The Removal Man of Egypt

Giovanni Battista Belzoni was born in Padua on 5 November 1778. He displayed such amazing physical strength and became well known for his ability to carry some 13 people. Performing at Ashley's amphitheatre. He was boisterous and good humoured whilst carting about all these people around a stage. He was adventurous and a gentle giant.

During the year 1815, May 19, this circus strongman set out from Malta for a business venture in Egypt to fit specialist water engineering apparatus. If he had been engaged in this for the rest of his life as was his plan...Egypt would have a vast site more antiquities. He was not successful with his water installations. So instead, he felt the yearnings of the age for collecting Ancient Egyptian antiquities that truly morally and artistically belonged in Egypt…private owners, museums and downright greed robbed Egypt of so much of her past that you feel tears rise at the squalid plunder. Love of the cultural beauty, mystery and the supernatural identity of the animism of the deities of ancient Egypt all provided the splendour demanded to satisfy world-wide collectors.

Salt, Dravetti and Giovanni Belzoni, all helped themselves…in the feeding frenzy within the stunning art of a people they would never understand, not really. Criminal…is the only description. The sting was slightly lessened when Belzoni was given the tip off regarding a most unusual temple site near the small village of present-day Abu Simbel. This turned the course of history for Egypt's past present and future for the clearing away of huge quantities of sand by the team of men under Belzoni's guidance and with local knowledge of how tricky sand shifting can be until it is wetted and moved in a certain manner…

Eventually, through sheer slog in tremendous heat and sweat the opening to the main temple door entrance became accessible.

There before the astonished workers was an interior of such beauty grandeur and intrigue that they knew it had been conceived in a time of great rulers.

This was no less than the famous 'Great Gateway to Egypt'. Ramesses II had this magnificent temple built during his reign in the 19th dynasty…to declare his rulership over the two lands…serving all the great gods of his time…and its tremendous beauty served a dual purpose.

The Builder Ramesses II designed and aligned this astounding temple to allow the sun to enter and penetrate the farthest most sacred sanctuary during each equinox and witnessing this exceptional light piercing the gloom until reaching four seated figures beautifully carved from stone seated at the farthest wall of the temple. Twice a year during the equinox, three were illuminated by the sun's rays, but one at the far left was left in darkness and of course this is Ptah the god of the shadows. A temple to Hathor of Habshek…Hathor's most important Nubian shrine is at Abu Simbel where Ramesses II (1279–1213 BC) built two temples where he is shown worshipping himself and Hathor who is recorded to have had many aspects but it is her gentler self that is represented here as a goddess of music and sexuality. The smaller temple he had built for his favourite wife Nefertari and is some short distance away. These great buildings also served as a warning to any wishing to do harm in the land of the Pharaoh. The message carved beautifully above the massive opening states…

Beware this is the land of Pharaoh Ramesses the Great…and he will retaliate. More or less. The message is not subtle. But one asks an obvious question—how many were as educated in the ways of the highly valued scribe, artisan, or learned viziers and certain well-versed Pharaohs in the Gods words—the Medu Necher. Nubians and the enemies of Ramesses were made aware through other signs entering Egypt and Ramesses II had a short fuse and although was around five feet six or seven inches, red haired and rather temperamental. He was excellent at PR…a great showman. Born today he would be a very wealthy television personality with his own reality TV show. Interestingly, although he honoured Nefertari with her own temple at Abu Simbel her statues are smaller but next to him. Also their daughters have a place, this is unique in the manner of pharaohs. Oddly, and remarkably perhaps Nefertari's most beautiful tomb in The Valley on the West Bank bears no sign of him on the walls. Ramesses The Great lived a long life into his 90s fathering some 120 children. He outlived many of his offspring. The most famous of the Nubian temples Abu Simbel has a spectacular history…when the building of the Aswan dam flooded the area some 155 miles southeast of Aswan. Abu Simbel was threatened The largest of these temples was dedicated to Re-Horakhty, Amen-Ra, Ptah and of course the deified Ramesses II. Few know that prior to Belzoni it was indeed the great explorer Jean-Louis Burkhardt in 1813… who found the heads of Ramesses II protruding from the sands…but had not the means to correctly identify the site or the means to clear it. No, this was achieved by Belzoni four years later. There is even more to add to Abu Simbel's history.

UNESCO during the 1960s moved each piece painstakingly to higher ground, to 213 feet higher in fact…The new site is constantly visited by thousands of tourist's historians and Egyptologists every year. Moving the temples was a great fete of dedicated engineering. Seeing this spectacle for the first time is utterly inspiring…the four colossal statues on the main temple are 65ft high! The lady that intrigues us all even more than Belzoni was his wife Sarah who came from Bristol in England and displayed immense flair and courage. Famous for her large hat and black silk neckerchief, she moved with a certain confidence amongst groups of women on many journeys with her husband. He was so keen on sharing all he experienced with her and gave her a section of his great book 'Belzoni's Travels. The section is named...Mrs Belzoni's, – "Trifling Account of The Women of Egypt, Nubia and Syria."

(Amira always felt a passion about any women involved with Egypt in the past. They had nothing like the modern conveniences of the twenty-first century. They applied great boldness and if fearful, fought it down'.

Amira particularly loved their honesty and their refusal to gloss over some dreadful experiences. Sarah Belzoni's ability to point out how badly treated so many of the native females she met were. Also, how inferior their lives were and how this made Arab women so secretive, furtive and observant over every little event and detail.)

Sarah invented a recipe of oil with scorpions in it to aid recovery from their very venomous painful bite. Even today, Luxor has many scorpions and a great many people are bitten. She invented an eye wash to reduce the dry soreness in her own eyes brought about by the hot winds. Sarah discovered that by daily washing them in Aqua Vitae gave her clear sight, in fact she claimed due to this her eyes became clearer than when she was in Europe. In fact, Sarah swore by this treatment and claimed her eyes were never better. She describes much of her endurance and in particular the trickery of certain women she encountered. However, she drew on her great resourceful nature to endure much. Her belief was so strong in all her spouse Belzoni endeavoured to achieve.

Amira finished the write up and began on the schedule and itinerary notes. These could be double checked on the flight to Cairo and photocopied in the Antiquities office...She could buy folders there to keep the papers clean and tidy. She sent Yasmin updates along with the plane's arrival time at Cairo's International Terminal. Security was strong due to terrorism. Her Antiquities Visa would only carry her so far.

Sally had turned pouty and was packing for time with her father and his new wife who was not at all as Amira had expected and stank of cigarettes which also had made her complexion poor and muddy. The family access law however had to be adhered to unless you were truly wealthy...at least some of the holiday was to be taken up with time in the Rockies...consequently, Amira bought Sally a new warm coat. The dear little girl was practically exploding with excitement. Her father's parents were pleasant people who genuinely loved both Sally and Amira. They would be going on the Rockies adventure also. This in itself gave Amira great assurance that Sally would be genuinely understood and well cared for. Amira rang them and they were adamant that Sally would be 'Watched like a hawk'. They wished Amira a safe and successful trip. They were astounded when they heard about her horrific ordeal because their son had left out telling them anything about the terrible mall shootings and Amira's involvement and her incredibly brave and amazing escape until Amira was at Sonia and Jack's, In a way they were not surprised because they had witnessed first-hand their son's callous attitude towards Amira.

They remained loyal to their daughter-in-law and were considerate and determined to care for Sally. They had the worst role to play being such gentle unassuming people…they could not understand his vile attitude to their daughter in law. Amira made it very clear she adored them. Sally did rather get her own way in their company. Amira planned a talk about this…that night when they were packing her little duds. They often sent money and gifts…dear people. This sweetness in the aftermath of the messy divorce made Amira wonder how they had ended up with such a spiteful thoughtless son. In stark contrast he was very good to his new wife. So that was something. Life is so strange.

Sally had all her pouts on full display and showing off honed to perfection the night before her trip with her father. Amira had carefully explained why this time was dedicated to packing and 'The Talk'.

"Are you packing Binx darling?"

"He was first in but I'm not taking my flute, Mummy."

"But darling, Mrs Simmonds rang me and told me you were really making headway and you're becoming skilful, shame to let that slide. Take it and keep it up Mrs Simmons is such a lovely teacher…you said so remember."

"Suppose so. Sadie is good too…I am going to miss her we do a lot of pieces together."

"Yes, and that's all the more reason to keep it up I'd say my sweet girl."

"Grandpa keeps asking me what I like at school."

"You are very lucky; they care deeply about you."

"It's a big responsibility, isn't it, Mummy, looking after me?"

"It certainly is."

"They won't let me do anything on my own."

"Ah that's called love and protection, hon…grandparents are just about the same all over the world…they sign a book when you are born…its title is 'Unconditional Love and 24/7 protection'."

"Noooooo there isn't, you're fibbing, Mummy."

"No, it's true and look this is a big pile of clean undies…try to bring some back, won't you, darling?"

"Doh! I'm not a baby."

Amira laughed.

That night, all the toys were lined up for the big story read. Amira lay alongside her scrubbed and perfumed daughter who had pouts at the ready. Just in case.

"And you will write and 'FaceTime' us, won't you, Mummy?"

"Absolute scout girl's honour; if time zones are peculiar I will text you. Got your mobile charger safely packed?"

"You know I have."

"Right, this is last snuggle until morning."

"Kiss my toys please, Mummy."

Amira gently kissed them all and tucked Sally in…her last act to kiss her daughter's nose.

"Best nose this side of the Rockies."

She pottered about quietly until Sally began steady little snores. Amira breathed deeply as she stood in the doorway of her daughter's colourful bedroom. One last look before tip-toeing to her own room. Falling asleep the minute her head touched the pillows.

The next day was horrible—her sneering 'ex' pulled up at the roadside called impatiently from his driver's side window to Sally and she obediently trundled her case to the car from where he hauled her in barely allowing her to wave to her mother. He drove off without a word. Amira stood outside until the car vanished around the curve of the avenue. Back inside she put on her favourite music 'Cowboy Junkies'—The Caution Horses…and packed for Egypt.

Light cotton…plus classic smart suits of an excellent cool material made up inexpensively in Cairo.

To allow for ultra-coolness a few dresses and huge headscarves which were totally necessary for certain occasions. Good shoes and walking sandals, a few books and accessories completed the pack. She owned a minimum of bangles etc. Maps, compass, sunglasses and swim wear and one pair of shorts. Mossie spray and sun cream she would buy at the airport. Tickets, money, passport were all in her one good flight bag. A clutch would do for nights out, if there were any. She carried her Egyptology laptop with her into the cabin in a special flight bag. Never left behind was her tiny lucky Isis figurine which resided in a suede-lined pouch. She had a photo of Sally and her grandfather mounted on stiff card with a quaint stand-up feature for her bedside table and a tiny alarm which served her well. She also packed her favourite book with the unnerving title of "*The Viper Gives Birth to Live Young.*" Tristan was the last to call her and wish her well and a good flight.

Detective Alain Veldour had volunteered to drive her to the airport. She knew now of course why Mumblechuckler was so quiet. She'd garaged the old car and it didn't take "Brain of Canada" to see that the Detective had grown fond of her. At the airport she gave him her car keys, a kiss on the cheek, and said goodbye to Indie and Bindie…all were a little misty eyed.

It had taken a shot in the side to bring her and Sally many new pals, a lover and two poodles. She was still, if honest, rather unclear on who the real lover might be. She had noticed her neighbours were smiling very knowingly…

Amira never let out that special sigh of relief until the jet reached its cruise altitude and the booze was in her hand. Today was certainly no different, sleep was intermittent, but she had a horrible feeling she had snored because her throat was dry. Eventually after many hours, the Pyramids were spotted and cries of joy went up. Real joy, and then there followed the bumpiest landing in aviation history. Wind gusts from the desert no doubt. The well-remembered smack in the face of hot air made Amira cry out, "HELLO EGYPT," as it always did. That old familiar opening of the oven doors syndrome…which always announced,-

"The Land of the Pharaoh!"

She wiped tears of joy away while she sat with her fellow passengers on the airport bus across to arrivals. She binned her scuffed to hell and back flight shoes and slipped on cool pretty sandals. This was a big thing…it was called (When in Egypt do as the Egyptians do). Love of the Arabic language made her giggly as she slowly recalled phrases…she immediately saw Yasmin who was holding up a card saying:

WELCOME HOME AZZIZI

It is never a good idea to show Egyptian men a woman's name.

"Oh my God, Yasmin, how fantastic."

"Inta Jamill."

The old college chums hugged.

"Asif habibti, I forget you are shot by those fucks."

"I'm okay more or less now, but oh what a treat…you look so pretty Yasmin."

"Still not the engaged woman azzizi."

She held up her rather delicate hand pointing to the naked ring finger.

"Plenty of time for that…you have to get the right one."

"How I meet this right one. You tell me dillwatti."

She pulled Amira out of the path of rushing people and helped her put on the hijab Cairo style.

"Shame to cover such gorgeous shar but I am not making the custom."

"It's okay really it sort of makes me feel really here."

"Inta magnoon."

"Nam, ana magnoon"

They trundled Amira's things to the pickup point and the department's driver waved them over. In minutes they were zig-zagging through the chariot race from (Planet Crazy) which is normal Cairo traffic.

"Nothing has changed I see."

The driver flung back a laugh to them.

"You say the true Madam Amira…you say the true."

He took them to a restaurant first as they were all terribly hungry. Amira and Yasmin rushed to the washroom for a freshen up, while he ordered a good meal. Amira fell into step with (The Way) She knew if she ordered, the price would treble. When they were all seated, the sweating waiter gave the table a good beating to clear crumbs. Amira gave out a huge happy sigh which the men at the next table copied laughing. Soon many were joining in and the lively music added to the good feeling.

"Welcome home, habibti."

"Shukeran warda."

This was the trigger for several men to call 'Warda!'

Yasmin pulled a face.

"They love the women with pale skin."

Amira laughed she had missed Yasmin's language blunders and then covered her face quickly. In some circles, it is considered bad for women to laugh too much in public. Yasmin waved it aside.

"Mafeesh mushkillah henna…not to care so much…here is free to laugh restaurant." The food arrived and Amira had an opportunity to carry out a quick 'send to all' text message.

The department had arranged for Yasmin and Amira to share a reasonably updated flat and as soon as their driver relayed their new instructions, they waved him off and took the lift up. Amidst ridiculous giggles about nothing in particular and everything in general they flounced through the adequately furnished flat and sprawled hot and dusty across a massive couch.

Yasmin found the Egyptian music channel on a television that had seen better days and nights…then promptly lit an incense stick and proceeded to dance a foolish mish mash of East meets West style raks. All the time rolling her eyes melodramatically. Throwing her clothes off and making awful faces which were meant to drive men wild with desire.

"KIDDIYANNI."

Shouted Amira and left her to it and drawing a bath she sank into bubbles and was soon singing along with Mohammed Mounir. Finally, only intending to rest on her bed for ten minutes she fell into a totally blissed out sleep. Yasmin was off doing God knows what…God knows where.

At 8 pm, the sound of Yasmin's key in the door woke Amira…so she ambled to the kitchen and filled the kettle for chai. Yasmin lolled around the doorway with a smile as incandescent as a toothpaste ad.

"What have you been up to dearest Yasmin? You are the very image of naughtiness."

"Ah while you snore your heads off…I am finding out much gossip."

"Oh brilliant, so what's hot and what's not."

"Our lovely Japanese guests are already here in Cairo…staying at a numero uno funduk of course."

"Not slumming it like us then."

"Laheh habibti."

"What news on them."

"Halwayat, ghani, mudhik."

"Smart, rich, funny. Wow sounds good…better sharpen our best pencils, Yasmin."

"You can, I'm going to see if the man in my dreams is still in the funduk next to this building."

"Not out late tonight darling surely, we are up early don't forget."

"Habibti this my only chance of love…tahally…keep my time one time Amira…you will see him. This is a job for white girl not black girl come on get dressed up…and pile on the booby props and lip gloss. Pleeeze for Yasmin."

Amira did all she could to be as glamorous as her friend demanded and finally they trotted out like one trick ponies with well brushed manes and tails. All look and no substance. Yasmin cared about fake 'frou frou' too much. But for now however, Amira kept her opinions zipped. Yasmin was happier than Amira had ever seen her. The poor girl was mentally dancing on the hot tiles of the Cairo rooftops and wanted to capture some unsuspecting male.

The women selected (in Yasmin's expert opinion) the perfect table and gave the order for chai with mint…this sometimes arrived with dear little sponge cakes in a faint mimic of the honey cake which all good Egyptian women are famous for making.

Tonight, was no exception so they sipped daintily and nibbled delicately. Men passed and stared which they of course were meant to do. Yasmin was panning for gold and so laid out all the bait. She was very beautiful in her expensive wig…red lips and shadowed eyes. Amira in contrast was blonde, delicate, with barely there lipstick. This totally opposite look of both women was dazzling.

Unknown, unseen and non-descriptive, a gardener plied a hoe over the hotel garden which was dusty by day. In the evening however, it enjoyed a coolness and invited the eye. Fairy lights lent a magic which was false…the gardener muttered rude remarks about the women—Happy to judge from his distant court of weeds.

Yasmin had her notebook page open in her mobile and suddenly gave a sharp intake of breath and tapping quickly—handed it to Amira who read… ('The One' is here.)

Amira tapped… (Which one…not the one in the pale linen suit?)

Yasmin tapped quickly.

(Yes. Smile…if he sees you…you can go over and ask for a light for your cigarette.)

"I don't smoke oh no really Yasmin I will cough."

Ignoring her, Yasmin pulled a cigarette from her pack and gave it to her.

Luckily or perhaps absurdly pre-ordained, the tall fine-looking Egyptian gave off an excellent smoulder from his corner that would have given Tristan a lesson in smoulder to scorch all within forty metres.

He took a call from his flashy expensive mobile and sauntering over confidently to their table, placed a white card on Amira's side plate and strode off the terrace of fairy lights into the busy main foyer of the hotel.

Yasmin rapidly settled the bill and practically dragged Amira from their very successful bower bird creation.

"It's worked…Yasmin, it's worked. God, that was clever."

They took their time walking through the guests. He was nowhere to be seen.

Up in their apartment Amira read…his card…and telephone number, but of course…and his name in gold Arabic lettering and English—'Mohammed Bogarde Hydro Engineer Consultant'.

Amira never understood at the time why a cold breeze danced over her forearms.

"Oh, Yasmin, I have gone goosy."

"Yes, you go goosy I will go meet him."

"La! La! you don't know him, wait a night…meet him in a group…not so trusting darling please."

"Are you magnoon this is my one chance with him…he is the one…to go stale now is big foolish."

"But to run after him it's dangerous for you Yasmin…what is this crazy idea."

"You talk like my jadda."

"A wise move would be to invite him with the group tomorrow or the next night…look this Japanese chap Riku Takeo—my goodness Yasmin he is a top Hydro Consultant…what better mix can you make."

"Laheh laheh I want be alone…if I am alone, I can talk sweet Kateer Kateer."

She ran to her room and soon came back in a new outfit with the wig frou frou'd to new heights. Amira was exasperated. This foolishness was beyond comprehension. Standing in the hall Amira tried reasoning with Yasmin.

"A good Muslim girl can lose every chance of a good safe marriage by such rash choices."

Sadly, Yasmin covered her ears and left the flat.

Amira sat down on her bed. She blew out a huge sigh that came from the 'You lost that argument'…part of the cosmos, then actually smoked the cigarette which was mild and rather strangely comforting…she tried to contact Sally but without success. Laying out everything for the next day, setting the alarm on her mobile and as good fortune would have it…managing to locate her tiny travel alarm she set it up right next to her bed alongside her treasured photograph of Sally and her grandfather Mikael. It seemed her head had only just touched the pillow when she was frightened awake by the most awful racket. Totally disorientated she grabbed her dressing gown and struggled to the front door. It was daylight and there stood Mahmoud the driver!

"What the hell has happened?"

"Come on why you not ready and Yasmin not outside I ask her…please be ready outside."

"Look some problem must have happened. Come in I will be quick as…"

"Not allowed…yes be very quick I will phone ahead. Hurry, Madam Amira."

Amira was galvanised into action threw water on her face and cleaned her teeth…dressing rapidly was her forte' after the many times when Sally was on one of her 'go slows' set aside for school days.

She was so relieved to be able to pack in the carefully prepared schedule into her briefcase. She repeatedly yelled, "YASMIN, COME ON WE HAVE OVERSLEPT."

Still no response so she began hammering most impolitely on her door which automatically swung open to reveal a very smooth bed and generally scattered outfits but no Yasmin. Disbelief held Amira trancelike… "YAS."

The flat yielded no sign of a note or explanation…so Amira called Yasmin's mobile which went to voicemail instantly. Amira found the flat keys and because she was so pale with worry managed to apply blusher in the lift down. Mahmoud the driver started the car at first sight of her. She clambered in the front passenger side.

"Why you not have Yasmin what she play at."

"She went out with her new man last night and didn't come home."

"Da giga you say this the true?"

"I say this the true."

"Fucking no way…this crazy girl I see she is playing game with her life…but she will be losing job."

"Please, Mahmoud say nothing at the moment."

He drove carefully to the pickup point jabbering on his mobile with it clamped expertly between his shoulder and chin but still guiding the large car through the Cairo morning madness. He pulled into the forecourt of a stunning hotel where another driver called him to park up in the VIP bay.

"They are very understanding, Madam Amira. Shukeran Allah for he is with you in heart today. Come inside for coffee with them they insist…we must obey."

She followed him and gave way to a gasp of awed pleasure. The concourse was a blaze of colour, light and grandeur. A smart Japanese man bowed low, and Amira found herself bowing back, she was ushered to a table groaning with breakfast coffee pots, croissants, fruit and dishes of unknown but tasty looking titbits.

"Here is Madam Amira your Egyptologist. We apologise we have much traffic."

They were wonderful. Only the truly noble are generous, and they made her at home and fussed over her gently and yet excitedly at the same time. Amira had no words but kept up a grateful nod like a joke dog in the back of a cheap car. There were in fact only five Japanese men, their aftershave constantly wafted around. Subtle, exotic, uber expensive. Riku Takeo, she recognised instantly by his photo. She could not help but notice him he had a smile like dynamite igniting in a mine. There is a point in all our lives when we know a very different path is opening to us…we see a massive gate flung back and the exquisite new world spreads like caviar over the finest cracker money can buy. This was the caviar moment. There was no mistaking it. They held court with her and she felt like a Princess of Cairo. They all talked at once and only Riku was silent he was not as rambunctious as them and indeed seemed to be held in thrall by this pale blonde woman in the seat of honour. Amira was unaware of this as so much activity, laughter, antics and croissant passing was in play. Waiters seemed to bounce about with cups, glasses, tea, coffee, even a fine malt whiskey made an appearance.

Amira felt that herding cats would be easier than managing this wild bunch.

She sipped her delicious coffee and nibbled breakfast hungrily, aware all the time that she was in her best suit. Life can be marvellous. Her mobile lit up and she bowed politely and managed to get to a quieter corner.

"Madam Amira, can you entertain them as best as you can…we have a call from Madam Mubar her daughter has migraine…very badly."

And he was gone this was it. And that was that. She looked at their driver and he nodded. He came forward.

"These men like you I can tell so half the battle is won. We shall drive you all in five minutes to the New Egyptian Museum out on the Alexandria Sahar Shara."

"Two cars…"

"Convoy, Amira, convoy."

They left in a rush of laughter revving police cars, flags and all pennants flying in the Cairo sunshine…Amira was seated with Riku who quite obviously is a highly respected member of this already powerful group. He had a strong presence which was challenging in a way she had never encountered before. A thought came to her that perhaps a part of her psyche was being invited to appreciate men again for the first time in many years. Perhaps even for the first time. She looked at his casual air of enjoying the journey. In profile he had an excellent bone structure. His hands though were the most fascinating.

There was a great capability to him. A strong history played about his features. Owning what the French refer to as "visage de magnifique". You sensed his ancestors had planned every cell and he was the result of a fineness of their combined spirit. She had the most wonderful urge to say this. She held back of course her confidence certainly had not yet grown to quite the height required. All her past experiences were of no use to her at this moment she felt flung to the sunshine and dispersed. Happy just to be alive. She was however not on vacation she was here to work. As they emerged from the limousines the heat and light swooped down on them all as fierce as a giant wing beat. They all gasped and even failed to recall later what they actually saw first…awestruck by the massive gold façade created as an illusory image of a mirage of pyramids rising out of the Sahara Desert. This is how Amira beheld the architecture… everyone will report differently of course. For it truly was as if the exterior of this massive undertaking with its breath-taking interior was accessed through a peculiar opening in the base of a pyramid. Yes, it is truly as if some passing giant has stooped and kindly lifted the whole architecture just at one angle, amazing! Through a window especially structured to withstand pressure heat light and dust storms – is a view of the Great pyramid of Khufu. Surely, the whole spectacle is the work of competing magicians. Breath-taking…pride fills Amira.

All earthly senses are assailed by shafts of light striking upon and splintering in all directions. Swooping to engulf and lead every eye to the colossal stone figure of Pharaoh Ramesses II striding emphatically out of his 19th Dynasty in order to show them round. Fearsome and fabulous.

This truly was Zep Tepi!

Henhalegen Peng so in tune with the (in the beginning) feeling and influence of this totally 'out there' architect's adventure with shafts of light landing majestically upon the Alexandria Desert Road.

Passing into the buzzing concourse gallery functioning as a great arena of magically shifting light dramatically aligned to illuminate and give each visitor a thrilling journey of discovery…Amira felt as if she was transported into "The Sailboat" painting by Lionel Feininger—the German New York born artist… who had attended Walter Gropius' Bauhaus Movement Art School during the early years of the twentieth century. For it was Bauhaus that gave a completely different awakening to the light platform of the arts from furniture to jazz to engineering, photography, film, and after a feeble struggle—architecture. The great impact that had seduced their senses outside was even more powerful inside.

Riku Takeo took her gaze and held it.

" Excuse me please my ankles have swollen to twice their size in this sauna of heat."

"Oh, do let me give you some grapefruit oil to massage on them."

The massive structure allowed for a strange and direct intimacy…nobody noticed them break away and Amira helped Riku to find a chair behind a workman's screen. He gratefully took the tiny bottle and between them they managed some application…of the fragrant oil.

"Humanity is dwarfed by such as this."

"Ah yes I have had the good fortune to be presented to the Pharaoh's influence before you see."

"One can be overwhelmed."

"That's the whole point. Egyptians are great stage makers. Panoramas to them are meant to be dressed up."

"This is such a nuisance you are taken from your work."

"Necks are meant to be worked though aren't they…what I mean is so much for your friends to look at lets me enjoy your company."

"How charming you make it sound to look at a Japanese man's toes."

Amira laughed…

"This was not what I expected this morning as we rushed through the crazy traffic…have a little more oil, Mr Takeo, your right ankle is very puffy."

"You are the kindest. But please Riku call me Riku."

"Forgive me Mr Takeo,…protocol…I think your name would look well on the billboard of a film about warriors sort of jumping through trees brandishing swords. An ancient warrior."

"You compliment me greatly and the strangest fact you bring to light. My name means Wise Sky Warrior."

"Oh, how fabulous."

A message plinked through to Amira.

"Oh, it's from home it's Jack. Look Mr Takeo this is my foster brother Jack, oh my he has news of an asteroid which landed in Gloucestershire on a family's driveway. It's now being examined at the Natural History Department. Astro physics comes to The Grand Museum."

"Most apt."

They soon caught up with the group and Amira introduced them all to a heavily made-up woman in her fifties.

"I have pleasure in introducing Juliet de Mettiamenmy my tutor of the 18th dynasty the great golden age of change and the peculiar reign of Akhenaten the Pharaoh now thought to truly be the father of the young Pharaoh Tut Ankh Amun...whose name literally means... Living image of Amun. He was like a golden god to his people...his early death would have been the most terrible disaster for his court and devastating for his wife the Queen Ankhessenamun who was actually his half-sister... Her father also being of course Akhenaten. (The Aten is Justified). Her mother was Nefertiti. Intermarriage such as this was normal within the Royal sphere. The bloodline was safeguarded, but there were terrible consequences from such intermarriage. Tut Ankh Amun's mother was a courtly lady and obviously favoured by Akhenaten. All these pieces of information are now consolidated through the processes of modern science DNA and dating brought about by MRT scans and Archaeology...we can date trees through similar methods and of course the contents of tombs...seeds, flowers and fragments of bone, even strands of hair. All this is brought into play...here we will conserve repair display and continue research. This is the greatest museum on Planet Earth dedicated to one civilisation on Earth." Amira caught sight of Riku and hoped he was okay. There was much to see so Amira happily caught up with Juliet on Departmental news. The group were all talking quietly awed as they followed the women who took them to the section dedicated to the newly assembled Tut Ankh Amun collection.

It was the oddest thing but the whole world felt it owned this young Pharaoh of the 18th Dynasty because so much had been written regarding him. His life cut so short and still surrounded with many unanswered questions. His controversial discovery by Howard Carter. A rude but absolute genius of a man. Who simply refused to give up on his search for this Pharaoh's tomb and its original intention to hold a female...no doubt of royal birth...the totally dramatic and singularly unique discovery on November 22, 1922.

They crowded around his intimate belongings. The sticks he used to walk with and how they ranged from each being made precisely suitable for a child to a tall teenager. He was beautiful, disabled and yet God-like. There was also a tenderness of humanity about him not present in other great leaders. The much recorded touchingly devoted scene of him with his sister wife can bring tears to the eyes still.

One recalls Howard Carter saying, "I want to talk to him." Oh yes, this disabled little dark eyed child who used a stick to get around his palaces and temples. All his life this young pharaoh suffered many health problems.

Turmeric played a vital role within the lifestyle of the ancient Egyptian household and there were seeds of this pungent spice stored in an anti-chamber for the teenage Pharaoh to use in the afterlife. Also, the bows he hunted with as a small boy and their sizes ranged right up to full size for hunting in the marshes...and perhaps while balanced precariously on his chariot while trying to guide very lively horses.

He quite obviously relied constantly upon his personal physician and his young Queen Ankhessenamun who was constantly at his side and exquisitely depicted in so many artistically designed furniture and fine alabaster vases, one of these is an exciting unique design of a two layered technique. When the interior is lit by a candle or a wick in oil...the exterior becomes a brilliant domestic and loving scene of Tut Ankh Amun and Ankhessenamun. A fabulous expression of the ceramist's ability.

Even his clothes have semi-precious gems sewn into them. This wonderful collection is now within his very special section in the new museum and is of course as you can witness for yourselves carefully preserved, also, and I think I can stick my neck out here...lovingly displayed.

Recent discoveries made in Luxor have brought to light many of the missing sections of his solar boats which were part of the collection found by Howard Carter...and are now reunited with their counterparts.

Flowers that were placed upon Tut Ankh Amun's breast during those final moments with his loved ones have been the cause of much discussion. Some shed tears over this touching reminder of how much his wife loved him. One, is led to conclude he was a gentle person. His battle dress...called a 'cuirass'...(we know he took this part of his duties very seriously due to him conferring many titles and honours upon his military commander Horemheb, we know that this commander would have served Akhenaten first.)

The 'cuirass' which was designed with great detail and is delicate and bears much gold, has been worn away along the edges from use in battle. One theory is he was away on a campaign and tumbled from his chariot and this most definitely would have added to the problem of healing him so far from home.

The irony being that Pharaohs such as Tut Ankh Amun had huge resources at their disposal and his vast wealth was taken care of by his treasurer Maya – (1336BC–1327BC) Yet these could not save him. We know Tut Ankh Amun's soldiers were very active in the city-states of Syria due to fine reliefs of Syrian Palestinian prisoners being led before Tut Ankh Amun which are most wonderfully depicted on the walls of Maya's tomb…but none of this would help him. Antibiotics were still a miracle for the future. His multiple injuries were far too serious. So there he was interred far away in his female tomb in the Valley of the Kings KV62…a strange story in all ways. The site is in actual fact two valleys. If you approach the valleys along the mountain path from Deir El Medina, as the craftsmen would have done some 3,500 years ago as they trudged in the early light to work upon the tombs. You can feel the power of the place enveloping you with its strange nostalgia. Your senses collude with the very rocks leading you to hear ancient whisperings.

When the tombs were excavated during the ninetieth and twentieth centuries the greater part of them had tragically been robbed and disrupted. Except for Tut Ankh Amun's because although that too had been entered, extraordinarily the robbers were interrupted and the tomb chamber seals were intact. Yes, perhaps, it had been saved by the necropolis priests. Some even suggest Djedi priests.

As I mentioned before many people today become upset by the faded flowers placed upon his neck and shoulders to adorn and comfort him. They are dried out but although thousands of years have passed some colour still clings to them. There are those that talk of their fragrance having come back from the fields of their beginning.

Now their very preservation seems vital to convey the truly emotional side of his life. Symbolic of the tenderness of love. We can easily visualise his distraught wife placing them with loving care…for he was greatly loved.

The Sneaking Monkey

Ay (c. 1327–c. 1323) An army commander soon manoeuvred himself into his desired and no doubt much coveted role of King of Egypt. He appears however in a strange and unsatisfactory light. E.g., when we see the tiny tomb for Tut Ankh Amun and the presence of Ay performing the ceremony called— (opening of the mouth) we feel instinctively that something is amiss. He stands opposite the dead king shown in his bandaged mummy form wearing the double crowns of Upper and lower Egypt. Usually, this ceremony is carried out by the Pharaoh's son the rightful successor to the throne. Ay has taken on this highly significant role without the blink of an eye…also Ay is dressed in official priestly attire complete with leopard skin! When in fact he is only a servant to Tut Ankh Amun and his grieving widow the young Queen Ankhessenamun….

Today.

Ay's name has been efficiently hacked away. His tomb dismantled and the sarcophagus dashed to fragments. His mummy has never been found! Some say Horemheb had a hand in this but proving this is another matter entirely.

We know that Tut Ankh Amun's grief-stricken half-sister bride suffered greatly and was inconsolable. For not only was she in mourning but under threat from Ay who thought marriage to this exquisite, beautifully educated young girl would be within his right as Pharaoh. To her this was inconceivable. As a consequence, in her desperation…Ankhessenamun wrote many letters to another King, even sending letters to her country's enemies asking if she could marry one of his sons. She stated categorically that she was under pressure to marry a servant… Not only too old for her but despised by her. Any attempt for these rulers and Kings to send her a royal son with a royal blood line as was befitting of her status…came to nought—they were waylaid en-route and vanished, most likely killed. No doubt by Ay's well paid soldiers or spies. Whatever the outcome Ankhessenamun is not mentioned again and vanishes from history. Many suspect foul play on the part of Ay. He did not reign long, which was obviously not what he so religiously schemed and connived to achieve. He was not considered a loss. His reign was just four years and was far from noteworthy or even legal. A man lacking in regal qualities…no, his reign was more of a…a monkey dressed ridiculously in ermine sort of reign. He was replaced hastily by Horemheb.

Much discourse surrounds this period, and many believe Ay was in a race to bury Tut Ankh Amun and take the throne before Horemheb returned from a vital military campaign. One of the truly tell-tale signs for a reason to suspect this being…the black mould on the walls of Tut Ankh Amun's (inferior) sized tomb…as spoken of before…the grave goods although beautiful were a hotchpotch gifted by other royals. The Canopic jars are exquisite and of a fine transparent alabaster but are the likeness of a young royal princess.

I conclude by saying the more we try to investigate this young royal Pharaoh…the more questions arise.

Eventually, the lively Japanese group declared they were thirsty and after leaving a particularly wonderful display of art laid out under a galaxy of stars of the night sky, the tour was concluded. They all meandered out with a great deal of lively excited chatter to the cars. These vehicles were now terribly hot to the touch…with interiors like ovens. The drivers had to open all the doors for a few minutes. Not that this made much difference. Air con on full blast made some sneeze. After a short journey they were all seated comfortably in an excellent restaurant.

Immediately it was clear they were all expert at ordering exactly what they wanted. Amira noticed Riku had cleverly managed to select the seat next to her. Designer flasks of whisky (no doubt)…kept making appearances. Amira thought they would all be either drunk as lords or dehydrated. Probably both.

The drivers were joining in and the whole restaurant party became raucous. No way would they be doing anything else that day.

Amira signalled to the driver to meet her outside.

"They will be rolling around soon we must get them back safely to the hotel."

"We will get the Maître D' to pull the bill on them and as they pay it, I will literally call them out to the cars. No excuses got that?"

He got that.

Returning five raucous very happy rich men to a hotel which has a reputation to uphold is dangerous and a little wishful in the thinking…they were on red alert and spotted (how the hell do they know these signs above premises) a particular type of club. This one was smoky and sleaze oozed from every lurid curtain. Cairo's most worst for wear exotic dancers were in full sweat and handsome Japanese men obviously unshackled from disapproving wives and mothers-in-law…as well as being spoilt and rich… Well, the high octane energy music soon had two of them gyrating with three exotic girls who were wearing fake pearls and not much else. While a dispute over who saw who first, kept Amira and Riku in gales of laughter. Never had Amira laughed so much.

Their driver was pulled into the melee by default while the other driver took photographs. Amira wiped tears from her eyes and Riku was suddenly snatched up by a lustrous eyed girl with rubies in her ears and belly button…whilst very small triangles covered other intimacies. The drivers flopped down eventually and shouted above the din.

"So, this is how we get them back to the funduk."

Thankfully, there was a lull in the music, lights came up and everyone staggered outside. How the safety of the hotel grounds and concourse were reached…remained a mystery to all. The group insisted Amira stayed at the same hotel in her own room at their expense…and she ended up under a shower with a white hotel style negligee rippling invitingly across the gilded satin cover of an exquisite bed. Sleep was almost instantaneous and when she finally woke. Her first thought was…

"Jeeze, do I still have a career."

They were all hung over and it was five no shows. Mahmoud the driver called her…

"Hey, princess, you slept good I think?"

"I am in shock still; the extravagance is overwhelming."

"Don't worry I lied for you and the itinerary picks up again tomorrow…let me take you to the apartment."

"Shukeran siddique."

She left a note thanking them all at reception requesting the clerk to place it in Riku Takeo's pigeon hole. Once back in the very contrastingly dingy and sobering apartment she sorted herself, her notes and the grubby and creased good suit out. There was an excellent launderers and cleaners close by thankfully. She checked the time difference and called Sally to set up a face to face with her and her grandparents. Praying her eyes did not give the game away… Sally was over excited and had trouble sitting still…she showed Amira her pirates hoard of new clothes toys, and gadgets…courtesy of grandparents Lucy and Simon…they came in on the face to face with everyone talking at once. The perfect conversation. They were all a little tearful at goodbye. One thing stood out clearly these separations were never going to get any easier. We tend to trade off so much in our lives.

Her world of Egypt filled with gold and bustle and ancient wonders. Her home life of preparation, childcare, bills and responsibilities… Small wonder she enjoyed the bright lights and freedoms given so freely by the close proximity of wealthy people. She didn't want to cross any line. She longed to know what Mahmoud meant when he clearly stated that he had lied for her.

She called him quickly…

"Mahmoud inta Quaisie…"

"Hamdoolah."

"Excellent you know last night was pretty wild."

"Mmmmm for some."

"You said you covered for me."

"Oh it was a late call from the department asking how the group responded at the Grand Museum."

"Why didn't they ask me I wonder."

"Oh there is old misogyny thing, you're clever Amira…you can work it out…you know, were the men made happy…"

"Oh, I get it…but why did you have to cover for me…I don't get that bit."

"They are all screwed up about stuff…to use your expression."

"Stuff?"

"Yasmin is not getting a new contract."

"Oh, so there is more to this."

"Yes, they suspect her of some wrongdoing. Her mother covering it up."

"Well, if sleeping out with a stranger is off limits."

"She is big Muslim Amira so absolute off limits for sleep about with the men. Parents can become very sticky about a daughter's purity before the marriage…even dangerous."

"Oh so they think I might follow this example."

"It's a fresh sting for them so they worry about you…I exactly told them you are busy looking after Mr Riku because he had horrible swollen feet from the heat here…also he is much old married man."

"Oh thank you and it is completely true. Let's hope they don't look at him closely…he is a little older yes…but astonishing features."

"Of course, the true and he contacted them and expressed his gratitude to the department for selecting a good responsible and knowledgeable historian. Mr Riku tayeb gibden…"

"Yes, he is kind. So they know nothing of me staying at that fantastic hotel with them just rooms away."

"No, and now…they have much bigger worries."

"Fundamentalist activity for one."

"This the true."

"Do we have clearance for the early am visit to Giza and Khufu's pyramid."

"This is going to be the fantastic."

"What time should I be outside for you."

"Sabba."

"Excellent…should I call their hotel."

"This my next thing ma alesh. Don't stand outside in the shara, come down by lift at my missed call."

"I wish you an excellent day Mahmoud."

"Allah kaleek."

Never had Amira had to deal with such a strange set of incidents. Life was becoming a whirl of events. At least it was not dull. Her mobile trilled into life at 7.05 am the next day and she scrambled for the keys and noticed that the flat needed a good mop through. There were even pathways she had made through the Cairo dust crossing from bed to loo to kitchen to lounge. The washing machine was slushing and grumbling over the bedding…

She had already located a new bed cover and pillowcases…which were a nightmare to change. Being like giant tight-fitting sausages…just another of Egyptian style wackiness.

Mahmoud held the door open for her handed over a latte from the brand new café across the shara.

"Wow you certainly know what a woman needs at 7.10 am."

"Ha! Please to tell to my wife, she is make the big shout at me today."

"Why?"

"Who can know what is to travel in the woman's think abouts."

"I will never forget your unique turn of phrase, Mahmoud."

"I am too unique for driver my mother she says this."

"What would you like to do."

"I have only known the way of Cairo. Yes, but not same you. Mine is all about where prettiest dancer live and what best market."

"The reasons are obvious your knowledge is specialist just as mine is… Hence good team."

"Hamdoolah, Madam Amira, you speak the true. Oh, by the way you go over Giza by the helicopter."

Amira looked forward to this immensely after all a Cormorant saved her life…of course in the skilful hands of a pilot and his exceptional medically trained crew. The awareness of this would always stay with her... within the unspoken depth of true joy of living. Of having... 'Come to be near death'.

A rushing thrill of life ran through her. She scanned her notes. This had always been her decision that at the height of understanding this strong will to live would continue only if its needs are in a force of constant renewal.

To sit in the ruts made before by others...is a mistake. Acknowledge and add. Or rethink.

Her constant mulling over the true nature and concept of Harmakhis Khepri Atum Ra...and whether this immense sphinx-like creature with the much-disputed features...which constantly reminded her of a true lioness, or Djoser...an Old Kingdom 2686–2181 BC...3rd Dynasty ruler whose features have a strong jutting jawline...more than the weak faced Khufu...it is her own conjecture...but more often her feelings ran with a song of thanks to the Sekhmet Red lion Goddess of old time. A song or praise chant tells beautifully of a slave family who were lifted out of desperate circumstances by serving the 'great one' placing before the 'Red lady' offerings laid respectfully between her massive paws...they soon lived in a pleasant home and gained wealth. Amira also became aware few historians had come across this song of thanks. They are still to this day to back this up...

Traces of red paint have been found upon the lion's body...and we know now he/she was painted red for hundreds of years. Harmakhis Khepri Atum Ra has a powerful enigmatic presence...all know this lion who faces the place of the Horizon and is constantly watching with passionate intensity the great heavens. Patient and mysterious. The quest of mankind in the battered face gazing upon the majestic cosmic flow. If this indeed is a match to the age of Leo we must examine...

Age of Leo 10,960 BC–8800 BC
Age of Cancer 8800 BC–6640 BC
Age of Gemini 6640 BC–4480 BC
Age of Taurus 4480 BC–2320 BC

Our own epoch circa AD 2000 the vernal point is poised to enter the Age of Aquarius.

Is this great figure a reverence and dedication to the majestic Leo constellation? A twin concept. The true mirroring of the constellations. Amira had met those who had shouted her down about this great lion's magnificent aura.

However…she still obeyed an inner instinct regarding the vital energy surrounding the Giza site. The group knew nothing of her personal opinions… she gave out only academic findings. She conducted herself calmly at such moments when she wanted to say how her true instincts ran. Her instincts kept her silent.

Destruction and Plunder

The Great Pyramid…has what we can express honestly as an accuracy of orientation that cannot help but draw the eye, fascinate the mind, steal the attention. The four corners have almost perfect right angles.

North East 90° 3'2"; North West, 89° 59' 58"; South East, 89° 56' 27"; South West, 90° 0' 33". When complete it rose to a 481.4 feet. The final 31 feet stolen away. The sides angle at of approx. '51° 52' to the ground. Area covered by its base 13.1 acres.1.11.

At the end of the ninetieth century, Caliph Ma'mun the wayward son of Harun al Rashid of Arabian Nights fame drawn by a mistaken belief that it was crammed with gold and treasure…broke into it in a clumsy foolish manner. One wonders at his awful, disappointed face…when finding rubble and huge blocks! Until this destruction, the pyramid although robbed of anything worth carrying away by furtive means was by its exterior appearance intact. This started the fashion for stealing most of the wonderful shining Turin limestone and the cap stone as well as huge chunks of precious granite from the apex. This horrendous plundering acting as a copious quarry providing for the building of bridges houses walls and buildings…within neighbouring Giza village and Cairo! The interior is the true magic of this house of eternity… Contrasting with the pyramid of Meidum. The Great pyramid was engineered in a transformative set of internal wonders.

Corridors of massive proportion i.e. The Grand Gallery. Chambers with shafts leading out to point unmistakably to particular heavenly constellations…whose true purpose was only recently fully understood. It does have incomplete recesses. We wonder at their function. Time may reveal this. This was such a huge undertaking of more than twenty years. Hundreds of workers…all to one purpose. Many would die and sweat and blood and tears would blend with stone. The great shining star on the desert would demand life and death. Eventually, Khufu would be carried aged and frail to gaze upon this splendid work of architecture. The Reincarnation machine. Perhaps, it had truly worked as he was never found inside apparently... Or perhaps by a twist of fate he was taken by his own secret request to Abydos to lie in stately grace within the sacred radius of the great Oracle and the gathering of all the ancient gods.

We shall probably never know.

Flinders Petrie's conclusion being that the Grand Gallery held sway over the vastness and dimensional mathematics engineered into the second phase of the construction. Many years of toil undertaken by Pharaoh Khufu's subjects to ensure a tall gallery. There had to be a purpose. Answers lie within 'That which is in the Amduat'... The 32 trials of the deceased Pharaoh as he traversed the underworld.

Amira had carefully photocopied this presentation and enclosed them in neat cream folders. They may end up in drawers in faraway cities in Japan. Mahmoud drove to the private owner's hangar of Cairo. VIP passes were presented and a stern-faced official took them to a beautiful dolphin nosed Airbus helicopter on its helipad. Shiny new rotors began the slow test turn. Her wonderful group were all beckoning her and she was welcomed aboard... To her happy surprise Riku was in the Pilot's seat and Itsuko was acting co-pilot. The day promised to be very different. Thrills exploded from every nerve end as they gained clearance from the tower the pearly fat bellied bird rose into an ochre sky. They swung over the skyline and as Riku confirmed his co-ordinates. Haruto and Hirotsu gave her the thumbs up.

They all wore headphones...Amira watched the 'spiritual' runway to the stars open out ahead and pale shuddering dust clouds assembled and dispersed. A melting vanilla sun climbed rapidly into a treble mirage of shimmering trembling heat haze. The vastness of Giza flooded their visual field. Amira spoke out clearly...

"Egypt's very own runway to the stars The Plateau of Gizeh."

There was a gasp of pleasure for indeed at this level and on this particular swoop line of approach there was a fantastic runway appearance to the carefully orientated site ruined slightly by the tourist signature symbols...ticket hut, and security wall tacky, unsightly. Shameful low modern walls are an eyesore to control the crowds. A sad fact of life.

Everyone was held spell bound. However, at the last minute they were not given permission to land... Instead, instructions were given in a direct order to veer away and Riku was given distinctly clear and vital orders and clearance to land immediately at Meidum.

"There has been a dangerous incident and we cannot enter the pyramid today…just permission to fly over and land at Meidum."

Amira sadly declared. Then diplomatically added…

"Just as exciting but in a very different way."

A group such as this actually seemed to prefer changes and added excitements and took it all in their stride. A text came through from Detective Alain Veldour…astonishingly accurate it read… "Avoid Giza there is word of an attack planned by fundamentalists." Amira mouthed… "Oh bloody hell no." As the rotors screamed on the landing swoop, they all prepared to scramble through the disturbed dust Amira fastened her scarf across her nose and mouth and put on sunglasses. As they dusted themselves down, her mobile trilled.

"Mahmoud!"

"Amira, you okay?"

"Yes, we couldn't land at Giza."

The group gathered around her.

"Shukeran Allah habibti."

He was crying.

"Siddique laheh laheh efie?"

"Those fuckers kill my friend and many tourists blow to sky in the bus…oh my god Amira keep away keep away."

He was gone. The group were in shock they found a small group of fellaheen…all glued to mobiles.

They gestured to Amira to come to them.

Seats and chai seemed to appear from nowhere.

"Howgad howgad, eshrubi chai?"

The fearsome heat of Giza was tempered at Meidum by a lively breeze off the desert which was obligingly on the doorstep of Egypt's first true pyramid.

Sneferu (He of Beauty). Was sensible enough to finish the structure after Huni had departed his kingdom on Earth.

"Your friend Mahmoud is heartbroken."

"Yes Riku we are thrown into turmoil by grief."

"We hear very early today a whisper at the hotel."

Amira gave him her full attention.

"There was much discussion about even coming to Egypt. I want to keep my friends safe…so we made this back up plan." Amira had the overwhelming desire to hold him close…to comfort as one human to another. Just to feel better… They were alive and the tragedy of people once excited by the thought of light heartedly being on holiday and visiting the Great Pyramid had lost their lives. Their families would soon be in deepest mourning. She knew about such things.

He nodded towards the Airbus H155…the remarkable dolphin nose and dorsal fin recognisable anywhere…cruise speed 150 KTS…Max speed 175 KTS. Range 463 nm-… Expensive…screamed from the exquisite bluenose of her quirky beauty…against the backdrop of Egypt's most unusual pyramid. A small boy with a huge old male camel were seemingly gazing in adoration at the gleaming technology of 'now' juxtaposed against the technology of 'then.' The then—being-The Old Kingdom 2686–2181 BC.

This, the great period of classical Egypt. When Memphis was the capital selected by those old kings, and their country had reached its zenith of refined building…the constructing of pyramids enters the psyche of a people who are star struck. This of course followed a period called the, – Thinite 3150–2686 BC… Which was united with much struggle under one King. Religion, government, art and script become fixed almost in the final form. Tragically after Sneferu the first king of the 4th Dynasty… there were minor rulers. Which some claim to lead to the weakening of Egypt in so many ways. By the time of the 6th Dynasty…often regarded as a marking of the end of the true classic Old Kingdom 2686–2181 BC… came Teti, Pepy, Merenra.

Pepy II.

This ailing old king ruled so inefficiently and for far too long. Nobles lost their lands and anarchy ruled. Fields lay fallow and crops were not tended. Famine gripped the land in a grip of iron. Then began the first Intermediate Period 2181–2060… The 7th Dynasty shrouded in mystery. Totally unknown. Maat was not in the land. Slow reversal of fortunes. It is often spoken of when Ra and Amen are cleverly respectfully incorporated within the Pharaoh's name…Maat flourishes. If the Nile rises correctly and to the safe height of inundation…Egypt flourishes.

The question all ask…what about when the Nile water is stolen by another country what then is in store…or (not in store) for Misr…Kemet…Egypt! Death comes on swifter wings than humanity can conquer.

Who shall we turn to…Harmakhis Kephri Atum Ra.?

So, Pepy II weakened the country by too long a reign making ineffectual decisions (perhaps senile). Anarchy…a series of petty-minded kings…deprive the nobility of their property…no crops grow and famine strikes its fangs deep. And the great lion of Giza marks time by shadow sun and star. All this is so far away…Amira as an historian is forced to see the constant flux of reality of empires rising, falling and rising again. Riku is listening to her speak about these times and all the group have become hushed as her steady voice relates the Kingdoms of the past and as a finale, she gestures to the boy guarding the great Airbus while he holds onto the fraying bridle of the camel…who seems to take it all in and is saying… "Mmmmm now that's very interesting…"

Munching his breakfast laced no doubt with a little weak marijuana.

The men of the village give cheers in all the places where she speaks of Sneferu and mutterings of Mish Quais (no bloody good) when Pepy II is spoken of…all charmingly predictable…and yet…there was something more about all this.

They leave the true pyramid after a session of photographs with the dusty robed old village men who wittily managed to extract a little baksheesh…why not…thought Amira. The chai was very good after all. They flew over Cairo with Riku busily keeping up a constant response with Cairo's Domestic Flight Tower.

Amira heard the familiar…

"You have clearance H155…altitude…airspeed…" Finally, the hotel came into view. The great blue dolphin helicopter finally settling her massive ass on the helipad as daintily as a bee lands on a daisy. What a morning. Amira was about to be spoiled again. She wondered at this unusual turn of events. Ringing the department brought only voicemail. She reported in all they had achieved and gave her present whereabouts. The schedule was torn up completely by now obviously… That evening she bought a lovely cool dress from the sale rail at the hotel shop. The go anywhere suit desperately needed cleaning after Meidum's dust. She washed her other things in shampoo… Spreading them out carefully behind a handy plant on her high balcony. Using her little clothesline and pegs… All her life, she had learned to save money and avoid ill treatment to her clothes with such little tricks. Hoping the wind would not snatch up her bra and whisk it across the Sahara.

She arrived sporting a new hairdo piled high on her head. The dress was admired by everyone. Riku most of all. "This so special with your eyes…"

"I am fully complimented Riku…I am very grateful too…thank you for this wonderful, unexpected treat." She waved her hand over the opulent scene. Waiters bounced about and did all their bidding. Amira allowed Hirotsu to fasten very ceremoniously a huge napkin of purest white to protect her clothes. Everyone followed suit accompanied by gales of laughter the whiskey glow doing its work. Life is filled with such charming opposites. Haruto Sato managed to gain silence (not an easy task) he raised his glass to the happy state of being alive in the company of good rich friends. Rich enough to buy a Holyrood distilled whiskey. Riku was attentive and Amira found his company more liberating than she had ever thought possible. He clinked his glass to hers slowly and gently.

"I am smiling outside but inside I have a need to confess some vital development in my life."

"Well, you are among friends."

"My life has been blessed with such great fortune we have two lovely daughters—but for the last two years my wife has asked for a divorce. Today it is granted. Soon I will be sent the final paper."

Amira was genuinely shocked.

"You are talking about Decree Absolute. Oh my God, Riku, this is terrible."

"Her rights are that I buy her a home."

"And you have to do this."

"Yes, all these decisions are decided by lawyers. So, I have complied… She will not change. My heart is very bewildered."

"Any way that you feel is bound to be sad."

"I will have special right to be with my daughters."

"What are their names."

"TsuTsu and we call our eldest Fragrant Rose shortened to Lily Rose. They feel it most acutely. My wife has told me she met another man and wants be within his family."

"Divorce is never good or easy for any family."

"The time of our absolute youth was the happiest…we somehow lost the way to be happy."

"This is hard for you I am so sorry."

"I don't want to make sadness but it comes of its own accord. My wife listens always to these very cold women…they tell her go on diet you get too fat. This is foolish…she makes herself take this shallow philosophy as reality. I ask her—

why you need to please them…please yourself. I liked her the way she was. She takes on this horrible diet…her body does not change the right way…her face becomes like old woman…so she had." He tapped his face trying to find the right words.

"Cosmetic Surgery?"

"Yes, the cost was very high and now her neck is like scrawny hen. So, I ask her…what has happened to you where are you? She told me; I want a divorce you are never here. I am working hard for my family. My children want to attend a good school and own fine things. They don't fall off cherry blossom tree."

Amira touched his arm very gently.

"I am only allowed to do small things in this country…to give you comfort."

"This is a big thing that you listen."

"You want your family again."

He stared into the night beyond the window…into the richness of the swaying palms.

"Money does not buy everything, does it, Riku?"

He slowly shook his head.

"These hands have made my company but the price the price ah! It was very terrible."

After the meal which was a delicious one, Amira hurried up to her room and rescued her things from the balcony. She sensed Riku might marry quickly to avoid loneliness. She saw his difficulty. A strong business profile in the world of the capitalist demands a huge amount of input. Setting up a face to face with Tristan was the weirdest thing. He seemed faintly accusatory, but this probably was just her being over-sensitive perhaps. He was on the opposite end of the financial spectrum. He was also sulky…she noticed the more she knew him the more he leaned into moodiness. He was turning into less of a lover…more of a cantankerous oaf. This she excused due to the ankle taking far too long to get to rights. Perhaps if he had not tried so soon to turn somersaults! A faint niggle came into her mind that she was judging him against the worldly Riku. Whatever it was, she was glad to get away and into a shower and at the point of pressing her beautiful bedside light she was practically nodding off. Her night was restful and dreamless. The following morning the department sent a new driver who was spiky and had none of Mahmoud's wonderful warmth and wit. The new plan was to fly direct to Hurghada to visit a new experimental programme in a desert location, which was under the watchful eyes of the Egyptian government. The idea was to expand development of growing food and to impress sufficiently enough to showcase investment (Probably, the whole point of the group's visit to Egypt). She quietly briefed the group and arranged the flights to Hurghada. She would accompany them. But first she must quickly clear her belongings from the apartment. She promised that all being well and security in place…they would see Luxor. To her this was indeed the highlight of the trip. Of course, next to The Grand Egyptian Museum which was still to be tested by time. The driver agreed to come for her sharp at 4pm for the six pm flight. She told him to give her a missed call and she would come down at once and leave the apartment keys with him. He pulled a face of such scorn she almost gasped…

"Please don't tell me my job."

She gave him a curt nod and vanished indoors. As she closed the lift door she whispered.

"Plonker face."

Packing up and setting to rights all her notes she also lay out all she would need on the flight…then ran a warm bath. Refreshed, she took a long time to set up her hair and grabbing keys money and mobile while wafting soapy perfume she hurried across the busy shara to sit in the café opposite where Mahmoud liked to hang out. She left a voicemail miss you such a lot my colleague message and told him see you soon and salaam in case his wife listened to the message…she also added many respects to your family. No sign of him of course so she ordered coffee, water and cake and set the alarm on her mobile. Returning to the flat, she saw the driver sat with his mobile clamped to his ear. Well at least he would be on time It was just 3.30 pm…At 3.50, he rang her and said curtly.

"I am here for you…please to come."

"Thank you."

She nodded curtly to him at the airport and with a huge sigh of relief entered Internal Flights. The group were all there waving and smiling, what a lovely sight. Truth being she was horribly lonely without their lively company. Riku showed his lovely manners when asking if he could sit with Amira on the flight over the Eastern Desert. She entertained him with a most unusual history lesson. The proof of some of it laid out below for all to see. "Cairo is now so huge and sprawls away with new satellite villages and building programmes stretching further every month into less and less comfortable surrounding desert. Heat in Egypt will never be conquered. It is a fact Egypt grows hotter every year some report as much as one degree and in August it is unbearable, and is often called (the killing month). However, in contrast it is becoming increasingly colder during the winter by up to two degrees. A felucca Captain Ashraf Farag owner of a huge old wooden style felucca moored on the Nile near to the old Novotel Hotel well, he related to Amira how he had scraped thick icy frost from the canvas awnings and wood fittings more than once in the winter. Amira explained how she became truly alarmed one season in Luxor to see monstrous black hailstone clouds with their familiar silver edges. She had pointed repeatedly to them and told people to seek a doorway or some shelter… or a coffee shop…but they just laughed. 'No, no my lady its all okay.' But she knew the signs and kept right on hurrying to her favourite Nubian coffee shop in the Souk. Making it just in time. Hail stones like golf balls hammered bare heads and faces. The big cry in the middle of the storm was…"Allah mercy Allah." Many of the new homes have an irreverence to real people. Low ceilings and small rooms that encourage the hand to reach for the takeeffi switch.

"If you cannot afford the electricity, you just sweat in the sleepless nights. Often in Luxor on the West Bank visitors taking balloon rides in the very early mornings witness families sleeping out under stars for coolness. Because often whole roofs are deliberately missing from homes. If you go up too high, the house taxes go higher also. Often the very oldest homes have stone steps leading to a rooftop room with strong home-made pallet style beds or wicker style woven affairs—anything that could make a sleeping platform away from heat, snakes and scorpions.

"I have often met people who were forced out of Old Qurna in Thebes…such dilapidated homes had originally been excavated partially underground hundreds of years before because this gave immediate coolness. Many dating back to the old dynasties. This eventually naturally gave rise to an instinctive tunnelling desire towards the tomb clusters close by. So much of this tunnelling became conspiratorial in that old ideas of robbing tombs lived on and any excuse for easy money must have proved a great winning recipe. The outcome was inevitable of course, people were caught and the law showed its teeth to them.

Also, a man walking casually through the village of Old Qurna swinging along gaily no doubt singing softly some sweet little popular song—suddenly found himself falling through the road. The tunnels had undermined the village so much that it all sort of gave way. The authorities were on this like a duck on a June bug. Showing up not best pleased and many residents were called out and the next thing the village was world news… New Qurna was built and foolish architects designed the ceilings of these new homes far too low, therefore trapping stuffy heat. Such cheap homes were miserably inadequate for purpose. So many of these homes were cramped and the families naturally dismayed.

The Tomb Robbing Culture…began due to truly ancient scores that needed settling within the older 'Old Qurna' residents. Much resentment still thrived in certain communities. Apparently, a certain Pharaoh…buried in the Valley of the Kings had not paid his workmen and artisans. They had families to care for, responsibilities to be met. To work for nothing is to starve if you are poor…and a Pharaoh covered in gold was asking for trouble. And got it…Life has its vicious injustices…the odd mummy plundered…led to a gold grab of a kind only witnessed in the South African gold mines…searching for gold is ever a pastime of mankind.

So, the great break in began and then the chuck 'em about tear 'em apart and dismember limb from limb with gay abandon all carried out of course by flaming torchlight. In their haste, many things were missed in this great secret searching for gold, lapis, precious stones…and well anything that could be flogged to anyone anywhere any old how really. Humanity is this mixture of resentment and need, happiness and greed. I made a cine film of Old Qurna right before the big pull-down programme and 'relocation' of families."

Riku had not meant to laugh but he couldn't help himself. "So, it is true that the people that buried the grand pharaohs viziers and wealthy nobles became the very people who knew how and where to target them for making money."

"Tragic of course for the complete historic picture of Ancient Egypt…but we can see why it happened. You don't have to approve to understand. Later of course it was for a different reason. But the total outcome being all 'that which was sacred and inside'—is now pored over minutely and is outside!"

They drank refreshing chai that the flight attendant brought to everyone and just relaxed.

Riku began to fidget.

"Madam Amira if you don't like to talk about your private life, tell me instantly…all I ask is you don't throw yourself away on some worthless person."

"No one wants to marry me, Riku. I have no plans in mind no irons in the fire…"

"Wretchedness in marriage is particularly hard on women."

"I have a divorce to prove that already. My life is sweet at this very moment…I don't see how I could improve on this."

"Are you including me in the sweet moment."

"Oh didn't I look from the window and directly at you. Strange, I thought I did."

"Yes, you caught me between 'sweet' and 'this'."

"Shall we try and get some of the honey cake Riku."

"We shall, and I have a little of the whisky for such times…I will order."

He stood up and swayed in the slight turbulence caused by the aircraft passing over high dunes. She knew in that moment they would end up together but how and when was the question. They were so right together. There was none of the trying to be a shitty dominant husband constantly threatening divorce and slapping to get all his own way. To be with such a thoughtful man such as Riku was a breath of fresh air. She felt so good about herself in his company. Proud to be by his side. There was the comfort of tender feelings within the excitement of him as a masculine lover…and protection of the kind that is hard to give a good description of. She had been told about a meeting like this about four years ago by someone…but who. They had said distinctly—

'You will meet a man so right, and you will feel so right, that you find yourself and himself loving deeply. Just be patient let time sort it…because it will darling it will.'

He returned with chai laced with whisky and a little sugar. For some reason the sun streamed in over them at that precise moment…perhaps the jet had changed course ever so slightly. A realignment of necessity. A cosmic approval. Or a demonstration of something not yet discovered by any science…

"The sun has come in to join us Madam Amira."

The drink was nectar.

She remembered everything…it became a mental treasure.

Two days in Hurghada was more than enough for Amira. They spent most of it by the pool getting tans…with the brief but necessary stint out to the desert to examine one of the many government experiments in agriculture by reclaiming desert (Which several thousand years ago was rich savannah). These experiments were vital for feeding a growing population and therefore fulfilling the 'brief'…The question asked of course is how long does it take to look at a type of leek…Riku was involved he had incredible insight into aquifers and knew of the stored water in landscapes that appeared totally devoid of life. Wadis are old dried up river courses. Naturally, he examined his own peculiar maps. These were of as much fascination to him as a baby with ice cream…he tumbled them about in the gentle wind and they all helped him by holding them down on the bonnet of one of the cars. He did not talk but worked inside a tent like structure and made notes on a laptop. Finally, he stood up straight in the strong sunlight. Thanked everyone...Amira helped fold away the precious maps. She was extraordinarily proud of him. Feeling a glow spread over her whole being as she watched his strong features in concentration. She suddenly knew his specialist knowledge was why they were all here at this pinpoint of time in Egypt. Truth be told the type of plant was growing but it truly was so boring. This of course is why diplomacy is in the dictionary for such cases. The feeding of more and more people being crucial in Egypt this cannot be overlooked. He concluded his report, made a phone call. Now they headed back to base camp.

As the cars shifted through gears and 'found' the correct route back to Hurghada...a wispy dust column rose to the left-hand side of the minibus. Amira pointed it out to the others and the mention of a Waltzing Jinn, and the request of shwia shwia to their driver. He lowered the back window and they witnessed one of the strange desert phenomena of a rising dust column, their excitement mounted as the column seemed to form the shape of a woman and rose erotically waltzing. One second she was playing a game of—'Look I'm coming to get you.'...then...'No I've changed my mind'. The Waltzing Jinn played and danced along the desert growing to some fifteen or so feet...then dropped down once more sand and dust to sand and dust. They all sighed in unison and the driver speeded up once more and returned them to the hotel.
'The Five Star Playboy Club'...Well, that was Amira's secret name for the hotel – gave up all its luxury goodies and Amira had Sally and her grandparents in fits of laughter telling them about the 'Waltzing Jinn' dancing and all the funny things they all got up to. Sally was peevish at the end of the link.

Amira cried later in her hotel room. The flight across to exciting Luxor was the highlight of the whole venture in Upper Egypt for Amira...even as she took off and the Jet steadied at cruise speed she was preparing... The talk on Tut Ankh Amun's tomb and the subsequent desperation of his young widow. Which led to one of the strangest pieces of correspondence in history. The letters of Ankhessenamun.

The Young Widow, Ankhessenamun

(Her life is of Amun). When her husband Tut Ankh Amun was finally interred with a muddled preparation of the tomb and a heart-breaking ceremony with all its clumsy haste…so much so that Ay even instructed the bewildered workmen into vandalising one of the coffins by sawing it off literally…at the last minute to make it fit and accommodate its occupant for all eternity. Because of undue haste…certain measurements had gone awry and this in a land where the 4th dynasty pyramid builders had only been inches out when completing The Great Pyramid…it does seem a twist of irony that this adored teenage Pharaoh is given a speedy hotchpotch burial.

But we know why, don't we?

Haste according to Ay's scheme was of the essence…for any day Horemheb… would no doubt come storming in back from a campaign… protecting Egypt's borders and interests…So Ay must have been lording it up…planning to capture the pretty widow with all her own personal wealth… Many see her pleading within the letters as a true insight into what was really happening. A document found in an ancient Hittite capital date to the Amarna Period of Egypt. The so-called Deeds of Suppliliuma I. (A Hittite ruler) – while being in siege at Karkemish received a letter from an Egyptian Queen. The letter reads:-

'My husband has died and I have no son. They say about you that you have many sons. You might give me one of your sons to become my husband. I would not wish to take one of my subjects as a husband I am afraid.'

This document is extraordinary as Egyptians consider foreigners to be inferior. Suppliliuma I is amazed, exclaims to his courtiers. 'Nothing like this has happened to me in my entire life. 'The Hittite Chronicles say she is called Dakhamunza…a transliteration of Egyptian title TAHEMETNESU… The King's wife.

'One of my subjects,' could be translated as. 'One of my servants.'

Ankhessenamun was born with the given name by her father Akhenaten of Ankhesenpaaten. She was the 3rd daughter to him and his wife Nefertiti…

She appears on monuments of Amarna roughly after year 5 or 6 of Akhenaten's reign.

King Suppliliuma sends an envoy, suspecting quite naturally in the circumstances, a trick. Later he relents and sends Prince Zananza—who must have been very brave—he dies trying to reach Ankhessenamun.

Foul play is suspected. Ay no doubt sent spies and murderers to waylay the young Prince. Ay does take the throne of Egypt… Four years later he is dead…Horemheb succeeds at last and as there was a certain justice possibly outstanding, he has a reign of 14 years. Ankhessenamun vanishes from history.

Amira loves 'her group'…she has taken this possessive expression due to them showing such kindness in every part of the exchanges between them all. Riku carries much weight within its dynamic energy. A conversation with Itsuko sealed these most certain conclusions with the stamp of…the emperor… So to speak.

They had been met from the Hurghada to Luxor flight by an ostentatious limousine. Amira thought a low-key affair would have been much safer in the present climate of hostility towards visitors.

They were still sorting luggage in the foyer of the Jolie Ville Hotel…it was extremely busy, and it became obvious a loud voiced tourist and his exuberant wife were discontent. The actual cause of this of course was unknown.

Itsuko came and flumped down next to Amira with his clowning mannerisms. Much loved within the group he was often given the job of breaking the ice on tricky subjects…with magical wit and the hilarious misuse of grand protocol.

"Oh, it is a relative of mine…they probably sent the brunette pole dancer to his room instead of the blonde!" He pretended to listen and turned one ear towards the loud pair and cupping his beautifully manicured hand with a ring to shame all others glinting in dull beauty.

"Ah yes this my Uncle Fred; he always makes this problem."

Amira shook her head smothering laughter.

They sat back patiently as a waiter came courteous and efficient…they soon had cool juices with bobbing ice shapes…pyramids…yes pyramids.

Amira clinked glasses with him… "Here's to a melting cliché'."

He smiled and setting the drink down he looked deeply at her she responded at once giving him full attention.

"We." He caressed the space over the Japanese group…

"Have the greatest respect for the warrior."

"Riku."

"Yes…this is a story of love for a man who is brother of our hearts. My life was totally cruel by my father's hand. He made us tremble; he was unfair on all levels. I know you are one that understands life does not give all people enough to eat…a kind father and mother and sufficient clothes." She wanted to say…

'How would you know such things'. He raised a hand in the gentlest way to give reassurance.

"My life was such. I took up the task to be father when my father was sent to prison… He was a bad man. I cannot make a cover story for such as he. My mother made old by his beatings could barely walk. So, I would rise up very early help her make cakes, some sweet some savoury…and load a cart with all we could sell…cover with canvas and trundle through rain, sun, snow, wind to sell in the market and when all were sold, I would trundle home…run to school and learn all I could. The day came when we learn that the newest local offices like food delivered. I am fourteen now and tall, so one day I take beautiful food to Riku's office…I am not aware who he is…how do I move in his life…only in the delivery…he thanks me and tells me I am undercharging. He gives me a new job and I am to help him in so many ways."

Amira is astounded. "In two years, I am full personal assistant then his company are on the point of making a new conquest with a business but I have seen this new business man in his office and know he is a cheat and does not obtain permission with authorities governing taxes and such…you understand."

Amira nodded fiercely. "Dangerous."

"Exactly. Of course, this is fatal in Japan. I panic and with great secrecy in my voice I take Riku to a quiet office and tell him all I know regarding this man. You see nobody really see the sandwich boy."

Amira tapped her forehead.

"Exactly…Riku stares at me and believe…he withdraws with a clever diplomatic move…like a quiet bear he gently tip toe out of the deal backwards with his company's money still intact. He is ecstatic with relief. I get to hear eventually that this other man go to dangerous levels with his dealings and government take him down. I am proud and Riku is so happy with my honesty to life, and to people, he gives me my own company. We still watch each other's backs…this correct saying?"

"Exactly."

"We never see him care for another woman the way he is care with you. Trust to me you are loved, and he will walk through fire for you. This is private conversation you understand."

That night

Amira woke from some strange dream. She sat at the edge of the wide bed shaking and tearful. This was a flashback to the mall shootings and the river, its broad watery sheen, the friendly skiff. The noise of the downward thrust of wind from the Cormorant's rotary blades whirr.

She rang down to reception and ordered hot chocolate…the night porter was concerned the moment she opened the door.

"You are shaking madam do you need me to call you a doctor."

She shook her head.

"La shukeran."

He left quietly closing the heavy door with respectful care. Amira found a pack of cigarettes kept for such occasions, took everything out to the tiny balcony and sat in the black whispering night with the naglas rustling each other in a conversation they have been engaged in since the beginning of the world.

The next morning delivered normality. Luxor was as lively and crazy as ever. Amira took them all down to the Old Souk but not before she had told them to leave all their watches and cameras in the hotel safe. Luxor has an interesting reputation…that must be acknowledged with respect.

Shouts of 'BASSALL, AISH, SPICES'. The Kalash carriages with their snorting stamping horses, jangling harness. The love she felt for this nutty place was as strong as ever. Stall holders called out to her in friendly recognition. Saying funny things.

Riku wanted to know everything they were calling…

"What did he say to make you laugh."

"Oh, it's a funny thing… Smile, because you smile before you die."

"And egg on your knee."

Amira cracked up…

"No no eggeree. Go home!"

"What to us."

"No, it's funny it's just joking… Sometimes they call out… Go eat with your father."

"And."

"This can be insult…especially if the father is dead."

"This one just call to me kallissy."

"Kallistaha."

"And."

"Shut up your mouth."

They all loved the old souk in the sunshine, the rich splendour of its hot golden rays reminding Amira so much of the art of the 18th dynasty with the sun disk spilling its molten droplets of golden light over the people. They found a wonderful worker's restaurant and sat in a circle on low stools with broad wooden tables…they soon tucked into spicy foul and fresh aish with chicken and hot minty chai, Egyptian Salata…Baba Ghanoush, honey cake…

The whisky flasks were most carefully and secretly passed and some of the workmen watching noticed this (they never miss anything in the Souk) and they grinned with pleasure. This very beautiful malt was purely medicinal…of course. They were very chuffed with Amira, who of course knew about such typical back street workman's cafés. She greatly encouraged this choice. After all, why shouldn't the poorer businesses get trade.

It was a wonderful meal the laughter never ending…the bill was tiny even with a generous tip. Much was made of them in a friendly gruff down to earth sort of comradery. On leaving, they were waylaid at every turn by all the traders merchants, merchant's donkeys and small children. Motorbikes growled their passage through the narrowest of spaces, sometimes with four boys perched grinning and calling out to Amira. Even Kalash carriages muscled through. A few tired donkeys looked at them from shadowy recesses. As if to say. "Yes, and what about my photo for your collection." One donkey leered with bared teeth at Riku as he asked Amira to stand next to it. She flatly refused.

"Riku, you stand next to him he wants you to buy him that's why he is showing such huge old yellow teeth."

The owner told them…

"He likes to go to Japan by tiara. He makes like this face to show love you."

This had everyone in hysterics. Riku took lots of photos and Amira was so nervous that young souk pick pockets would home in on the very desirable smart phones. Riku became very intrigued by a tiny desert fox that had been through the hands of a very inept taxidermist. This creature appeared for all the world like a snarling cartoon outside a very dusty ceramic and junk filled shop. Riku took its photo. Amira was greatly puzzled as to why anyone should want to record such a creature.

They soon all expressed the opinion that this was quite enough for one day. Amira guided them out to the wide servees shara and waved down a couple of taxi cabs and they all tumbled in. Amira had quite a task negotiating the fare. They had so many bags of loot comprising of incense in gaudy tins (the real stuff): Cashmere headscarves…or their cheaper alternative. Trinkets of dubious manufacture and even more lurid but most necessary scarves...the taxi drivers...were laughing as they called out...

'HAMDOOLAH' to all the other drivers. Horns honking, one played the 'Land of Dixie'. Amira groaned.

Whatever happened to—going under the radar—with much laughter they made it safely back to Jolie Ville in a chaos of shouts and whiskey. As they opened the taxi doors gifts fell out at the hotel entrance. Amira said under her breath... "A Japanese invasion of the funniest kind and there was me worried about 'THEIR' safety."

Riku was helped in a diplomatic manner because he was rather tipsy...and was on his dignity a little to retain a certain class and elegance. However, he was obviously relaxed and happy. The whole point of the excursion. A hotel called Jollie must after all be allowed to live up to its name. A call from the department in Cairo to check with Amira that they were enjoying themselves and were happy, gave her an opportunity to hold out her mobile as she replied laughing.

"Er, I think I can safely say they are settling in comfortably."

Welcome to wonderful, naughty, friendly Luxor.

The true purpose of the call was to ascertain the security of the trip out to 'The Valley of The Kings.' ...and the need for an escort convoy. Amira requested one from the Department. It was provisional on the local police giving the go ahead.

The night that followed left Amira relaxed because she had such a good feeling slipping into pure white sheets, and with the gentle hum of the takeefy cooling the air she was sent quickly to sleep. At three, she awoke breathless sweating and clutching her side, it was throbbing horribly. Vicky had warned her about the possibility of this happening out of the blue. Luck can run in and can run right out again...the mind is a mystery of selected memory and the primordial instinct is still being unravelled. She made a tea with the hotel courtesy kettle. Sitting outside she watched stars stretch to infinity...it came to her then why Riku wanted her to stand by the bad-tempered old donkey.

He was trying to sneak a picture of her. Bless him.

Amira sent a text to Tristan...he would understand this night thing after all he had survived the same atrocity. To her surprise a call came from him.

"Tristan!"

"Sweetheart...I was online; I can't sleep the news in Cairo had me shaking."

"Me too...my bullet wound is throbbing like blazes."

"Poor darling…they are real fuckwits…and you should be here with us."

"You are sweet but I can't."

"Yes, you can…the Mall families service was held and of course gained huge coverage by the networks."

"You were there."

"Of course, Detective Alain Veldour also, he stood with mum and me. Dad, couldn't he has a huge job on he's helping with the overhauling of a beautiful yacht called Pagan Arrow."

"What a fantastic name."

"She is fantastic, love to go on her they are all off to the Med'. You should come with us…bring Sally…see it as an adventure. Mum wants you to come."

"Pagan Arrow…sounds like a once in a lifetime experience."

"Fabulous yacht darling…when you come home we will all go down and see her… She's about a hundred feet or something, fast lines and huge white sails constructed the old way…she has been on oceanic voyages and is as tough as a miner's thumb."

"I'd have to get permission for Sally but home schooling is all the rage now I might let out the house."

"Great…see…aren't you glad I called."

"I am."

"Sleep well."

"Goodnight."

Amira felt hope return. For the future was opening before them. Possibilities and opportunities. She watched the naglas shift and whisper along the extensive garden right to the water's edge. Of course, it was the Nile, this great river the longest in the world that was soothing her… "The father of all the rivers."

She whispered to herself…returning to her bed she left the balcony windows open, a slight risk but the faint distant calls in the night soothed and sleep returned.

The next day when she flicked on the television…a channel was showing a special dedication to Bob Dylan and Amira went into overdrive with her own version of one of his famous songs…

"Tangled up in blue…

The sun was shining,

and I was wondering

if her hair was still red,

Maybe we'll meet again
someday on the avenue…
Tangled up in blue.
She was married when we first met,
soon to be divorced.
I helped her out of a jam I guess
but I used a little too much force."

This world-renowned number seemed to fit exactly into the mood of a new defiance that she had most definitely woken up with. There was a something she had brought out of the dream with her…it kept escaping and then returning to her thoughts. Like some old travelling pedlar from a forgotten city.

This enigmatic dream truly was an old traveller which had come back to remind her of youth, rebellion, and a whole other self as she used to be. She grabbed it delighted from that dear old pedlar and it was here in the room in the lyrics of a song from long ago …from an old LP she was certain was called…

'Blood on the Tracks.'

She said it out loud and caught it up with everything that was now.

Over in the breakfast room…the group spotted the difference. Those tawny gold flecks were like sparks in her eyes. Also, a remark was made about their upward tilt at the corners being the same as a cat's…Riku was very animated by her presence as she lay out the map of the Valley of the Kings… "We can visit here, there and of course Tut Ankh Amun…but things can change direction like a moody snake out here."

The Divinities

Amira gathered her group around her precious map of the Theban Necropolis. She placed her excellent compass on the map and proceeded. With a small pointer indicating the choices.

"We have just a few hours allocated. I am pleased to obtain permission even for this. We are as I have said constantly alerted to the possibility of instant change. The convoy will accompany us to here. We are travelling by two nondescript cars. I have chosen them due to their ordinary everyday look. We cannot flout wealth and status. This is neither the time or place. The vital component is to play down our presence…we will slip under the radar. The convoy is fully armed. When it veers off here…we will look like average folk going to visit relatives. This area here is named 'The Valley of the

110

Monkeys'…we begin there. Next…I have arranged for our tickets to be in the cars and we will proceed directly to Tuthmosis III. From there I have taken the liberty to choose KV 62. There is a minimum of visitors allowed we have to be vigilant. Your safety is paramount. We have been given clearance for these three sites I hope you understand."

A murmur ran through the group.

"We will leave this tomb and proceed to the restaurant…where we have plenty of time for refreshment. We will return here to the Jolie Ville you all know me a little by now and can feel free to ask any questions during our tour. Tomorrow, we have managed to secure a visit to The Temple to Montu. Not an average tourist destination."

"We have not heard of this place before Madam Amira."

"Precisely…"

They all walked heads bowed to the rather scruffy cars. Well aware of their comparison to the ostentation of pearly white limousines.

The drivers were dressed down also. Amira made no apology for this dress it down approach. She strongly believed this would allow a certain freedom and surviving Thebes was her only aim. The group were subdued. Amira thought it would do them all good to experience simplicity and live. She had already expressed this adamantly. The department knew it was all a question of reality and were in total support. Riku was nodding and so the rest of the group fell into step staying within the convoy. The serious side of Egyptian travel due to fundamentalist activity dictates…you accept certain realities or risk your life. Most set aside personal opinion…in the face of terrorist extremists. The deaths at Dheir el Bahri are a terrible reminder. The horrors of Cairo fresh in memory. Egypt cannot forget such atrocities They would be very close to this controversial zone near Hatshepsut's Mortuary Temple. As a country Egypt is aware…of the fine balance required. People demand to see Egypt's rare treasures… The economic vitality needs people…but the governing bodies must do more to keep these people safe. The same as any country with such immense borders.

Monkey Business

Their drivers Mr Neefty and Mr Sahidi respectively, soon earned the nicknames Nifty and Shifty which they loved and constantly talked to each other on their mobiles amidst much laughter. They all should have guessed really that this would be no ordinary day… Sometimes maktoob sends a special day to keep us all from going nuts. This was that day. The drivers for some reason (best known to a bunch of bananas in the left-hand stall at the Old Souk) missed a turn in the road…or did they…?

A dusty village loomed and Amira suspected commission was behind the stunt…but gave it the benefit of the doubt. They cruised through…windows up at her command, a swarm of the happiest, dirtiest children ever seen ran from every household…the cars picked up speed until only one tremendously stout hearted little individual gave an Olympian burst of speed…and held this for nearly ten seconds then dropped back still waving energetically. Everyone cheered him. Riku leaned over to Amira… "He will go far."

"Yes, he just did."

They soon by a twist and turn and a couple of backings up drove to the site. The excavations of some workshops Amira figured, about twenty, and areas still under tidy up and sieve gently instructions…in truth the site yielded few wonders…Amira explained with respectful ease that… 'This truly is the realistic side of preparation for the afterlife'.

Pointing out various functions behind the remains…most of the site had been used to clean and no doubt repair funereal goods and furnishings. Little was wasted. Thankfully the group were interested…after all a workshop is a necessity. As they quietly and carefully picked their way about, a cloud of dust and a rowdy group of village fellaheen came streaming over the broken cliffs. They were all laughing and holding out tablecloths, tee shirts, pots and alabaster figures…

"Laheh laheh nastaclere."

Amira whispered, groaning very loudly. They were soon surrounded by sellers of badly assembled packs of napkins with geese on, and massive stiff white cloths were held under their noses. The leader of the pack had obviously been eating his lunch or brunch…when 'the call to arms' came because the last of these delicious nuts were being spat into Hirotsu's darling face. Luckily, he soon saw the funny side when Amira shooed the man away and wiped Huritso's face clean as a mother would a child's. This natural concern had the group involuntarily laughing. Eventually, the bloody tablecloths were all held in line and some trading was in play…but it was all one-sided. Japanese business tycoons are not in the least bit interested in cheap table ware, no matter the number of the thread count of the cotton on badly transfer printed squares.

The line was drawn in the rubble-strewn sand and Amira led the group out of the valley of the shadow of the mummified monkeys or whatever…back to Nifty and Shifty. Once in the comparative safety of two very dusty taxi's they all laughed their heads off.

Amira asked Mr Nifty and Mr Shifty to take them all to Tuthmosis the third tout suit. They sheepishly ground a few gears and left calmly… A misunderstanding of a rictus grin on both their faces. Tears of laughter were still being wiped as they drove to Biban el Maluk.

Tuthmosis III (Born of the God Thoth)

A great deal of jealous behaviour and a hacking off of names and destruction of Hatshepsut's monuments, likeness, and cartouche was carried out during this Pharaoh's reign. An immense surge of aggression was released from the deep psyche of one of Egypt's most famed and powerful Pharaoh's.

The god Thoth is represented by the baboon…due to this creature's desire to sit out on its ridiculous bottom and receive the first warming rays of the all-powerful sun. The baboon of course is no god but a bit of a bully who likes to sunbathe…how the mighty are fallen. They really do have a horrible derriere. However, in an Egyptian myth… 'Thoth is the Master of the divine word.' Wisdom and truth should also be in the brief.

All that has gone before should be torn down…does this hint at anarchy, rebellion? The reverence surrounding this god and the animism represented holds a position within the divine purpose. The pharaohs' purpose being to obey the will of the gods.

This pharaoh was exceedingly dangerous… His place in history falls directly into The New Kingdom 18th Dynasty 1570–1070 BC… Perhaps we should look at the great female Pharaoh before… Indeed, because there, we really do find a wealth of knowledge…for it is none other than the wonderfully quixotic, charismatic Hatshepsut.

We need to carefully unravel such strange outcomes. Emperor Constantine (AD 312–337) removed (stole) an obelisk from its true home in Thebes…it was transported to Alexandria for shipment to adorn Constantine's new capital of Constantinople. Constantine died before this Tuthmosis obelisk even reached Constantinople. Excellent outcome some would say. Also, he did not live up to his name.

The idea then fell upon Theodosius the first to set it up in the famous Hippodrome of AD 390.

But it is Tuthmosis III...we speak of surely...

Yet, as in so much of history we often look at a figure through opinion and little hints.

Champollion 1790–1832...found he was able to study and learn how to decipher hieroglyphic texts by identifiable names within the Royal cartouche of Tuthmosis III and Ramesses II.

The pharaohs were not the only ones to be buried in Biban el Maluk others were given this honour also. At one point in Egypt's great history, rebellion amongst the priests led to those without royal connections to be given a shaft tomb burial there.

Within KV64 was found a valuable (time capsule) to show us a strange period in Egypt's history. For it contained two women, one of an earlier time...of some 500 years before...robbed of all her finery by tomb robbers. They showed much contempt and haste, because the mummy had been tragically ripped about by anger and greed leaving it exposed to vile decay and horrible desecration. The tomb left open exposed to insects. Masses of wasps' nests cover the interior walls. Her 'Ka' may have departed to go elsewhere. She was of royal birth...but this fact did not aid her. Loose sand and rubble was strewn over her... Very sad. A new occupant was placed there. This leads us back to a time of great anarchy and rebellion within the Priests of Amun. She is said to be the 20-year-old daughter of a high priest. Her role within the temple of Amun being Chantress to Amun. Her name is Nehemes Bastet. Within her simple wood coffin, she was found to be very skilfully mummified and intact. The coffin is covered in beautiful and delicately intricate artwork. She was found holding an exquisite wood tablet painted with great loving care...depicting her as an exquisite, pale chantress honouring a symbolic figure representing several divinities. This wonderful find was by a hard-working Egyptologist the highly respected Susan Bickel.

Going from the simple to the grand, we talk of Tuthmosis III—who prepared a splendid tomb for his favourite wife. Hatshepsut Merytre. Also, Rekhmire—vizier and Pharaoh's first minister the most important official in the land...his tomb reflects numerous activities and is one of the most attractive with diverse artwork which wonderfully conveys vital information...depicting a wonderful and illustrious career. His titles and duties were many... (The corvee)...

compulsory state labour, was organised by this man....also steering (The ship of state).

Rekhmire was close to the king serving him well and helping him in all manner of duties. Conduct impeccable. (He makes this statement)

"I was the heart of the Lord, the ears and eyes of my Sovereign. I was his skipper and knew not slumber by night or by day. Whether I stood or sat my heart was set upon the prow rope and stern rope, and the sounding pole was never idle in my hands...I judged rich and poor alike. I rescued the weak from the strong...I defended the widow. I established the son and heir upon the seat of his father...I judged great matters...I caused both parties to go away satisfied. I did not pervert the cause of justice for reward. I was not deaf to the empty-handed. I did not accept anyone's bribe..."

This vizier certainly earned his informative tomb...it is located in the village of Qurna...near the valley of the Kings.

Tuthmosis III...KV34. Arranged for his own highly sophisticated tomb to be cut into the cliff some 30 metres high up from the valley floor. And deeply excavated...it is remarkable...the site enjoys a certain isolation in the furthest wadi. Obviously only fit people can gain access. His facial features are in some people's opinions 'eerie' his stature slight for he was a nimble warrior and at only 5ft 3in...short. This is misleading because he was excessively successful as a campaigner...extending lands...for Egypt's wealth increased. His reign 1479–1426 BC...gives him a reputation as one of Egypt's greatest Pharaohs.

The Discovery of the Tomb

Workmen under the guidance of Victor Loret...who was born in Paris on 1 September 1859...died in France (Lyon) 3 February 1946. Victor Loret was an enchanted man, fascinated by all things Egyptian and became Archaeologist Director General of Egyptian Antiquities. His service was impressive producing a brilliant portfolio of excavations at Sakkara and Thebes. Regarding Tuthmosis III...the excavation was meticulous. Loret proceeded with a method of 24 square grids. Nothing considered too small (which eerily echoes the ancient people's ideology). Sadly, tomb robbers had left mere fragments of funereal furnishings. The once beautiful sarcophagus is badly smashed. The orientation of the tomb means the entrance lies North.

The vestibule hewn out at roughly 90 degrees holds two square pillars...with strangely unusual designs... A remarkable wall decoration lists 741 of the divinities who appear in the Amduat which is unusually depicted as a frieze along the great walls of the burial chamber. Four excellent annexes used as store chambers strongly indicate this was a richly furnished tomb overloaded with the greatest and richest of treasures. All stolen. The beautiful cartouche shaped yellow quartzite sarcophagus had been placed on a limestone plinth. This must have been a magnificent tomb richly glowing by torchlight.

In the Belief System of Ancient Egyptians

Death was not the end. Food, beer, medicine, herbs, even clothing and loincloths, jewels, bows, arrows and the delicate Solar Boat. All manner of everyday necessities were stored in the tomb for the 'transitioning' Pharaoh to undergo some 32 perils of the underworld. Priests at one point had secreted the mummy away. This was located hundreds of years later by Maspero in the Dheir el Bahri Cache in 1881.

Returning to the eerie scenes upon the pillars...which are hauntingly simplistic and yet they convey an energy, as do the stick-like cartoons of the long lines of figures in the scenes from 'that which is in the Amduat.'

There are cracks in the blue ceiling with its myriad of stars...the cracks are clumsily treated...but still preserving its meaning and tell a story of its original brilliancy in the finish...

This is the great tomb of a powerful warrior king.

Amira told the group it will always be the one place where she felt 'observed'. Her down to earth approach was greatly challenged here.

They stumbled out into the glare of the powerful Egyptian sun.

Once they had descended to the Wadi floor, Amira quietly led them on the long hot walk through the Valley to the exact opposite in tombs. After walking down some sixteen steps to see what was once a vibrant young Pharaoh Tut Ankh Amun...they were astonished at turning left into a tiny area... This world-famous teenage Pharaoh lay with a true solemnity. Reduced to lying in a glass container viewed from a modern wooden balcony. Simplistic art (in comparison to the weird figures of Tuthmosis Ill Tomb) surprised Riku most of all. He quietly stood near to Amira...as he loved to be near her at any opportunity.

"This is a huge contrast."

"I knew you would all be surprised. Also, it was intended for a woman."

Hirotsu waved a hand over the simple scene.

"This boy was buried in one big hurry."

Amira took her laptop and showed them how he would have looked to Howard Carter in 1922. They all gasped.

"Ah this is big difference…they could not leave this once the press had exposed it in all its detail."

"Correct, the one true statement over there on the wall…do you all see the peculiar shapes like tadpoles…well they are like a code, a strange message…"

They huddled close and watched her as she translated.

The symbols for time itself… The artist was very different to any living in our time. He made an eerie prediction that his young Pharaoh Tut Ankh Amun…the living image of Amoun or Amun…will be spoken of for thousands of years. He is stating here that his name will never die.

"He invented a kind of forever for his king."

"Yes Riku."

The blackened mummified remains held them within a hypnotic lonely connection. Both these tombs had one thing in common they both declared emphatically that an earthly death…was just the beginning of a strange journey. To all priests imbued with the spirit of these rituals, this was but a beginning. Tut Ankh Amun's black body inside the glass case seemed so simplified. All the news and stories surrounding this tomb had been talked of worldwide. Here however, confronted with the young boy himself…one could not ignore a strange powerful energy…the spell was soon broken. His teenage frame and scull appear frail…upon the walls around him…the poor artwork done in such hurried clumsiness… it had failed to dry and was sealed in such haste before the paint had dried … producing an unsightly black mould spotting. There upon the wall with baboons and the correct prediction detailed and clearly pointed out by Amira, was the sneaking scheming of Ay the one who seized the throne with such haste upon Tut Ankh Amun's last intake of earth's air. Ay donning the garb of a sacred priest of the temple…the sacred leopard skin upon his old body. His eagerness to be seen here… The one who may have even married the exquisite Ankhessenamun. Grieving and fearful, she wrote those despairing letters…to a King of a quite another country… "Please send me one of your sons."

Tragedy befell her…many conclude…her fate being – never to be mentioned again in her time.

Ay is sneaking in the back door of the palace… As he carried out the opening of the mouth ceremony. The task of the next 'bloodline Pharaoh'. Such haste, such acting.

All so long ago.

Outside they meandered silent, thoughtful.

Hirotsu…walked with Amira… "Do you feel sadness…?"

"Of course Hirotsu."

"I am haunted by the pathetic look upon this boy's countenance."

"Did you feel strange in Tuthmosis tomb?"

"Madam Amira, I will not forget this day…all the time I am in front of those spooky stick figures in that warrior tomb ugh! But with this boy…a sadness that he died so young in some shady circumstances…I feel."

He shook to emphasise the shivery feeling.

"I agree it is in Tuthmosis 3rd tomb I can honestly say the only one here…that makes me feel as if I am constantly being watched."

She took his arm gently and guided him around a stone enclosure…a dig was planned here…some new evidence of a chamber…the report that the tomb of a physician to the Royal Court had been located.

Chapter Four
Back in the Coils

By the time they had reached the restaurant, they were all hungry. Ordering far too much…but Amira did not complain…the drivers were keen to return to the hotel. Amira said that would be impossible…they could go and come back, but this was the group's rest period. The sun was strong now. So they shut up…for once chastened no doubt due to the monkey business of the morning…which had backfired. Amira knew the badly educated Egyptian Muslim likes to rule everyone and ends up ruling a car radio with his feet up. His cigarette smoke burning away his hard-earned money and usually as broke as he started out. Their lives were held within a self-inflicted futility. Riku sat next to Amira…they raised glasses of fresh juice and clinked for good health. Hirotsu called,

"Good health, happiness and pretty women."

This brought the whiskey flasks on the scene again.

"How do they do it Riku my friend?"

"How pleasant to be called so…you honour me Amira."

"Bless your heart…how are your feet holding up in this heat."

"Hahaha…much better…these waiters suffer far more they are almost running to feed us all."

Truly, they clashed and clattered swerved and served. This the busiest of times. Food appeared and everyone rushed to scrub their hands and wash quickly…returning with clean hands, merry faces. Japanese food is served very daintily. Egyptian food is brought in a stream of dishes but in this tourist style it lacked finesse. Nobody cared…they ate hungrily and jokes flew. One of the men called out … "Hirotsu you need me wipe your pretty face clean?"

Amira blushed to her roots. Hirotsu stood and thanked the joker.

"My thanks to you."

He bowed very low. "For reminding me of the beautiful moment when our dearest historian…"

Flourishes in Amira's direction… "Look after me with tenderness."

This had tables whacked and the joke had lovingly backfired. He then bowed graciously to Amira and everyone…and returned to his seat to murmurs of polite approval.

"You are such a gracious people Riku."

"Oh, you honour me with too much kindness. You are our pride surely you know we hold you in much esteem."

"I do now."

The meal slowed to chai served once again and whiskey once more boosted the chai.

The miracle to Amira was they never seemed to get dehydrated.

She sat back to watch a busy party leave their table and a woman came and began to move cutlery… Not exactly moving it as pretending to. She turned her gaze upon Amira…there was simply no mistaking the venom of hatred in the look…Amira felt the sweep of a chill breeze pass through. Her side throbbed. She began to tremble all over. Riku stared at her…

"Amira Amira…"

His voice echoed in her head…gripping the edge of the table she tried to speak. The horrible woman vanished into a crowd of new visitors… Her look was that of a snake, a vile poisonous serpent that has struck once and longs to sink its fangs once more. Riku was soon at her side and had steadied her…preventing her from falling. He gave her a glass of mineral water…he had seen the way she had stared and her trembling reaction.

"Amira what is it tell me let me help you." She pointed.

"There was a woman like…" He followed her gaze but there were so many milling about…the woman in the black head scarf had melted into a crowd…she was nowhere to be seen. Riku knew Amira to be a calm person…not given to histrionics.

"What is it…you look as if you saw a Snake Woman."

"I did…she looked at me."

"This we call ill omen…who do you know here to wish you harm."

Amira snapped to and looked at her hands they were shaking she tried to control them… "The water might help."

"Damn to that here sip this it is the best in all the world."

She took the cup hiding the golden fire of whiskey.

"Fight fire with fire."

"Yes, now you understand…us. When something like this happens, we say water and tea just make you want to pee. This is medicinal…" She drank the glowing fire slowly; it revived her senses and her trembling eased. Perhaps there was truly something in this backward logic. Whisky for shock, water for peeing. She laughed…

"That's better…we have our strange little ways."

"Some of them really work."

"Don't try to stand, stay here in the shade we will take care of everything."

He returned quickly and they all trooped to the impatient taxi men. Thankfully the rest of the group had been too busily joking and settling accounts… which was less than peanuts to them…only Riku had witnessed the whole thing.

Back at Jolie Ville he came to her door and asked politely if she was well. She invited him through to the tiny Egyptian balcon.

"Are you truly recovered?"

She nodded.

Her perfume from the cooling shower filled his head…he was like an intoxicated creature. Amira felt so comforted…and yet excited by his presence. There truly was something of the Warrior Lord about his whole demeanour. She felt a real desire to lie down and kiss him with passion. Well, they called him 'The Warrior' didn't they.

"Don't be alarmed, Amira…the others are aware of my singling you out…but I am considerate to your professionalism. However, there was such a terrified look on your face at the restaurant."

"I know it's all so odd…there was just a split second of a fainting feeling… that's all."

"No, I am aware of more than you know…I have young daughters…this was not a faint…this was all due to your seeing a face…you were pointing into a crowd of people and trembling. Did you see someone who wished you harm?" She shook her head honestly.

"I sincerely wish I could explain it Riku…really, I mean that."

He nodded.

"I can tell by your eyes that you are mystified. I think you see Nure Onna a Japanese yokai. We refer to these as supernatural monsters…or people who have been taken over by them. In our folklore…this yokai is bewitching, attractive, calamity. There is a connection between blood and water. The creature is a reptile with a woman's head. They inhabit coasts, rivers, places of water. Yokai the snake woman began her life as a normal human but her emotions ran too deep and she ended up transforming into a monstrous creature."

"My goodness, Riku, how knowledgeable you are."

"This can be told to you by even the smallest child in Japan."

"These are strange times; don't you feel they are strange Riku."

He took her hand and held it…

"Perhaps we shall have a solution very soon."

She made him tea with a Japanese style tea sachet from the guest tray…

He sipped it and she drank her own dreadful concoction (no doubt to his palate) brought from home. "Our paths have crossed Amira…we cannot uncross them."

"I never guessed in my wildest of dreams that I would meet such a calm kind person as yourself Riku."

He breathed deeply.

"Our time now is lovely because so small. When I return home, it will be with much work to contemplate. Will you think of me a little…?"

"There is a saying in the tribal cultures of the First People…as they are called. My heart soars like a hawk when I think of you."

"Then I am happy. Do you know the schedule for tomorrow?"

"Yes, a choice…a visit to Luxor shops for carpet and jewellery or Temple to Montu at Tod."

"Can you split the group…we go to Tod; the rest vanish into carpets."

"Do you mean like Cleopatra Berenice."

He laughed out easily…happy in her company.

"Perhaps you help more than you know Riku."

Breakfast brought the group together and Riku was keen to see Montu Temple the rest held back knowing smiles and happily wandered out to the taxi on the forecourt and waved friendly sayonaras. Amira and Riku were secretly thrilled…this was the first and last time they would be able to talk quietly together in Egypt.

Montu is hidden in plain sight…its ruined temple which was once so vital to the Warrior God Montu is found amongst the purely agricultural villages and reaching it they travelled by local taxi and all the sun of the bright morning came warm and soft. The vegetation rose as if it was impenetrable and seemingly parted only at the last second to give them passage.

Magnificent nagla palms paraded their beauty and moved within a rhythmic dance of their own imaginative device. Amira spoke to the old men who sat pleasantly smiling at the entrance. She gave them money and they gracefully led them both through and one also followed quietly. Amira had visited twice before. The excavations had been sympathetic. All laid out with their original positions written in the succinct text of the archaeologist. Now they appeared to be patiently waiting for a giant to come to arrange the ruins just as they once stood.

Of the circumference walls (once so deep ancient Egyptian families built little houses into them). One structure remained complete with windows and a small figure could be seen hanging out washing which would be dry in ten minutes in the powerful sunshine.

The most delicate looking of the old men took them with extreme politeness to the remains of the Sobek temple where the female crocodiles would come for offerings from the priests. Many people get an uncomfortable feeling on seeing this. In ancient times some of the amphibians even gave birth and remained in safety for free food handouts.

The carvings into the pale stone revealed a well-designed crocodile…in the stance of a human. Quite odd to see. Quaint and wonderful in retrospect. This is a strangely quiet place. All the numbered ruins seemed to be held in a trance within their separate suspension of time.
Archaeology is like this, the ceremonial and ritual power of the past returning though the struggles of passing time. Living again. Amira amused Riku by bending to the stones and whispering. "All the people that built me wish they were still here."

She continued with a quiet reverence.

"The earliest mounds and sacred remains date back to the Early Kingdom. A witness to ancient farming methods. The proximity of the Nile is the clue of its importance to priest and warrior Pharaoh and many a traveller of sacred journeys."

Amira and Riku strolled about sometimes together, sometimes a few yards apart. Riku now and then talking gravely and looking with great concentration into his mobile then gravitating back into her company with light footsteps… There in the central position of the site…stood a sacred Tamarind tree. There are stories of the god Osiris hiding in the Tamarind… As they walked beneath its delicate fragrant needle-like leaves where all the passing decades had built up cushioned layers of perfumed crushed flowers…giving each a sense of entering a room within an invisible world.

All of her life, Amira would recall this new birth of herself. Evolving, barely able to breathe for fear of breaking the spell. The fallen blossoms were tiny yet formed a sensation of greatness at the same time. Riku stepped towards her and they sat together on a fallen pillar. Without a word spoken they fell into a dream spun by ancient minds.

Not used for sacrifice anymore, the site of the temple to Montu lies by the longest river of them all. A gentle ambience now lives amongst the fallen temple stones as if everything had worn itself out. As Amira and Riku left, the old guards invited them for mint chai…they followed and children stared as village children always do, partly from mischief mostly out of curiosity.

Women were clustered about but said nothing. Amira and Riku passed from blazing sunlight into the cool black interior of one of the better homes…that consisted of a warren of rooms…which seem to be a requisite of Egyptian life. Amira sat on the family bench seat feeling relaxed and cool as they drank gratefully of the strong sweet chai. The lovely old boy who had shown them Sobek was gentle…yet as the children clustered around the door jamb peeping, giggling…he became impatient. He waved them away and they immediately scattered. Amira offered to pay for the strangely refreshing chai…he tutted politely shaking his head. Outside, Riku took many photographs of Amira standing within a growing crowd of children.

They left in the taxi…their driver also had been given hot chai…he spoke up as they drove away amongst a scampering throng of noisy children.

"This is rare for these people few come here. Madame Amira…you are obviously special to them."

"I wrote a thesis on this site…when I was a wild little student."

Riku sighed audibly.

That last night at Jolie Ville was bittersweet. Her dear friends which she once had referred to as 'The Japanese Group'…were in subdued mood. Part of the meal was given to watching a screech of a female trying to sing. She was almost as awful as someone long before…but not quite. They took their drinks out to the pleasantly lit terrace gardens and waiters tried to bring sickly desserts but were waved away. Amira had a delicious coffee which Hirotsu had daintily splashed a little whiskey into. They exchanged happy grins. She gulped at the idea of them going. Yasmin had missed a beautiful experience.

Out here in the evening light that closed in and crept up first over their feet and then nibbled the edges of every tree and flower. A transformation via the twilight of the gods in which one is transcended.

A great many mutterings began then Hirotsu stood up and walked to the back of Amira's chair… She attempted to stand but the others grinning with pre-planned events in their eyes all begged her to stay. Hirotsu fastened a necklace around her neck. She was speechless. The necklace was a stunning true Egyptian design. The weight told her it was excessively expensive. The gold glowed rich and warm, lapis lazuli of the finest quality with a living utterly thrilling depth of real blue. Fire ran through tiny stones between the gold links. An Ankh of the most exquisite workmanship finished the piece in a balanced design. Amira was looking at them all laughing, crying, astonished. She could not speak.

Riku stood facing her… "We all thank you most warmly, humbly and with certain sadness. Madame Amira…our time with you shall be treasured. You are unable to speak…this happiness in your eyes…is saying everything."

The cheers and table whacking and bows…were tremendous.

She did manage to stand.

"My friends from Japan…when I was told to manage on my own…there was a nervous flutter I confess. There is an admission to be made…you surprised me with your nobility and generosity. Meeting you is my pleasure."

She bowed to them as they had always done.

The table went wild with joy.

Riku took her hand he spoke a few words, she had no idea of their meaning, but he raised a glass and once more the expensive whiskey flew about on wings of fire. Returning to her room was so lonesome. She folded the last few things into her case and a quick shower left her cool as she slipped into cotton pyjamas. Her mind whirling. She slept eventually and deeply and with her fingers constantly touching the necklace for reassurance that it had not all been some glorious dream. They were already gone when she woke up to answer the seven am alarm call. Her flight was at 2 pm the taxi due at eleven… There was an ache whenever she recalled Riku. She had given him her email and home address. There would be many moments when she could not take in the truth of them all going home. If the feeling stole her over that it was not real she had only to touch the necklace…she had recalled Riku walking apologetically away once or twice to look at his mobile screen and chatter quietly into it…when they were at the Temple to Montu.

Now she knew what had been planned. She cried with a feeling of great happiness that lies in the heart and only tears can express. The flight to Cairo was oddly sobering and thankfully, uneventful. Reporting in at the Department in Cairo was a revelatory experience all of its own. The feedback was tremendous, and two contracts were apparently under discussion. Naturally, the Department gave all credit to Amira's personal abilities.

Unwinding in the newly polished apartment… Amira ran a good bath of bubbles…kindly left behind by another historian. She folded up a towel for her neck and lay back in bliss. If anyone called or knocked now, they would be ignored. Relaxing done in such a manner leads to snores and soon Amira slipped accidentally into the sneezy bubbles. Laughing, she emerged and pulled the plug on all past discontent. Contacting everyone with 'message to all'…she added her flight and landing in Toronto details. The time zones were at play now so everyone in the Grey Dominion slept while she togged up and popped a scarf over a ponytail. This gave to her height all it took from her in glamour. She shrugged.

There was a certain relaxation now in the schedule. Trying once more to call Yasmin resulted with a big fat nothing doing. There was definitely some fishy business surrounding that mother's excuses. No point in distressing herself. Amira did wonder candidly if the parents had forbidden Yasmin to work within the department any more due to its access to men…fun for Yasmin was obviously forbidden. Perhaps they considered Amira as bad company. In this lay great irony. She had begged… but Yasmin was under the 'influence' of true romance…from her overtly sugary books.

She carefully fastened on once more the gorgeous necklace. No way would she leave this in the flat. Wandering down the Shara she found a small restaurant and was soon scooping foul up with aish freshly made. The cake shop yielded some sweet concoctions, and an apple seller gave her one to munch noisily as she swung along… She returned to the apartment after a few purchases and packed up. She had ordered a taxi through the department. They insisted she did this. Personal safety being paramount.

There is always the possibility that there will be no familiar face at arrivals… she should not have worried. Sonia, Jack, Sally and Sally's grandparents were there and everyone jumped for joy together. No Tristan of course he was away from Canada with Cirque de Solei. At the instant she saw her daughter, Amira was delighted and let her case fall scooping up Sally with a great big hug laughing into each other's faces they kissed and Sally laughed out... "Mummy, my mummy my lovely mummy."

Grandad gathered up the dropped luggage and the little parade wandered towards the car park all talking at once. A meal was planned at Jack's and so all were excited. Jack sat with Amira. "Welcome home, Amira." Sally couldn't stop chattering and was cuddled up as close as she could possibly be.

"Mummy, I went out with Indie and Bindie."

"Oh, that's a big surprise who else was there."

"The detective...and I told him you were coming home and guess what he said Mummy guess."

"Oh I can't darling you will just have to tell me."

"That he thinks you are really brave...there I told you."

"You certainly did darling...thank you."

There was a silence in the car after this. Past events thought about and mulled over. Sonia drove into the wide space in front of their modern classy home. Amira gave Sally another cuddle and kiss then headed for the shower. She knew questions would be asked regarding this trip, especially who was in the group. Riku so noble looking was of course very evident in her mobile gallery. To top this off the necklace was going to cause a stir. After she'd freshened up. She gave out gifts. The men received Egyptian after shave. This was a success. The men of Egypt are very clean as a rule and barbers and facial services are on almost every shara. Sally loved the doll dressed in an opulent queen's costume. Tacky...so therefore adored instantly. Children love colours. Sonia was in genuine raptures over her cashmere. Grandma was helped to drape a stunning mixed weave. This exciting addition to her otherwise sombre wardrobe was much discussed. It was a tourist piece yes but had a certain style. The design incorporating the iconic ankh on each corner, so she accepted it with such a look of bliss...Amira laughed out... "Well, this is a hit!"

Grandmothers love to be remembered. Amira was hugged a great deal that evening. Sally snuggled close to her in bed that night but even after several stories her excitement and the new Egyptian doll all added to difficulties in sleeping. She constantly snorted in Amira's ear and her mother adored it all.

Telling her mother over and over. "I saw you first, didn't I, Mummy? I saw you first."

"Yes, you certainly did my darling…you and Binx." Eventually, the steady breathing told Amira she was away…and Amira breathed in and out in a sigh of happiness and slept. Breakfast was busy, Jack spotted the necklace first…Sonia gulped. "My God girly that's some trinket. Buddy how about that who in heaven's name?"

"Oh, it's from the group…they kindly presented it to me on the last night."

"Hey, Jack get the eyeglass."

Jack guessing a demand for a similar gift was coming wisely high-tailed it to his truck and after crashing through gears zoomed off.

"Whaddisay."

Sonia asked the coffee pot. Amira's laughter silently muffled trying not to spurt waffle crumbs.

"Jeeze Amira he zipped out of here faster than a bear with an ass ache."

"Do bears get ass ache Mummy."

"Jack bears honey Jack bears. Please don't repeat that in school do you promise."

"Well, if I can take my doll and Binx…I am calling her Divinity."

Sonia was still looking for the jeweller's eyeglass. The drawer was not yielding this particular prize.

Other things manifested however and were tutted over and rejected.

"I gotta go…ooooh come here Tindy Pindy Rindy gimme kisses."

Sally was squashed into submission with lipstick kisses. Then Sonia was gone in a flurry of hat, coat and very expensive brief case and car.

Amira drove Sally to school in Jack's Ranger…the little girl was sulky at the school gate and Amira had to wave her in…with nods and blown kisses.

She drove over to Tristan's and had the best greeting from Felix who was on his way to work at the boat yard. "Ludovic is waiting on you hon, go right through."

"Hey there darling girl come right on through…he's prouder than a prairie dog with puppies to see you up and working and doing so well."

"That's real nice of him…is Tristan coping with the troupe…Manchester isn't it?"

"Don't go there, hon…he's a handful and no mistake. He will do all the things he is told not to do…the result is he's laid up yet again."

"I brought you this."

"Well, darling girl, ain't this just the prettiest scarf. Thank you. I love things from other lands it's like a little universe all its own don't you think hon…well, would you look at that."

"Glad you like it the very rich Japanese group bought me this."

"Oh darling girl…you must have made extra good history about those mummies!"

Amira loved Ludovic…and the two women carried a tray through to the cosy sitting area to catch up.

"He is never going to make it honey…this I just know. All the time spent on those classes were just a waste of money and energy."

"I feel sad for him…it's like he will not give in and gets even further from the awful truth."

"He won't hear of anything else…and it's all we can do to keep silent. Felix is asking around…you know for apprenticeships. Honey, he'd do more good serving pancakes to moon bugs."

"I understand Tristan though Ludi it's awful to give up on a dream."

"Not in my book…he has to come to terms with the limitations this goddammit injury has inflicted."

"Perhaps he will get access to newer treatment in the UK."

"Canada is ahead in all medical matters…France may be good…but even so the surgeon here is telling him the ankle cannot take repeated trauma. That's it. If he was teaching…well then fair enough. But he has been taken off the flyers cus' he's a liability."

"Oh, he can't possibly work trapeze with an ankle like that."

"He's found that out the hard way. Stubborn, impulsive and now downright pig—headed."

Amira cuddled Ludi.

"Sally must be the happiest little girl in her school today."

"She is in her element loves to show off…bought her a really tacky Egyptian Queen doll in all the correct but garish clothes…so popular out there."

"Did you enjoy it hon, the heat must be something else."

"Yes, but you acclimatise. One thing…my god Ludi my naughty student girlfriend Yasmin went off with this strange man…my first night in Cairo…slept out…got caught by her parents…they can't let anything happen to a daughter like that…strict Muslim tradition you see…a spoilt girl is considered…well like a harlot in their custom…she's been (let go) the department cannot go against the Islamic code of conduct. So, I managed five very influential tycoons. They were also supposed to be going to the pyramids at Giza but there was an appalling terrorist attack you must have seen it on the news…instead, the richest and most influential one of all—hired a helicopter a huge Airbus and you know it had this dolphin nose…bright blue. We flew over the Great Pyramid of Khufu with its satellite pyramids over to Meidum instead."

Ludi looked very like someone who has just heard intimate customs about a tribe on the other side of the cosmos.

"Well I hope they appreciated you honey but judging by this jewel fest around your neck I'd say they just about adored you!"

The two women laughed with the pleasure of just being alive and all the nonsense of everything.

Sally wanted to go 'home' home, so Jack and Sonia drove them over to Grandfathers' place as it always had been, and always would be called. Mumblechuckler started up easily and Amira took Sally to the local market for fresh foodstuffs. They made a good meal with sticky ribs, salad, and a meringue dessert that could have sunk an iceberg. The new doll was called Divinia Emmilina now and Binx was married to her by the end of the meal.

Amira was happier than for a long while. Tristan managed a link up while a sleepy Sally in pink elephants pyjamas showed off…fit to bursting. They were very alike Amira noticed when it came to attention seeking. Sally ran off to fetch Divinia Emmilina the Queen, now married to a filthy old rag toy. Bet she wished she'd stayed in Egypt.

Tristan blew kisses and told Amira she looked fantastic. She wanted to be thrilled by him…but some awkwardness was there and Sally luckily zoomed in front of her and saved the day. Wackily weird. Oh, and lucky.

After a couple of days normality set in with its homely pleasures. Detective Alain Veldour came by and Amira told him to sit down while she located some after-shave…made him a snack. Then she told him about the incident at Dheir el Bahri. He listened very carefully. When Sally had to be picked up from school, he drove Amira. Sally was bubbled over already due to an excess of popularity. Tacky dolls are in—apparently. Two poodles doing excited prancing waiting for you at school gates…take you way over into the fame zone.

Amira shook her head. The seven-year-old world is in a galaxy far, far away. They all enjoyed the park. Amira in old jeans was free to try to run with Indie and Bindie…Sally changed into her play clothes. They were like a little family.

Alain was relaxed for the first time since his student days. He wondered why he didn't know about family fun way back…but he hadn't. They ended up at an easy going 'Take Out' where the dogs could sit on the long benches on a green. Children were drawn to them because of the handsome dogs' playful faces…eager bright eyes…slobbering chops. Sally grew tired so they drove home, and Amira managed by a miracle to get her washed up and settled down in minutes. Sally's happy eyes closing instantly…she cuddled the doll as if her very life was at stake. Amira clicked out the big light…the roundabout of the elephant's night light glowed smugly. Alain poured a wine each and they watched TV…no way was it romantic in inclination. Amira had a paper to complete for the department. Tomorrow was going to be back to work day. There is a saying. Or is it a song…'What a difference a day makes, twenty-four little hours'.

The full impact of truth came by news of such horror – tucked between a delightful 'thank you' card from Sally's grandparents and ads for garage doors…was a letter of great grubbiness. Amira thought it might be for Binx. The contents however…wiped the smile right off her face. She remembered the first night in Cairo with a vivid recall on reading a very unfamiliar address—

'Light goods and supplies Souk'
Beshay Family
Garden City Shara
Cairo.

Dearest friend Amira,

My parents have taken all my things they have locked me in with the Qur'an and the rules of Islam against the woman who is as you call puton….My father has beaten my back raw. When I cruelly left you that first night, for which I am truly truly sorry and ashamed. I met the man who gave you his card. He only wanted sex with me. You were right. How stupid of me not to see, not to know. My head turned by his handsome face. My heart overtaken by a crush on a man who want just the body.

My friend please, please, try to forgive me. I am foolish and have paid very much dearly for my mistake.

My parents have treated this behaviour with strong arms…beating me every few days. I cannot sleep on my back any more. This paper was brought by

Samier… who was with us for the first year in college. Her parents stop paying… (they had sickness so ran out of money) Samier is the good one of our group.

All you told me is correct. Why don't I listen? The heart was overtaken by this man's face misleading me. He cannot be trusted. Treating me the same as bad woman. I was virgin and not bad woman believe this dearest Amira I long to turn back time.

Now I am prisoner of correction until I learn my mistake thoroughly. Samier remembered the old book she had of all our addresses and numbers. Do you remember as student when we enjoy together those innocent times. Oh, how I long for them. My passions trick me my own heart betray me.

Rescue me help me escape before they kill me by this overpowering correction. Samier is clever, resourceful…the word you use. We plan daily my escape. My parents think she lectures me in moral behaviour. She shouts at me for their ears to be satisfied. Then we whisper and write things. Help me from my prison. They plan my marriage to very fat, old, merchant widower man… Oh good Amira please get me out. I am now the very contrite Yasmin who is deeply sorry. Write to this safe reply address only. Samier is good person but has no money but what they give her in the shop. Peanuts as you say.

Beloved friend

Diamond friend—

Help me…

Yasmin xxxxxxxx

Amira read and reread the horrible outcome for Yasmin's decision to have a romance. She was paying very dearly for this decision. Her anger at first made her want to tear it up. Why now… Then good sense and her own kindness and desire for fair play took over. She begged Ludi to come over. Ludi drove in as Amira put a good casserole in the oven and clicked the timer on. Hurrying to the door.

She hugged her…

"Thanks for this…do you want some tea or beer?"

"I just had one darling. What is this dreadful news, Amira, you are not one for dramatics…but your voice?"

Amira handed her Yasmin's plea for mercy.

Ludi read the letter carefully, open mouthed.

"Oh my God what a vile thing these parents are so so…I can't find the words."

"Evil, cruel, stupid…reacting with extreme. The laws there are all laid down by these ancient expectations for the women and young girls moral conditioning."

"But this…"

"They have a structure for family around a code of clean living and obedience. No exceptions."

"Yes Amira quite possibly, but I can't cope with the beating and imprisoning."

"We are living in the free world Ludi."

Ludi was pale under her usually excellent colour.

"I must tell Felix…" She telephoned him at once reading it through. They discussed it thoroughly. Sighing she paced about the kitchen.

"We have to get her out Amira, Felix feels that this is a great miscarriage of justice…he is incensed. What a pair of harpies."

"Yes but how will we accomplish this. She will need paperwork, a safe passage, money and an excuse to leave the room the house rather. I will struggle this month to meet all my responsibilities as it is."

Amira phoned Detective Alain as they now referred to him…who was now a greatly respected friend.

He regarded the call immediately as deserving of his attention. Once the letter had been read…he responded calmly.

"Yet another example of the Muslim intolerance…even towards their own children."

"Felix thinks a meeting would serve us all well."

"My role can only be advisory within the confines of International law."

"Oh of course…we would want a voice of reason but the ideas are so…far…

1. Fly out break in and snatch her.
2. Take a ship and moor up at Alex then find a reason to treat her medically outside the house and have a car ready…
3. We don't have a third plan yet."

"The second plan truly has sense to it…but will take a while. Also, the port authority…dim view…kidnap etc. We might need that time to lull her parents into a sense of relaxation, as for kidnap…Amira…the law is clear. This marriage to an old merchant… Is that happening sooner or later?"

"As soon as she learns her lesson."

"My advice is to at least get her out of the house…perhaps for dental or medical treatment."

"Yes."

Amira wrote to Samier…and told her plans were being made at once…and the idea of a dental visit and subsequent car waiting. She would need a safe mobile number…not contract phone…a pay as you go…

Sally could not be told anything. All her chatter could endanger them all and the whole plan scuppered. It would not be the first time she had shielded her daughter from a truth. Sally was perceptive however, so caution was required.

That weekend Amira was obliged to allow Sally's father his legal access,… hating the idea would not serve.

She followed up on Ludi and Felix's invitation to visit the sailing ship he was helping in fitting out and making ready to cross the Atlantic culminating in a cruise of the Mediterranean. What an opportunity! Amira had to sit down and fanciful thoughts ran amok regarding them all going…no, no, don't be silly, she told herself. Still, she mentally argued the case for, and against.

"Ah wait a mo."

Addressing the coffee pot…a Sonia tactic.

"Didn't Tristan invite me a little while back when I was in Egypt!"

Packing Sally's little duds. She made a cardboard bed with some linen napkins and placing Binx in with Queen or was it Princess Semolina as she called the exotic doll…much to Sally's acute annoyance…of course.

"No, Mummy, you are not doing it right…they are in bed as cuddle up friends and her name is Divinia Emellina…not Semolina."

The sheer determination of her daughter to align the pair to absolute perfection with all names intact drove Amira to hide in the bathroom with the most awfully inappropriate fit of the giggles.

When she waved her off Sally the darling child was blowing kisses. A tear fell. Amira hated seeing her going off with that pig of a man. Funny how lately she had settled on this mood against all he represented. Legal obligations seemed to dog her at every turn in her life.

Alain (he had earned that name now) was at the door at ten to pretend to look at Mumblechuckler who was going noisy again. He pinged the bonnet.

"She's an old gal needs more TLC."

"Like you and me then Alain."

He grinned close mouthed. Head to one side. His life was changing since the neighbours had brought him snacks. Curtains don't twitch on their own. He had a brilliant mind and steady self-assured intellect that often proves useless with truly beautiful interesting women such as Amira. Pity they don't teach (romancing in the real world)—in evening school. Heading…

How to Woo the Woman of Your Dreams Without Fucking It All Up.

He smiled with a sad smile. A wire in the car had been stone jumped loose. Fixing it and generally tinkering he soon had the old car mumbling and chuckling. He could sense Amira in the house. She had such a brilliant attitude. However, he could not get into the life he so dearly craved with her and the little girl who had won his affection. Awkwardness handicapped his phrases. All his team knew him as a good friend…clever and full of abilities in the field of detection. When it came to dating…they saw him blunder magnificently. The dogs stood a better chance. Late in life this opportunity had headed in his direction. Funny really. Never a tremor before.

Amira watched proceedings from the kitchen…without a hint of what was really going on. Drying her hands on a towel she stood at the door.

"Sticky ribs and salad, okay?"

He nodded with oil on his chin…Indie jumping about playing dance and prance playtime with Bindie. A neighbour held his binoculars to the happy scene.

"You know Denise that nice chaps out there again. T'would do them a lot of good to have a great sort of handy man like him permanent."

"Frank you old fool, stop watching n' matching them up…she likes that sexy young 'looker' in the jeans…and who could blame her…come away you nosy buzzard."

"Jus' saying is all…jus' saying."

After lunch, Amira cleared up and while Alain played with the poodles throwing a ball chewed to rags in the garden…she changed into suitable yacht wear, plimsolls and a crew neck over the necklace, jeans and scarf. The look was very cute, even she noticed. Chatting madly at her reflection.

"Oh I see and oh I say…jolly old main brace what Midshipman Carruthers Magrew go make the stew…then watch them spew!"

She was happy and it wasn't down to the vitamin pills either. A certain Japanese man had sent her emails of great affection and had requested with much charm that she should look out for a mailman.

She had become coquettish and downright happy replying with fervour, news, and much love. He naturally sent her loving hopeful messages in return but Amira sensed a restraint. He was obviously still intertwined with his wife mentally and legally. It was a waiting game.

"Looking out…for mail man." She trilled down the stairs.

Sonia was outside with Alain…oddly, Sonia instantly recognised 'the look' in Alain's crinkly eyes.

"You still tinkering with that old lump of scrap iron. Amira darn well loves that old gal to death and back. You hoping for a cuddle you naughty old detective you…well come here and get a taster." Helpless, Alain stiffened in the breeze as the heavily made up overtly sexy Sonia suckered him on the face. He was red for ages. Amira was watching her daredevil friend but didn't dare laugh. As Sonia sauntered naughtily back indoors, she collared her.

"Sonia, you wicked wanton…he's shy…you shouldn't."

"Well, Miss keep it in yer drawers cus I just did, so whaddya gonna do about that eh, eh." And with that she slapped Amira on the derriere. Poor Alain. Amira laid out lunch for the three of them. At the end of his visit Amira and Sonia thanked him cordially for all this pampering of a car that really had been given yet another stay of execution. They waved Alain away. He'd blushed up the instant Sonia touched his arm.

"Well, there's a man who ain't been laid for quite a while."

"Sonia he's a good hearted and very serious detective."

"Stuff that! He is still a man, can you imagine the tremendous sex you can have with a man so starved. You wouldn't walk for a fortnight gal a fortnight…!"

And with that awful exit, she climbed into her fabulous on trend vehicle, then waited for Amira to lock up and follow on. Sonia was meeting up with Jack immediately after the visit to Pagan Warrior the fabulous sailing yacht that Felix wanted them to see. Amira knew Sonia was so right for Jack and thought the world of her. But, she really could be very, very outspoken. At the busy boatyard crews of other yachts were ogling Sonia and Amira…avidly. Amira pretended not to see. Sonia played up to it with the most dreadful wolf whistles in reply to theirs. Ludi knew exactly who was coming and ran along the stunning light wood planking of the yacht's gorgeous decking. Two cats yawned and stretched on a cabin roof. Winkles and Don't Touch. Named specifically and descriptively…

"Welcome aboard."

"Hey you sexy French gal, is there room for two saucy wenches…?"

And other much more blush to your roots remarks.

Felix emerged with a very unusual young man close on his heels both drying their still rather oily hands with old tee shirts.

Sonia naughty to the beautiful bone gave the younger man a look that cannot really be described without publishing censorship.

"Hello Sonia, hi Amira, this is Mattie…" Dear Felix polite to the finger nails stood aside while a man with great litheness in his physique and the high cheekbones of the true real first nation people of Canada nodded…years of past abuse still made him acutely aware of white people treachery. Bronzed in summer, pale gold in winter he gave off a (highly tuned to life air) in his manner. Amira had met Bedouin people that knew great sacred secrets of survival… This man held himself with the same understanding. She had written papers on these wonderful men and women.

"Hello Mattie."

Sonia went quiet. It was so odd. They all joined Ludi who with her excellent skills had rustled up drinks and nibbles…a tall refined man with a merry mischief in his eyes sat in the cramped seating of the Mess room. He nodded with that sort of look that says, mmmm, I'm going to need a while to ascertain whether these women are right or not… Felix made introductions.

"Amira, Sonia, this is Captain Charles Coulson owner of Pagan Arrow."

Sonia sat down with a mug of tea. Amira used to unusual meet ups stretched her hand to the captain. "Pleasure to meet you Captain."

He appraised her and nodded slowly.

"You are the woman who speaks Arabic."

It was a statement not a question. Nodding briefly, she sat down and sipped the hot tea.

Thinking instantly of Riku, she involuntarily touched the necklace.

Charles watched her like a hawk.

"Inta quais al youm."

Amira smiled broadly. "Hamdoolah shukeran sadeek."

Everyone laughed loudly, the ice was broken.

Charles scrambled out after all the food was eaten and called Amira to join him…without ceremony he took her to the chart room.

"Pagan Arrow is a yacht of the first order she's fast, sound in her line and can handle bad weather. That's if you do come with us…I'm still figuring stuff." He pointed to his crinkled platinum curls… He had grey eyes like the sea in the light off the Labrador Strait. Amira knew she was in the company of a reasonably sound man.

"You are the one that pinched a skiff rowed to safety with a terrorist bullet in your side."

Another statement. "Mmmmm."

"Can I?"

He pushed the neck of the crew top jumper down…the explosion of colourful jewels met his gaze. He approved. "You appreciate this yacht I think…not to look pretty…but you know she can do the bloody job…bit like you isn't she." Amira blushed up.

"Sokey, I'm known for a direct line. We are gonna get along just great."

Amira had a lot to ask…but her way was to go easy in new country. Watch out for mines, traps, tricks. "You know North Africa."

"Egypt a little."

"A little she says…inta killem Araby…beautifully, you have heard all the words I know today."

"I'm quite ignorant really there is so much to learn, takes a lifetime." He laughed loudly and pointed to a chair. A very beautiful chair.

She sat down.

"This is the room where we plot and chart our way across a fucking beautiful totally unforgiving set of swells. You understand. Our life at sea is spent reading skies, responding and planning."

"And enjoying it."

He tapped the side of his nose. She saw his playful smile come through and caught it in the air between them and pointed to the partially hidden whiskey. His true smile burst out. "Now you're talking."

They examined the whiskey, the golden fire.

"The group I just said goodbye to in Thebes were great aficionados of this miracle of the Glen's. They were Japanese."

He stepped outside and called Felix to him…Felix smartly nipped up the deck and gave a quick automatic nod.

138

"Yes Captain."

"I need this woman on my vessel. Speaks Arabic don't you know…and more importantly is going to do well on the wheel."

He pointed to the great ship's wheel of Pagan Arrow the very beating heart between the hands of the mariner and the deep mystery beneath her bow.

Amira was shaking her head.

She scarpered back to Ludi.

"I can't go on the wheel Ludi I don't know what to do."

"He won't expect you to just do it automatically darling. Charles is good with people. I trust his judgement; you wait and see he will teach you and you'll love it."

"Do you love it?"

"Yes, no, I'm not cut out for it…my forte is here…"

"Ludi!"

Amira soon found her naughtily flirtatious pal it wasn't hard because Sonia was watching Mattie (who wouldn't).

"Hy hon…fabulous yacht I wish I could go…Jack won't leave the business, too risky."

"He could be crew surely, he is as strong as a bear."

"No he won't leave the warehouse its primed for expansion and he can't trust anyone else. But yes, it would be a marvellous experience. Sally will get quite an education."

"Thank you, Sonia…you have just given me the third motivation."

Sonia looked pleased and puzzled…she was usually good at connecting dots…Amira gave her a loving squeeze. Amira drove home with a great deal of what the devil am I getting into. Charles was fun at times, stern at others…bossy, wickedly accurate and had seamanship. Felix came over…the next day. Amira was completing the main draft of a paper on 'The Tamarind Tree'. All sorts of hold ups were getting between her and her research. Then the front doorbell tinkled its merry tune. A parcel with beautiful stamps and Japanese writing which sent a thrill zinging through Amira. Felix the father of one of her present love interests Tristan…was probably not the ideal observer of the contents. Amira blushed in the hallway and slipped upstairs to secrete it away in her bedroom. Felix was screwing up his face at the house. He wandered outside and rubbing his chin looked at the peeling exterior. "Do you trust me, Amira?"

"Er yes."

"We could pay Jack's company to sort this out. I have a proposition, do it up and why not let it out while you are away. Families are desperate to live someplace like here… Good amenities, school connections."

"Complete interior and exterior. Felix, my bank account won't stretch up that far. Although as a starting gate I could sell stuff off with a yard and garage sale."

"That's the way Amira. All the world knows Jack will be very generous about a mate rate and we will cover the short fall. So, no demurrals. Also, when Tristan gets back perhaps the trip on Pagan will force him to face financial facts… No way is he going to be even teaching dance let alone working within the fiercely competitive world of performing arts. It's tough enough when you're super fit."

"Oh, Felix he will be so angry. Don't you think you should be careful…he's proud of his ability."

"Don't you think also he's old enough to grow up."

"Ouch! If someone told me to give up Egyptian History. Well."

"You're proving your skill; there is no comparison."

"Handled carefully, he may be open to local school work. He's good with little ones. Just don't bludgeon him too much into submission. He has the rebellious streak."

"You noticed."

"Pretty much straight off, he has an impulsive immediate love or hate personality. Magical yes and irresistible? Very. Surely, this can be channelled."

"Oh you are a generous woman Amira, but it's all theory…he is impractical we have to carry him, literally."

"It's not his doing, Felix…we are traumatised survivors don't forget."

Felix was a good sort of bloke but his carpenter's life was limiting his outlook. He only saw his own effort. There was a possible disagreement rising. She was rather relieved when he left. Also, there was a creeping truth that Tristan as husband and father material was a long way off…perhaps never. She was already making excuses and even entertaining the sublimation of her own desires to accommodate. The road into love…sure was a very different road to the one out of it.

Also… The Greeks have a wonderful saying 'Love goes in by the eye and out by the eye also'. Her parcel from Japan was waiting…she just had time to open it and then settle to her work. The parcel was so exotic that she turned it carefully in clean fragrant hands. Everything connected to Riku was irresistibly sensual. His way of looking at her, the tenderness. There was no mistaking such desire.

The stamps gave a hint of artistic beauty to come…of course…she carefully opened it and smoothed the surface of the paper and then drew away pale blue tissue…a short kimono of the purest silk almost slipped like a river through her hands. Pulling it on, she walked to the long mirror in the hallway… Who was this woman before her, the deep scarlet was enhanced by a pure white crane rising into curve edged clouds embroidered in pale creamy white edged with gold. The seduction of her heart had just begun.

Flowers chased delicate friends here and there. The look was so ethereal it defied description. The beauty of the style, its deceiving simplicity of tailoring and structure meant it could be worn with a long simple dress or with elegant evening slacks…

Or if you felt daring, nothing.

The thought of standing this way in front of Riku made her shiver with the thrill of it all.

"Oh no oh no." She stepped to the mirror and pressed herself very carefully to the glass. Riku appeared before her she kissed the glass longingly raising her left leg and then stood quietly heart racing…going to her bedside she stared at her pillow and then caressing her body through the silk of the rippling kimono she fell into the bed kissing the pillow with real passion… Flinging her hands back, she lay looking up and suddenly with such intensity began arching her back and imagining his hands on her breasts then in her hair. Imagining he was deep inside her while a great flood of ecstasy enveloped her.

Shaking and trembling much later she stared at the ceiling. If his gift alone could do this, imagine what his real presence could do. She laughed out loud. For some reason she couldn't stop smiling. Looking into the mirror. She glowed. Her voice belonged to someone else.

"Riku, what have you done to me?" Her husband had constantly expressed to her his sexual disappointment.

Forgetting that not all people have huge experience before they marry. He thought she should be well versed in all sex matters and yet a pure virgin. What an idiot. Well, he was wrong about everything. Tristan had easily woken up the little devil in her.

However, it was Riku who had opened the door of want, desire, love and a something that had no name no expression. The power of bittersweet. Under the tamarind in warmth, safety, caught unawares.

"Can I have two men please?"

The answer came back.

"No!"

Reluctantly she slowly removed the enchanting silken artistry of the Far East. The parcel also contained toys for Sally. They were perfectly quaint, dramatically bright. She would love them. A pale envelope of creamy stationary displaying on the back a red flower dark and mysteriously pressed into a seal of red wax. The paper inside was fragrant and filmy as gossamer.

'Amira please look upon my gift with kindness…I have to explain myself. My darling… When we were together in the old temple, I began to come alive in my heart again.'

She read and re-read the lovely words. Breathing in deeply, the idea came to her…she would live with him. Correction, 'they' would live with him. But how would this come about. Hanging up the silken kimono on a covered hanger…she touched it longingly with her fingertips. Eventually, she came out of her bedroom after throwing on sweaters and jog pants and opened her lap top. She had to work her way to him. She had to earn him.

The crossing on Pagan Arrow would be the proving ground.

The Tamarind Papers

Throughout mankind's history on planet Earth, there has been a constant need to explore to discover and to bring back to castle, palace, mansion, cottage…cave—something new and exciting to try for the first time an exploration in taste touch smell or curiosity. After war, there is a desire for rest. To try the spoils, test the value of herbs, spices and seed pods.

Ointments, plants and within them the great discovery—hot, cold, weird or unpleasant. Nice, nasty or their great preserving qualities. Who planted the first Tamarind in Egypt who knew of its shade (A truly precious comfort in strong sun?) The flower and its properties to produce a harvest…when dried to a cake to make a drink. The Egyptians were open to trying anything.

The Tamarind is so obliging. The older the site is where it sheds blossom and leaf, the more fragrant the cushion of its comforts…underfoot the tree creates a precious carpet. Disturbing the petals and leaves arouses its perfume. The refreshing drink made from the cake…is pleasing enough. In addition is a magical story… The temple to Montu at Tod in Egypt some twenty-one miles from Luxor hidden within the agricultural region within the simplest of villages next to the Nile… A symbolic planting of a Tamarind took place many years ago.

Within the arts…

The Tamarind Tree is often simplistically portrayed…one example painted delicate and expressive appears upon the wall in a tomb of the (18th Dynasty) subject…'Tamarind fruit harvest of Menna'. The reason being of adherence and remembrance of the symbol of Osiris. Osiris was the first man to be created by the gods. Therefore, first Pharaoh—ruling kindly, benevolently with his sister-wife Isis. They were clever, introducing farming, agriculture, cattle raising. Causing prosperity to come to his people. The land prospered. But a terrible jealousy grew within the heart of his younger brother Set, some call Seth…who, spitefully, cruelly, conspired against him.

Set built a large chest of strong wood…and as inducement provided a banquet…offering the chest as a prize to the man who fits perfectly into it.

Many guests naturally tried but of course to no avail being too big or small too long or too short. When Osiris tried…immediately Set pounced and battened down the lid trapping inside the astonished Osiris…his own brother! Set soon sealed the chest with molten lead, casting it into the Nile where it floated eventually out to sea.

Eventually, it washed up in the branches of the Tamarind tree on the shores of the Phoenician city of Byblos. Over time the tree grew to an extraordinary height, its branches supporting and enveloping the chest containing Osiris' body. The king of Byblos saw the magnificent Tamarind and ordered it be cut down to act as a pillar in his palace. The extraordinary scent permeating from the wood was so bewitching its fame soon spread… News reached the grieving Isis who with her sister Nephthys (Set's wife)… transformed themselves into falcons in order to search the world for Osiris, they soon heard of this 'perfumed pillar'…Isis immediately saw the significance of the tale. Isis travelled to Byblos…and after discussing everything with the Queen of Byblos managed to appeal to her for help in persuading the King to part with the chest. Isis returned triumphant to Egypt…found her husband inside the chest and promptly hid him in the swamp. Tragedy struck again. Set on a hunting expedition discovered the body and in his enraged state he vile monster that he was totally dismembered the body into fourteen parts scattered to all directions. Except the phallus which Set threw to the crabs and fishes in the Nile and they consumed it.

Isis set out once more and found all the pieces and fashioned a phallus from wood. With the aid of Anubis, they accomplished the first act of embalming. So with the great knowledge learned from Thoth the god of knowledge, Isis created her fine husband once more. Again, she transformed herself into a bird hovering above his body while she fanned him with her wings.

During these moments, their son Horus was conceived. Fearing reprisals from Set…she carefully hid Horus the young infant from him with great cleverness. Many say Isis hid Horus at Chemmis a beautiful place near Buto in the Western Delta…where great stretches of papyrus grew in close thickets. Here he was well hidden. Turning once more into human form Isis set off and travelled the world within this disguise. She constantly relied upon the kindness of strangers. Only daring to return to Chemmis when Horus had achieved manhood. Old enough to avenge his father's double murder. He achieved this by besting Set in a number of contests (called the contending's) which were judged by Osiris's and Set's father—the great Egyptian god Geb.

Montu, a Witness to Passing Humanity

A temple situated upon the fringes of Luxor deep, hidden in the village of Tod. Famed for agriculture dating way back into the Early Kingdom and all its attendant Palaeolithic foundations. Where there is evidence of axe heads and settlements through chopping and clearing. Manmade resources of food gathering. Bedouin low desert skills in reading sun shadow fall. Timing with seasonal food resources and dry spells…Inundation of the Nile…commanding crop rotations.

Archaeological findings of significant treasures at one time among them certain small bronze figures of Osiris representing the cult status…these apparently were found in the Saite period of the 26th Dynasty. The partially preserved barque shrine of Montu the warrior…built by Tuthmosis III.

Restored by Amenhotep II…then Seti I. Amenmesse and Ramesses III and Ramesses IV. As previously discussed, there is a beautiful Tamarind tree within the ruins of the temple to this day. Perfumed wood and medicinal cures were constant sources of the physicians of Egypt, all we read of their knowledge today is astounding. Sadly, antibiotics were still a long way from being discovered.

Tut Ankh Amun would most likely have been saved by these. Or the Djedi priest's knowledge. His tomb had previously been excavated and cut out simplistically for a female occupant. Due however to his sudden death strength of opinion favours that on Ay's instructions the plan was to inter him there. Perhaps even temporarily. Alas the young Pharaoh remained. He was on his death around nineteen years of age (a teenager).

There is another way of looking at this…due to the female alignment orientation and entrance setting of his tomb, plus the researched description of many things hastily gathered together to act as funerary furnishings, even the beautiful white artistically magical white chest, a gift no doubt from Nefertiti… tomb robbers had only penetrated so far, jumbling things together in their fearful haste perhaps after only having stolen a few things. Perhaps caught or frightened off by guardian Djedi priests. Because, upon the tomb's eventual discovery in November 1922 by Howard Carter…the very nature of its sealed intact state brought to light a near complete hidden history. This was to provide world interest, investment and constant investigation.

Amongst the 'wonderful things' lay a significant treasure of boxes containing harvested fruit, seed pods and herbs. The very vital turmeric stored in abundance held a history alongside mankind all of its own. Treating many digestive problems and numerous uses within the physician's skilled hands these were invaluable to Tut Ankh Amun in his next life. These boxes ended up lost in amongst the dispatched boxes sent for storage in Kew Botanical Gardens London. They have now, after almost a century returned to be examined and displayed as part of the most incredible 18th Dynasty collection at The Grand Museum of Egypt.

So far, we are thinking life simply goes on according to the evidence…after the 32 trials of the underworld Tut Ankh Amun would be in blessed union with friends' family and his own dear little daughters…together in the field of reeds. With all the daily domestic ornaments, clothing, food, medicines, furnishings, bows with arrows, magnificent chariots were found, also treasure boxes of fruit and grains seeds all harvested and carefully stored.

Turmeric had an important role to play in Egyptian life, and is one of nature's outstanding gifts. There are some 100 components. The Main component of the root is a valuable volatile oil containing turmerone…as well as colouring agents that were used in medicine, foodstuffs and cosmetics. Also reported benefits of treating certain skin cancers.

All these goods clearly demonstrates that he was to come to life again through resurrection...even his name offers up a world of meaning... Living image of Amun. 'Living'.

Amun's presence is often represented by the great Djed pillar so powerfully depicted at Abydos by skilled artists under Pharaoh Seti's instructions, who in turn had been instructed by none other than the most powerfully influencing priests of all Egypt's great history...

This famous leaning pillar representing the back bone of Amun...Amun ra...depicted with, and attended by, skilled and mysterious magician priests of truly ancient Kemet... The Djedi. One cannot imagine today their influence and all-pervasive power. Their name is within part of the utterances....Heteru Meteru...Zep Tepi... The first time.

Akhenaten certainly hated them. Jealousy and pride with a lust for the sun disk the Aten to be served instead, led him on and on to strange ideologies. His very name banished all idea that no other would he serve. Some stories tell that he ended badly. The 'Maat' balance so vital to Kemet's place in the worldly, cosmic, and spiritual order of harmony in all things was dismantled by this misshapen Pharaoh. An elongated head with protruding lips and oddly feminine hips announces the inbreeding mistakes. Rather than hiding his defects he displays himself with instructions to all artists painting and chiselling his likeness to be totally honest.

Was he cursed...and in turn because of his banishment of the Djedi and followers of Amun Ra... Did his young son also suffer the effects of this curse?

Ay himself a servant to the court of this strange dynasty attempted to tamper with the very order of things to gain the crown of mighty Egypt for his own gratification. All questions lead to more. We know Tut Ankh Amun was married to Ankhessenamun but her name while her father lived was Ankhsepaten. One thing stands as simple witness. Ay missed the clever planning of perhaps Tut Ankh Amun's beloved wife Ankhessenamun.

Perhaps there was too much for Ay to supervise...she saw her chance and had the artists clearly cleverly paint into the walls of the tomb chamber the vital magic words...announcing that this Pharaoh shall Indeed live forever. The gods' words of life everlasting—Amun's gift to the young Pharaoh.

Why do I think this...because she lovingly placed flowers across his breast and women are excellent at fine detail.

Ay surely did not possess the knowledge to read the great sacred magical texts. He owned the mere cunning of the moment…missing the 'long game'… His desire for instant gratification proves he was poorly equipped.

He set himself up as Pharaoh…he was not in line. He forced his hand.

He set himself against Horemheb's energy and certitude.

He tried to play for the young widow Ankhessenamun in marriage…she felt insulted by this – called him a servant. Ankhessenamun…who, while her father lived answered to the name Ankhesenpaaten…translation…she lives for the Aten…this name was cast away by Tut Ankh Amun for he may have wished to appease The Djedi that his father had disbanded.

The symbols… The medu necher…God's words.
We must always study these for they are like the seeds of mankind… tadpole-like symbols that declare in their thousands of years, a message that defines time itself. Within their strange code the life of Tut Ankh Amun takes on a new consequence.

For if like Ay you believe the pharaohs were chosen by gods to rule. To perform tasks in the Duat. The facts are there.

Ay only lasted some pathetic four troubled years. He was truly overtaken by death, his heart would not have been light against the feather of justice… in the great weighing of the heart ceremony. His heart would be too heavy.

His pursuit of Tut Ankh Amun's widow in itself was cruel and wicked…she must have feared for her life increasingly with every passing hour after the internment of Tut Ankh Amun's mummified body.

The young foreign princes who were journeying to her were soon dispatched. Likely Ay had too much to lose to care who died. However, he remains a failed usurper in total.

Indeed, the great followers of the Djedi priesthood were by Amun to embellish Tut Ankh Amun with the eternal life that Ay attempted to secure for himself. History can now tell a far different story. The truth is today millions know of the young, crippled boy Pharaoh…it draws tears to think of his brave way of hobbling about on his stick.

To picture him in battle. How would he have been able to balance on the precarious chariot floor…with lively fast horses galloping…across a battlefield. However he died then—he is world famous now. His name continues to draw many thousands of visitors.

Also, the very name of Djedi gaining a complex strange rebirth within the script of a contemporary film. One cannot help but wonder of their opinion of this twist in the rope of destiny. Though certain demonstration of their immense power of time over time and within time itself. We have found so much in textual evidence. They held such secrets. The very universe gives them space. They alone have the spiritual essence of all the lives of man in the cosmic order, for they serve Amun.

Amira finished and also enclosed a short email to the Department. If they remonstrated with her over this…so be it. Sally returned from the parental access visit very tearful.

Amira had to go to the car and ask what the problem was…Sally's father was ignorant at the best of times, now he ignored her completely. She sighed audibly thinking all the while… He is ignorant so he ignores. Amira wondered if the courts could see him now how they would judge him. She collected her little daughter's things from the boot of the car. He merely scowled and did not answer to anything she said. When these things occurred, Amira put it down to his crass stupidity. She closed the boot with an efficient clunk…just as Alain drove up…Sally resurfaced and ran to Indie and Bindie…neither of them registered the departure of her father.

"You are most definitely welcome. How are you?"

"Good yes, all good…I 've been upstate."

"Yes, I heard."

"And how is dear Sally?"

"Oooooh can I change Mummy and play with Indie and Bindie."

"There's your answer dear pal. Sally, please ask Detective Alain if it's okay but wear your boots the garden's wet."

"Can I?"

"Hello Sally and yes but." Sally galloped off on an imaginary pony with the dogs hot on her heels.

"On her behalf…hello. She was crying when her father brought her back. In those circumstances… The brain of the child usually responds to what they want, not what you want so Alain I'm truly sorry. Poodles however do like to play with children don't they?" Alain laughed and held aloft a bag of rather high-quality shopping. Amira cheered by such fare…bowed with a low flourish… "Enter oh chief of the cooking pot."

"My goodness Amira, that's a lot to live up to."

"Oh I'm sure you can manage."

"Do you ever…"

"Ever what."

"You know think about the future…and a relationship that would give you financial stability."

"All the time dear pal all the time." They soon had a grand meal laid out… Sally appeared in the doorway bootless and filthy. "Shower please now darling but first, undress right in front of the washing machine." Alain was open mouthed…the dogs were even grubbier. Amira merely shrugged.

"You better supervise the four-legged culprits of the muddy school."

She gave him several old…very old towels. The barks of joy told a story called 'Play with the hose and get washed with any luck'…was now in full pursuit. The dry yard was soon transformed into the wet yard. A damp band of pilgrims arrived at the table.

Amira kept bursting into giggles. Alain was kitted out by now in one of Grandfather's lumberjack shirts and trousers of such ancient cord that little plush was left on the darn things. The dogs were making snuffling noises in their nether regions. Sally was carefully spooning in delicious meatballs obviously beautifully prepared…trying not to draw any attention to herself. Her damp hair combed away from her face made her look cherubic. However, her pyjamas sporting witches and frogs amended any mistaken identity. It was terribly funny and an enormous sneeze from Bindie quickly rendered all seriousness futile. The meal was a resounding success. Sally was tucked up in her crowded bed like a bug in no time at all. Her toy cult all a tumble. The new Japanese toys were under the covers with Princess Semolina and Binx…soft snores…told Amira when to tiptoe away.

They sat down to watch a rather foolish unwind serial. "I enjoy all this, Amira, you know I do."

Amira was simply not on the same wavelength. She was writing a list of gifts to buy Riku and his two little girls. A letter with all the right words would be easy. She wished for so much.

"It's good to relax I had an excellent day wrote a good paper on my wonderful Egyptian history, well, I thought it good, but perhaps that's my ego talking…" The telephone jangled…Amira leapt up to stop it waking Sally.

149

"That's Felix, they want to take me and Sally for a picnic on Pagan Arrow."

He tensed up she saw it but ignored it. Amira began yawning…rather theatrically. He gave her a lopsided grin and called the dogs.

Watching him go out to the car and with a wave drive away. She felt good and at ease. There was never going to be any romance with Alain. It just wouldn't be. He might call again, and then he might not.

The next morning Sally had a puzzling time about which two toys to take. She eventually tramped to Julia's car. That morning, she favoured Princess Semolina and a Japanese bird of a puzzling species. Sadie very smiley was vigorously waving a doll in camouflage gear. Amira sighed…all so different to her own schooldays when with a rumbling tummy, holes in her footwear, she would shiver off hearing her mother snoring off an excess of booze…there was as per usual nothing in the kitchen to eat. She shook off the memory and set to making friends with hoovering an untidy house which is a sobering pastime. When she'd finished…she posted all outstanding correspondence. Sonia wanted to meet up so Amira showered, then pressed a good dress and donned best boots and jacket. Drove Mumblechuckler to Sonia's office park up. There were clients chatting away with Sonia, so Amira drew up a chair and sipped water from a tiny, waxed cup. Reading glossy magazines made her peevish so she watched Sonia's office in action.

Sonia shook hands with a tall, smart, obviously well-healed buyer. Escorting him to the door she turned on her very expensive heels and beamed.

"Amira, you look great let's go for lunch at the Commerce." They were soon comfy with menu's held high. "I can't afford this, Sonia."

"It's obscene I know but we gotta get you with some rich dude and they do not go to greasy knives."

"Spoons."

"Yes, and those. Did you meet someone in Egypt, you are glowing!"

"That obvious…eh…"

"You are a single gal so enjoy. I want to tell you darling now listen to Mummy are you listening Amira look around."

"Where?"

"Here, sweetheart, why dya think I brought you here, not to admire the decor. Now there look there the one with the cream suit…that's best wool hon. Just look at that smile costs a fortune to keep teeth like that in your head. Drives a pricey car bet you any money."

"I can't back it all up Sonia…it's no good."

"Let them fall in line with you…not the other way round."

"I feel good though you're right."

"Whaddi tell you. Read the signs, flirt. Tristan is a lost cause."

"Don't say that Sonia."

"He is sweetheart he is. The chances of him being father material are zero. He can't even keep himself so look upon him as the occasional romp in the hay. You need, Sally needs – stability. Look I have no child this is true but I have the best guy going. Stability."

"Yes you do I will concede to that."

"Big of you darling…now that you look great that's when you run up your colours."

"I don't think Alain will get past the first stage."

"So what…he is not the only fish in the Atlantic baby. Just cast the net higher."

"I hope you're right."

The trip with Sally to see Pagan Arrow was a maker or breaker. Amira wanted to talk with Riku…tell him all her news. A sharp pang filled her at the thought of him with someone perhaps he was also starved of attention. Now his divorce, so surely he had a friend to…to…oh no…it was unbearable. Being human was full of pitfalls, guilty memories and cul-de-sac romances. Stability was important. Sonia had a point.

Alain hadn't rung but she knew he wouldn't. The complicated nature of his work and shyness with her made him a non-starter.

The more she thought of Riku the more she knew Riku would be the life partner. This was a growing need. Needs and wants all over again. Life made one settle for stability…no choice Sally needed a dad.

Riku is a father. He has two daughters. Would he like a third?

They drove to Felix and Ludi's house and after tucking old Mumblechuckler into their copious garage…everyone bundled into their big off roader. Sally singing with Felix about blowing the man down.

Perhaps this was the answer. The trip, decisions, rescue Yasmin…Amira momentarily had forgotten all about Yasmin… "I am a truly selfish shallow woman." She spoke into the window of the car.

"What did you say, Amira, I didn't quite catch it."

"Oh, Ludi I just remembered Yasmin…how she used to be."

151

"Mmmm I don't think Charles knows quite what to do about port authorities or something."

Amira sighed from her deck plimsolls right up to her warm crew neck. "Forgive me for saying this Ludi, but if she had just listened to me and waited a day or so none of this would have happened."

"She sounds silly."

"She is suppressed and grabs like a lot of Muslim girls and young women at any bit of romance."

"Which is a fantasy."

Amira looked at Ludi. Thinking—I don't think you're right. You're underwhelmed by certain criteria obviously.

She also set aside for closer scrutiny later that they had spoilt Tristan…had not prepared him for the real world. The thought that Ludi was hoping to be a mother-in-law and subsequently coming into daily contact with Sally…it all lost appeal. Amira saw her own maternal instincts becoming sharply focused.

The critical nature of people kicking in after they had ruined a child. Parenting is a skill. She herself tended to indulge Sally…overcompensating perhaps…her father was usually reasonable regarding his little girl and it was unusual for him to demonstrate any harshness towards her. With seven-year-olds, tears came easily… They stopped at a coffee shop…treating it like the last chance saloon.

"Come on, everyone, let's get stuck in, god knows what Charles has in store for us."

Felix locked up the off roader and they trooped in. Amira seized the chance of neutral ground. "Darling, why were you crying when daddy dropped you off."

"He said I was acting like a spoilt brat…and pointed at me."

"What had you done or said."

She shook her head… "I was playing with Divinia and Binx and didn't hear them call me for supper or something…it was me just playing my special game…"

"Is that the one where mummies and daddies all cuddle in the bed laughing together."

"Yes…and when I told him…"

"What happened?"

"He got all red and shouted…YOU ARE A SPOILT BRAT!"

"He's wrong to say that."

"I hated him for a while. Sorry, Mummy why is he mean? Why doesn't he say hello to you?"

Amira sighed. "Hon, those are the questions that divorced couples ask constantly. Shall we look at the menu together sweetheart."

"Can I run to the cloakroom promise I will be good I won't talk to anyone promise."

"Good idea see you in…"

"Quick time, Mummy, quick time."

"Do you want me to go with her, Amira."

"No, we are all grown up at present…on a roll." Ludi laughed. "You are such good pals, you two…it's really great to see."

They enjoyed good hot coffee and Sally tucked into a sandwich and hot chocolate as if she was starved to death at home. Amira kissed her forehead.

"I'm eating it all up, but they can't cook like you and Alain…can we have some dog's mummy."

"God in heaven no darling, we don't have enough towels and provisions for ourselves let alone domesticated wolves."

That produced a chain reaction of laughter from their table to the next and so and so on. A man stood up and showed his near empty wallet. "You're sure as hell right on it lady they eat me outta house n' home."

His wife shushed him and waved her hand for him to sit down.

"Whaddi say Mummy?"

"You are as funny as Sonia sometimes, hon."

Felix laid out a map.

"Right, this is where we need to sail Pagan…weather permitting. Charles insists we have real sea experiences we can't simulate it."

"Do you like going on the ship's wheel Felix… It's my new dread."

"Oh yes, it's sensational. She handles well and don't worry if you can't you can't but it's vital everyone learns all kinds of seamanship. Have you heard anything from Yasmin."

"Their mail isn't like ours…the Egyptians are renowned as post stealers…it's in the history."

"Excuse me."

"Interception problems. Felix…all we know and understand here is thrown on the pile of (ha ha and so what)…out there."

"Do you think in all honesty Amira we can literally smuggle this poor girl out of the country."

"Sometimes I think yes, but when I'm fully awake it all seems like a daft nonsense."

"What about other members of her family…can't they help us."

"Er nooooo but astrology might be useful…well it served in the past. Or we could throw the entrails of a mythological creature and read them. Or, or how about reading runes. That's it we will consult next Tuesday."

"I get a feeling you are not hopeful."

"We need real money Felix. How do we law abiding citizens of Canada get to know fraudsters cheats and forgers?"

"Ah yes there is that. When I told Charles, he said he just thought the whole thing would be a beep beep circus."

"I like him already Felix." Sally wiped her mouth with great exaggeration on a huge paper napkin. "I like him too, Mummy." Ludi put her head in her hands and shook with laughter.

The map was old worn and impossible to make out. Amira shook her head sadly.

"The crew are sailing into the unknown with crazy ideas of rescue of an equally crazy woman… Sorry but I'm getting a totally up to date map…were the Navajo responsible for this design. Look Felix it's all worn here…is that where Big Chief Chew Me Moccasins…kept jabbing his thumb to mark out dangerous rocks."

Ludi couldn't speak and Sally was cuddling into Amira…

"More Mummy more."

Felix put away the rubbishy map and sat with a forlorn hurt expression.

They all trooped out.

Pagan Arrow was massive she needed hard work to gain wind in the great sails. Her speed was frightening and all the time Amira was on board she was terrified Sally would fall overboard. It felt like a bloody daft idea. Captain Coulson was however aware of what can be learned. Amira fastened a grumbling Sally into a special child's life jacket and said it was a death sentence to anyone who helped her out of it. Chastening words. Captain Coulson agreed wholeheartedly. A new chart of clear instructions of headlands rocks shallows deeps and nautical terminology became the bible of all planning to go. Ropes were given names that Amira was puzzled over. Things called dead eyes…sheets and cleats. How to vomit downwind preferably not at someone else. Being really tired and heaving and trimming entered her dreams. Ludi was quiet and Sally dressed up Winkles in an outfit that would draw tears of laughter from the most serious of onlookers. 'Don't Touch' held his dignity with explosions of hisses and horrible growls. Well named.

Sally gave him a wide berth. Winkles obliged enough anyway for both cats… He held court at about 10 am…and sauntered in Paris style mannequin elegance the long deck. He was as daft as a brush…his ensemble changed daily. All the world loves a clown and a Tom cat in a dolls bonnet takes a lot of beating.

Sally had assembled a classroom of Binx, Winkles, Princess Semolina a new wooden doll (with a gruesome leer) made for her by Mattie. A bird from Japan, the ultra-tacky Egyptian doll Divinia Emmelina and a teddy with one eye.

The general consensus of opinion was that her ghastly classroom made more sense than the crew. Amira wanted to talk about dignity for Winkles but a voice in her head persisted with… "Oh no Winkles is not a real cat he is a born again pop star waiting for his big moment."

All the world.

Amira tried to be one of the crew but the thing she feared loomed constantly. The wheel terrified her she would carry out any unpleasant task in hopes of avoiding contact. Mattie labelled a lot of the fittings on board…also amusing names appeared on galley utensils. On the kettle he had fastened a label announcing…SHEEP…

Then on another day on the wheel…appeared a luggage label saying… BENGAL TIGER…

The day Charles saw this, he laughed loud and long. Called Amira and handed her a good warm Jersey looked her up and down and said, "It's time."

Amira felt her heart zunk zunk zunk in her chest…he put her hands in the same positions that he placed his own and told her where to plant her feet. Placing his hands over hers he let her get the tremor of the keel the tug of the tide and rise of the swell. Remarkably, the wind felt as if it was pulling the great yacht into the maw of the sea even on a quiet day with so little swell, it made no difference to Amira. Her terror was apparent.

Every day, Charles patiently taught and gave her nods and instructions. The lessons were hard. Then the pull tow slip and great crash of power gave Amira a feeling of flying. All the world was shut out…she felt the deep…it was a world without cease of movement wave tops seethed spray like snakes writhing.

A soft wind caught her off guard. Her alertness to each timbers tremor spoke to her. The world beyond Pagan Arrow failed to exist. She suddenly gave her heart to the sensation of sailing.

She began laughing into the cold sun and sparks up the nose wind. Planting her feet firmly, her hands began to move intuitively a strange mood overtook her and she began sailing…Mattie was close by one day and she suddenly told him to ease a cleat portside.

He saluted smartly. "Aye aye."

It was carried out.

When Charles let Felix take the wheel, he watched her reaction…she was stern. Amira was watching the sails luffing and she wanted to correct them.

He called her into the Chart room. He took note of her reluctance to leave the deck her eyes swooped up to the great mast. Searching along the stays.

Now was a reckoning and it was a beautiful one. "Sit down Amira." She nodded a closed mouth half smile.

"You love this feel of her, don't you?"

"Yes…"

"You are a very different person now when you handle her."

"It's a shock…I was terrified."

"And now."

"I feel the collect I feel her collect the power of the swells and use them…to speed through."

Charles gave a laugh. "I knew you would love it."

"How, when I did everything to avoid it all the time in the beginning, how."

"I was exactly the same."

Her smile docked into a serious line of puzzlement.

"She truly comes to life."

He nodded. "Everyone here does it by correction…you sail by instinct… from love."

"Really you think so it's like I am flying through a whole universe…I feel the tingle of her as the swells take her leave her as she flies…I can't tell it only do it."

"You have a lot more to learn but you have the feeling for her."

"She's beautiful fast and so sound…she speaks to me." Amira clamped her mouth shut.

Charles poured two small shots of whiskey handed her one clinked glass to glass gently, the sound was good. Amira nodded and drank the liquid fire.

Home seemed so dull and after weeks of sailing they all felt that their work was gradually becoming easier. The house was cleared and a garage sale brought in a little boost to the coffers. Decorating began in earnest and the slow changes at last began. Tristan was coming home.

The last day of the painters and decorators was here…and Amira invited Alain, Jack, Sonia, Felix, Ludi and the Pagan Arrow crew members to a meal. The house was packed, they over-flowed into the garden…the weather gods had been on their side for a two-week weather window of a fine dry if a little too dry spell. Then the truth hit…Canada was undergoing serious fatalities through climatic catastrophe…heatwaves of appalling ferocity and wildfires. Amira ever the black humour expert thought well at least fresh paint smells nicer when it burns fiercely. Alain allowed an over-excited Sally to be with Indie and Bindie…as long as zero water was in the mix.

Chapter Five
Icarus the Boy Who Fell Out of the Sky

Yasmin lay face down on her bed. The room was in darkness, but it was impossible to sleep until the raw burning on her back had died down enough for her to cry and the relief of tears gave way to the silence of nothing. She had heard her mother let Samier in and this staunch friend was told with drama and hand wringing that…

"This monster daughter with harlot ways this ungrateful daughter refuses to marry our chosen one. Not only is he good rich and hardworking but a believer. She is saying no. Who is she to say no. Tell her a father have the broken heart. She only has a broken skin…nothing next to a broken heart."

And on it went. Samier with meek sobriety listened and quietly…answered.

"Let me try again, good mother."

Yasmin heard the key turn and light sprang up like a good fairy into the room. She heard her mother tell Samier she would bring her chai. The bed was large and apart from the stand for the Quran the room had a chair and a fold out table. Heavy exotically coloured drapes adorned the window. The view beyond was of rooftops over Cairo. Outside, the innocent sun was setting low and a few deep pink and orange clouds gathered up heavy skirts to follow their solar bride to her next country.

"Habibti…she has gone to the kitchen."

Samier scrabbled in her bag and brought out a soothing tube of cream…she tenderly drew away the black blouse and applied with gentle cool fingers the balm that eases fire.

"Oh my God Samier yarrup yarrup the bitch gets worse I swear."

"It's very broken near the shoulder…sorry darling oh my life such a nightmare."

"Any reply yet?"

"No, but don't forget Amira would have to write back instantly for anything to come this weekend."

"Of course...oh Samier if I had listened to Amira, quickly my mother's coming Samier put the cream away."

"Yasmin, please do your wonderful parents bidding please be good girl...they love you and want the best outcome." The mother nodding shuffled through in her schlip schlips...depositing two glasses of chai and a plate of cake carefully on the fold out table.

"Ungrateful girl...all we have done the cost of the Cairo tutors all was done for her happiness but Allah is merciful in his wisdom."

She often slapped Amira's raw back...but this would offend Samier so she pointed in her daughter's direction instead. Tutted and left the room shutting the heavy door with a resounding click.

"If I live through this Samier...there will be a funeral."

"Drink this chai habibti keep up your strength. I brought you the strong needle, scissors and thread you asked for quick hide them!"

Yasmin carefully stood and wincing at each step hid the packet in the folds of the curtain.

"Please Allah they don't decide to remove these. It will be harder to hide them."

"No, they probably don't even see them anymore. She's making supper I can hear the bigger pots clanking. My brother is coming this weekend he will give me his old phone."

"Oh how fantastic. Once you have the number tell Amira by the email..."

"So, you really think the department will give me such information."

Yasmin squeezed Samier's small hand with gratitude. "In sha Allah." They sipped chai.

Pagan Arrow

Amira stood behind Sally holding the little girl's shoulders, then every now and then tickling her under the arms...so much had happened since they had trained to be tough little sailors. Amira was thrilled. With the house so beautifully painted...it did not stand out any more for all the wrong reasons. The other houses now paled against it.

This was a real first for Amira and Sally...the interior was cleared of junk... De-junking interiors was more fun than they ever imagined. So much

159

decluttering gives a boost…they were tired though. Sighing they giggled as the powder blue paint seemed to sing. Their house really showed up all the rest now which was a new sensation.

"She's smiling, isn't she, mummy?"

"Are you convinced it's a girl house, darling?"

"Praps shudda been painted pink."

"Your grammar young lady is slipping badly…don't copy Sonia she came bottom at school almost every year. So no more and PLEASE don't speak about this."

The unsold junk was waiting with the accusatory stare that only really awful junk can manage. Luckily, Alain was helping load it and take it to the municipal dump. He was on time too and they changed into their scruffy gear and kept Indie and Bindie whimpering with disappointment in the back of the car. Mumblechuckler was perfect for municipal dump trips. Time was whizzing by and there was a heatwave of 49 degrees all over the news. The West Coast was preparing for a Wildfire season. Amira felt what was planned was crazy, to leave her home freshly painted etc. One thing glowed on the horizon Riku had responded with loving kindness. He had managed to make a link, not a good one but it was a connection. Sally was totally amazed that this kind strong-featured man really loved her mummy. When he had sent gifts, Amira was blown away. Tristan had never had any imagination he never sent her anything…Sally was the first to speak of this.

"Why can't Tristan send a pretty card, Mummy?"

"Men are all different, darling…anyway you can ask him yourself tomorrow."

The gorgeous toys Riku had sent were making Sally very popular at school. Amira wasn't sure that such materialistic showing off was so good in the long run…however the whole world practically fell over itself to do just that. Was it so bad to see her so happy. Amira could barely complain she was sporting the most stunning necklace after all.

So were they coming out of an old life. Pagan Arrow demanded so much time and attention that it was an email from Samier that really shook her.

'Friend of Yasmin I am Samier,

Dear Amira,

Hello, my English is hard…so to tell you truth is hard. We ask if you can come Yasmin is upset and beg of you forgive all the foolish things. Her parents are big ogres, and her back is ruined. She cannot lie on it ever. My acting is fool her mother by pretend to tell Yasmin off and make her obey. All time this pretend—if I say the true to her mother, they will block the door and bolt it forever against me. Come quickly to me this my address in Garden City. (There followed a totally undecipherable few short lines.) The mobile my brother give to me will be need fix. Then when I do this, we can speak me in Cairo…a friend to you Samier.'

Amira replied instantly.

'Thank you, Samier, the problem I face is to persuade the captain of the yacht to berth at Cairo. The Port Authority will confiscate his valuable yacht if any breaking of Sharia law is uncovered so it's a big deal.

But you say Yasmin can escape by marriage or we could arrange a dental appointment then get her away by hired car. What about a blonde wig she likes those? Look, do the best you can. Amira Kinov.'

What she really wanted to say was…Jeeze what a mess.

Tristan was flying in that evening so naturally Felix, Ludi, Jack, Sonia, Sally and Amira were all going as one big cheering, welcoming committee.

Loving him the way she used to was impossible now…her nature was to be honest. So much had come to her unplanned. The awful truth was Tristan was probably going to be forced to train in quite another career or perhaps just suffer a sinecure.

A man reduced in this manner is not in the right place mentally to have his girlfriend dump him.

Amira felt honestly this 'engagement' did not sit well with her any more. She needed to face facts and how to gradually persuade him. The voyage on Pagan Arrow would provide opportunities. Amira did not want to give up on him as a friend, but did not want to give up Riku. Any future viewed this way…was precarious.

Voicing it would create an emotional tsunami. Which must be avoided at all cost. Sally would be upset enough in her life experiences. Her teachers were also to be persuaded that perhaps many months out of conventional schooling would be replaced by an exciting once in a lifetime opportunity.

Sailing across the Atlantic Ocean in a 100-foot yacht named Pagan Arrow. With ports of call in many countries along the North African coast was preferable to reasonably safe to and fro car rides to her conventional schooling in a seven-

161

year age group. This would mould her ideas for life. Persuading her father was going to be tricky.

Amira wanted to create a piece of writing to satisfy both parties. Three big obstacles stood out. Rescue Yasmin. Take Sally. Persuade Tristan into a job he would loathe. The crossing seemed to loom up ahead as something more than just an adventure.

Life was complex, how to accommodate a truly wilful and probably now resentful Yasmin that was bloody impossible surely. Amira saw a similarity, after all they both had parents who had treated them cruelly. Plus, Amira and Yasmin shared Egyptian history as careers. Well, more like callings really.

Also how much are forged passports…in Egypt for runaway Muslim girls disobeying their strict family who live by a code of honour, duty and ridiculous expectations as to what kind of man their daughter they are beating near to death should marry.

Put like this there was going to be trouble ahead.

Ludi drove over and read Samier's emails she picked up on the facts. There was a distinct emptiness to these women's lives. Empty of choice. "Those parents of hers sound monstrous counting mentally what she is worth on the marriage market.

Well, they are reducing her value with these beatings…and as for her mental state, she must truly loathe them…"

"I'm not so sure Ludi…the way of Islam is not so simple as you might think. Yes, now she hates what they have so cruelly done…but a whole lifetime is a long period to never see them at all or forgive.

Strong feelings are in play here now and as for anger of course yes—but passing time can alter thinking, remorse, and hatred…hatred can bend towards or away."

"This is surely proof Amira as to why your mind is that of an Egyptian Historian and not a cleaner in a school or a shop girl."

"Shall we see you at the airport Ludi darling?"

The reply was a kiss on Sally's nose and a gentle hug for Amira.

Sally was in overdrive as to which toy should go to the airport. Amira was just a little bit irritated by her daughter's shallow approach. It would do little good to set up a resistance now. But this lesson on life was well overdue. Her daughter had manipulated the Toy God to do her bidding. Amira was on a losing wicket to even mention…we are meeting someone who has nothing to do with flipping Princess Sodding Semolina. A huge sigh from her mother stopped Sally in the hallway. "Ooh, Mummy, you're ever so cross with me aren't you?"

"Yes."

Amira shoved Princess Semolina Concertina…into a shopping bag. Grabbed up all the keys and hurried out, turned the key in the ignition without swearing too much…started Mumblechuckler and watched without bursting into giggles as Sally kept her head right down and gently closing the front door hurried to the car. Less than half a mile down the highway they burst out laughing.

Everyone was at arrivals and they soon spotted Tristan hobbling towards them. He looked very attractive. So much of life is anticipation. Amira had such mixed feelings… He was in great discomfort, and they journeyed home to Ludi and Felix' house with an uneasy question hovering over them all. A buffet had been set up. Tristan hobbled best he could to freshen up.

Sally was talking to Ludi's cat called Mike. Mike had no social graces, he was extraordinarily gifted in the awkward department and went purposefully heavy when anyone picked him up.

Sally carried him about like a heavy shopping carrier. He mewed piteously and Amira told Sally in hushed commands.

"Put the poor thing down Sally, let him go."

Horrible pouts followed until Amira close to screaming took Sally by the hand and led her to the spare bedroom. She closed the door and sat her down.

"Right young lady, tell me why you are dragging that poor old reluctant cat about."

"I thought he might like to…play."

"He is neither a toy nor a school chum. He is however very reluctant and miserable."

"But Indie and Bindie…Winkles!"

"They are young playful animals. Mike is a cushiony style puss."

"What does that mean Mummy?"

"It means…he's like (Don't Touch) but without verbal threats."

Sally ran to her mother and cuddled herself into her neck.

"I love you Mummy so much."

"That's just as well then actually, isn't it?" Sally kissed her mother all up her arm.

"Do you want to go downstairs…have some buffet."

"Yes…Tristan might have brought presents."

"And Winnipeg will fly over Gibraltar and drop cooked puddings plum flavoured."

This set Sally into the most awful giggling fit.

The buffet was great. Awkwardness was for dessert because Felix dropped the bombshell of Tristan returning to the hospital for X-rays again which could only have one outcome. Tristan struggled up and said he was tired and was going to bed. End of. Amira embarrassed said bye to Felix and cuddled Ludi in the kitchen where she was hiding. Sally pulled her coat on saying a huge thank you. They were waved off.

Sonia and Jack whispered…outside… "Oh bloody hell."

Kissed Sally and Amira and drove off pulling whoops! Faces.

Never had a meeting at an airport gone so badly. Amira conveyed her daughter home. A daughter who was puzzled why Tristan had not brought her gifts. After all her bedroom was crammed with other people's offerings. Binx sat at the head of the ensemble with both eyes crossed with indulgence. But it was lovely to be home in the decorated house. Felix had got that right. However, the very idea of all of them being on Pagan Arrow in this (Elephant in the room) flavoured mood was without attraction. In fact, it was bloody painful to think of because there would be no escape. Perhaps that was the point. Amira had horrible jobs to do. Sonia was 'minding'…their personal bits. It had zero appeal to leave those in the house for any strangers to gloat upon.

Advertising the house was also in Sonia's hands. Jack was putting together a letter to bribe Sally's father into giving the go ahead for Sally to go on her Atlantic adventure. The same for the school. Jack thought if one line would swing it then (valuable life lesson) and (the true experience) of learning about sailing over the Atlantic in a fantastic yacht with full supervision twenty-four seven, would be a truly once in a lifetime experience for Sally. She is so excited. The round trip will take in various North African ports. There is the great opportunity to visit Egypt. From there, Captain Coulson is sailing Pagan Arrow to Crete and certain Greek Islands, winds permitting. The Piraeus is included, and the return voyage will resume with a charted schedule…again, winds permitting. Sally will be (Yacht Schooled) learning the names of countries, marine creatures and star-based navigation. Seamanship and charting mathematics to suit her age group.

Within the letter, they included photocopies of the crew's certification and the Captains Master Mariners Ticket and papers. Amira was so impressed with Jack's letter she typed it out again to give to the school.

They had an uncomfortable wait. Sally accompanied Amira to the school's head teacher's office.

To their delight, it was like nothing they expected. Permission was given under the proviso that Sally indeed would follow a school set routine of learning. They emphasised that although this was permission with rules it was to pave the clearest way to opportunity. Sally's father was not convinced. He insisted on meeting Captain Coulson. Amira didn't feel any qualms about this. She prepared Captain Coulson. Explaining how Sally's father had hit her across the room when she was pregnant with Sally. This alone made the captain tut and draw in breath. He said quietly.

"Amira, don't worry I know a great deal about handling and managing difficult men. Giving orders and even persuading reluctance to become acceptance."

Amira breathed out…recalling her own resistance over handling the wheel. Look how that turned out.

When Sally's father came out of the chart room, it was obvious they were going and it was a done deal. The house belonged solely to Amira therefore she did not need permission from Sally's father to let it out.

Nice families showed up over the next two weeks but the family with the little lad of nine and the 'laughing' golden retriever proved absolute favourites. Sonia was in charge of the reference and did not hesitate to take it up. Sonia's agency would manage the financial areas. Amira and Sally would be financially 'okay' but only just. There could be no extravagant purchases. All basic living expenses had to be covered and pulling their weight. They also were expected to pay a small share of any berthing tolls whilst in port. The excitement of course became palpable. Sometimes things just work out. The chart room of 'Pagan Arrow' held less and less terror for Amira. Charles had fantastic charts and he did not hesitate to lay out the route of the passage across the Atlantic…Nautical mile upon nautical mile. They would put in at Bantry Bay. Cork, Ireland. This was the planned Pagan Arrow's first destination. On the day of the departure the graceful wooden sailing yacht came magically to life as she slid romantically, majestically out of port. Everyone they knew was shouting and waving from a bustling quayside…Amira thought somebody might fall in it was so crowded.

All the crew apart from Captain Coulson who was glued to the wheel—were waving and someone let off fireworks…not the best idea with so much oil and fuel about.

They were soon out of sight and yacht life took over in a very serious manner. All had to obey orders and attend chores…no exceptions.

Amira showed Sally the Longitude and Latitude lines, told her how this wonderful discovery was made by Greek Astronomer Hipparchus—190–120 BC. As coordinates he suggested a zero Meridian Line passing through Rhodes.

Modern Technology of course meant a great many technical tools were at their disposal. The way they would navigate would be by Satellite Navigation. They were taking on other crew members. Pieter Vostonski and Jim Cray—friends of Mattie. All chores and duties had been allocated prior to the sailing date. Excitement of reality and the new kingdom of priority after weeks of preparation and deck training…learning how to handle themselves in storms, crisis, fire (and possible piracy). The actual voyage held an edge. Amira sensed her 'land mind' was being replaced by her 'yacht mind'. There were two loaded guns with up-to-date papers on board. All kinds of drills, fire and shipwreck, vital first aid. This prep alone was a huge education for Sally she did not pout or sulk once.

Winkles the ship's cat…also was not without work. Title, Booster of Morale. Don't Touch was considered too unfriendly to be in any crew, scatty old tom cat. Both Dont' Touch and Mike were left with the boatyard owner, a genuine cat lover…poor man. Amira worked with Mattie a great deal. Tristan barely spoke to her. There was no falling out he just distanced himself from her and Sally. Felix was reserving judgement Ludi still hoped that Amira would be their daughter in law one day. Sally was puzzled and kept tagging along behind Tristan everywhere, but it soon became obvious that he was just not the same man. Amira asked him to sit with her for a chat. He shrugged.

"This is a funny sort of carry-on Tristan."

"Oh, I think we both know that I'm just not going to make it in the 'providing father' category."

"Have you any thoughts on how you will move forward Tristan…after this adventure on the high seas."

"Dad's decided I'm to complete a course of choreography to join the staff of the local school if they will have me."

"The Cirque experiences must have been painful."

"What do you think."

"I think, excruciating. That ankle was never going to hold up."

"Well, you know everything then, don't you?"

"We came through the same tragedy Tristan. We survived and it's of no use falling out with each other as friends. And we were lovers too for a while." He breathed out the biggest sigh of sadness.

"I was going to marry you, but I am too proud…defeat is a humbling reality Amira surely you as a teacher of history know how fallen hero's end up."

"I won't lie to you. If I remarry my ex won't continue the same financial agreement. He will always make some contribution. However, the roles will be how shall I put it—clearly defined."

"How is he on friendships."

"One look at you at Julia's party was enough to persuade him that we were very attracted."

"Still attracted, but short of a miracle."

"The Cirque must have been a very rude awakening."

"I almost dropped a man."

"Ahhhgh."

"Yes, it was at rehearsal…we had nets. But the choreography demands thrills. They nearly fucking had one that day. The flyers go into a sort of swing by ankles gripper hold and it makes for fantastic viewing. My upper body is excellent for other stuff but I can't even tumble properly now. It's the collect at the end…you're supposed to carry the momentum on…I can't quite make it look smooth and effortless, in fact it's well you know you've seen the act."

"Yes, it relies on a fierce strongly timed momentum."

Tristan looked at the deck. Amira wanted to grab him kiss him and make love to him all in the same second. If she had done so events would have turned out very very differently.

Instead, she picked up a luggage label that Mattie had fastened to a coffee pot at one time it read…MOUSE In fact there was a faint smudge of coffee on the reverse of the label, that really looked like….a mouse! Methods and madness.

Mattie was a serious imaginative contender for a new dimension… somewhere in another universe. Binx sported a label on his filthy leg…or what passed for a leg. It read.

ENDANGERED SPECIES.

Sally adored this naturally.

Tristan broke the silence.

"How was Cairo…mum says we are going to attempt to rescue a friend of yours who went off with a man she shouldn't have. Sounds a bit nuts."

"Yes, poor foolish woman had her head turned by a well-cut suit. Captain's not getting involved obviously because he cannot risk Pagan Arrow."

"Fantastic yacht, isn't she? You're the flavour of the day I hear on the wheel."

"Absolute heaven. I was frantically avoiding learning. Now I'm longing for my turn every day. Look, Sally is confused Tristan…you can play with her you know, I don't think children ever really get the adult thing."

"I will try but…I hear you had an admirer in Egypt."

"The group I was allocated were surprisingly kind, incredibly clever businessmen from Japan. I was sort of forced to manage alone when Yasmin didn't show up on the first day at work…literally, and so they gave a glowing report about me to the History and Antiquities Department. I believe two business contracts came out of the visit."

"Must feel good."

"Certainly does." Amira heard her name shouted on deck. "That's me speak later okay." He nodded and kissed her cheek briefly.

One can view it anyway you want but the hopes they once had of a future were truly dashed. Sally needed a real father figure. Amira had to refuse any compromise in that consideration. Tristan simply was not the same man. Verve gone she supposed. One thing standing clear above all was the actual thrill of the adventures on Pagan Arrow this was the highlight of everything and if they could fathom a plan for Yasmin, well that would be grand…Alain had also waved them off with all their neighbourly pals, friends and families. Mouthing the advice. "Amira, be careful."

Within his heart he held a message that Amira and Sally were one helluva missed opportunity. His tongue had always tied the second he wanted to change friendship to romance. Amira had time to contemplate the rescue of Yasmin who cried piteously from her beatings…who wouldn't…this would need the aid of nearly all the Gods of Egypt. Who by the way were NOT Muslim. They had great imagination in those ancient times. All swept away by the invasion of the Roman Empire and then Turkish and Arab interference. Perhaps she should go forth like Peracles with a highly polished shield to decapitate the head of the Medusa. In other words, slay Yasmin's parents. How about a burnished copper disc.

Surely they could buy one in North Africa.

Mattie was standing with Amira in the wheelhouse showing her the photos on his phone of all his family. Two black-eyed infants with chubby arms grinned like miniature copies of their beaming father. His wife was plain, sturdy. Twinkling mischief sparked from her eyes. Tears of jealousy for such happiness in marriage welled up in Amira.

"You lucky man Mattie, they are the ultimate in happy. You should be beating your chest in victory."

He was a tactile man and tweaked her hair playfully.

"My wife is the best any man can have."

"So I see. What is your advice for me in marriage?"

"You will go far far away I feel…great things wait for you."

"And Tristan?"

"No, he is small here." Taps his head.

"Well, Mattie, we are supposed to be learning charts."

"The Sat Nav, she do the work Amira. This is backup…look swing the tool this angle and read me the reference on the nautical marker you see for me."

She did as he asked.

Later, Sally pushed open the door.

"Mummy, Captain Coulson needs you on the Main deck."

"Thanks, sweetheart."

The wheel of Pagan Arrow had a crisp new label which read…HEAVEN Amira picked it up and turned it over. On the back, it read. SAME. She laughed and placed herself carefully behind Coulson. Covering his huge hands with her small ones.

"I know I am truly at sea when Mattie starts to write this sort of thing."

"He is so spiritually aware."

"He is so nuts you mean."

"Well, I suppose following his orders might prove chaotic for the crew."

"Might, it would replace calm with anarchy."

"You love him like a brother."

"We go way back. His family are so tough…had to be I suppose…Christ, his people had some cruel treatment dealt out to them in the past."

"First Nation should have more say rather than less. The world might still be pristine."

"White thinking will be this planet's undoing."

"Well, I know some other thinking that's not so clever."

"Right Amira push into this set of swells…that's it…don't stint." Amira laughed into the wind…Charles took a wool hat from his pocket and jammed it on her head tucked her hair in.

"In some tribes, that's a marriage proposal."

They both laughed and drank the coffee Ludi brought them. Parts of life take us into heavenly experiences. Amira was in hers. She saw now what Mattie's label referred to. Up here at the wheel she could be truly free…how the sails and rigging laughed and sang, shook and trembled…luffing rarely showed its antics when she was on the wheel. It was like orchestrating the music of the sea. But she was a beginner. The true test was waiting out there somewhere…and may not be so merciful. Tristan was on deck cleaning with Pieter, they were not friendly, but tolerated each other. Amira was able to watch Tristan, his lithe strength beautiful really in a different way than the conventional. It was a fruitless pastime. She concentrated on Pagan Arrow…beginning slowly to sense the lithe quality of her line and the oceanic powers. Captain Coulson was watching Tristan carefully.

"He's a nice-looking kid."

"Lots of women think so."

"Some men too shouldn't wonder."

"Ah not my territory Captain."

"Loved a girl myself once. Irish…lives in Bantry Bay."

"Ah but aren't we heading there, our first landfall."

Charles had walked away without Amira knowing whether she was in charge of the wheel or not she wanted to shout 'Hey hey I'm not ready for this'. But there simply was no point. He was gone.

That night in their cabin which was so tiny, they had very little leg room. Sally was washed and tucked in for the night. Story book open at her favourite page telling the story of a famous dancer who dressed like a firebird and now toned to perfection (who writes this stuff) was limbering up and keeping his muscles warm prior to his Grand Jette from the wings. Sally never tired of this reading but Sally had tired of the flute. Amira had tried so many bribes, but the flute lay silent. There was a time and place she supposed. Missing Sadie and her school chums no doubt, they are a huge part of any seven-year-olds life. Amira brushed her hair gently.

"Mummy?"

"Yes, darling?"

"Don't you think it's funny we have all the sea in the world but can't go swimming?" They started giggling and snuggled under the covers together.

Sally was asleep in no time…Amira needed a hot drink and slipped out throwing on a jersey and deck boots. She wondered what Riku was doing and by the time she'd entered the galley of course Tristan was there, but of course…there would always be him everywhere. You can't hide for long while at sea.

"Sally's fast away so I thought I would grab a hot chocolate."

"She's settled to sea life remarkably well."

"Mmm it's all terribly new and so far, not a real sulk, pout, or tantrum."

"I don't think teachings for me. Dad's on all the time for me to read this book about preparing for a year's trial in support teaching of light drama or some such thing."

"Sally is crazy about 'The Firebird' at the moment. I have to read a page over and over."

"Not the same page."

"The same."

"This is what I am simply not interested in."

"Repetition…or reading in general."

"Both."

"No, I guess you are action man personified."

"They dance certain acts from the Firebird at…" His voice trailed. He stretched an arm towards Amira pulled her into him. Kissing her hairline. "Snice."

"Yes, we were always great snuggler uppers."

"We were great at a lot of stuff if I recall, Tristan." Footsteps fell on the gangway…they flew apart. Felix came in bustling and red faced from the sheet adjustments.

"Hey you two, any chance of a mug."

Tristan struggled up and made a hot chocolate.

"Sally in her lifejacket?"

"Yes, she refers to it as her life locket. Kids are funny she pipes up with…we have all this sea, Mummy, but we can't go swimming."

"Excellent, she's a rare comic did you catch her with Mattie the other day doing leaps…?"

"Oh no that's from 'The Firebird'."

"They were totally into it. Mattie had tied feathers to their backsides and they sort of danced but it was with great squawking leaping and laughing."

"Mattie is such a character. Always up to some lark, full of fun and teasing."

"Yes, well perhaps he has more to fucking laugh over than the rest of us."

Tristan umphed out leaving them speechless.

"I must apologise for my son's rudeness. He's been like this a while now. We have a 'blow' coming Amira better get rest while you can."

He tousled her hair affectionately rinsed his mug and left.

The 'blow' was an understatement. For five perilous hours they drove into the teeth of a wind that was uncompromising. They were forced to tack and tack again sails down and sails up she was ploughing what Captain Charles Coulson called 'An abomination'. They had no choice but heave her out of the sea lane.

If they continued, she could flounder inside swells. Side on smacks of tons of water can drown out any vessels who tried to be clever. Soaking after soaking left them tired and exhausted with all hands-on deck and Sally slept through the lot. Amira was sent below deck first. She would be freshest when the lull came. Her first real time on deck alone with Mattie who would hold a vigil in the chart room.

She slept the second her head touched the cushions.

It also felt like nothing had happened when Captain Coulson woke her. Dawn had brought straggles of clouds and a warm front settled like a great damp goose overhead. No swell hardly at all just ruffles of tired foam strewn with strange weeds. God knows where these things come from.

Amira took her bacon sarnie and coffee up on a tray with Mattie's they nodded sleepily. "Sally, still asleep."

"Yes but restless and moaning."

"Dreaming probably."

Amira stood at the wheel and Pagan filled her sails under the new hands.

"She responds well to you—must be in your DNA."

"DNA…you're full of surprises, Mattie."

He clinked his mug against hers then went into the chart room.

It was a strange eerie few hours alone like that…one is tempted to sort of nod into the wind.

She had to snap her mind back constantly into reality. Weird and weirder…a shape in the clouds ahead brought her up sharp.

"What the hell?"

It was a plane flying low droning miserably, a search plane no doubt. She heard Mattie make the call sign response and identify himself as the Sailing vessel Pagan Arrow out of Canadian waters etc., their position…the pilot's voice cracked and inquiring…

When the plane had circled twice, it droned higher and finally veered westerly. Mattie came out and gave her a break. On her return, he was grim faced. Amira inquired… "Who are they looking for."

"Private vessel and crew of 'The Condor'."

"Is it bad?"

"She's broken up out there in the sea lane."

Amira took the wheel and scrutinised the stays.

"She's picking up wind North by North West knocking us about again Mattie."

"Fuck this tack…I will call Pieter and Jim." They came up quickly all froused up from sleep, irritable too.

Pagan was steadied up again but she took work, real work. They began a series of jives.

All the time Amira pulled out every ounce of concentration. The lovely vessel constantly obliged in her hands. Pride before a fall Amira told herself constantly staving off the smug values of a beginner who may be doing well. She took no chances and watched the luffing spread and tighten once more then she carefully preened the feathers of Pagan Arrow. Praising her talking to her…loudly… "That's it, my beauty."

A touch at her elbow started her out of her marriage with the darting yacht.

"She likes you, Amira."

"Oh, Captain Coulson, you made me jump I was."

"Talking to Pagan. Yes, I heard you. Go below and have time off."

"Aye aye, Captain." He took over and as she walked gingerly and unsteadily away…he called…

"Get a good dinner Amira, Sally is in the Mess."

Amira was saying goodbye to all she once knew with each nautical mile. The adventure to end all adventures. This could be the one. She had created calm places time and again for her and Sally but in the end noise, clamour, and the outside world had insisted upon being experienced. Once a quiet studious girl. A vulnerable foolish ninny falling for a selfish indulged man who was a pig once they were married. Yet here was Sally and she was great. Any sign of her being like her father as yet had not surfaced. Maybe it never would.

Bride

Yasmin was getting married. She had no idea what he even looked like. The following quiet ceremony at two this very afternoon would mean that tonight she would be sleeping with a complete stranger…Samier was allowed to help her get ready.

Dressing her friend and pulling on a heavy dress made of bridal material and yet tragically not for a happy bride. To Samier, it was sacrilegious, appalling, and making up the saddest face was a trial beyond anything so far.

"My poor Yasmin, your back is so bad there is no way he will want to sleep with you. This is the only blessing."

"Put the ointment on again please please. This dress is a misery against my sore skin. I truly will hate my parents all their days."

Samier gave her friend a tender kiss on her tearful face. She managed to ease the dress off again. Poor Yasmin's skin was in a terrible state. Samier thoroughly washed her hands before applying the salve.

"Put plenty on, if the dress gets ruined, so be it."

Samier did her best and an hour later her friend was at least dressed. The hairdresser arrived and he wordlessly brushed pinned and styled the long shining black hair. Eventually, Yasmin stood head down, thoroughly defeated by events. Her fate sealed by such vicious cruelty.

They left the house stepping into taxi cabs with no chance for Yasmin to make a break for freedom. The ceremony was brief and within no time at all she was giving obedient smiles to her new in laws. Photographs were taken. The bride solemn with a faint smile passing like the fleetness of a cloud over her face.

Relatives suspiciously nudged each other. Yasmin's mother repeating like a parrot. "My Yasmin is very shy. Yes, very shy." The groom of course was not an ugly monster, but he was far from the dream man a young bride wishes for. The cake was vast and ridiculously ornate…everyone had to be met and welcomed. Yasmin had to hold her hand out to people with graceful politeness. She had delicate hands anyway but these months without work had left them beautiful. Her new in laws thought her pampered, spoilt. How was she to clean and cook with such hands. The luggage was stowed away and Yasmin had one good piece of fortune on her side. All the time of her incarceration she had kept carefully sewn into the curtains in her room her beloved grandmother's deathbed gift. The gold and jewels which had passed down to each chosen woman in the family. Until they had reached her.

Yasmin's grandmother had overlooked Yasmin's mother calling her a spiteful woman. No way would she bequeath such honour and wealth upon her. She had chosen Yasmin instead…with the words and blessing of… "My little Yasmin, these will give you a good life and may even save you from a terrible poverty. Take them and hide them from your family. May Allah bless and keep you."

These family heirlooms were secreted in her suitcase which she had packed and locked very early that morning. Yasmin saw it herself as they left the wedding party. It was already safely stowed in the taxi with her other things. She would enter her husband's family and her life would be his responsibility from now on. She did not for one instance look at her mother or father. Luckily, this was read as meekness and obedience towards her new family. The ordeal of the night lay ahead. This was not anything like the thrill of sleeping with the charmer in the funduk. The very reason she was in such dreadful trouble.

The sisters of the groom were not particularly clever but even they suspected some secret was being kept from them. They sensed trouble lay ahead. When they helped Yasmin out of her bridal outfit, they were horrified. Mona the meekest of the two shrieked. She went immediately to her brother, running into the room he looked at Yasmin's terrible wounds inflicted by her father. Tears of pity and disappointment fell onto his wedding shirt.

"They are barbarians."

The sisters immediately called their own doctor…to examine and dress the wounds. The question promptly asked…and what of her mental state.

The Burnishing of a Shield

There was now a whispering lull on board Pagan Arrow. Ludi Amira and Sally were requested to create a halfway party. Like many grand houses a quality yacht has a dressing up trunk. Literally. This was dragged forth. Stores were plundered and tasty dishes appeared, Ludi was an excellent Patisserie chef. She was blessed with patience and was enjoying Amira and Sally's companionship. Amira however had a gripe. She had not been asked to take the wheel since they had recovered and repaired after 'The blow'. All the while she had brooded after being (caught) talking to Pagan. Ludi knew there was something new in the air around Tristan and Amira so presumed this to be the area of the brooding. She had read in the ship's log that…

'All crew are satisfactory in duties. A bad blow has tested mettle and sacrifices were made without oath or shrug. We are making good time. Amira has shone at managing the wheel duties. Her instinctive feminine intuition is exceptional. Pieter and Jim must now prove all their qualities. We have a calm warm front heading towards us.'

She saw while on her party preparations—Amira going to the steps of the gangway and listening far too often.

Ludi knew the matter well enough.

"Amira you are distracted a lot these past two days."

"Oh that obvious. It's just that."

"Just what."

"Captain Coulson has not ever asked me to go on the wheel again he used to lay such praise on me and my love for the job. Now, nothing."

"Oh, I can clear that up in seconds. Sally don't handle the pastry any more darling It will be like a brick…pop it in the fridge…that's right. Will you fetch me the apples not the sweet one's hon but the sour cookers." Once the little girl had skipped off happily…Ludi stood very close to Amira whispering. "I took the captain his meal yesterday and as he wasn't in the chart room he must have slipped out briefly, well Amira I read the ship's log."

"Oh my word, isn't that sort of really private."

"Whatever it is I read the absolute truth. You are mentioned as exemplary. The boys Pieter and Jim as you know are at the start of their real training or whatever is the correct expression…oh you know the Mariner's Ticket or something. Well, they have to learn all aspects of handling the Pagan Arrow, so they of course have to learn really learn the wheel. Mattie is with them mostly… He is instinctive like you."

"Oh, so my work is approved…oh now I see."

"More than darling. Sally wash those apples and dry them for me please." Amira swelled with pride. So she was able after all. Able Sea Woman Amira sounded rather well she thought. The party began at dusk and it was beautifully timed with a run of fine calm breezes. A meal taken with a calm sea on deck by lamp light with the port, aft, and starboard lights twinkling tiny messages into the night sky is like no other. They were all togged out in funny clothes and Sally wore a drawn-on moustache, Winkles sported a fine blue Jersey…a doll's cast off. All present were tipsy and tales were to be told with acknowledgement towards tradition. Captain Coulson waded in first.

"We were out on Cape Cod…I was fourteen and keen as mustard for adventure. My eye was caught by old Captain Tremain. God, he was a hard man. I feared and yet half respected him. He caught a man shoving another about and brought him to task about it. The seaman instead of acting contrite began a diatribe on his ill luck. Captain Tremain had him locked up in the rope store to cool off. The seaman was furious and maintained a terrible swearing and cursing all present. We all secretly laughed at his foolishness. Then there was calm but at three bells there was this horrible screaming. In the end, they had to let him out. He was gull breast white. His hair also, like snow. No one could get a sensible line out of his head. The captain was forced to get him to shore at first chance."

Sally who was wild-eyed from the tale. Stood up. "Captain Coulson…what was wrong with him did you ever find out."

"Never my lass, never."

Sally pulled an ever-obliging Winkles into her lap where she petted and stroked the affectionate creature. Amira pulled a 'well I never' face. Jim was next. "I'd had some leave and was back on board…an oil tanker 'The Hygromia'. She was bound for The Gulf and empty. All on board were alert naturally cus' the vapours can be very lethal because they're volatile so naturally we had security measures to take and maintenance to carry out.

Thankfully, my stint was finished so I was walking along one of the maintenance passages when I saw a chap coming natural as you like. We take pride in all being pals and mates on board. So, though I didn't know who he was I said 'alright mate', and he nods me a hello. Back at our quarters I shower and have a few beers in the mess. My cabin mate comes in and I ask him, "Did you know we have a new man on board?"

He stands up and looks over the whole of the Roster for a new name. He says… "No, Jim, sorry no new name on here."

We both look really carefully. He's right. We know everyone so this needs some explanation. I go to the captain…he's a steady calm man. I ask him if someone new has been taken on. Perhaps some specialist air lifted on…while we slept. He was quick to answer.

"No Jim, sorry can't help you out there."

I am puzzled to this day. Never saw the man again or have any idea who he was. Everyone was hushed." Captain Coulson looked at Amira. "What about your Pharaohs Amira, there must be some fantastic stories about them."

"Oh, there are some very spooky places but beautiful as well. There is one place that I have never been able to explain satisfactorily."

"Go on tell us."

"Well, it's an 18th dynasty tomb belonging to Tuthmosis the 3rd. It's a grand tomb in the Valley of the Kings. He has the most expensive…one could say truly sophisticated and very unusual tomb which truly has a weird ambience it has this odd way of making you feel like you're really being watched and not by modern cameras or security. It's the only tomb in the whole of the Theban Necropolis to my knowledge that has this strange quality. The tomb has four chambers which were once full of fantastic treasures and funerary furnishings.

No doubt the very finest of its day. Alas, tomb robbers have stripped it entirely. All that is left is the smashed sarcophagus, also of course the strangely sophisticated art which fools people into thinking it's actually contemporary, because the figures depicted are like no others in the whole of Egypt. They are actually stick figures…it's as if an artist from our time has designed them. On top of all this you feel watched. Many feel this. Some people say they feel overlooked…others shiver. Many consider it could be its lay out on an unusual North East alignment…also access is only possible via a high set of steps some 30 metres high up in the cliff face."

"Were you there recently?"

"Yes, I took a group of five there. They felt uneasy and found it inexplicable."

"Do you have any ideas you know as an Egyptian history woman."

Amira quickly rephrased the questions meaning.

"I'm a keen researcher in ancient Egyptian lives through textual evidence which has led me to believe strongly the 'observer' is the very 'Ka' of a highly aggressive Pharaoh made restless by the vile tomb robbers. You see, they stripped Tuthmosis of his goods for the next life his very reincarnation…in the field of reeds."

"One heck of a really pissed Pharaoh."

"We, perhaps need to be a little more sympathetic. The 'Ka' is a complex double of the living person. An all-powerful spiritual essence."

There was a silence. This ideology was beyond the rough and ready approach of handlers of canvas rope and wood.

Many slept uneasily in their bunks that night.

Sally made it very clear that she wanted to dance with Mattie. A bit of a crush had formed. Amira thought it fine as she had switched her admiration from Tristan who was extremely moody.

Mattie, Pieter and Sally were very happily working on a special act from 'The Firebird'. Days of sewing and scrabbling for old outfits, searching in corners below deck. Mysterious whisperings and covert operations were amassing Props'…Woe betide anyone who did not take this comedy seriously. Art comes in many guises.

The night of the 'The Firebird'…heralded a great deal of permission given, much pleading and boundaries being tweaked.

Lights and music and calls in the dark brought great magic to the main deck of Pagan Arrow which moulded imagination in the strangest directions at night.

All actions were designed by Mattie (who else) Amira had shown her special Mattie designed ticket at the 'door' which was a curtain of dubious colour and manufacture slung across the side planking. Refreshments were stale crisps kindly revived by Ludi at the last minute.

The cast hurried off to get ready. It was very exciting. Felix and Pieter rigged up some rather simple but colourfully effective lighting. This was in itself atmospheric. Captain Coulson went off to find the recording of The Firebird…an exciting ballet by Igor Stravinsky who had been commissioned by Sergie Diaghilev in 1909 to compose a fabulous entirely new concept of drama. So, the genius Stravinsky chose a Russian Legend which tells the story of Prince Ivan who defeats the evil witch Kaschei with the help of the firebird—who offers one of her enchanted feathers to Prince Ivan after he spares her life while hunting in the forest.

Amira was beginning to think Sally multi-talented but all mothers think this. Dance had once captured her own heart when her beloved grandfather had so kindly removed her from her drunken sots of parents.

She had always escaped into the world of 'Corps de Ballet'. Tutus and blocks (when she was allowed).

Her favourite ballet—*The Nutcracker*.

Followed by…well…all of them. And the more tragic the better. She was however too wild in her choreography to gain approval from any mediocre examiner which filled the school system in those days. Her grandfather encouraged as much as an elderly man could…bless his old heart.

Modern thinking now thankfully dominated dance and music and she hoped one day to give Sally the advantages of choosing music dance and imaginative choreography. Sally had written out—and with Mattie and Pieter's help—had actually produced a funny play which was in the format of a comedy sketch. Pagan Arrow quite naturally featured as the stage. Amira gave it her thumbs up. Mattie loved his involvement and entered into the full spirit of the arrangements.

Little invite cards were designed by Mattie…who else. As soon as chores were completed all those not performing assembled excitedly to see…

The Terrible Spell of Kaschie

The stage was set and Stravinsky's 'Firebird' music began—making them all jump! Lights sprang up and Pieter as the terrible witch Kaschie entered wearing a dress which was of a very oriental design. Amira stopped herself snorting with laughter, he looked more like a drag queen in some low-budget movie. This may have been the desired appearance of course.

Ragged at hem and high at the throat…to hide tattoos and tan. His hair was a horrible wig of scouring wool and cotton scraps escaping from a good hat gone to the bad end of witchery stitchery. He wore high heeled peep toe sandals, painted toe and fingernails courtesy of Ludi. He must have been in discomfort with those shoes. But high art does demand suffering, fortitude and clean teeth.

He leered horribly and sat down clanking a wooden ladle around the galley's largest pot.

"Hear me Hear me…

Cus yesterday I stole a maid

I cast a spell and to me aid

I drew a frog from a stagnant pond

A bag of fleas

and a French almond

I set my spell and lo the maid

Is lain down dayed.

She is, I know, a funny bird…

but filled with magic So I've heard.

I have no mobile phone or telly. Just a rumbling in me belly."

He turns the ladle noisily in the pot to reach an awfully loud crescendo of Firebird music as Mattie playing Prince Ivan enters pretending to be riding his horse through a forest (a sheet over a mop)

With eyes, nostrils and mouth sewn carefully on. The back end of the grand chevalier sporting a tail of rope especially frayed for the purpose…(much imagination is required) He comes galloping on the spot due to lack of space. A clacking of coconut shells (where did they find such things) closely and cleverly clippity clopping.

Applause followed for ingenious effort.

Then the lights swing onto Sally covered in an ensemble of feathers brilliant and totally wild… She played a few birds notes on her flute and then cleverly vanishes. Mattie makes his horse rear up and dear Sally firebird appears from stage right performing a reasonable Grande Jette with heavily made-up eyes and brilliant feathers flying…where did all those feathers come from is on everyone's mind. Kaschei stands up and shakes a wand at Sally until she gracefully with much feather fluttering lies down. Winkles sees this as his cue and oddly and most artistic within fortunate and accidental timing, runs from under Felix's legs to sniff at the feathers…to meow piteously at Sally's head. Mattie takes advantage of this and declares from his horse…

"Ah the good Shaman 'White Wolf' with his great powers has shape-shifted into a good ship's cat and breaks the spell with a touch of his magic paw."

Sally jumps up and pirouettes in feathery grandeur. Flies and leaps off the stage followed by a mystified Winkles tail aquiver and held rather theatrically aloft. The scene ends with a triumphant Prince Ivan holding on high the enchanted feather with a defeated Kaschei dead at his feet…Sally enters and twirls exotically and triumphantly to wild applause. All players assemble with Winkles running to the 'stage' mewing and looking at everyone with a most bewildered expression. The applause made him sit down in front of the bowing players with an air of polite but humble gratitude, which comes across distinctly as…

"Yes, thank you, all my own work don't you know."

Looking at the hysterical applauding audience.

Crackers divinely crackers!

Amira had a great deal of trouble getting Sally to settle for sleep that night. "I was a Firebird wasn't I, Mummy?"

Was all the dear child could say. "You most certainly were my darling nobody can deny that."

All agreed it was a good if somewhat unusual rendition of the original. The return to the cleaning, sailing requirements, cooking and daily management was very dull. However, reluctance is cured by necessity. Crossing the Atlantic is a wonderful accomplishment although done often by so many, for Amira and Sally it held a heady mixture of firsts. The wind was such a powerful force and after 'The Blow' as Captain Coulson had called it…Amira was not approached about the wheel. However, after Ludi had read what appeared in the log, she felt comforted by the fact that she'd done well. Maybe proving herself capable in an emergency was the main issue. This was a constant in her life. Perhaps, being judged unfavourably and unfairly so often by her drunkard father…gave her foolish excessive concerns. She was determined Sally would not be dubbed inadequate. The remark her 'ex' had made about (spoilt brat) had made Sally feel she was in the wrong when in fact she was playing quietly. The bastard. Was he going to pick on her now in just the same way he had picked on Amira taking advantage of her darling grandfather's death? Seeing her vulnerability. He had taken pleasure in hitting her violently across the room when she was pregnant. Well, at first opportunity she would remove Sally from his nit picking.

This feeling swooped through Amira like a great bird. She was determined to lose the reliance on any child support which the law had decided upon. If she stayed with Tristan if she married such a poor provider, how many more insults, remarks, black looks and sneers…would she, could she, take. The answer was coming. She wanted a showdown one that would get rid of her ill-tempered 'ex' forever. Could she really take Sally and live in Japan? If Riku truly was sincere would this lead to him proposing. You can't hurry love. Time perhaps was not on her side anymore. If they could live with him would the culture close down her freedom? No, surely his gentleness with her was not just a front. She had to learn the value of trusting a partner once more.

Yes, her parents were woefully ill equipped, but her grandfather had given her and dear Jack… Oh no she couldn't leave Jack and Sonia but surely Jack was entirely settled in his marriage with fun loving flirty Sonia. He had clearly made his own life so she must make one for Sally and herself.

Amira buried her head in her hands. This was not solving anything. The possibility that Riku would take her and Sally into a whole new world was exciting but the loss of the world they knew meant official change. Also, Rich men can be very dominating…she was sick of finances being the dictator. Riku may not want a foreign wife. Yet he was so loving. She gently pulled open the parcel containing his brilliant kimono she read and reread the precious letter. The trouble he had taken. She put it all carefully away.

Pagan Arrow skimmed through the wild swells of the ocean. Amira showered and felt better. Brushed her hair and went on deck. Mattie was on the wheel. He waved, she replied with a salute and pretended to drink. He nodded, she made them both hot drinks added cake. Ludi's special apple cake always a favourite.

"Can't sleep."

"No…I have a decision to arrive at, the time has come."

"It's the halfway feeling."

"Oh yes, I suppose that's it. I even thought Captain Coulson was joking when he said we were heading for Bantry Bay."

"You will learn he is never joking about landfall, ports or decisions over crew and vessel well-being."

"Starting to learn that."

"Sailing is mind work."

"Oh yes, it is. Being on a flight makes you aware also but in a different way."

"You look different."

"Oh, Mattie you're always so easy to talk to."

"My wife was like you. She was fearing marriage, the step a woman is making is not the same as a man makes."

"I know, having children makes for vulnerability and with a violent partner…GRIM."

"You cannot take Tristan for a lifelong partner. You need older steady man, one who has proved his strength…not one who goes to anger first. Tristan will always go to anger first. His parents have softness with his making…he needed firm teaching. Life took from him but instead of learning he sits in bad decision to be selfish. What has been cannot be unbeen."

"You are wise beyond the stars."

"Where you hear such words?"

"Spending time with the desert dwelling people changes perspective."

"Charles is proud to have your spirit with Pagan."

"Truly."

"Why you take away your beauty and strength with doubt. That is white man thinking. Bear your spirit… Give life all its due. You are so clever to think in another tribes speaking. We go to the sand countries very soon. This is you. Throw away white teaching take strength from one who loves you."

"A Japanese warrior."

Mattie pointed to her throat.

"The one who behind such as this."

"Riku Wise Sky Warrior."

Her hand flew to her mouth.

"Oh my God."

"Yes, this his power token. Who behind this has very serious thinking. Not play."

"Yes, yes, we sat under a Tamarind tree in an ancient temple to Montu in Egypt. I felt such a powerful peaceful connection."

"How much proof you need."

Amira fingered the ankh the very symbol of life.

"This means big thing, Amira."

"Gift of life."

She took the mugs and plates down and washed them, Pieter was yawning off his nap ready to plot with Mattie the next part of the passage. She patted his shoulder affectionately he grinned back sleepily. Now it was truly the correct course she felt better, more than better. Happy. Her next message to Riku was a hundred per cent to the point. The Pagan Arrow's passage was on time and bearing up with fine weather ahead and a good sea running. All now was a vital learning curve. She told him all she felt, the absolute truth…and more important how she was drawing strength from just knowing him. The step had been made. The next three days were brilliant. Then they came, three flashbacks in quick succession. The thing—'with the way the mind works' that Nurse Vicky had spoken so carefully about. There was no warning. The sun may have splintered off a metal surface triggering corner of the eye thinking that no amount of inquiry can satisfactorily explain. Recalling Vicky, Amira felt some encouragement and scrabbled her fingers along the rigging sheets…then sat clumsily down on the deck. Tristan was suddenly kneeling in front of her…

"Amira, Amira, you okay?" His face was distorted. Nausea caught her in its snare. She vomited clumsily. Luckily, he'd moved clear as the fluid hit the deck boards.

She was shaking so uncontrollably that he called Ludi who came with a cloth and some water.

"Amira, I think you're having a flashback...Tristan help me get her to the cabin."

Amira was made comfy while Sally began wiping her face with cold water, she remained calm although terribly frightened and concerned. Amira slept and when the crew were told about the flashbacks Tristan was able to fill in gaps that not even Amira could figure out. Captain Coulson went down to the cabin and sat with her. Concern etched into his wonderfully crinkled sunburnt face.

"Do you feel any better? Tristan told us what can happen he told us all he could remember...how he had absolutely horrible recalls, some extremely close together... Is this what happened to you?"

"Yes, immediately like the flashing gunfire but unexpected so unexpected. I was caught off guard. I remember how the sunlight was splintering off a metallic surface that's all I got all I can remember. Could it be the firearm the sound and flash and the brain trying to you know."

"Whoa there, Amira, I have truly basic psychology, that's way over my pay scale."

"Thank you Captain Coulson, you are at least honest. It's all to do with the way the memory works or something...to store as a warning for my future fight or flight I'm not a psychiatric or psychology expert."

"Yes, a real mystery. My nursing extends to placing an antiseptic plaster on a wound and administering quality whiskey. So you may be better off chatting to Winkles at least he will purr contentedly. Does anything come clearer now?"

For the strangest reason she thought of the woman pretending to clear tables at Dheir el Bahri... Her pretence was certainly an issue.

For after all, terrorists entering countries pretended to be planning to live a better life, declaring their wish to contribute to the country in an altruistic way whilst planning murder of the innocent and unarmed. War and the new acts of war. Something prevented her from speaking. She closed her eyes breathed deeply.

He stood up and moved to the cabin door...

"Take it easy today...guess you don't have much choice. Look we all totally understand Amira just rest and come back on deck tomorrow. We can manage so...you know." She nodded and then lay down then sat up again nausea threatening. She was mentally back in the skiff and who was that fucking woman why was she so significant. Did she know her was this why there was such a persistence in her mind to deal with it. She knew what she must do. The first chance that came her way she would contact Alain… He would know. He knew all the peculiarities of the terrorists. Eventually she felt her body relax, and just as Captain Coulson had suggested the comforting purrs of Winkles comforted her. She slept deeply. Sally was up to the mark and looked after her mother with loving solicitude. In other words, surrounding her with cushions toys and love. A well-intentioned but uncertificated nurse. Who spilt hot chocolate but at least grinned an apology. Amira loved her so much tears prickled at the corner of her eyes every time her little girl brought tasty snacks made lovingly by Ludi in the galley. Love is sometimes a tearful emotion.

As for the crew on deck they were making excellent headway. Pagan Arrow flew along. As soon as she felt right again and to show trust, Amira was given her heart's desire…another turn at the wheel. Nothing like Pagan Arrow to restore the soul. Within a few days her equanimity was more or less restored.

She returned to schooling Sally and was keen that her daughter wrote an essay in the form of a letter to her school, and they settled at the table in the Mess and had a quiet session. Math was the hated subject. Dance and being in an adventure was favoured over everything.

However, Amira skilfully combined the yachts nautical progress so far with some general weather calculations with patient calculations and descriptions from Pieter who had a real genius within the field of wind pressures and thermals. He also knew a lot about Condors how they instinctively chose rising thermals in their mountain home in the morning. How they rode them and soared effortlessly. Of course, there were no condors where Pagan Arrow pierced the waves.

They were entering Irish waters…near one of the busiest sea lanes in the Northern Hemisphere. Shipping was accompanied by various gulls who swung low with incredible acrobatics which gave Sally an excellent opportunity. Pieter gave her a great deal of his spare time helping with a drawing of a gull's beautifully extended wings, pure white breast feathers. This kept her totally occupied. It was a good well illustrated essay with relevant drawings beginning to slowly emerge.

Meanwhile, the gull's acrobatics brought them nearer and nearer sometimes even landing on Pagan Arrow's rails. The crew then began the cutting and running for the Irish coast. It was utterly exhausting constantly tacking and jiving and they were entirely relieved when at last they hit a good steady run of wind pushing them magically towards the port of Bantry Bay.

Amira taught Sally a song which strangely delighted Captain Coulson.

"We're going to meet the bus

We're going to meet the bus

We'll meet the bus and say

Welcome to Bantry Bay."

She threw in a few extra WHIRRA WHIRRAS…for good luck.

Amira explained it was from an old school book called 'Pegeen'.

Sally delighted to see her mother working about the deck singing…

"Whirra whirra Winkles

He has a bell it tinkles

And his toes they twinkles

In the pale moonlight."

All were pleased to see land. Captain Charles Coulson had already booked a mooring in the Bay and everyone was super happy. The crossing had taken them just a few hours short of four weeks. All safe and well so a great success. The next part of the voyage would take them clean to France. It was doubtful they could afford more than a short shore excursion on the French Coast due to the cost of mooring the beautiful 30.48 metre sailing yacht Pagan Arrow. It cost very little to sail…it is stopping that is expensive. Amira kissed the deck and going into the Mess found a mug with one of Mattie's labels it read PINEAPPLE. Captain Coulson was breakfasting and gave Amira a mug of hot coffee.

"Come keep me company. I just had a message over the air that they are charging £140 for a plate of chips in London."

Amira smiled widely.

"Is that with or without ketchup?"

"Ha ha you have me there. I'm not one for the UK…its over-rated by any standards. Cold shoulders are bred there as a hobby and I don't feel the need to put into a harbour that welcomed slavers."

Amira shivered.

****

In a good area of Cairo…

Yasmin was alone in the pleasant bedroom of her new home. She was much improved in her physical health...sadly, her mental well-being was damaged. She hated her new husband and barely tolerated his gentle unassuming sisters. Their shock upon seeing her poor back they could not hide. The family doctor thought her parents should be prosecuted. Yasmin bitterly spoke up.

"And this would undo the wounds they have done me. Forget. Money thrown away." This was a terrible dilemma. Her husband was well off and not without good sense. He took her to an expensive, epidermis specialist. This clever man took photographs and examined her under a special lens. He made a report. It was not good.

Most of her back would heal and in some five years a great improvement would be seen. Grafting was spoken of but the deep welts on the right shoulder were far too large and too serious. The scar tissue was so fragile. Yasmin's father had been efficient, he had scarred his own daughter for life.

The decision was to allow natural healing as much as possible. Operations to improve could be done when the correct creams and treatment to the skin had encouraged this and natural healing had followed its own course. Yasmin was still young. Now while the skin was so damaged more harm could come from too much interference.

The long treatments under special lamps were most beneficial. As the weeks passed, she lost the stiffness and movement became easier. Soreness eased. Mental damage however, the hidden assault upon her mind. What to do about that. She would never ever forgive such cruelty. Her voice was once filled with laughter, knowledge and romance. But now she was instantly ready to swear and condemn at the smallest irritation. Her husband kindly and much confused gave her space. He spoke to his sisters...Mona and Hosna with gentleness.

"She needs time...naturally this is not what was planned. Her parents are like the barbarians of old. This poor girl we need to reconsider. I had so hoped for a child...but that must wait. Her mind is fragile. All my life all my life, the poor girl."

Mona cried. She sought refuge in their beautiful modern kitchen...baked beautiful cakes, made delicious food. Yasmin began to fill out. Her head was filled with avenging thoughts one minute and escape the next. If she caught sight of her back in a mirror, she loudly cursed her father. This was terrible to hear.

No amount of good food was ever going to return her physical beauty. That was history and where was Samier and Amira…Samier should have called the doctor and police to her parents.

Yasmin shouted out such curses when Mona applied the expensive healing cream which were working, also the medicines, healing lamps and tablets. All that could be done in the hospital had been done and done well. Her mental well-being…yes well that bordered on hysteria. Samier brought news to Yasmin of how Amira and her daughter were sailing across to Cairo…and explained how Amira could not be expected to take Yasmin from Egypt.

That was viewed as kidnap. Authorities could imprison Amira and she had a little daughter. Yasmin oddly enough softened at this fact. There could be other answers it was just finding them. She had the jewels they were intact. Perhaps they could buy her a way out. Just as her grandmother had suggested.

Samier patiently explained about the papers and passports. They were simply not within Amira's knowledge she knew no criminal types to forge documents. At this admission of the facts Yasmin threw a plate at Samier who withdrew frightened. Mona held her outside the bedroom.

"She does not mean it. The cruelty the cruelty…such horrible things happened to her… Samier, forgive her she will heal soon. Forgive habibti forgive." But Samier longed to leave forever the festering hatred in Yasmin' s eyes.

Her funny Yasmin where was she? The spirited romantic, where had that girl gone. The demons glowing in the eyes of this young married bride were truly terrifying…If Yasmin had subjected herself now to psychometric tests for mercenary missions, she would have passed. Yet, if she told Amira the truth, she would not come at all. Samier wondered if indeed she herself could escape Egypt. Many girls long to run from decisions made to rule over the unjust life of the female in Islamic tradition. Dangerous scenarios passed all the time through Yasmin's mind. On and on the discrimination the subjugation. How to survive became her only mode of thought. That and revenge. Amira would find a very different friend to the lively, intelligent, romantic…she once knew.

****

The whole crew of Pagan Arrow were grouped on deck in the crisp clear sunshine of Ireland.

Amira and Sally were in the first group to go ashore in Bantry Bay. Lots had been drawn to make it entirely fair. Captain Coulson had given them a little map and the list of provisions. Everyone was allocated a 'list'…First stop was a rather wobbly achievement as their legs were not used to land that stayed still rather than lurched. Of course, Sally took it one step further than required. She was such a funny little girl taking advantage of every opportunity to entertain. Or as some rather more critical observers remarked…(showing off) Amira let it all wear itself down…they found a bookshop and bought a new notebook and a book on ballet. But of course. The books all had so much charm and Amira didn't recall the last time she was choosing a book. These experiences were lovely— Being all so Irish perhaps. They posted mail to Sally's school including the essay on 'Life on Pagan Arrow'…A rather curl-edged missive with paintings of people in a dancing scene and for some odd reason Mattie with a tea and coffee-stained luggage label dangling from his old wool hat saying…BRILLIANT.

The self-same wool hat was also festooned with feathers from various birds and would draw tears of laughter from Sally's wonderful Head Teacher Aoife. A whole bunch of letters and cards (hastily scrawled to everyone they knew). Sadly, there was zero information about Aristophanes. He was a pure genius of comedy in his time coining the wonderful phrase—Cloud cuckoo land. These three words remained constantly in use and Amira was keen for Sally to benefit from his eloquent humour. Never too young to learn about comedy's foundation was Amira's new motto. Dinner was next and she found Pieter and Jim already munching through a typical Irish bacon sarnie or three. Washed down with Guinness. Sally piped up for the Guinness and this Amira did give a lecture over. Well, a two-second one…consisting of…no and definitely no.

Secretly however, Pieter gave his glass to Sally for a gulp to try as soon as her mother's back was turned. Sally made the most horrible of faces and declared it worse than medicine. She recovered her equilibrium just in time for her mother's return…and was thrilled to tuck into fish and chips and some peculiar pickles. Which she insisted on nibbling and then pulling exaggerated faces. Everyone in the café was entertained thoroughly.

Tay washed it all down and they shopped in a group for the provisions list. The taxi back to the quayside was an experience in itself. A wonderful man with two enormous ears which he could move independently had Sally in raptures. She was allowed to place filthy old Binx…who had resurfaced unfortunately…on the dashboard. It pleased her, although everyone else groaned at being watched by one evil eye out of a ghastly grubbiness of features. Nobody understood a word the driver said but a hand extended for payment is an international language. The rest of the crew left the instant Sally swung on board declaring…

"The fish and chips are fantastic."

She diplomatically waved to her (brand new pal) the taxi man, who also wisely waved to attract the other members of the crew departing from Pagan and heading into town. A smooth exchange. Amira was only too glad to put away the provisions and wash up. The excursion on shore having severely dented their budget…propelled her to fill her time with chores of a lightweight nature. The letter to Alain was also a sobering one. She eventually lay down with a huge sigh. Sally had become deeply engrossed in the dancing book.

A godsend!

The crew rallied the next day with various grumbles hangovers and a mystery girl waving and crying from the quay… No man was prepared to give away anything by waving back.

All wonderful events no doubt entering—The ship's log. They finished repairs, cleaning, and set sail two days later for the next chapter of Pagan's voyage of discovery. Tristan was attentive and Sally was defiant about changing the choreography of *The Nutcracker*. She told him… quixotically…

"I do know what I am doing."

Which reduced everyone to giggles, behind their hands of course. Amira sighed. There was a naughty little cheeky girl emerging but a voice inside said. 'Let it be'. She might need this energy of new confidence to resist the attempts to suppress the spirit of her youth which was no doubt…no doubt…arising out of the nit-picking father's corner. The crew were longing for distraction. So often after a day or so in port there is a mixture of suppressed emotions. Each can speak for themselves. As for Amira she felt that this was a long old way and slow as molasses in January… Yasmin's predicament weighed upon Amira's heart and a danger waiting if she dare make poor decisions. With the friendship of Yasmin in Cairo badly damaged by rash behaviour. One part of her reasoned… why the hell should she risk so much after all it was Yasmin herself who had neglected Amira that first night in Cairo then zipped off to have a rendezvous with a complete stranger. Such a foolish woman. However, one discussion with Ludi the ever fair-minded voice of kindness—was a new way of understanding. Of course, women had become intoxicated by men's lies from the very dawn of time. Also, men succumbed hourly to female allurements. Amira recalled her own losses and hadn't she been tricked by Sally's father. Add to this the loss of virginity in a tawdry hotel room…

The Islamic stifling culture of servitude and subjugation of the female in Egypt leading to being literally locked up. By the very hour religious leaders (men) were coughing out sermons of fighting natural instinct. Set aside desire and serve…the same old misery conveniently buried in mystery and lies. Life itself gives us a natural instinct to love and our bodies instruct us to make children…well most women…some escape this very neatly. Watch them closely. For marriage is suffering and loss through child birth. The faulty religions served by countless drudges' grudges and endless rules. Cover everything liable to cause offence. Being a woman itself is an offence. Was that why Amira was shot in a bookshop. Were her modest white top and neat clothing an offence.

The snake woman had to be shown her own reflection… Eventually, Amira calmed herself… Sally had come out of Amira's mistake.

For the next few days there was talk of little else but the rain. You would think being at sea the whole crew had learnt to ignore rain. They were lashed with it until the cabins smelt of drying out clothes. Sneezes and wet foreheads became the norm. Then the English coast faded, and Charles gave everyone whiskey. Sally sipped at her mother's mug and shook her head with disgust.

What a relief.

Amira sat with Mattie and as the rain cleared and the warm sun dried off sodden heavy canvas, wood, clothes and people…he spoke of the great and terrible evil that had come out of London in the disgusting guise of a Wesleyan missionary…one John Wesley entered this life 28th of June 1703 at Epworth.

Mattie's voice is tragic…as he related quietly…

"This liar and cheat…a fanatic…who's followers behaved like demented sheep travelling to the Americas and Canada…settled with their vile papers and books that shattered the lives of the tribes they found there. Small children stolen and forced to learn white lies. Their tongues tortured by mending nails if they could not form those white man's lies by talking rubbish. The land that had been spiritually gifted to the tribal ancestors from the beginning and was beautiful had been stolen. The foolish and weak and the browbeaten forced to accept some peculiar man on a wooden contraption with blood pouring. Horribly barbarian. An egotistical son of some god that these crazed white thinkers wanted to worship. Evil deeds done in this pathetic creature's name. All the avalanche of horrors brought to our land by this twisted body set on wood. The white thinkers showed no mercy and would not allow totem or ceremonies for our customs ever to us. We admire the speed and endurance of the brother wolf and the pack, the greetings and communicating by howling. Wesley peoples in their greed and ignorance misunderstood the wedding of the wolf…not able to grasp the spiritual unification of brother wolf to us. This vital unity of man and woman's spiritual strengthening and vital messages exchanged with the wild of the night. All the great rivers trees and signs that mother earth gives to her children. They assaulted and insulted the great mythical energy of the Thunderbird. And the final twist of the Wesley man's knife. Love one another! They did not love anything. Only a book of humiliation, lies torture. Love one another and yet they brought us misery shame and degradation. Alcohol replaced life. They brought stink, stench, infected blankets and disease, killing so many with their vile practices within contamination. A mockery of cruel snake tongues that came from more lies carried like a disease. They were disease. Now people want museums of the old life they had cruelly stamped on. The white thinking had no sense, no fairness, no beauty in it. Just theft of the soil. A cataclysmic event. A diatribe of failure to the planet. Its beauty its wonders. The peoples looked to the Thunderbird. The lightning birds. Nature spirit. The absolute reality of…the rocks and the water. They are the true spirits They are the real. They are the universe…from where all life comes. Not Wesley liar man, not blood taker vampire thief of the very soul of the First Nations. Not this poor twisted dead man on wood. They said Rome's soldiers do this torture to the dead man. Go to them tell them to change, what is this dead story to us. He is not here but the trees and birds are. This rape of the peoples and the land…was ever their shame. No law was set to protect the tribal nations only laws set for protecting their evil oppressors. Now the new way forces government to acknowledge the wrong done."

Mattie had tears in his eyes. Amira held his arm the whole time. It was in respect of these truths that Captain Coulson had not landed on British soil. Mattie bowed his head in respect of his forefathers. Amira also knew of the people that the French had gone into war against. Those who wished to save the creatures of the deep. A ship dreamed up by a visionary Chief…of his nation… A ship named 'The Rainbow Warrior'.

Only the stupid could destroy such a truth of protecting the great creatures of the deep from extinction. But they did.

Now such a cry has gone up the twist in that knife was from the Norwegian whalers who had 'run out of' whales.

The curses upon those vile whalers. Such stupidity. Twist of the knife. The near extinction of the Whale…the greatest spirit of the Sea…a book detailed the cruelty shown to these fantastic Whales…killed, horribly tortured and stripped out by evil. All the good world now weeps for this. White thinking it bleaches out the dark sweet mystery of Earth.

Mattie was red eyed.

His amazing face set to the wind. The winds of change with a soothing justice within its perfumes. Amira still held his arm.

"My brother under the stars…the true way to honour the Earth our only mother is now being breathed in the great chambers of government. Your ways were nature…the scientist will come to you on bended knee…"

"I need them stop their race to kill our planet. I need them stop now."

Sally sat calmly with her mother on deck. Amira was on wheel duty, and Pagan Arrow was set on a fair wind to France and the port of La Rochelle on the French Coast. Where once aristocrats had fed the guillotine.

Now statues appeared in museums of victim and victor alike. Words filled out books and trees were felled to serve the rights of literature. The fallen had paintings to represent them and music had turned into drudge and moaning. The arc of light on old paintings the golden circles of faith had become a drug cartel of need. A sense of failure entered city and town. County Lines took on a new meaning.

The new world had a new need. Art was now a great commodity. Vaults hid religious fervour and ghosts haunted the galleries. All this too shall change. Screechers like banshees from an army of thousands in heavy make-up feverishly signed recording contracts. The money god breeds mediocrity easily.

Fashionistas strutted in clothes costing the earth.

A new everything. Planes crashed and a pestilence strode towards planet earth. Followed by fire and flood. Icebergs collapsed under the weight of man's needs. The Thames Barrier was under improvement. Something was coming.

Amira strained to turn the great wheel and Pagan Arrow obeyed. The sea was stunningly lovely.

"Can we go right into La Ro Ro."

"La Rochelle darling."

"Yes…but can we?"

"That's the plan."

"Why is Mattie sewing a new shirt, Mummy?"

"Darling, that's a silly question now isn't it?"

"I'm learning Mummy I have to ask questions."

"Why don't you go and look for a nice clean pair of trousers for you and for me…please make a start at least."

As the child jumped up, Winkles thinking play, cuddles or food might be in the offing also jumped up to twirl invitingly. Sally disobligingly ignored these antics…and the cat stared after the skipping figure with hero worship twinkling in slanting green eyes. Amira reached across and tickled him under his clean white chin.

"Oh dear Winkles, you're not wanted below decks just at present, me old mate."

The cat on hearing his name sat and gazed adoringly at Amira the second love of his life. Well, for the present. Captain Coulson dapper in a brushed jacket and newly trimmed hair courtesy of Jim came up to Amira.

"Able Sea Woman Amira Kinov you are in excellent form today so go below for lunch and prepare to go ashore."

Amira saluted.

"Aye Aye, Captain."

She loved all these specific details. Even her name which although was sometimes incorrect was near enough and a nod to a blind donkey is the same as to a blind guinea fowl. Bliss comes in many forms. Ludi was perspiring and laying out food in the galley. Sally was plating up and the whole place was abuzz with La Rochelle.

Jim had plastered his frizz of unruly blonde curls into a kind of clay curl structure. Like Polyclitus the spear bearer reporting in with his new look. Contraposition. Balance and tension. The gaze of beauty which is truly in the eye of the beholder. Effeminate male beauty does not appeal to all. And it's understood…Alexander the Great's taste for the catamite will not suit everyone. Amira kept her eyes averted it was too much male beauty before lunch…she truly wondered if the ultra-staid and conservative French were ready for such an invasion. The tearful girl waving on the quayside at Bantry Bay was still fresh in her mind. La Rochelle offered them all the finest fresh foods and light crisp wines. Were truffles available and if so, why could they not afford them? France is so often a maiden fresh and fair lying out in southern sunshine. Amira also reminded herself of the fact that Leonardo de Vinci had died in the arms of an admiring grieving French King.

They, Sally and Amira were lucky once more and as Captain Coulson knew so many people here a dear friend of his came on board with his wife and two strapping sons to enjoy Pagan's beauty and keep a Weather Eye. The Pagan Arrow crew's party on the 'tender' was an hilarious and excitable experience. Ludi made it clear she wanted to be with Amira and Sally. Felix had soon sauntered off with his arm across Tristan's shoulders. A statement of father and son on shore and free.

Amira relieved as hell took Ludi's arm and Sally's hand and they went off to find the park with the plane trees. The men were happily selecting a good beer establishment…they wobbled along the quay trying to get land legs again. They managed to board a local bus which was thrilling in itself and soon they were walking through…dappled shade and sparkling light.

"Oh how lovely to see a tree."

Ludi threw a rug out onto crisp green grass and stretched out fully… "Oh how lovely no washing up."

"Yes it is exceptionally gorgeous up here, what a panorama."

"Let's pour out some lemonade Amira…Sally come back don't wander off like that when Mummy is busy."

"It's a new thing. My guess is Ludi that this voyage is giving her a confidence but without true knowledge of danger. So, I'm glad when people keep an eye."

"Tristan was dreadfully reckless he gave us nightmares."

"Still does I imagine."

"Why is he so headstrong we were utterly committed to his wellbeing and sat him down talked all the time never pulled sneaky stuff like some parents…we always communicated the whole works."

"It's impossible to know…we all have a different approach, I think you indulged too much. Yes he is confident but has to learn a lot about true disappointment in life and how to overcome obstacles."

"Gawd is it that obvious. What to do though Amira, he's all we have."

"I'm no expert. People tell me I allow Sally to take liberties but she has a nit-picker for a father. So, I'm guessing that my role is to pick up and perhaps overcompensate."

"No school teaches parenting; we go on through trial and error."

"This lemonade is the business."

"I'm so hot, Amira…do you mind if we get into that shade. Being in the galley is great but takes me from contact with real sun."

"Are you…now tell me honestly darling pal…happy on this voyage."

"Oh yes, it's brought Felix and me closer than ever. He, now keep this close to your chest, he is thinking of letting out our house the way you have done and going up to the snowline for a year, you know experience the real frontier life…before it's too late too crowded."

"What? Live like a troglodyte!"

"Ha ha ha ha…geezer life, yes like those Yeti people who suddenly appear at the edge of the forests howling like a wolf pack."

Sally flumped on the rug.

"This is in the shade, Mummy, why do you want to sit here."

"Questions City is where we live now, Ludi."

"I was too hot, darling…why don't you take my camera Sally and take lots of photos…it's lovely here."

"Thanks for that, don't be surprised if all you say is recorded and yacked back later Ludi."

"The determination and spark in the little girls of today is so very different to my time. We dared not do or say anything. We had to ask permission to take a comfort break." The two friends lay back with eyes closed and Sally sat in the sun with the camera exploring artistic angles.

****

In the clean comfort of her husband's Cairo home, Yasmin was looking better She had plumped out and was all aglow. Samier found her pruning flowers. A real luxury in Egyptian life.

Her sisters in law were dancing attendance and it should have been idyllic…but it was not.

"You look so well now Yasmin. Your face is filled out and your hair is glossy…married life suits you."

Yasmin wanted to snap Samier's head off with impolite sarcasm but felt it might be better to hold back a little.

"He's not pushed his way into my room so that's a relief."

"So you're still not really married."

"One way or another with those dopes for sister in laws…it's easy life…my father can't get to me and if that shit of a mother rolls up to my door here, I have easy access to the kitchen knives."

"Oh Allah does not like us to speak against our parents in such a way."

"I have no belief any more Samier. I wish we were still in the great Pharaoh's times when women could get more justice."

"Oh, don't speak like this it hurts only you in the end believe me."

"You are Omar the donkey these days look in the mirror you're like an old worn down jadda."

"This is the true. It's the shop…I can't stand much more I work such hours there. So many lovely young men come through and I must keep humility and modesty. I'm sick of the servile life."

"You should take all the money out of the till on the best trading day and clear off. Do you have a passport yet?"

"Yes, father had to spend out for us all he wants us to visit our family in London."

"Oh, is that the plan now. I thought he was marrying you off to the local fat old pig in trousers."

"I forgive you Yasmin the way you were treated makes you say this, I love you."

"Oh, blah and blah blah you all make me sick. Such acceptance of all the rubbish that this life here forces us to endure. Oh here come the twits."

Her sister in laws came out with trays crammed with treats and lovely chai, sprigs of fresh mint decorating the glasses of hot amber liquid.

They sat in the pretty garden, women without young lovers without hope of careers. Just the sun and gossip. Samier thought it really comforting and wanted nothing more. The sisters were content to munch on biscotti and honey cake for variety. They felt no yearnings. They beamed with pride at the work they had accomplished with Yasmin…pleasing to the eye. If they didn't think about the horrendous scars on her shoulders. The hard eyes. The empty heart. Allah is great. They eventually went indoors and washed up. They had long given up on allowing Yasmin to help in the kitchen. Her temper flared most there. The plates falling victim to her ready wrath.

"Here's a letter for you Yasmin, posted in a place called Bantry Bay."

Yasmin snatched it up eagerly tore it open and read a few lines looked at photographs threw it angrily to the ground spitting expletives.

"Oh, not good news."

"Oh, not good news…of course it's not she's about a month away…she's yacketty yacketty about her bloody life on a luxury yacht with her brat of a daughter in ballet shows or some rot…what do I care."

"She's not rich Yasmin that's unfair…didn't you say she had to let out her home to do this."

"Yes and have you seen her fiancé young, slim and tawell, plus extra special good in the bed."

"How you know he is good in the bed?"

Yasmin shoves the enclosed photographs under Samier's nose.

"Oh yes I see what a handsome boy."

"Yes, yes, boy Samier not old man with a stomach same as hippo. Boy…lucky Amira eh eh. I'm sick of you all."

She threw the napkin and envelope to the ground then flumped miserably indoors.

Samier retrieved the letter and carefully returned the photographs inside the colourful envelope with its fascinating stamps. Her eyes shadowed by despair and fatigue Samier gazed up at the rather lovely house with neat shuttering against the sandstorms that can surprise millions of Cairenes and reduce their eyes to red, itchy orbs.

"I only speak the true."

****

Pagan Arrow was plying a course towards the straits of Gibraltar and the Mediterranean Sea. They could sense the change in the sea and its colour deepened to a fairy story cobalt…inky, dramatic.

La Rochelle had been such a treat. Captain Coulson's friends had been immensely friendly and had made meals for the crew. Crab and extra fine wine became a feast for a royal yacht. Sally was thrilled to welcome on board their eight-year-old… terribly pouty quixotic daughter. Amira sighed and prayed no bad habits would be learned. Sally was at a funny age. There had been no need for concern. Adeline was fairly well mannered and tolerant of Sally's constant questioning. She showed off and Sally gave instructions on how best to dress up Winkles, who now saw himself as a nobleman at the Court of Versailles.

Not a plump ship's cat with yearnings for tuna and steak.

Adeline gave Sally a look of pure contempt.

"Noh, I don't dress foolish cats."

Fair enough. Now the many au revoirs were but an echo on the salty breeze and Sally had a new dress which was a preening aid. Jim made the most awful guffaws and giggles whenever Sally sought his approval. He was of course…the crush both little girls had invented for themselves and whispered over until the final moment.

Amira admitted they at least had chosen well.

Jim was chunky and muscular and had a tan of absolute bronze god of Athens calibre…finished off with dark honey curls. Green eyes that flashed a promise, or indeed a warning to all females within his radar. Amira thought it normal and did not interfere, it would fade soon enough. Life sorts all too quickly these across the age's affections. Sad eyes and soulful yearnings…end in tears if you're lucky. She had sent more cards home and a letter to Riku…she had enclosed photographs and had even posed in the kimono. Sally took a lovely photo of Amira with her hair in a chignon. The art of Japanese Geisha 'up do' was well beyond Sally's or Winkles hairdresser skills.

Winkles went through the straits of Gibraltar sporting a bonnet and special sun cream on his nose and ear tips via a request from Captain Coulson.

Amira was not on deck but helping Ludi, and the women chatted pleasantly. Earlier in the day, Tristan had pulled a very surprised Amira into his torso and kissed her several times.

Lovely though this was…Amira viewed this as all a bit out of sync. No opportunity ever arose to extend the kisses into full blown rampant sex. Which would have been fab…but a real spanner dropped into the new works. The photograph album grew and sea miles nautical and salt laden flew under Pagan Arrow's trim lines. They soon sighted Cuata.

Amira took pains to explain The Pillars of Hercules…

This of course is part of the ancient and classical world of the Mediterranean countries interwoven through trade, war and intrigue. The Phoenicians brought the first Alphabet to the known world, twenty-two letters on which other formations of lettering could be built. The great pillars of Hercules are so set into myth and legend that they are impossible to overlook. The Greek legend of Hercules tell us he had to perform twelve labours. One of these was to bring the cattle of Gergon (some say they were enormous) from the far west and bring them to Eurystheus…the Westward extent of his travels. Renaissance tradition says the pillars bore a warning…'Ne plus ultra'… Nothing further beyond. Some myths claim Hercules built the two pillars to hold the sky away from the earth. Sites are still not agreed upon…

Cueta a Spanish enclave military post at the Mediterranean entrance.

An 'autonomous city' on a narrow isthmus that connects Mount Hacho (also held by Spain) to the Mainland. Mount Hacho has been identified as possibly the site of The Southern Pillar…and Jebel Mousa (Musa) in Morocco is another contender. Amira set Sally the task of imagining these pillars and carefully drew a map for her using the charts in the chart room. She wanted to see if Sally could actually throw out an idea of her own and choose selective propositions. Huge ask. Amira had been a 'natural' within this field. History is decidedly easier when you love the fact that people lived it, made great things, evolved and showed bravery, conquered, lost and died. Romanced, made mistakes and became fathers, mothers, rulers. Some did all of this. They also lived to tell the tale. We see now certain individuals lived great lives. While others barely moved beyond a village. We work still today with this inherited story of Earth. The value is a price beyond all the gold mined. Amira went ashore with Mattie, he had voyaged here with Captain Coulson and Pagan Arrow before.

Pagan had been spotted from far off due to her trim line's and clean canvas billowing. A crowd had gathered. The Spanish appreciate lovely structure in yachts. Amira glowed with real pride for she was under instruction at the wheel when they dropped anchor. In fact, Pagan Arrow drew great attention in harbour due partly to her beauty but also a famous Spanish ship builder who had repaired her two years ago…after she had done battle through a sudden fierce storm on the Mediterranean… was there at the quayside with a crowd of tourists… He loved Pagan and was soon aboard slapping backs and shaking hands. Perhaps, it was the light and the clarity of the air, but Amira felt very comfortable in this famous port.

Mattie knew where to take her to find a shield. He understood such desires. Sally was happy to trot ahead of Felix and Ludi singing loudly. The words were jumbled but the general idea was.

"We are off to sunny Spain Vive Espania. We will sail the Spanish Main Espania por favor."

The words often changed places. Sally with a genius only a seven-year-old can get away with pulled it together with pretend castanets and flamenco. Youth has a charm only the young can employ. While dancing on the spot with spoons for castanets. Ludi and Felix didn't mind but Amira had been worn down by it. She needed a break. Amira and Mattie were not staying long ashore due to Captain Coulson going up to the great house of the ship builder to eat drink and be merry with his dearest friends. So, looking after Pagan Arrow was a big responsibility. Piracy on this coast was a possibility. They had cleaned and loaded the two guns the night before because along this particular stretch of coast you cannot take any risks. So Captain Coulson would wait until their return and then take time ashore.

Mattie was so dark he passed easily through the streets. Amira next to him however gave a contrast not easily ignored. Men stared at her fine features, blonde hair against the delicate tan. Her strangely upward slanting eyes. All this next to the rich deep hue of Mattie's complexion…his eyes and hair. They made an interesting pair. Mattie had an idea of where the perfect shop might still be trading, and after a cooling ice cream they made their way along the crowded-out markets…it was obviously a main shopping day for residents.

He found the shop which he had held in his memory. Amira was impressed and told him so.

"Mattie, you have a brilliant memory. I for one would never have found this place." They entered through a fly guard and the sultry atmosphere and remnants of some long burnt down incense stick gave an edge of a perfume reminiscent to Amira of Egyptian Souks. The balding man that grinned a hello from a shadowy desk area…made Amira slightly uneasy, she could not spend very much. She had given her money to Mattie as he was such a brilliant trader that they felt between both their reluctance to be big spenders they would not fall foul of the smiles. They wandered around and the trader kept showing them junk and even more rusty dusty junk. All seemed lost and then at the final tour of the dust laden muddle, Amira caught sight of a circle of what appeared to be gold fire peering from the gloom behind crumbling manky furniture that defied description. The trader was not showing any sign of weakening in his garbled descriptions which neither of them was really paying any attention to.

Amira gave the pre-arranged signal and so Mattie came to her side, and she pointed out the shield. Together as the owner garbled his nonsense, they extricated the circle of fire and took it to the entrance of the shop. This was perfection. The owner of course was not even aware of its existence until then but now praised it to the heights. He took it off them. How bloody rude. Then conveyed it like the long-lost shield of Achilles to his desk and rubbed it with a duster. This had zero result. Amira fearing some rogue chemical could be applied snatched it away and said she wanted it just as it was. "Ke!"

She nodded and Mattie jabbed her bottom…not as a sexual thing but as a 'let me please' signal.

She smiled and let the men shout jabber and generally argue all kinds of uphill and down dale penny pinch and general worrisome diatribe until they had thrown her money about and suffered masculine petulance and general wringing of souls. The price was decided. 35 Euro. End of…they at least had it wrapped in paper that had obviously been invited to many parties and had been around and reused since Noah had followed the white dove.

Once they had walked down and away from the shop. They both exploded with laughter. Bought cool beers and returned to Pagan.

Captain Coulson was very maudlin drunk and gave them bear hugs…left them in sole charge of the yacht while he and his companion of old…a roguish looking deeply tanned man who reminded Amira instantly of Pablo Ruiz Picasso left on the tender to continue the drinking reverie on shore.

She thought the two exalted drunks were more like pirates than pirates ever could be. Mattie declared…

"This funniest time since I was in Sally's play…Je sui famme."

They plundered the galley and ended up with omelette fin herbe' and set chips to fry. Sally was still on a spoilt rotten jaunt with Felix and Ludi. Mattie had chilled the Spanish beers carefully and they thoroughly enjoyed them as they ate and drank and went over the nonsense in the shop with the dusty rubbish and laughed until their sides ached.

Amira held up the shield which was actually a bit of alright once they had cleaned it the way they cleaned Pagan Arrows metals. They could see their reflections and wanted to read the inscription on the back, so Amira fetched cotton buds. She dipped them in a little hot soapy water first and faint lettering emerged. The shock on her face was evidently good news shock.

Mattie applied a little pressure with a new cotton bud. Puzzled as he grimaced and said, "Perhaps made in Calcutta…who will know."

"No, it's Greek Mattie…Greek."

He shrugged and plodded off to shower and Amira sat with the burnishing cloths and cotton gloves rubbing and happily crowing over her prize. For some reason Winkles was fascinated by the cotton gloves and as Amira pulled them on to start burnishing once more, he lay down and began wiggling on his back and proceeded to play pat paw with the gloves. He loved them…she tickled his tum and he began a game of boxing with his feet against her arms.

"You nutty puss…do you love white cotton gloves. You are so crazy."

He scooted away when she opened the polishing liquid.

Pagan was rocking gently at anchor and Mattie and Amira prepared Pagan for the night, they set her lights twinkling at mast head, fore, aft, port and starboard. The black sky of the Mediterranean came down to meet the cobalt waters. Peace reigned. On shore, Cueta life had swallowed the rest of the crew. Sally was staying in a cheap hotel (if there was such a thing) with Ludi and Felix. In the fair light of day, Amira thought it all a very expensive set up. People were finely dressed…Cueta had no sign of wear and tear… She kept first watch until Mattie took over, then showered and went to bed tingling from the damn good scrub she'd given her skin. Sleep was instantaneous without Sally tossing about. All in all, a successful day.

Next morning, she made coffee and Mattie yawned and went below to sleep. Alone with Pagan, Amira retraced her recent life mentally. No really unhappy thoughts came until she recalled Yasmin and her mistake…Captain Coulson was right, no way could she sail away with them…this was obvious. Even if they had the finances for forging vital papers…the risk to Pagan and her crew was too great. The only answer was to help her get a train to another part of Egypt. Perhaps secure a job as a guide at Abu Simbel.

Amira had vital contacts there. Yes, that was possible. Yasmin would surely have an identity card; travel was impossible without one in any part of the country. All new laws directives and government security had tightened since the terrorist threat had put red alerts on the country's long borders. It was a puzzle and no mistake. Going below deck Amira located the shield…sure it was probably a cheap tourist copy of some famous historical artefact, but it glowed beautifully now in the cool dark of their cabin. She hung it up on the wall in a spare space.

"Yes, that's exactly right." The snake goddess Wadjet suddenly came to mind. Amira felt quite mentally invigorated by this.

Sally and Ludi waved from the tender and were soon on board chatting excitedly. "I stayed in a proper bed Mummy, it was enormous. I had rolls and some onions and huge tomatoes on steak. Oh, and a fruit ice cream with a banana swimming in it, it was really funny then I got sick and went to bed. Where's Winkles?"

"He might be curled up asleep. Let me find your pyjamas…thank you, Felix, she must have worn you out."

"Yes, we forgot how you have to watch kiddies of her age twenty-four seven. Did you get your shield?"

"Thanks yes, it would not have been possible without you two and Mattie…we got it for 35 Euro, but it was a struggle."

"Well, she's worn us out with her prattle and so demanding…questions and then they require more explanations…I often got stuck. Ludi has a headache."

"Oh, I am so sorry does she need tablets I have…"

"All in hand we found a pharmacy."

"Look do let me pay for Sally's meals."

"Lord bless you, we mucked it all in with ours…you will just have to let it go…"

"Well, huge thanks I have had a real break."

"Excellent, I am on the cleaning duty this lunchtime so better get started."

Captain Coulson came back in the evening very worse for wear. Amira was very firm with Sally about noise and told her to behave nicely…give them all a bit of peace. Spanish towns cities and flamenco in general was quietened down to drawings of ladies with dubious outfits and Winkles sporting a black, home-made Mantilla. Which he was not happy about and eventually had a tear up to shreds boxing class with. Sally was mortified. Sulking was high on the agenda.

Amira was forced to hide from Sally because she saw the truly funny side of the shredding of the mantilla the way that Winkles fought this black lacy foe by scrambling it up in all paws and growling it into submission and finally tearing the ensemble to shreds. The final battle of the Mediterranean! Eventually, Captain Coulson surfaced. He looked pretty bad he must have had a doozey of a head and stomach by the way he grimaced. Amira took pity and made up some fizzing Seltzers. He drank it down and then retired to his cabin again. Being ill like that on a rolling deck is vile. Pieter and Jim filled the breach, and all was good on board as Pagan Arrow flirted her beautiful lines over the sea towards Lebanese waters and Tripoli. Phoenician traders once plied their cargos here and many living today along this coastline proudly trace ancestors back to the times of the great trading days. Modern El Mina covers ancient sites far too well for archaeologists to get to ancient artefacts. The rich history of Northern Lebanon. During the Ummayad, Abbasid and Fatimid periods Tripoli became a fascinating financial centre for the Phoenicians with sea trade extending throughout the

Eastern and Western Mediterranean. Their alphabet contained twenty-two letters standardising major sounds. Along with their famous purple dyes…sailors traded textiles, wood, glass, metals, incense, papyrus and carved ivory. It is said that noted merchant traders were colonisers of the Mediterranean as far back as the 1st Millennium BCE.

During this enervating part of the voyage, Amira began to come into her own. The nearer to Egypt she drew, the more alive she felt. At one point she even dived off the boat when they dropped anchor to catch a few fish…a rare sighting of a lively shoal had the men excited as fish were fewer now in the Mediterranean than ever before in history. Amira slipped into the water like a nymphet once they had caught their fill. Ludi was envious and managed with Felix helping her to half fall in laughing. The two women frolicking like dolphins…with all the happy landing of fresh fish going on, Winkles was driven crazy by the gutting of the fish for the freezer and demanded a head. This he chomped on with an appetite and then pounced upon another flapping individual…growling most horribly. When he let it go, Pieter grabbed the poor fish and dispatched it at once. Winkles looked disgusted and sauntered off to bewail his misfortune. Amira swimming happily with Ludi until it became a little chilly, they found getting back on board a lot harder than getting in due to numb fingers. What a lovely day that was. The supper prepared by a refreshed Ludi was the best anyone ever remembered. Fish fresh as any ever could be. Absolute heaven. Sally gave some of hers to Winkles who was crazed with delight. Pieter gave a speech.

"Here's to good fishing and the Med' Captain Coulson, Pagan Arrow and all who sail in her." The next day, Mattie was beaming…he had tied one of his famous labels on the tea urn…it read, QUEUE DE CHEVAL.

But of course…what else. Life was good now with sun, sea, sparkling waves and happy thoughts. Tristan was smiling invitingly at Amira, and she was writing love messages to Riku. Winkles strode about in an overtly official capacity of fish connoisseur.

He suited the part beautifully.

They all wanted to see Tripoli. The lots drawn gave Amira second visit. The tender went off with Sally, Captain Coulson, Tristan and Jim. A peculiar mix. All the world knows that headache tablets would be in short supply tomorrow. Although Mattie was good at so much, he could not really get his head around sketching. Amira gave it her best shot and drew their part of the coast from Pagan including a little of the rigging, Pieter who was very fine in his maths helped a great deal with advice on dimensional matters…to avoid rubber marks. The result was a reasonable rendition which Mattie was thrilled with. He would treasure this. Amira glowed with pride it was nice to thank him for his help with the shield. She could never have made that purchase. The merchant was such a difficult man, hard as nails.

When the tender returned, Sally threw up all over the deck the tender was 'bouncy' apparently. She was okay just needed a lie down and a wet flannel. Captain Coulson was a no-nonsense doc and Sally threw no tantrum and obeyed him. Amira delighted that Sally was totally fine and obedient for the captain went off with the others to Tripoli. For to miss this opportunity would be unthinkable.

One bouncing tender later, they all arrived and made a beeline for a restaurant that prepared kibbeh which is the national dish…it was lovely, so tasty a sort of emulsified paste of fresh lamb and bulgur wheat with spices. Mattie thought they should try to make it on board… What they loved about Tripoli was no sharp sneaking winds. The harbour being more or less naturally formed. The hive of activities, sailboats, trade and connections all along the coastline enjoyed by Turkey, Syria (when not in conflict) Lebanon and Egypt.

This half-moon shaped gulf of El-Mina provided shelter from the North East winds that create strong currents and deep waters.

The Port of Tripoli is independent both administratively and financially. The coastal breakwater shelter is a good Anchorage of 17.1–18.2 metres. There is a little humidity.

They walked about and finally took a taxi to the famed Mameluk Mosque built from 1294–1314. They admired this the largest of the Crusader fortresses. Amira knew very little of its history and earwigged in on a local guide instead.

When it was time to return to Pagan Arrow they were tired, but in a good way. The sea was calm now with the sun setting and the twinkling lights on board the beautiful Pagan welcomed them back in a cheery manner.

Sally was sound asleep. Amira showered off the sweat of the day and snuggled down in her bunk opposite and began sleeping instantly. A great day. Vital chores and minor repairs made the next day a normality and soon they were weighing anchor and heading back out to a stiff breeze that stayed on Pagan Arrow's aft for two days…courtesy of the weather gods. Captain Coulson was showing a new way to handle such a breeze to Jim and Amira.

'Lively as she goes' was a saying that Amira grew to understand meant a lot of little tweaks in the rigging to take advantage of such a direct kick in the ship's rear so to speak. Nobody was let off this speed driven nautical mile gobbling part of the voyage…then nothing. They barely glided over a smooth sea as if the Mediterranean slept.

"This won't last long; we will pick up a wind off the desert soon and that's a fast wind."

Pagan Arrow made excellent anchorage at Tobruk. Once an historic settlement named Antipyrgos offering a major harbour for the Hellenic states. This port certainly has seen incredible scenes. Oddly, it has never been systematically surveyed. During the Italo Turkish War in 1911 Tobruk was the landing point for 35,000 Italian soldiers.

Fast forward to WW2. The port became one of the most valuable deep-water ports in North Africa. Fortified by 12,000 British and Indian troops and 14,000 Australian.

The German General Rommel surrounded the port…besieging the troops resulting in the Siege of Tobruk.

Amira Ludi and Sally were happy to go off to a darling little café they were told about in the town. The men wanted to see the war memorials, and tanks etcetera.

Amira did not envy them one bit. The café/restaurant was brilliant, and they all tucked into couscous Garbanzo beans and minced beef with veg. The chef was lovely and so friendly and fun…he was more than happy to flirt outrageously with Ludi who longed to get the recipe to try this magnificent looking dish on the rest of the crew. Amira teased her as they left waving and blowing kisses to the brilliant staff…that with very little effort on her part Ludi could have married the lovely chef who was handsome, friendly and fun. She had to agree he had a certain panache. After a quick look in a shop that sold trinkets for dancers. Much to Sally's disappointment the merchant was wily fierce and unbendable. They left empty-handed. He remained empty tilled. There is stubborn and there is bloody foolish. Shame. They also noticed his shop was consistently avoided by all passers-by. They returned to Pagan Arrow to give Pieter Tristan and Jim their 'go'…Amira helpfully made a clear map of how to find the fun café with the delicious food.

There was no chance of the men drinking, as alcohol is totally banned in Libya…also there was a horrible case of alcoholic poisoning from drinking Black Market booze. So that source was far too risky.

No headaches no hangovers!

They returned to Pagan happy but truly worn out. Luckily, Ludi was saved from galley duties as the rest of the crew had stuffed themselves silly at the brilliant café.

"Oh God they spoilt us Ludi, no kidding…we told them you recommended them showed them the map. They are so in love with you, what hospitality."

"Glad you loved it. Amira was in her element there…it must be wonderful to understand people here."

They were soon all back on board and weighing anchor was done reluctantly… They would soon be in Egypt… A fair wind accompanied them to Alexandria, and they made it in 40 hours sailing before a helpful wind that was in Amira's terminology-

'The very breath of Isis herself the goddess of resurrection'.

Pieter was fascinated.

"But isn't that the name of some terrorist faction?"

"They stole it like they do everything…Isis is the winged one who sought her Osiris…when he was tricked by his evil brother Set into getting into a wooden chest. He bolted him down and threw him in the Nile."

"Oh, and this is big story in the Egyptian history."

"There is none bigger…in my estimation."

Ludi and Sally packed for the pyramids. Captain Coulson called them to the chart room.

"Your destination I think Amira. What I need to tell you is we have paid up for ten days here…it's expensive, but I won't play with your good sense. I ask only that you do nothing to endanger yourselves. Or, and this is most important, you risk nothing for crew and the safety of this vessel."

"My plan Captain is we take the train to Cairo, and we will be staying at this hotel. It is a three-star overlooking the pyramids.

Naturally, this may be Ludi's and Sally's one opportunity to visit in their lifetime. Keeping this in mind, we thank you most sincerely for our safe passage and will not endanger you or Pagan."

He hugged them all in turn.

They were soon in the tender with all the shipping around them. They took all the information they would need for returning to Pagan and once they were at the quayside reported to the passport and visa desk. Outside they found an Internet café and Amira located their hotel online.

She rang Mohammed's number he was chief reception there and the second he heard her voice he exploded with joy.

"Madam Amira, oh my God Allah Akbar it is too much for my heart. Sayeed tahally dillwat…it is our Madam Amira…"

"You are well I think habibi…"

"Me more bloody welled than well. Please to tell me how many coming."

"Three dear azziza…my friend Madam Ludovic and daughter Sally. Can you let us have a room please."

"I will build a bloody room if there isn't one. Let me see we have a balcon room you see great pyramid and it have two lovely single beds with room for small bed, your daughter will be happier there than at home. What time is your train, azzizi…"

"We make the midday train and will come direct to you."

"You need my car, dear one."

"La shukeran we will find good person to come directly. Ma fiche mushkillah habibi ashouf badayn Allah kaleek."

"Ashouf badayn Allah keleek."

Amira wiped tears from her eyes. So beautiful Mohammed was well and all became tears for her. She was in the land she loved.

"Oh, Mummy, you're crying does your side hurt?"

"No my love, Mummy is very happy to be in Egypt with you and Ludi."

They hurried out and Amira read the buses that squealed everywhere up down in and out for the people's servees. The station was murder…they found the ticket office and after queuing patiently and muttering a good deal had to run like Billy goats for the midday train, they were so out of breath they collapsed with their bags on the scruffy seats, and all blew out huge breaths of relief.

"We made it Mummy didn't we? We made it."

"We most certainly did…look Ludi the drinks trolly is coming grab it quickly…"

The laughter and the joy was uppermost and they even closed their eyes briefly. Sally was snoozing as she lay across her mother's lap. Amira stroked her daughter's hair…finding a brush she gently smoothed the pale brown curls away from her little girl's brow.

"There is something very restful about watching you do that Amira."

"Ludi, I know Yasmin is in trouble but being truthful I could not be happier. You will love the room Mohammed has set aside for us. He uses all sorts of funny expressions and curses like a cowboy. But has the biggest heart of anyone I know."

"Oh, I could tell you two were real old friends."

"He represents all that is good about Misr."

"Misr?"

"Kemet…Egypt."

Once they had arrived at The Pyramid Funduk…Sayeed ran out and helped them all in. Mohammed crying and laughing pulled them in and could only say…

"Allah Akbar Allah Akbar."

"What a day this is Madam Amira… my lucky stars this one for the television… I want you be happy here. Ah your friend is beautiful…this curly one is your Sally… come sit with Mohammed my honey cake."

It was useless to refuse anything, and they were treated to a lovely time… Mohammed was ticked off by the owner for neglecting other new guests. He may as well have talked to a wall. Mohammed bowed his head and as soon as the owner had returned to his office…Mohammed waved naughtily to the owners back and arranged for Amira and Ludi to be helped upstairs and they thanked him for all his hospitality.

Ludi and Amira once they had showered sat out on the balcon in a cooling breeze. The heat had been stifling.

All the world knows of the pyramids, so Amira kept quiet…let them speak for themselves. The sun was not far off from setting and Khufu's Great pyramid was gilded and the whole scene bathed in heliotrope colours like a massive film set. Except of course it was real.

Ludi rang Felix and told him how fab it all was. The men were planning things but work and watching Pagan Arrow was of course still going on.

"Gawd in heaven, Amira, it's a spectacular scene…small wonder you love this country."

Amira eventually rang Samier who was thrilled. A little tone in her voice put Amira on edge.

She related this quickly to Ludi.

"Something else is afoot Ludi, I just know it is. Egyptians have a way of using a certain voice…you know when they are holding something back."

"Can she bring Yasmin here. Isn't Yasmin living with her husband's family now?"

211

"Yes, and he is a really nice man apparently has treated Yasmin with great respect and kindness. Yet still she's wanting out."

"Well, we can only advise…to aid and abet her to run from a kind husband is madness. The police will be on his side. A Muslim country and all that entails. She cannot expect you to risk your passport."

"I won't, don't worry. A black stamp for such a breach of our visa conditions would be the end for me in Cairo."

"When you see her perhaps she will have calmed down by then."

Amira nodded but felt there was some awful premonition lining up, she knew Samier was not being totally candid.

They settled in and Mohammed was kind and attentive. He spoilt Sally but Amira knew it might do her good to have such a lovely example of a truly genuine fatherly figure for once…not that Felix was not kind, but she felt Sally would benefit from how real doting parents behaved. Her ex could learn a thing or two here that was for sure. Sally adored Mohammed and once was dressed up in a spotless outfit and 'helped' the tolerant humorous man by copying all his mannerisms. The guests of course were delighted and even those that were a little bit funny about precocious seven-year-olds let it pass. It was funny but Sally took to Mohammed so strong that he said she was him all over again!

Ludi was pulling excruciating faces at the pairs handling of guests and when finally, the owner returned to the hotel it was to many behind the scene signals… Oddly, he was just in time to see a little girl of seven scamper into the lift. The reception appearing as normal.

So, he scratched his head and went back to his computer screen to see how much money he was now worth.

Amira could enter the sites easily and freely, courtesy of her Antiquities Department status. However, as soon as they set foot on rubble and sand at Giza they were soon 'adopted' by a couple of noisy camels who were still munching breakfast and not well pleased at this disturbance. She haggled with the keeper for rides as it was beyond expectations to deprive Sally of such noisy company.

So, they were hoisted onto them and Sally clung on with her mother as excited as she had ever been in her entire life. The keeper loved to make her laugh which was not conducive to staying safely on. This meant of course Ludi had to be helped by a dear little boy. Naturally, Ludi was terrified. However, it was the type of terror that includes laughter but of a hysterical kind. They harrumphed around the site and Amira paid the keeper his dues. He wanted to wait for them like a taxi but Amira was firm, and instead took his mobile number…in case they needed him again. He was very happy at this and wandered off to invite some other tourists to ride Nefertari and Cleopatra, Khufu's camel daughters. Ludi was much happier to walk even in the stifling heat. They took Amira's advice and wore sun hats. Sally was in awe of her mother's easy manner with guides, camel keepers and guards, they all nodded in great easy politeness and deference to her as she babbled away to them all in Arabic. It must have been very beautiful to speak so nicely with these fierce looking people. Sally noticed her mummy treated everyone with very nice manners. These are the ties that bind. The sweet blend of understanding and diplomacy a visual living play in progress of how to behave in a country where the history goes way back to where rock art displays simple lines beautifully, artistically conveying a clear message of the birth of an intellectual civilisation 7,000 years in the making. Where a Pharaoh once held the crook and the flail.

In the hubbub of life, it is good to be in respect of such a history. Amira was soon surrounded by eager listeners…Sally could tell that here deep in the bowels of the great pyramid built to take Pharaoh Khufu to his gods in the afterlife…was her own dear mummy's office. It was funny really as she watched people ask her mother this and that and how her mother patiently spoke of the 4th Dynasty in Egypt with its thousands of workers, stone masons, carvers, artists.

Cooks' bakers and beer makers all orchestrated over one task which took twenty years to complete. And the fact that Khufu had vanished…there certainly was no sign of him anywhere. Sally thought he might have changed his mind and gone somewhere else. The thought of tomb robbers in the dark of these great carved out spaces gave her shivers. Her mother noticed this and politely told the people that now if they didn't mind, she wanted to be with her daughter and friend… They all tutted of course but let her mummy go. Amira led Ludi and Sally out into the sun once more. They saw Menkhare's tomb then headed for the restaurant and the toilets to bathe hot foreheads.

Once settled with a menu Ludi was curious.

"Sorry to make you work again Amira, but I don't get how they thought it would take Khufu to the Circumpolar stars."

"That's the way their belief system had instilled itself deep into their psyche. There simply was no argument. Only they called them the Indestructible Ones. The Pharaoh was not an all-in package holiday experience for them. He was a Golden God from a place they had been identifying with as 'supernatural' since they were babes in arms. Even in the bible of the Christian worshippers is the phrase,-'Our father who is our God who is in heaven'. Stolen liturgy direct from the Ancient Priests of Egypt. Which was called Kemet back then…but we won't go into that at present."

"Really, and they thought of them like a place you could get to."

"Yes. Priests prayed and chanted daily for the Pharaoh because his whole life was dedicated to this great journey into the next life…that's why the Egyptians made chambers to store so many of the things from this life to help them in what they believed with their entire beings was to be their next life. Also guiding the solar boat to the stars…"

"But if he isn't there Mummy, he made it to the stars then didn't he Mummy?"

Amira hugged Sally…she hadn't the heart or indeed the energy to go over the truth again. That some even believed Khufu changed his mind and sought the priests of Abydos and was interred there as a simpler solution to risking the wrath of enemies made in life who would not think twice about stripping his mummified remains for jewels, and ransacking the chambers for inlaid furniture and fine Canopic jars containing his poor old organs.

It was indeed a great thing to fathom.

They decided to view the Sphinx or Harmakhis Khepri Atum Ra as Amira named the great lion… once the sun had gone down. So they returned to sit in comfy cool seats in a special sound and light show the following evening.

This to Sally was even more exciting… her mother seemed to really love this great big lion with the bashed-up face. Sally decided she would watch everything.

Ludi stated categorically that the night was wonderful. She thought the sun much too hot. She also was more than a little afraid of the camels.

These things unravel gently to us. Within the wisdom of hindsight.

Amira admitted openly…

"Yes, Harmakhis is of a greater interest to me I admit. Once, some thousands of years ago all this area was verdant and lush with trees.

There were palms abundant with dates. Offerings of beer, onions and tasty treats, sheaths of lotus would be placed before the great lion. There is much strange information coming forth that the figure was neither man woman or beast but a symbolic union of all powerful deities which command attention and granted many favours over centuries. There were whole families of servants who tended this great figure. Nothing was considered too great to bestow and place between the paws. The fact is this great lion was even painted a deep rich red for hundreds of years."

Ludi had her mouth open.

"No really…that's amazing. You think it's older than they say?"

"Oh Ludi I cannot go into that. The controversy is too great."

"Oh I see."

They sat quietly as the Sound and Light show began and a version most acceptable and greatly watered down and dramatically adjusted for touristic pleasure was performed as to how and why the great Harmakhis Khepri Atum Ra came to be there in the site facing forever to the horizon. Patient, beautiful, and powerfully ordained…known the whole world over outside of Egypt by the Greek name Sphinx.

A mystery indeed a riddle still to be solved.

Amira could never forget the poems and verse songs (like hymns of thanks) left by scribes or priests one of these fragments of papyri…stating openly and more importantly without restraint of any kind…

"I place before her the goddess between her divine paws the offerings giving gratitude praise and all honours as she raised us up from terrible poverty this being truth for while we served her, she gave us our home and comforts. I place food refreshment before you great red lady the way you placed beer and refreshment before us."

Great red lady!

Was this goddess a truly matriarchal influence. What was their name those many centuries before the great changes of worship for this leonine figure serene and all knowing. Witnessing the myriads of years, the wheeling constellations.

The comings and goings of earthly beings.

No mention of Khufu or pyramid—(Interestingly.)

One mystery defies explanation—a rumour within textual evidence on papyri—that Khufu went to consult with Harmakhis where he should build his pyramid.

Many people sense a tangible 'sacredness' at the site…perhaps an even more ancient receptacle or shrine of gods and goddesses once graced this truly enigmatic plateau called Giza from its older name Gizeh. There of course was a great square stone once long ago with a massive carved bird…Horus the Falcon

215

god, the people walked around this clapping and chanting. A famous Egyptian director had included this within one of his really old black and white films.

The people still show this film during certain festivals. Whenever Amira asked about it from the village people, they would look a bit awkward...and say... "Before."

They would not elucidate. Amira thought this meant before Islam. Imams would not like to admit they had smashed a much older Icon of devotion. This covering up was such typical behaviour. People find it easier to pretend they are not an invaded country. Beheading is a ghastly provocation.

Amira always left more mystified than she arrived. Time hides so much with heavy veils of yesterdays. Returning to the hotel they all settled down with hot chocolate...it had turned chill out there so near the desert at night. Amira woke the next morning groggy and bad humoured blaming the telephone for interrupting an interesting dream. Scrabbling for the receiver she gave a hoarse.

"Yes, Asif, salaam."

"Amira it is Samier, Yasmin asks me tell you come quickly to her home I will come for you now and take you in my brother's sayyara we will come twenty minutes." Amira sat bolt upright fuming at such liberty taking to be ordered around in such a way.

She breathed in and out slowly...Ludi had surfaced with tousled hair looking across irritated and puzzled.

Amira stared at the receiver in disbelief and in hushed tones stated furious as hell...

"Samier you are not to blame for this bloody audacity... Tell Yasmin that we have all crossed the Atlantic and most of the Mediterranean. She can cross Cairo and come here this afternoon at 3 pm for tea with us to talk."

With this she replaced the receiver.

Ludi gave a look as if to say... She's got a bloody nerve. Well done Amira.

Ludi unpacked a travel kettle...they made coffee Canadian style rummaged for shop bought biscotti all the while looking across at Sally who resembled a darling angel with her tumble of sunny curls.

Sneaking to the balcony they breathed the tangy air of early desert perfumes that welled up seemingly from geological mysterious depths to tease and please.

"This is a splendour I will never forget Amira thank you for all of this."

"Ludi, do you know you make the best of all things...I love you for that alone."

"Did you love me when I jumped off Pagan Arrow that time so clumsily, I made you swallow a great galumph of seawater, was that my finest hour would you say?"

"By far."

They chuckled into their coffee cups.

"Tell me if I am wrong Amira, but that Yasmin girl is mighty bloody cheeky, good for you speaking out. I heard what the girl said I could not help that could I."

"You talk away dearest this is Yasmin all over. Wants to plan her day. She's probably shocked to hear that for once I am not following her orders. The nerve. We are three she is one, she can't bleat any more about being held prisoner."

"Sally is awake Amira."

They breakfasted properly downstairs and wore long cool dresses because the heat was already building, joined by a Cairo vanilla mist with an overlay of petrol fume laden atmosphere which changed every distant outline to a soft impressionism painting but of an Egyptian kind.

The receptionist sent a message through for them. "Yes Yasmin will come with her sister-in-law at three pm. Also, a Mr Captain Arrow? Will come at 4.30 pm."

Everyone laughed. Ludi was greatly amused and when the messenger left added.

"Captain Arrow with his lady-wife Pagan."

"Captainess Pagan wore clothes of shimmering gold she was not so very young, yet not so very old."

This 'naturally' set Sally off singing it to everyone and anyone in general. Dancing with the jolly and incredibly tolerant waiters who adored children. She helped them clear tables and was very precocious indeed. Amira snatched at her skirt as she once more hurried from the kitchen and being stopped in her tracks in this manner was most put out.

"Now, young lady, we are cleaning our teeth and strolling to the souk. You are coming with us."

The little scamp giggled, escaped, and then took several more plates to the kitchen defiant and triumphant. Then with compressed lips meekly came up and said, "Sorry Mummy."

Amira set her face firmly and all three trooped out with nods and apologetic walking.

217

The souk was shaded…which Ludi was grateful for. They found a few souvenirs for the crew, Amira held up a fabulous scarf with a very deliberate manly design and mouthed… "Mattie."

Ludi and Sally gave the thumbs up sign together. After this, a little café of a scruffily quaint school of design caught their attention and they sipped cold drinks. Sadly, the toilets of this establishment were a cross between a hole in the floor and a midden of stinky mucky urine. Amira handed out wet wipes…Ludi tried not to breathe deeply and was forced to hide a real grimace of distaste behind a scarf drawn across her mouth. Sally, not yet finished in diplomacy school niceties gave exaggerated Ughs and Oh yuks. Which were at least accurate.

Everyone nodded as they paid and left. Amira's Arabic led to a moderate charge and not an inflated one.

"They seemed not to think of mops and disinfectant in there did they Amira?"

"I know Ludi, that's the worst I ever saw in a long time. Perhaps we could post them a mini mop and some bleach!"

"Oh darling stop, they would probably keep it as too clean and precious to use like in Stella Gibbons 'Cold Comfort Farm'."

"There have always bin Starkadders at Cold Comfort Farm."

She managed to get out before giggles set them all off.

This of all things that had unfolded that day set Amira laughing with tears rolling down her face.

They sauntered back in heat that could cook an ox. Showers were followed by exhausted snores on their beds. Phew! What a time it was. Before Ludi fell asleep she said softly to Sally.

"Nobody told us it would be so amusing all this history."

Amira smiled and closed her eyes. Bless.

Strangely, it was Captain Coulson who showed up first for the afternoon tea party. For that is what it turned into.

Amira ordered some food as they had all missed lunch and anyway, they could enjoy eating much more during this cooler hour of the day with the umbrellas shade to sit under and cold tiles for soothing the feet. Sally was happy to sit with Captain Coulson who was noisily drinking down light beer and smacking his chops for Sally's benefit. Amira thought…oh hell this will lead to naughtiness of the irritating kind.

"Captain Coulson, I wanted to say thank you for all this and to let you know Yasmin is coming to say hi."

"Oh, let out of prison now is she."

"Yes, married and feels better. She's as bossy as ever so I will apologise in advance."

"Yes but a man can steady up a flighty dinghy very quickly."

Sally ever alert for humour and possessing curious ears spouts up.

"No Captain, she's a girl not a flitty dinghy—duh."

Any reply was cut short as a waiter brought a very chubby woman with only a slightly less curvy one to their table...the scuffle for chairs and two extra places covered up a certain awkwardness.

Amira hugged her old pal. Thinking 'jeeze she's filled out'. Both Egyptian women were in Western garb of a faintly unfashionable blend. Yasmin had her large shoulder bag and carried a holdall. Which was as mysterious as it was lumpy.

"It's so good to see you at last... This is Mona my sister-in-law. Hosna wanted to come but felt too tired."

Mona smiling while she pulled constantly at her unfamiliar skirt. Missing her long dress...which hid her ample figure so well. "My English shwia shwia."

Captain Coulson came to a gentlemanly rescue. "Don't worry, lass, you're among friends...do you like chicken and salad c'mon eat up."

And she did. Food being her constant refuge she munched daintily with her dear little fat sausage fingers, smiling and appreciative. One of the young waters taking sneak peaks at her round chubby face. High plump breasts. She was obviously to his liking! Yasmin sneakily wrangled the seat next to Amira and whispered.

"The other sister is ginormous...my husband is like a hippo darling, Amira, you have to get me away. It's like being a kept haroof fattened for Ede."

"I don't ever lie to you Yasmin; we don't know how we can bring that about. Egypt is a country with very different laws customs and regulations and the like. We simply can't aid you to run off and leave him."

"Why not."

"Oh, darling is he cruel to you like your mother."

"Don't go into any of that now Amira I want to visit that fabulous yacht, he's the owner isn't he the captain the one belching beer."

"Yes he is the owner you can ask him about a couple of nights on board with us... It will be a squeeze."

The kitchen brought them even more food and a waiter hovered with fresh minted chai.

Amira thanked him.

"Thank you, Madam."

He nodded polite and good natured as every person here under Mohammed's skilful management was.

Yasmin wiped her mouth and bold as ever visited Captain Coulson's side of the table.

He stood and took her hand.

"You must be Madam Yasmin—Forsa Saheeda."

Yasmin cleverly smiled and pulled out her best charm incentive. A chair came and she sat with the smiling eyes of a cobra beaming upon him. He poor fool fell under the spell of the snake who knows exactly how to subdue prior to the strike. Nobody but Amira of course knew of this tactic. Their conversation was subdued, and Amira had to listen to Sally talk nonsense about two kittens that were under chairs in the cool, playing with dropped food and pouncing on imaginary prey in the shadows.

"Oh, Mummy, that little one there oh are you sure they won't let me pick them up. Oh, so so sweet. Pleeeeze, Mummy, you can't know all the cats here in the hotel."

"These are from a feral mother Sally they don't get handled they are nothing like Winkles."

Sally impetuous to the point of anarchy ran to Captain Coulson at present mid drool over the charms of Yasmin...who was busily pouring forth the nectar of false modesty and sexual favours as a possibility from every pore in her now voluptuous body. No man could resist her almond eyes of dark lustrous promise. Edged delicately with kohl and a strong possibility of naked on a bed scenarios. He, the stupid fool was under the spell and false crooning of the siren on the rocks.

He was a 'gonner' and Amira knew he was a 'gonner'.

Nobody else caught onto this including Mona who was at last replete, and trying to mouth the word RECIPE...from Ludi's expert teaching. After all they had much in common.

Everyone else chattered away and Ludi continued a very odd conversation with Mona who was now scoffing her third piece of honey cake and slurping more chai greedy and content. Some are easily placated.

Sally was tugging impatiently at Captain Coulson's sleeve.

Amira thought this was excellent and saw how Yasmin shut up…

"Captain Coulson, Mummy said that these kittens." Points under the adjacent table for back up.

"These kittens."

"Yes, darling."

"They are not like Winkles."

He scooped one of the tumbling bundles up looked at its pure white tum and stated.

"Yes, I'm afraid the old chap Winky Woo has had no part in producing these pussies."

Sally furious tries to take the wriggling kitten but it won't have it and as Captain Coulson bellows out laughing, he drops the little chap on the tiles where it scoots like a miniature tiger for the bushes.

"See Sally my sweet matey not a bit like that randy ole Tom."

The tables were in uproar as he drank down another half glass of beer belched and then got stuck into half a roast chicken.

Amira was laughing with everyone else…until Sally proceeded to stamp about scolding the air. This was reminiscent of her father's antics…there was no doubt of that.

Amira took hold of her hand and marched her around the corner and with a very determined voice reprimanded her daughter soundly.

"Now, young lady, that is more than enough…"

She took Sally by the arm and led the child tearful and pouting fit to kill back to sit on the seat. Playing with a white napkin.

People said things like… "Such a naughty temper…too right, she has to learn."

The waiters having witnessed all…gave the corrected Sally sidelong glances. Which spoke volumes.

'We dare not interfere…guests you see guests'.

Amira explained,

"Sally is terribly sorry, over-excited by the kittens you see."

"I think we won't keel haul her today we'll grab her next week."

And with that Captain Coulson returned to making eyes with Yasmin.

Such a triumph is but a short-lived mist laden cloud in a hot desert sun.

Then the decision was made. Captain Coulson would be responsible for Yasmin and manoeuvred the next stage of the programme. He took her sister-in-law to a taxi and sent her home much frightened and rather mystified. All protest ignored. He'd won that round.

Then he got the staff to give smug Yasmin a room and as he'd already assigned himself one went off after generously signing the bill for all the food.

All Amira could do was sigh. Ludi came to her later in the room and sat with a much subdued Sally.

"Amira these things happen. All the world can see she's up to something, but men like him well they have different rule books to women."

"He will rue the day the great dumb fool."

"He will be sober later you'll see…he'll change his mind. Men do you know."

"She is not the same girl I knew, her mind is twisted. She will just use him I know it I know it."

"This is out of your control Amira. How were you to guess such an outcome."

"Well, she had better behave in our cabin that's all I can say. Sally, would you get ready for bed now please. Yes, and darling brush your teeth."

The little girl was quiet now and red-eyed. Life had these peculiar twists in them. She adored her mother and knew all too well that stamping in temper in public was a really big no no. Her heart was heavy but she silently trusted her mother's consistent fairness in this. Without which, well, she did not want to be with anyone else.

Amira never let the sun go down on her anger and read her subdued child a fairy story and tucked her in with Binx who was back on centre stage once more.

Amira kissed her daughter's little sun-tanned nose and snuggled her under the cool sheets.

"Night night darling."

And she whispered back, "Night night Mummy."

The little girl chastened and quiet. Closed her eyes.

Amira found her cigarettes and joined Ludi on the balcon.

In the distance the Pyramids were ethereal in a violet dusky light. An Egyptian moon half hidden in cloud cleverly chipped at the corner of one pyramid as if a light had been switched on in a room inside the great blocks of stone laid so dexterously in the 4th Dynasty. Ludi also lit a cigarette...it was that sort of evening.

"Look, Mrs Khufu is just going to bed."

Amira reached out to her pal and rubbed her shoulder affectionately.

"Gawd in heaven what a day it's been Ludi."

On Reflection

Captain Coulson took himself off complete with hangover and Yasmin to the station. They would be on board Pagan Arrow by midday all being well. Yasmin had left a sarcastic little note for Amira at reception. It read...

Ashouf badayn. See you later!

This was yet another going off with a strange man incident.

Ludi was stifling giggles and taking Amira's arm said candidly.

"Perhaps we will be back on board ourselves by four, so we can catch up with her 'little tricks' then don't you see?" Amira who was busily trying to plait Sally's unruly curls saw nothing but trouble ahead for the male members of the crew. She also sensed a weird outcome but had no clue as to what the hell it could be.

They packed up their clothes and duly mopped Mohammed's tears. Promising to return at the first opportunity. Many photographs were taken. To this very day, there is one on the main reception area of him standing with Amira Sally and Ludi. He was such a kind soul. His waiters gave Sally a little gift of a cat brooch. Her joy knew no bounds.

As they fastened the pretend diamond glitter to her blouse, her skips and laughter said all they wanted to hear. Amira tipped them all moderate amounts. Waving and tears were combined with Sally bouncing about in the taxi.

Amira prayed no kitten would show up. Ludi held a box of snacks made in the kitchen on Mohammed's orders.

"What a lovely hotel Amira, how lucky to know about it."

Amira hid her eyes it was upsetting for she had the oddest notion that she would not see Mohammed for some time.

"I have taken many groups there you see...it's moderate price and so close to the—"

"Pyramids."

"Yes."

The train was so busy they were lucky to get seats together but halfway to Alexandria the majority of people in their carriage piled off taking huge bundles bags and produce with them. The stifling air soon cooled.

Hot chai came around on the little trolley and Sally after an age spent admiring the 'diamonds of despair' as her mother called them…fell asleep. Children wear themselves out with pleasure.

"I wonder how Captain Coulson is faring now the gilt is finally off the gingerbread."

"Oh, darling Ludi, what a thought. Perhaps she will direct her gaze on Jim next."

"What do they call such women in Egypt?"

"Charmute."

"That's pretty actually."

Amira sipped truly refreshing chai and gazed out on villages wondering about the hundreds of lives of Egyptian people. The hard working the jealous and the serene.

On board Pagan Arrow Yasmin was sitting on deck with Tristan and Pieter. Mattie had taken against her at first glance. He spoke up to Captain Coulson…sober now as two judges he regretted wholeheartedly his foolish U-turn of letting such a salacious snake on board. Sober emotions having dictated a very new scenario.

"Why you bring a snake eyed female to Pagan… She is poison Captain… some cruel picture stays locked in her eyes…you not see this because a glass was raised!"

"Mattie, she will be leaving tomorrow and so will we. I have said okay okay okay to you and now want you to shut the fuck up."

"Mind she does go. Crete is my favourite island of them all I don't want her foot tainting it."

"She doesn't have papers so stow it. Find me the chart for Cretan waters make yourself useful."

Yasmin was as physically close to Tristan as she could get. He was driven along by sexual hunger for a woman. Also, he had a way with females and knew how to caress their egos. Yasmin thought him fantastic. Yes, he would serve her purpose very well. The jewels were safe in the cabin. She had hung them up…hidden in plain sight. Amira was such a pushover and even if the captain threw her off the boat. So be it. She caressed the beautiful ropes and shining metals. Taking a cloth as the others were doing, she polished vigorously making sure her derriere moved a lot and her breasts jiggled. Easy, easy, easy.

Amira would be pleased to see her at work. Wouldn't she? Those fools of an Egyptian husband and his water buffalo sisters would surely know by now they were history. Mona would be in deep trouble the fat bint. She had zero wit and as for Hosna…who would ever marry such a lump. Yasmin laughed as she recalled their simple-minded kindness their fine black moustaches across their top lips. She sang her favourite song 'Ma fiche…' an old one but a good one. The words seemed terribly mocking and strange to the men on board. They had absolutely no idea what the song was about. Her voice haunting and lyrical. The words in fact spoke of tragedy.

Mattie cursed the air around her. She gave him warning darts with those snake tongues in her dark cruel eyes. She had indeed become something very strange. She now engaged with dark secret forces of a design no man can configure. Oddly, it was because of those darting eyes Tristan wanted her. She knew this as fact. In his were a mischief all of their own (this pretty man this fiancée) stolen so easily from Amira. Yasmin laughed and moved along the deck next to him and shone what he had just shone.

He smiled as he watched her firm thighs. Yes, she would be a great and satisfying fuck. He lay her out mentally and shoved her legs apart…women loved that bit. He would lay heavily on her and get her worked up then as she panted and pleaded, he would tease her…oh that would do nicely. Yes, he wondered if she had access to money. She wore gold. She would be easy to manipulate after just one night of good sex. He sensed he could be hard and rough with her, in her and on her, and she would beg for more. He laughed and yes, he could certainly oblige.

There are always scenarios playing out in people's minds and Yasmin didn't like the cold winds off the quays. She soon went to the mess and Pieter ladled her out some delicious soup. The bread had run low, but supplies were coming on board that day. She tucked into the food hungry from so much fresh Mediterranean air.

Pieter was sweet but a little too gentle and well-mannered for her. She worked on him with her glances though because you never know when he might come in useful. Coulson was off the list. She had found him very unsatisfactory in the bedroom department. He'd slumped into a snoring heap after about a minute inside her. What a useless pig of a man. His breath stinking and his crude leering comments. She had hurried to Amira and Sally's cabin the instant he had started snoring and slept well with the gentle rocking of the yacht. Shame it belonged to the wrong man and not Tristan the beautiful. She noticed he had a strange sort of limp every now and then. Perhaps, it was the unsteady deck. Yes, that's what it was. By late afternoon, she was fully revived so she cleaned her teeth and then stretched out again on the bunk. Suddenly, she flew in a panic to where the jewels were hanging in her large leather bag, she adoringly began spreading them out on the bed covers crooning to them softly as if they could hear her. Folding them into their velvet nest once more she returned them to the shoulder bag. As she hung it up, a glint of metal caught her eyes. Amira had carefully burnished the old shield until it shone out like a sun in the tiny cabin. Yasmin caught sight of her reflection, so magical was the light radiating around her hair's rich raven black lustre.

She tried to smile but the shield suddenly distorted her image horribly and a ghoul with red eyes came back at her. She jumped back her hand flying to her mouth in horror. She threw a jersey over the shield in superstitious fear, dressed and went quickly back on deck. The quayside's busy clamour cheering her spirits once more. Her heart lifted strangely at the sight of Amira Sally and Ludi pulling a little wagon filled with luggage and a boy behind with another wagon… The provisions had arrived. All crew had been alerted and Felix woken up. The deck became a reunion of hugs and miss you so much cries.

Winkles stretched and ran to Sally who dropped her parcels and gathering him up began crying, "Winkles Winkles there you are."

Yasmin felt a tiny spark of her youth ignite as Amira hugged her along with everyone else.

They soon unpacked and Ludi happy to be off the train chattered with her beloved Felix once again as they got cracking on a feast to celebrate returning and congratulating each other on work achieved.

Amira soon had Sally fed and settled down. Yasmin actually helping.

"You are so lucky Amira this is a fantastic ship, I mean yacht. Ha ha I'm cleaning things Amira, actually tidy upping."

"Who would have known it Yas."

"Captain Coulson is very kind, but I see I can't stay magnoon to think I could."

"So, you will tell your hubby to expect you…We weigh anchor tomorrow we have to leave before a certain time you see Yas' because of the authorities

226

they will charge us for another whole day. We can't mess around with winds on a yacht like Pagan we get a sort of a clear window of opportunity. Wind and tide wait for no man."

"Ma alesh."

Amira relieved as hell that it all been understood snuggled down in the bunk beside the softly snoring Sally who had placed Binx close by on the tiny shelf and the diamond cat alongside with her other little gifts. A child's treasure trove. Night fell softly through the quay over the sleeping vessels…here and there a light flickered, but eventually all settled to rest.

Amira felt greatly satisfied that all had turned out so well in the end. Yasmin so quiet under the covers with her eyes closed. Amira fell fast asleep happily squeezed against Sally. Cuddled and snug. In the hours that followed. Only the chink, chink, chink of rigging offered sounds upon the breeze. Other noises too on the quayside, tiny scuffles and clunks. Perhaps seabirds restless with the coming dawn.

Gradually light slid perilous and pale like a shifting shadow through shara and suburb. Gradually a buttery glittering gold touched windows and far away down the Nile the pyramids seemingly sighed heavily. Taxi cabs waited with engines snuffling and grumbling at the early hour. A door closed and the beautiful Pagan Arrow returned to the magical embrace of sleep.

Ludi was disturbed by something which was unusual for her being such a sound sleeper. All was normal in the cabin, so she closed her eyes and drifted off again. For many years, she would wonder if she'd just been curious, things would have turned out very differently. But sleepy after travelling and chores her dreams claimed her once more.

Pieter was on night watch duty…anchors can drag and winds can rise he had not slept of course he was reliable on that score. But he had played games. He was a good sort of chap and strolled the deck from time to time in the night ensuring all was secure.

Captain Coulson showered himself awake and hurried to the galley to get the breakfast coffee rolling. He knocked at Jim's cabin which was shared with Pieter and Tristan. Pieter was soon sniffing in the dank morning air. Listening to the familiar sounds as other vessels came to life. Jim woke on his knock he had to take over from Pieter. So threw water on his face. He couldn't see Tristan so stumbled along to the Chart Room and looked over the route planned for the

Cretan Coast while he dried his face on a towel. Captain Coulson knew as soon as he sipped his coffee that something did not quite feel normal.

Jim came in and handed him an envelope.

"Good morning Captain, I found this in the Chart Room."

Reading it through twice, Captain Coulson stood up and whistled then lounged at the entrance to the Galley.

Jim felt prickles of danger over his skin.

"Pieter is going down for shut eye…"

"Of course, of course. Here Jim read this it will be common knowledge soon enough."

Jim scanned a few lines…

"Lumme this is fucking outrageous. She's soft in the head anyone could see that…"

"Yeah well, we don't all have your razor-sharp accuracy on personality Jim…she used to be clever…apparently."

"Tristan surely has an ulterior motive perhaps there is money in it somewhere."

"Nah I'm thinking a bit of running away for the thrill of easy sex and then he'll dump her."

Below deck Amira was woken up by Winkles scratching at the door…

"Sally, are you awake, let Winkles in or he will damage the paintwork… Yasmin's up early. No wait a minute, she's gone with all her stuff and the blooming nerve of her she's taken my bag with all our shampoo with her!"

"No Mummy, it's here…look." Sally had opened the door for the cat and so handed a heavy shoulder bag to her mother.

"I can't think straight without a coffee…but this isn't my bag."

"I can get you coffee Mummy, wait there."

Sally keen to make amends scampered off with Winkles to the galley her small bare feet barely making a sound on the boards. Amira opened the bag and stared at the folded jewel case beautifully velvet smooth and so neatly hand stitched.

She stared in disbelief…

"What the heck on an anointed Pharaoh's head is going on."

Then she realised Yasmin's easy mistake. Both bags were almost identical purchases from the same shop. In the darkness of the cabin, blue dyed leather would be like green dyed leather and vice versa.

228

There was no note. Yasmin had sneaked out and all the world knew where she had gone. The French Riviera was very high on her personal wish list, but without the hoard of gold…she was entirely sunk.

Amira dressed in some nice fresh clothes before placing the brilliant gold and jewels so exquisite in their old settings carefully away. Sally would tell the whole of Alexandria, not to be naughty but from sheer joy of discovery. Kids!

Sally brought coffee and was sucking noisily on a popsicle. Not an ideal breakfast for a growing girl.

Amira let it pass. She scrambled up the companion way and yanked the cleaning equipment out of stores. Then she saw Ludi!

"They've gone off together…"

"Sorry, who…oh right wait a minute Yasmin's sneaked off…"

"With our son."

"Ah I see. Well, it won't last…they have absolute zero in common."

"His father is furious. Amira darling, I have never ever in all our marriage seen him so livid. He won't take him back in. Never, he's sworn it."

"Oh dear Ludi he will, of course he will it's the shock. Tristan has no money. Well about twenty dollars or so and that won't get them to the Riviera."

"Do you think so do you really think he will take back such an ungrateful son. No Amira he will not."

"Come and have coffee and breakfast with me…no point in starving."

"You seem awfully upbeat for a woman who has lost her fiancé…"

"A not quite official one Ludi. No ring."

"I know you better Amira you know something we don't, tell us please."

"She's only got those cheap gold ear bobs and wedding ring…mmm let me see three sugars?"

"Yes, for shock. What do you mean I'm not with you?"

"They each think the other has money. Romance dries faster than tears when the…forgive my crude way…when money is spent and the sex has lost all its honeymoon edge."

"Well, yes I suppose but they don't even know each other."

"And both bad tempered. Sorry to tell you such a horrible truth at such a time but Tristan likes all his own way and has been…"

"Indulged…yes go on I know it's true. Such foolish spoiling. Our only child and no more came along."

"No good beating yourself up."

"Well, let me say it once Amira and I will try not to ever again…you're mighty calm and cool over your friend pinching your man."

"That's true, but tears would be wasted on such runaways. Hardly Romeo and Juliet. She is not going to stand his tantrums. Nor he hers."

"Well, you know her."

"Not this new version. Sure, she was great fun in our student days but this staying out for sex with a stranger my very first night back in Cairo well that finished off our real friendship and those doting parent's generosity. They are dreadfully culturally driven violent people under their clean clothes and pious prayers. How horrifically mean beating her. Now she has cruel eyes because of it…or I thought so. Once she was so, you know, maybe a little flirty yes, but nothing dangerous…now I wouldn't put any type of trickery or manipulation past her."

"Stop stop. I can't bear it. This hussy you describe has taken our son off to do God knows what God knows where."

"Surely you saw how she connived her way on board by flirting with Charles…he's a man, isn't he?"

"Yes, but surely he."

"He had plenty of opportunity and was squiffy. The old sayings are the true, Ludi when women go to the bad, men go right after them…but they don't stay! Tristan will come back…probably will be there waiting for you when you get home."

"I hope you're right Amira I hope you're right."

Captain Coulson was as chastened by the events as Sally had been after her ticking off and Pagan Arrow went out on a cheerful tide ploughing through a deep cobalt sea. He simply refused all begging from Ludi and would not wait around. After the crew meeting which was as noisy as a monkey temple at feeding time. They all trooped to various extra chores…being a man down. Captain Coulson shrugged it all off.

After all, he knew plenty of lads on Crete who were longing to ply the oceans in freedom with a good dinner thrown in. Mattie had kept his own council throughout. He soon chummed up at the wheel with Amira who was back on under occasional supervision. This crossing after all was now one member short. It took a day and a half give or take and they were on a fast steady run of swells. Mattie made for tiny adjustments and eventually spoke.

"My mind is tell me you are holding a secret Amira my good friend of the seas."

"I did wonder when you would click to it. Knew you would, sixth sense—and great insight."

He gave out a mighty laugh.

"Great wild bears know it all, they always smile through their eyes when the berries are in." Amira almost lost control of the coming set.

"Oh, that's priceless. I have not heard that since grandfather died bless his soul."

"Indeed, bless his spirit and all his far away dreams."

"You haven't made a label in a long while…why is that, Mattie."

"Oh that is a good idea wait there."

She thought that last remark highly amusing and watched the main sail tighten and relax, tightening and relaxing.

She called to Jim… "After this set, Jim…"

"Aye Aye."

And he scampered to the cleats.

Mattie was soon in attendance with her.

"Down hard starboard Amira she's not liking these side smacks." Amira adjusted and the deck became alive with all hands as the orders rang out. Felix eventually gave the order to…'steady as she goes'… The wind grumbled but remained steady. They were halfway now. A curtain of mist no doubt left from early morning, transformed into droplets sparkling in a myriad of colours like sequins which flew past her like some phantom from an unearthly kingdom.

"Weird stuff out here Mattie."

He was busy tying a label to the shiny brass on the wheel. She read it aloud.

"Golden Galleon Of Amira's Sea."

This silenced her with its accuracy.

Sally joined her and the three watched the sun climb feeling the heated anger set into its rays. Felix came back and took over. They swayed on the boards unsteadily as they went below deck.

Pieter was refreshed and sat down with Amira. Sally went off on an errand for Ludi. Peace reigned.

"She was a strange snake-like creature so Mattie says."

"Yes Pieter, he is spot on everybody listens to him."

"Tristan will only want money and sex we have seen him change very fast."

"Oh I think he was always like that Pieter just seeking an opportunity."

"I liked him sometimes."

"Well, he is a man's man."

"Mattie made an instant judgement he respects only you and disliked her on sight, saw trouble. You know…" He lowered his voice to a whisper… "She got into the sack with old Charlie boy."

Amira suspected it. Looked at the coffee pot and thought (of course of course).

"She had to get away any old how. Needed one man to help her and another to cover her track…Allay Captain Coulson's suspicions."

"Snake girl is Mattie's description."

Amira recalled very sharply and whistled. What was it Riku had said about these women in Japan.

She would ask him later. He knew such amazing things.

"You don't seem upset…I would be, a tawdry girl like that nicking my man…or…anyway you don't."

"What's done is done. I have a child to raise, after all it's a strange fact that recently he saw no future in anything sensible so maybe 'Strumpet's Clown' as a career might suit."

"Putting it that way, he had no natural yearning for working on this yacht he was a little blasé one could say."

"A lot blasé Pieter a lot."

Then they each ate a good dinner and returned to the extra work fairly divided by Mattie.

They eventually took a good run into a sheltered Cretan cove and dropped two anchors for safety.

However, at least they were no longer buffeted… This short blow had been forecast so Captain Coulson had wisely taken them into the cove as a precaution. Once Pagan was 'bedded down' he called them together and set to spreading a colourful map of Crete out on the galley table.

"We are here which costs nothing and the blow as expected has moved Easterly over here beyond the point. It can get nasty off Crete, often prevents the ferries from putting to sea out of Heraklion."

"Amira you have her history what can you tell us. I know you do know."

"Thank you Captain. Yes, over the past centuries almost the whole of the Mediterranean was trading to and fro various fine goods with Crete called Kriti as written so beautifully here…especially amphora because they are so useful for the vital storage of wine, oil, grain etcetera and so elegant and beautifully worked. We see them crop up in many archaeological digs they produced a stunning design with an octopus."

Amira produced a photo.

"From here…she pointed on the map they were trading in the Bronze age with all these Mediterranean ports. Phoenicians, Anatolians, ancient Egyptian. Egypt was called (Kemet) so I am informed. Kemet the black land where the land was black from the Nile's silt from the inundation. Deshret from the red land of the desert. This tiny place," she pointed to Matala, "takes its name from the Talon, an ancient coin once used by Romans. They were here and apparently placed their dead in these recessed little caves along the cliffs. You can see them still today. I am informed the hippy trail walkers used them to bed down in, but the Mayor of Matala soon stopped that."

Amira sighed loudly then continued…

"Crete has a violent history. The famous palaces were reduced to rubble by fire and some report of many earthquakes. The islanders were invaded time and again. And then some sites totally rebuilt by the people of the next age. We know a tsunami struck at one terrible time or maybe more than one…Santorini's and Thera's volcanic eruptions have given rise to the stories of the great floods which affected all this area. While I was walking on Crete as a poverty-stricken student, I was amazed to find seashells high on the hillside. Very mysterious. Several arguments surround that. There are signs of more than one earthquake and many tales exist amongst the Ionian group's poor farmers.

Cephalonia has had many fatalities and a colossal loss of homes from earthquakes. Tremors are still part of life for the people.

Everything in this Mediterranean basin is interconnected…tectonic plates and one of the deepest rifts in the earth's crust are in this region.

Santorini's volcanic eruption and subsequent implosion leaving Santorini with a culdar.

All this ties in with the island we see before us today.

The great stories of ancient Kriti…are splendid. A man by the name of Sir Arthur Evans made great discoveries at Knossos and Phaistos. These buildings laid out with names like Palace of Phaistos, Knossos, Malia and one he named Piano Mobile…have a whole history of a civilisation concocted by him called 'The Minoan'—Many no doubt would like to find the actual names of Crete's real history…until then. You can see for yourselves a beautiful series of wall paintings friezes, etc., at Malia, Phaistos and Knossos.

You will also find a peculiar attempt to make up a sort of jig saw puzzle of parts and shards into a figure of an athletic youth with pieces found by Evans. Incorrect, but he really tried he really worked hard.

As for the famed Minotaur and the great stone bull's horn symbols… historians constantly talk of a Mediterranean bull culture, which reached as far as temples in Luxor. I know this because I was there recently in the Temple to the Warrior God Montu at Tod. A massive bull is depicted quite beautifully along one of the temple's remaining walls. They were much larger than any bull alive today.

Now we have the ruins on Crete where a great rambling labyrinthine palace stood. This it is said would have been a matriarchal society. The shrines once standing here were of the finest and most advanced of their time. The palaces vast and full of passages. We can see how the myth of the minotaur sprang into life. This…"

Amira produced a small book with a female goddess figure depicted holding aloft in each hand…a writhing serpent. The whole forming a 'Y'.

"This female icon must surely represent a kind of oracle or even a culture of snake handling somehow conjoined with a matriarchal religion…I am still researching the fact that she is indeed seemingly brandishing them…perhaps this could also be interpreted as a warning. They were isolated on this island and seemingly originated from Anatolia during and perhaps even before the Bronze Age. Cretans are strong in the heart and the Greek they speak is slightly different to the mainland—Ochi is no. You might hear Malista for yes also neh. They say efcheristo and that's to give thanks…like the word Eucharist from the Orthodox sacred service…Byzantine influenced. They have a whole bunch of men…or rather did have…in Chudetsia…a village high in the wild of the hills. So dark and swarthy like Turkish men. Because they are in fact descended from the time Turks made wars and invaded Crete. However, these men hated wars and hated their vile generals even more…they wished to live in peace and stayed and intermarried happily with Cretan ladies had children sat and smoked and learnt Greek so they could chatter amongst the other men…"

Everyone clapped. Amira was much loved on Pagan Arrow. Sally beamed with pride.

"Tourists love Crete…there are many people from all over Europe living in fine Villas and the like.

A real warning. Here to raise the hand flat like so towards someone is wishing the other person to go to hell. It's taken very seriously so don't do it even in jest.

Don't touch or even approach the girls. Cretans know anyone from a yacht is not to be trusted because they are usually only passing through. To reinforce this I will explain…they have armed guerrilla units in the mountains and have done so for decades. They have a fearsome reputation. Quixotic swarthy, really brave fighting men are scattered throughout these hills. They will defend their own. This is an island like no other on earth. Crete only joined Greece in 1913 under the leadership of Eleftherios Venizelos.

The ancient sites are still a mystery. Until these are more correctly researched and administered it's what we have for now. Many would say it is the best we can hope for at present. The Palace remains are truly beautiful at Knossos and Phaistos when viewed on the skyline. A bull leaping ritual was considered a strong form of early Olympian prowess. Paintings of young incredibly lithe athletes (which included females) have been artistically represented here. I think it is a site at Phaistos that depicts laughing and smiling curly haired beauties sitting in the similar pose of the Egyptians. The food is very Mediterranean very natural. Yoghurt with honey…after a swim. Ifasima!

Many classical stories talk of Icarus the winged boy…the much loved but headstrong son of Daedalus, who many claim designed the under-floor heating and water system in one of the great palaces here.

Daedalus it is written wanted to escape, he felt that he had done quite enough for the ruler King Minos of this island.

So, he set to with his son to invent a sort of flying apparatus made of feathers and joined very cunningly with wax. There was a problem. The day they chose to fly was a very hot sunny day and as they dressed and sealed themselves into these flying contraptions or wings…it grew hotter. They must have made an amazing spectacle as they took flight… You can imagine against the rich clear blue of a Cretan sky…

Daedalus, the great builder architect and his young son taking off appearing like gilded gods with the sunlight shining on them.

Daedalus being such an adventurous inventor gave strict instructions to the eager and excited Icarus.

235

"Follow me close, do not set your own course!"

He went on with absolute determination that Icarus would listen.

"Icarus, do not fly too low over the sea lest the water wet the feathers. Or fly too high near the sun lest its heat should melt the wax. The pair set off from Crete in a north-easterly direction. They were doing marvellously. They flew from Crete to Naxos then on and on they flew to Delos and Paros. After they were leaving Lebynthos and with Calymne behind on the right, Icarus was overtaken by youthful exuberance and disobeyed his father. He rose higher and higher. When next Daedalus looked over his shoulder Icarus had vanished. Flying too high Icarus had entered the dangerous part of the sky where the sun was very powerful. The wax had melted and Icarus had fallen out of the sky into the sea to his death. Daedalus flew around until the body returned to the surface. Daedalus became grief stricken at the sight of few feathers scattered on the water. He carried the body of his dead son to the nearby island now called Icaria where he buried it. There is a beautiful suitably sad poem written about this which I can look up if anyone cares to read it. Remember always, this is a proud people. Aghia Galini is a fishing village that turned into a tourist village. Respect and diplomacy. Also flip flops may come in handy because it's a pebble beach."

Felix hugged her.

"Amira, you talk with such knowledge and, and great passion."

The crew were very kind in their comments to Amira…

After a restful night, a very playful wind kissed Arrow's sails so as the Cretan dawn brought a myriad of soft colours, they raised anchors and sped on a pillow of bright fresh wind to the private moorings of the 'Villa Melpomene'.

Amira and Sally had unwittingly crossed into their new life. The crew meeting was unusual.

Captain Coulson stood up and gently shook her hand which almost vanished inside his. "I know I speak for all present dear Amira. Thank you."

He compressed his lips slightly… "On a yacht like Pagan, we soon discover each other. Amira has proved herself an asset as you all have.

Crete is a place I hold dear in my heart. You all know my love of the sea, now I can show you quite a different man. We are here in this private mooring which as you are well aware was the very devil to manoeuvre Pagan Arrow into, but we managed it. The 'Villa Melpomene' belongs to Sofia and Yiannis Glavas—a married couple who are my very dearest friends. I was here with Mattie and a whole other crew some two years ago. Sofia is a brilliant philosopher, she sometimes lectures in Athens. Sofia met Yiannis came here married into his family and now refuses to leave Greece. She is often begged to go to America to lecture there. She has resisted.

"We will stay with them. Pagan Arrow is secure here. So apart from a couple of daily checks on the anchors and general safety we can relax. All chores can wait, no lots drawn we go together. Please lads don't chat up the exquisite girl here she is a feisty lesbian, and you WILL be clutching delicate areas.

Sally this is a very child friendly island so enjoy. Sofia has several servants so we will be spoiled. I have to find two more crew members so keep your ears open."

Everyone went outside talking at once.

"Mummy, Mummy what's a lesbian and delicate parts."

Felix on hearing this found his humour and gave a short laugh. Still hurting deep inside from Tristan's sneaking departure.

"Darling a lesbian is a lady that desires romances with other ladies. I think Captain Coulson is saying that she is best left alone."

"Like Don't Touch."

Amira nodded trying not to laugh.

"Exactly like Don't Touch!"

Eventually the crew all trooped along the gang plank…a precarious one that led to a path climbing steeply through fragrant flower bushes to Sofia and Yiannis' absolutely splendid villa.

"Oh, Amira what a pretty place. I hope Felix buys me one like this."

"Exactly…"

Sally skipped ahead eager no doubt to meet a lesbian as feisty as Don't Touch.

Although the path was rather a puff to walk up the villa spread backwards into the rock face…and had sturdy storm shutters, miniature garden areas, with secret winding trails that led to tiny, well-tended terraces.

All the time while the world of tourism remained far away, the villa really did live up to its name. There truly was an air of suspension and drama about the place.

Amira had the distinct impression that if you walked into the wrong terrace and looked back…the whole building would have ceased to be…it would have been spirited away. Captain Coulson carried Winkles to his own room while a stern-faced boy carried his bags. Sally and Amira were shown to a wing of the luxurious home by two servants who took their work so seriously that Amira wondered if the ambience of such a place could meet a small girl's needs.

She needn't have worried. Their room was delightfully and tastefully furnished with a set of steps leading from an elegant veranda to a miniature seating area. Away to the left leading back towards the sea was a path with a fish as a notice board which sported a bluebird extending one wing pointing the way...the bird was perched upon a turtle. Amira appreciated the joke... A bird can marry a fish but where will they live. Well here...obviously.

Sally exploded with joy and ran to the garden...pointing over and over to the bird... "Mummy, Mummy."

"Yes darling it says Grotto."

She twirled and arabesque'd with such ecstatic pleasure the stern servant clapped and followed Sally dancing her own Greek version of the same joy. Some joys captivate all.

Amira called out to nobody in particular.

"Ah not so stern after all then."

There is a strange undercurrent now in all Amira's decisions. Thrilled by the entry into Aghia Galini...she sensed to the very hour that they had set foot upon the pretty beach where Sally can safely swim...a change of fortune.

Yasmin's chagrin would be in the ascendant. Reflecting upon her terrible error.

Yasmin would be reaping a whirlwind for all her misuse of Amira and those who treated her kindly upon Pagan Arrow. The yacht was having her last say for such falseness.

After all, a deep blue velvet case filled with golden valuable earrings watches, necklaces, bracelets and rings is a strange exchange for shampoo, conditioner, toothpaste tubes and a very pretty pebble with a starfish painted with a certain delicacy upon it. Oh, and the soap dish. Never forget the soap dish.

Tristan is poorer than anyone she has ever known. Without a career. He limps on land far more than on the deck of the stunningly lovely Pagan Arrow. Yasmin now sincerely treads the path of broken dreams.

Amira is silent now regarding the runaway incident. Sally is far too busy running about being seven with an audience of grownups waving as she pirouettes and grand jette's to her heart's content. The Greek people warm to her antics she is never seen alone and stray dogs find her a wonderful companion.

Also, a small white cat with black cap markings prowls about like the true owner of the place. She watches all from a carefully designated distance.

On the second day, Sofia joins them all in the massive dining room. High and well-ventilated it sports a mural of a mermaid and a merman having a tea party on the ocean bed. Sea horses, fish and urchins, starfish, weeds and roses… Excuse me, ROSES! All jostle for prime position. Sally is pointing with dirty fingernails along the exquisite artwork, finding new delights all the time.

Amira is exasperated but does so not want to get into a state over such a trifle.

"Sally look San San has brought you a bowl…"

San San is an invaluable 'aid de camp' in the war of persuading Sally to wash her face and hands.

Amira sighs but the others laugh and call out… "Relax mum."

San San takes the strain and coos like a dove around Sally who now sits on the floor washing her face and hands while a doting beautifully natured San San gets most of the dirt off one way or another. Amira whispers…

"I feel it's all a dream in an alternative universe."

Pieter tucking into a huge omelette with salad pipes up.

"Well Amira, mon felos oh Santiago we ARE in an alternative universe."

A lady in a pale silvery grey dress with a vibrant amber necklace at her tanned throat enters the room.

They all shuffle about and stand up totally mesmerised by her calm exterior and low-key entrance.

"Please do sit down. I am Sofia…my apologies for not greeting you sooner. I thought to let you settle in."

Ludi quietly turned towards Sofia…

"Thank you Sofia, we are very comfortable. Your home is lovely."

Sofia sits at the head of the table while several dishes are brought to her.

"My husband will be here tomorrow…he is the genius of entertaining I am only a poor substitute."

Passion is a strange word, people talk of this and that being a passion, but to open your home in this way to allow strangers to share it and be totally at ease. Surely, this is a passion for people.

Whoever they are.

Later, they are all enticed by the wonderful aromas of coffee and baklava to go out and finish off a truly lovely meal on the terrace allowing an exquisite

Greek girl to clear away. This must be Ariadne and in truth there is a beauty within her features only seen in one lifetime. The men look but steer well clear.

Ariadne looks inquiringly at Amira admiring the fine face, with the high structure of cheek bones light hair…then she looks musingly away.

Sally scampers after Winkles who has an entirely new job…the description of which comes in as:

EXPLORE
SLEEP
EAT
LOOK FOR LADY PUSSIES
EXPLORE
EAT
SLEEP.

Winkles only glimpses the villa's other feline presence briefly.

Avoidance is a word that springs to mind. Superiority of mannerism might also fit.

Mattie is occupied all day with an old friend and is rarely seen without this companion.

Although he does promise Sally to look out for grottos.

Charles is busy within his own circle of friends in Aghia Galini.

Jim and Pieter swim and sunbathe and swim again!

Ludi and Felix stroll about.

Sofia is a calm person and works her way around within the group as a special friend does when other's comforts moods and well-being are paramount.

Amira senses her presence as a prickling along the skin of her arms but in a way of wishing she had known a mother like Sofia. They may have met before in another life perhaps. What should have been.

Gods and goddesses had the final decisions back then but one feels now life has with deliberate beauty of heart brought the correct meeting into being at last. Sofia soon catches Amira alone.

"Amira, please stay with me a while."

"Of course, I want to say thank you for everything."

"Sally is seven I believe."

"Yes, but nearly eighteen some days in her demands of diva ballerina."

"Does her father have a good profession…it is an expensive training."

"No, not one bit of it. My plans are thankfully being redrawn and I want to make a good decision for her sake naturally."

"Oh indeed, the child is besotted with graceful movements and her little heart wild to express itself."

"A natural ballerina in the making."

"Rare wouldn't you say."

"I'd say Sally has a natural drama…"

"Charles has possibly talked out of turn but you alone can judge, he told me a very spiteful girl pulled tricks on all of you."

"Oh yes and it hurts all the more because Yasmin was once such a good friend. Something triggered this. Her parents beat her so the hatred and resentment against them must have…"

Sofia touched Amira's face with such tenderness…Amira felt a rush through her entire being.

Her life was hung in a balance. A vibration from the deep earth had shaken her from a past which was incomplete—Into a dream life. A new reality beckoned like a star in a void. She reached out to it with eagerness.

"Yes, a girl who was once a dear friend of mine from student years went rogue, I think you would say. She ran off with Tristan, Ludi and Felix…well, he is their son."

Amira felt directly Sofia's calm acceptance of such a strange tale.

"What is to come about is the making of you Amira…both you and your daughter. Don't hesitate."

During the next hour Amira patiently typed a long message to Riku.

She explained truthfully how she felt and wanted him to answer her truly. Was there a future for her with him? Could she and Sally come to him. She told him about the villa, Sofia, the runaways the velvet case of jewels the Pagan Arrow moored up for the next week or so. The impending voyage to Athens the capital. How if he approved, they could fly out to meet him in Tokyo.

All her love was in the writing she glossed nothing over including all about Winkles. Sally's love of The Firebird her yearnings to be a dancer. An artiste. Their future lay in his reply. It was a spell-binding wait. Amira if she was honest already knew his answer. She recalled a poem by Robert Frost…

"A voice said look me in the stars and tell me truly men of Earth if all the soul and body scars were not too much to pay for birth."

Like all times in paradise, the days wore down to the last hours at the villa…Amira requested time with Captain Coulson…she wished to stay here in Aghia Galini to sort her head and heart. Of course, she didn't blurt this out. Amira belonged to the college of 'Demonstration of hysteria leads to Valium'.

So, they sat calmly together with lemonade under the big umbrella on the terrace. Winkles held court on Captain Coulson's lap no doubt sensing the gravity of the occasion. Sally was on the beach with Mattie looking for more grottos. The one at the villa having sparked great interest in all things cave-like mysterious and smelly.

"You're not coming with us to Athens, are you, Amira?"

"You are such an insightful man. No, I'm waiting for a message."

"Dare I put forward the possibility of a love interest."

"I'm no yarn spinner Captain Coulson."

"Now we are no longer involved with Pagan hierarchy, call me Charlie."

"Okay but you must not phrase me if I forget. It's true that Riku is at present working on Sally's visa and although mine is prepared, I need to be here to go to the next phase. Well, you get the general gist."

"Do you feel you could settle there. It is the most fascinating of countries but won't you miss The Grey Dominion."

"Miss friends dreadfully of course, but no not much else. Especially terrorists in malls. Sorry, that's below the belt."

"Top reason I'd say Amira. That evil Yasmin was totally blasé about your near-death experience. I dislike very few people in this life Amira but she is right up there. Yes, I know she was knocked about by her unwholesome parents and of course that was wrong and cruel. But for my money in the light of following behaviour the scheming heart was in there already."

"You would get on well with Alain my friend a wise Detective back home. He had huge theories about that. In their DNA…so to speak."

"She's unlucky to lose your friendship. Your calibre of character is rare. Riku is a wise chooser."

"Ah his name is translated out as Wise Sky Warrior."

"Ahhh now that's a good start. A man with ability, loyalty and maturity I hope for both your sakes."

"He is an astute businessman with good and loving ways oh and a brilliant sense of humour."

"I'm not sure we can let go of one of our best wheel women, this means a lot of sacrifice on our part. I may have to read the articles of war."

Amira was at ease now laughing easily.

"Oh no not the terrible Keel Hauling punishment."

"Oh, a far worst cliché than that…put you in the long boat at the very least. Mattie tells me you have a special secret. Yasmin left with your bag. And you have hers. Yes, Sally has been tremendously gossipy."

"Well, it had to come out. Yes, Yasmin picked up the wrong bag in the dark when she sneaked out with my once upon a time lover."

"Good, well let's put it down to karmic retribution."

"At the risk of sounding trite…yes let's."

"Enjoy yourself Amira, riches are not to be sniffed at in my philosophy. My whole life has been governed by counting up adding up and taking away. Mostly having the taken away and never returning lesson."

"Me too and how."

"Well, there you are. Sally will benefit. There, is a diva ballerina in the making if ever I saw one."

"You have to spend a fortune on all their kit alone. Oh and the price of Tutus. Riku is really looking forward to that he says he has three daughters now!"

"He must be pretty special Amira he sounds good for you."

"I liked him instantly…we are highly in tune and empathetic."

"My, that is special."

"I can talk the hind leg off a donkey about Egyptian history but telling people how I feel…"

"You fell in love together. Simple really. Do you have sufficient funds to tide you over until he sends you the visas?"

"Hope so, we might have to grab the visas and tickets, ferry across to 'The Piraeus' and sell some gold and with that pay for a taxi to the airport. All in one fell swoop."

"Exciting stuff you will keep in touch with us all please tell us the developments."

"Absolutely, in our life there is always room for Edmondson's *The Faery Queen*."

"You have me there. I don't follow."

"Just being happy."

He stood up and shook her hand…loving her frankness, her inability to play games. She was going to a well deserving man who understood her. A rare match.

Amira was able to sleep now without fear. All her past had vanished in the mist burnt out behind her by just being honest to herself and admitting to loving a very unusual man met in very unusual circumstances.

Sofia was working on her next lecture and so although Amira dearly wanted to thank her for everything, she kept busy reading about Japanese wedding customs. Packing their clothes as quickly as the staff brought them to her freshly laundered and pressed.

Smuggling amongst them dear little sachets of Crete's herbs.

A collection whose perfume would enable Amira to recall instantly these last few days on Crete. Strange that both her case and Sally's contained such fragrance.

The idea of servants was a very new experience. An opportunity to learn from, some might suggest.

That evening Riku telephoned and told her… "My lovely Amira, it's best you collect everything together at the airport desk. I am dying of impatience to see you both."

"I love that you are as impatient as me thank you my darling. Riku!"

"I'm right here, Amira, what is it?"

"Are your daughters happy that you have a new…er…person in your life."

"Person ah! No, I told them 'special lady' did I do wrong. They are doubly happy and are rehearsing a Japanese version of Stravinsky's Firebird because they know Sally loves this so. Yes, excited and they will I am afraid to tell you be treating Sally like a little cute pet. We will have to watch out for this. Children here are so pampered."

Amira suddenly recalled her doorstep vigils in the cold with hunger gnawing at her while her parents attacked each other in drunken brawls inside in the warmth of the house.

She had certainly come a long way. She pushed the image aside.

"Sally won't grumble she is at that absolute show off age. A good fatherly example will settle her wonderfully."

"You and I will be just big toys to them all Amira, don't try to be too real."

They laughed out together. They blew kisses but refused to say Sayonara. Bad luck in their estimation.

Amira undressed quietly that night, close by was Sally curled up sleeping soundly. Apparently, Mattie had found her a truly smelly but magical grotto. Also as the last act of a loving true friend to them both.

Mattie had given Amira a tiny bag, beaded with a bird stitched in blue flying across one side. She admired it constantly.

Mattie had also given her one last label.

She found it the night before they all said farewells and sailed away.

It read…TEARS.

So, Pagan Arrow had sailed away slipping her knots of restraint and with new crew members she had swept out like some beautiful dream over the inky seas.

The villa felt the loss greatly. Of course Winkles was gone. Sally felt very strange. The small Greek pussycat that prowled and pounced and seemingly wore a little black cap as part of her markings was odd to the point of an acute eccentricity.

Sofia claimed the cat thought herself as a Tragic Queen from quite another century that had claimed the villa as hers by a strange sort of birth right. Which considering the Villa was named after Melpomene was not an entirely wrong assumption.

For hadn't The Fates and The Muses all colluded to create the very foundations of Greece…Melpomene is one of the nine muses, patron of tragedy and lyre playing. In Greek art, her attributes are the Tragic Mask and the Club of Heracles. According to some traditions, the half bird half women sirens were born from the union of Melpomene and the river god Achelous.

Tragedy is a foundation of nearly all of Greek history.

Poets painters and story tellers have gleaned and woven from this exquisite and tortured tapestry.

In Brueghel, the Elder's painting 'Icarus'…we are held in a terrible fascination…W H Auden writes:-

"About suffering they were never wrong
The old masters how well they understood
It's human position; how it takes place
While someone is opening a window or just walking dully along

How when the aged are reverently, passionately waiting
For the miraculous birth, there must always be
children who did not specially want it to happen skating
On a pond at the edge of a wood.
They never forgot
That even the dreadful martyrdom must run its course.
Anyhow in a corner, some untidy spot
Where the dogs go on with their doggy life and the torturers horse
Scratches his innocent behind on a tree.
In Brueghel's Icarus, for instance: how everything turns away
Quite leisurely from the disaster, the plow man may
Have heard the splash, the forsaken cry
But for him it was not an important failure; the sun shone
As it had on the white legs disappearing into the green
Water; and the expensive delicate ship that must have seen
something amazing, a boy falling out of the sky,
Had somewhere to get to and sailed calmly on."

****

The resident feline watched all departures and changes at the villa from an obliging tree fork which had seemingly grown for the purpose of spying on any human inhabitants…of the Villa.

'Amusing'—is after all a very telling description and this puss made it very clear that cuddles and dress ups were the playfellows of foolishness and promptly scarpered at the first glimpse of Sally leaving no chance for any type of friendship.

However, Sally knew that Mummy was very happy and had inherited enough of her mother's fortitude to see past all the losses and hold ups with paperwork waiting to be resolved.

Amira emailed Sonia telling her where her divorce papers were and the file was labelled (DNDA.)

Unmistakable.

They had birth certificates and passports etcetera with them already of course.

Sonia had located it and had sensibly sent it direct to Riku's office in Tokyo as only the original documents were acceptable.

Sonia used to such vital documents knew exactly what to do.

Sally had noticed her mother had a book about Shinto Weddings and studied its contents as if her life depended upon it. She laid it out at bedtime and learned of the exchange of nuptial cups called san san ku do.

San means three, Ku means nine. So San San ku do…equals three, three, nine.

Saki drank three times each from three different size cups called sakazuki.

The couple typically wear kimono, sometimes even a Uchikake, a heavy highly formal style in red mostly. And made from a very heavy, expensive brocade.

White expresses purity. Amira was going to be wearing pure white Riku thought this would echo the day of ethereal beauty they had experienced whilst under the tamarind. Her hair would be swept up yes, but not in a severe style. No, they had chosen a much softer flattering look with a flower on one side. This flower was to be chosen by herself. She had told Riku she loved the peony in deep pink. She was very keen on this. Riku was delighted. He was also to be resplendent in white.

He had lovingly said that he had requested their names were embroidered inside his kimono.

White is for a completely different reason in Japan… White expressed the brides 'desire' to be painted by her new family Amira learned that Japanese couples were fond of Western style wedding rings. Amira and Riku would be choosing theirs together to be sure of the absolute perfect fit to represent 'them'. The brooch he was having made was a surprise. He had ordered a tiny copy of a tamarind tree.

Sally was to be dressed as identically as his daughters. To Amira and Riku, this was a symbol of her being the one to complete the family.

Sally wanted to dance at the wedding…which was awkward. So Riku was arranging that a little troupe would come to the house later, as they would have a wedding party in the family garden where public formality could be dispensed with. This allowed Sally to join the little girl troupe and therefore feel she was contributing. Riku is an exceptional, steady, kind man.

Amira thanked him sincerely.

She was learning some Japanese names and descriptions. They had no cohesion to her present mood but were chosen because she felt happy saying them.

Ninja = skilled in camouflage
Umami = deliciousness.
Bokeh = out of focus part of a photograph.
Emoji = picture character or letter.
Tofu = very popular beans
Rickshaw = a hand cart drawn by a man very quickly on large light wheels. Colourful.

In a few days, a massive jet would transport them to a land where the people prided themselves in bonsai, and stunningly lovely art often with cranes. These to Amira were birds from another dimension. They belonged to a land of Moss, Zen, Stone and tall whispering forests. The Japanese knew about the conversation held above in the sky between cold leaves that once held sunlight. Blossom time of the cherry was a special celebration. Sophistication and custom adhered to, and young girls hired lovely costumes from the past during this festival.

All was preparation for the physical mental and the spiritual.

That night Amira quickly stripped down, she had to cleanse, pamper, trim, and shave. Her scar from the bullet's entry had once shouted its livid presence. But now thankfully, the neat mouth was magically healed and pale, barely there. Silently talking of survival. She caressed it saying. "That which is." Massaging had reduced its raised appearance. She felt now Riku truly would understand what this meant. She was now the sole real survivor of the actual shooting. Tristan was wounded far deeper. Far more obviously wounded. The added burden was ironically perhaps due to a life of soft treatment. He had not had the benefits of tough. Amira had. She was refined by the experience.

She showered and began to follow a list of female cleansing from a beautifully translated Japanese book of preparation for marriage Japanese style. This was a practice run.

Suddenly, word came through and somnolence became action stations and much laughter and a very peculiar visit from the cat queen who strolled into their room and mew mewed. Amira told Sally it was saying goodbye. Sally…learning fast said,-

"No, Mummy, she is saying good riddance!"

As they had their luggage piled into Sofia's car outside and were driven away the servants were waving and San San was tearful. Sofia drove them to the ferry and purchased the tickets while they shopped for ice cold drinks. The ferry was not always well stocked. The crossing was usually 23 hours. Amira and Sofia said nothing sad just practicalities aired. They all hugged and 'andio' hung about in the air. Passengers bustled Amira and Sally along the well-worn gangplank onto the scuffed strumpet of a ferry. Sofia smiled…they were going to be very happy…one can tell such things.

And so at last it had come, the ferry crossing to the Piraeus.

Islands loomed up out of the blue then gradually vanished behind them while others grew before them like magical kingdoms glimpsed from afar but not visited.

Love had caught up two people in the temple to Montu and now it would have its final say.

The airport became a mad rush to them. Those days of quiet rest at the villa all gone.

They breathed huge sighs of relief as they finally sat in the departure lounge.

Sally telling everyone whether they would listen or not that she was going to be a ballerina in Tokyo.

"Yes, I know it's going to be very hard work. Yes, that's my beautiful mummy over there. Are you going to Tokyo too ?"

Patient non-English speakers nodded politely.

"Yes, and this is Binx."

Amira rescued a very patient glazed over businessman and took Sally back to their seats.

"Would you like a drink darling we have quite a wait still I'm afraid."

"I like it here Mummy. The last bit of Greece Mummy, and then Japan, aren't you excited. He's very handsome Riku like a singer."

Amira was well aware that seven-year-olds often bowed to a certain hero worship and or crush of any singer, actor or greasy haired teen. Poor Riku had fallen neatly if somewhat temporarily into this 'collection'. Amira thanked all toy gods for not producing a version of him. A marriage to Binx would have had great appeal. Princess Semolina having been 'divorced' some weeks past from the selfish Binx.

The people nearby giggled behind their hands and even Amira laughed.

They were very fortunate to be flying deluxe/exec class or something and their flight attendant who looked fabulous was wonderful to Sally bringing her a Japanese doll from the airline's special gifts selection.

Amira was given a beautifully wrapped gift. She opened it with great anticipation. Makeup and a mask for the face, lovely perfume and one of those sleeping masks.

Sally as can well be imagined was thrilled. Japan suddenly became the land of free toys. Paradise. Sally began a conversation of hair raising ability about who this 'doll' could possibly marry!

The flight attendant had such skills in care for those flying, they were pampered like poodles. Amira wanted her to be in charge forever.

She knew her job inside out. They were soon settled with beautiful food, magazines, cool wine for Amira and a soft drink for Sally. Games were available television and music, but Sally exhausted from matchmaking soon fell fast asleep. The delightful flight attendant helped to stretch out the amazing seats into really comfy beds.

Amira who took full advantage of the time and privacy stretched out with the ridiculously expensive moisture mask carefully applied, she fell into a light doze. Not a good idea. When she woke, the mask had done its work…dried out and had slid unattractively skew whiff. There are worse things that can happen. The stopover was the best fun and they loved the swanky hotel that Riku had upgraded them to. Sally had found plenty of playmates and was tearfully waving to cheery patient staff as they packed the luggage into an airport taxi.

The flight to Tokyo was packed but they were exec again and so rested well. Food now became truly influenced by Japanese cuisine.

Sally pulled lots of faces and Amira ordered some very plain things for her instead. She loved the flavours herself…but saw no point in making Sally miserable and hungry. They snuggled down and Amira told her the story of schoolgirls in Japan. Sally was a little bit tense so Amira quietly whispered to her that she might like to draw an outfit to wear perhaps describe a first day at school with new chums and how they would have dance classes. Amira drew on all she could imagine putting her child at ease. Of course, Sally wanted a kimono for Binx. The ghastliness of this vision…had the gentle flight attendant giggling out of control.

Amira sighed audibly. Riku was going to have to step up to the plate sharpish… Poor Riku.

An all-girl household. But of course, he was only allowed to see his daughters Lily Rose and TsuTsu on occasional weekends or school holidays! That was harsh. She made a wish all would be well.

The photos of them he had sent showed them dancing in very cute outfits. They were twelve and fourteen. A sweetness in their faces told her they were very gentle courteous girls. She let out sigh after sigh hoping they would like her. Such a risk. All anxieties collided in a rush of 'What if's'—and dreads of rejections fell like an avalanche. Wondering if the girls were so indulged they could make her life thoroughly miserable, and as for Sally's oh god oh god. Good sense kicked in and she told herself off after all Riku is a sensible man.

Conventional yes, but not unbending, he was a real 'man'. Totally gentle. But what if the girls were shrewish like their mother. Oh, and the letter sent to Sally's father stating the fact she had chosen Riku.

Mmmmm she would like to be a bird peeking in her ex's window when that particular line hit the brain cells…the jet drone was almost menacing by now and Amira…noticing they would be landing in an hour frantically hurried to the washroom.

Tying a scarf around her hair she cleansed her face and generally cleaned up best she could. Some excellent perfume was at her disposal, so she sprayed a little. Before Sally woke up…she carefully made up in the best light possible—but oh no it was all so smudged the dreaded turbulence (which waits for you to apply mascara). She steadied up, breathing slowly and cleaned up the smudge. She stood back and gave an honest appraisal of herself… Not so bad after all. Jeeze she still had to clean her teeth.

There was so little mouth wash left due to the allowance on board being minimal, and Sally had used up most of it by gargling noisily for entertainment.

She mixed what was left with mineral water to stretch it out. This, many months later became a funny memory of her old (eek out everything) lifestyle.

She was so distracted she cleaned her teeth twice. Brushed her hair into the ponytail style she had favoured in Luxor's sticky heat. Returned to Sally who was yawning loudly and going into the goody bag again. She was happier now.

Their lovely flight attendant brought them sweets for the landing and a little mineral water.

She oohed and clapped her delicate hands over Amira's hair style and came back with a flower which she expertly fastened. Sally fully awake by now and screwing up her face sat sucking her sweet well before the wheels were even lowered. So, Amira distracted her with a makeup mirror and the blusher. Taking a risk but hey ho. She tidied up Sally and tied a ribbon on Binx. Who was going through his awkward phase again.

Jackets at the ready. Saying farewell to the flight attendant was very hard. They bowed and thanked her repeatedly. They wobbled down the tube and were directed with VIP speed through all kinds of securities which were waived.

"Well this is a fabulous experience," Amira muttered.

Sally kept saying, "Will he like me Mummy, will he like me?"

"Yes darling, he loves children and don't forget he has Lily Rose and TsuTsu."

Sally was nodding in agreement, but her mouth set in a prim line.

There before them stood a group of extraordinarily smart people waiting. One held a card above his head it read—

'Welcome to Tokyo, Amira and Sally Kinov'.

This was a shock, there were so many people. Yet still no sign of Riku. Her heart began beating madly. They bowed low and gave her the most beautiful flower in a sort of handbag with a see thru window. it was a sign and not the first that Riku was a truly noble man for it is a fact that only the noble are truly generous.

Amira sensed that his 'Warrior Class Status 'was a really big deal here and this was 'the team' he had spoken of. But where was he?

She felt a tear fall but retained her composure by quietly saying… "Thank you, thank you how lovely."

Everyone responded with bowing. The conventional gracious Japanese.

They soon had their luggage checked through another set of security and then instead of leaving the terminal were requested to step into a little shuttle car and Sally was given a wonderful toy kitten in a beautifully designed see-through attaché case. She stared at it in total disbelief. "Mummy look, it's waving at me look look Mummy."

"Aren't you lucky sweetheart. But where is Riku?"

Everyone nodded and pointed ahead. "Yes, but where is Riku!"

One smiling and understanding young man said confidently…

"Not to worry, Madam Amira."

But Amira did worry.

They climbed out of the tiny shuttle bus and there on the tarmac was the most beautiful pure white helicopter. Amira thought it might be a Sikorsky, a very very expensive exclusive piece of aeronautical equipment. She had a strange recall of another helicopter.

They lowered their heads as the engine and rotors began their noisy whirling…Sally was fastened in and could barely breathe from the excitement. She cuddled both kitten and Binx tightly to her and held Amira's hand as if everything might dissolve as in a fairy-tale. Amira saw the twinkle in the men's eyes just as she was about to protest once more. For quite suddenly, Riku called out from the pilot's seat. "Welcome to Tokyo Amira and Sally."

She wanted to kiss him but knew this was always going to be their private intimacy. After all, things were completely stood on their head in fascinating Tokyo. A smiling attendant brought cooling drinks and Amira sighed from sheer happiness as Riku expertly manoeuvred the helicopter through Tokyo airspace.

There was a brief moment when vital thoughts returned her to how she owed her life to another pilot.

Fumbling in her flight bag, she drew out the photo of another helicopter with its crew of paramedics standing with Pierre Tremblay in front of the Agusta Westland CH 149 Cormorant.

The End